THE CUCKOO BOY

To my Mum and Dad who gave me all the love and support
that the boy in this book never had.

First Published in 2010

To Hell with Publishing
44 Ossington Street
London W2 4LY
info@tohellwithpublishing.com
www.tohellwithpublishing.com

THE CUCKOO BOY

Grant Gillespie

to hell with

Up.

He'd had a twin for company,

Down.

But his twin gave up the ghost.

Up.

And the first grown-up to welcome him?

Down.

Gave him to someone else.

His first photograph was taken.

Noticeably absent was the tired-but-happy mother, the proud father, the over-eager grandparents. This picture – a small one – was for publication in *Be My Parent* magazine. And he was inserted among a host of other children 'looking for adoption'. They all gazed out longingly. He also had a biography, which was naturally rather brief. It neglected to mention the death of his brother, his disinclination to feed and the problems he had adapting to diurnal behaviour. It focused on him being *normal* – that was the keyword – 'A normal baby boy who deserves and needs love and attention . . .' : a child's right.

Indeed, there was nothing abnormal about him, at least not physically. There was nothing remarkable about his limbs, which were present and in full working order; his tiny penis was only as tiny as it should have been; and his shiny black spiv-like hair – of which there was quite a lot – crowned a regular-shaped head.

In any case, the photo and life-story had the desired effect. Parents were procured. And the lucky pair who were to take home the baby boy were called Mr and Mrs Gardner, Kenneth and Sandra.

ONE

Sandra and Kenneth were in their late twenties. The wife was suburban pretty, with a small, neat nose and prim, plump lips. She was quick-tempered and protective, like a robin. The husband was schoolboy handsome, with grey-blue eyes, like stones in a stream. He thought a lot and said very little. They were both slim with dark hair, and everyone said that when they had a baby it would be extremely beautiful. But several years of marriage had already elapsed and still there was no child to call their own. Any sex that they'd enjoyed had been recreational or – as some would see it – fruitless. So they decided that they'd take their fertility into their own hands and go, somewhat shamefacedly, to the doctor expressly to have their fears assuaged and be told that there was nothing at all to worry about.

When the tests came back, Mr and Mrs Gardner were sitting tidily beside each other. Kenneth was statue-still but Sandra was paddling her fingers nervously in her husband's palm.

The doctor asked Kenneth, rather bluntly, 'Have you ever been exposed to any industrial chemicals that you're aware of?'

'He lived between every factory in the county as a child,' Sandra explained, before Ken could part his lips. 'You should see the view from his parents' house, chimney after chimney, big towers pouring with ... I don't know what.'

The doctor nodded. 'Well, it's not definitely the cause, but it is likely that ...'

'His mother never once took him to the doctor when he was ill, you know,' Sandra interrupted, stroking the mount of Venus on her husband's palm. If Ken had been *her* son, she'd have taken better care of him. She planned to cure him of his past and rescue his future. But before she could expand any further, the doctor informed them in his mid-range breaking serious news voice:

'I'm afraid that my tests conclude that ... you'll never have children. I'm sorry.'

There are moments in life that should be accompanied by a gong being struck. Sandra's now frozen fingers fell away from her husband's hand and came to rest on her lap. There was nothing to be said. They took their disappointment back to their empty home and wrestled with it. After days of reeling and tears and repressed blame, they decided to adopt.

The young couple devoted days, months, years, to making telephone calls and writing letters. They'd never been so united in their resolution. When the first blow came, it was from the hands of the adoption agencies themselves, due to conflicting medical reports. Husband and wife were obliged to attend umpteen interviews, presided over by panels of professionals. Each rejection brought a period of bewildering bereavement.

They were *good* people. That was how other people described them – especially concerning Kenneth. He had, by all reports, a good sense of humour and a good degree of humility. His colleagues at work – he worked in insurance – said that he was one of the good guys. High praise indeed. Of Sandra, people said that she had a good heart, which is only moderately different from having a big heart.

Eventually, though, their tenacity was rewarded and Kenneth and Sandra's biggest wish was granted. Now they could take to their hearts and their home a rather sullen – but certainly normal – baby boy.

They rejoiced for several days. Finally they could be just like their contemporaries. They could go and buy baby things . . . and that little room, which was already decorated for a child, would finally be put to use. Yellow: suitable for a boy or a girl.

After this euphoric period, doubts started to form in the fringes, ready to scuttle in, like roaches, the second that darkness fell. What if they could not love or bond with this child that they'd fought so long and hard to get? What if *he* didn't like *them*? But it was their whole-hearted intention to treat him as their own. And, for better or worse, that is exactly what they did.

Children change everything.

On the fateful collection day, Sandra and Kenneth arrived at the adoption agency early, dressed to impress – in Sunday best – and anxious, as if it were their first day at school. A young woman called Angela met them. Angela – so as to seem unthreatening – had no surname. It was Angela No-Name's responsibility to conduct the handover.

The parents-to-be had expected a preamble, a chat, as they walked through the building, but they were led through the first door that they came to. Sandra pictured a boy being conveyor-belted up the corridor, room by room, until he arrived at this one, closest to the exit, where he was now patiently lying, waiting to be picked up. It was a spacious, magnolia-painted room, empty except for a few posters and a cot.

And then, there he was, before them, this small, dark-haired, blue-eyed baby, staring benignly at the heavens in nothing but a nappy.

Sandra had rehearsed this moment time and time again. She would smile at him, a smile burning with love, and he would smile back, a broad smile brimming with recognition. In that instant they would choose each other. For ever.

The reality was somewhat different. She looked at this . . . this thing, this . . . someone else's child . . . and love was not a word that sprang to mind. Fear was closer to the sensation she was feeling, fear mixed with an unwanted wave of revulsion. Nor did he smile back at the brave upturning of her mouth. He looked through her, entirely unmoved.

The moment was over. It was not love at first sight. Sandra, in her panic, turned practical by reflex, forcing away the unfamiliar.

'What are those blue patches on his skin?' she asked, as though taking a blouse up to a sales-girl to try to get a reduction on the price.

'Oh, just pigment accumulation. They should fade,' Angela No-Name assured her.

'Right,' she said. 'Should?' Maybe she wouldn't buy it after all, unconvinced the blemishes would come out with one wash.

'They will fade eventually, but it can take a little time.'

'And his belly button . . .'

'Yes, that's the cord end.'

'It looks like it's glowing.'

'There is a little inflammation and some discharge, but it's very common. It'll heal quickly. He also has nappy rash and a small tongue' – a pre-emptive strike.

'A small tongue?' Kenneth spoke for the first time.

'Tongue-tied. It's where the expression comes from.' No-Name said it again, 'Tongue-tied,' and tucked her hair behind her ear.

'How does it become untied?' Kenneth wanted to know.

'It'll catch up with the rest of him, there's no need to worry . . . Now, there's some paperwork,' she told them, as though she were in a hurry to close the deal before they could waver.

After the formalities were over – and Sandra always found that formalities restored her confidence – they were all set to take their son.

'How funny. Our son! It's like the first time I said, "My husband".'

Kenneth looked into the middle-distance, wistfully.

'Our son,' she said again. The moment was almost too much to comprehend. Her eyes filled with tears. A baby. A husband and a baby. She was so lucky.

Kenneth listened distractedly to the little compartments of advice that were dished out, like an aeroplane meal, while his wife quelled the rising urge to snatch the baby and make a dash for the door.

'Yes, we're aware it may be difficult to adjust at first,' Kenneth admitted.

But Sandra knew that she wouldn't find it difficult at all. She would thrive, come alive again. She was adjusted. And this slip of a girl giving them advice. There she was, trying to tell them about her son's history, his birth, his birth parents, perhaps his brother. She brushed it all away, as she would have dandruff from a stranger's shoulder. He had no past, as far as she was concerned, only a future, a bright, bright future, with her in it.

'I'm sure you've held lots of babies before,' the girl said, tucking her hair behind her ear again, 'but you must always –'

'Support the head, yes,' Sandra said, and the words pushed her into picking him up for the first time. Her hands were shaking.

He squirmed as though she was hurting him. She looked to the girl for encouragement.

'That's it. He's a bit of a wriggler.' No-Name then handed the husband some 'Helpful Tips', typed out on green paper. On the bottom was a hotline number for the social worker. Kenneth took it and thanked her.

'Keep in touch,' Angela said, with a smile and one last hair adjustment.

If Sandra hadn't had her hands full she would've cut that lock off, or secured it in the hairband. But instead she looked away and said, 'Of course,' knowing that this was a lie. She would do everything in her power to wipe clean her memory of the whole place. She didn't believe in retrospection. This was a fresh start, a new beginning.

Before they left the room, the wife stopped and took stock. She could afford to be less brittle now that she had everything she'd ever wanted. 'Thank you, Andrea . . . for our son. Thank everyone here. You all do a wonderful job.'

No-Name, whose first name was in fact Angela, smiled until the Gardners had gone.

They didn't own a car.

'It's not a matter of the cost,' Sandra insisted to people who asked, and often to those who didn't. 'I mean, unlike a lot of our friends' – she was referring to their automobile friends – 'we've been abroad, to Spain . . . And not just the touristy bits . . . What is it you say, Ken?'

'Cultural travel is more important than convenience travel.'

'That's it.' Sandra exposed her insecurities by trying to conceal them.

But for this special occasion they'd managed to borrow a car from their friends Margery and Neville, who lived along the road. Margery and Neville, who did everything together, had two small children, 'one of each', so the car was equipped for two babies: their new son and perhaps – had he survived – his twin.

Sandra held the boy tightly. She was going to love him, even if it killed her. Normally, she'd have been in the driving seat. She'd passed her test a few years before her husband so – to her mind – that made her the better driver. Only now she'd relinquish the wheel in favour of the baby reins. She looked at his tiny hands and gave them a finger to hold, but they ignored it. They were locked into fists and no gentle prizing would allow her to worm her way in. Nor did he move his head in her direction. He looked nowhere and saw nothing. She tried not to be offended by this snub. It would be all right once they got him home and he became settled, Sandra was sure.

'Ken, will you slow down? The car's bumping him.' This was the first in a lifetime's worth of new reproofs.

As he slowed down, a gearshift happened in their relationship. No longer were they Sandra and Kenneth. From now on, they would be Sandra, Baby and Kenneth. A child: the clichéd filling in the sandwich, adhering to one slice, or the other, but forever keeping the two apart. Their previous existence together as a couple came to an abrupt end, and so all the vignettes – the story of the lovesick teenagers; the disapproving parents; the shambolic wedding; the holidays in Spain – were now unceremoniously dumped, like used nappies, on the roadside, left for landfill. The rest of their lives would be devoted to propping their baby up; book-ending him in. They would try to take care to leave enough room for his story. They would try.

'Kenneth, put the kettle on please,' Sandra said, as she took the wriggling baby upstairs.

'Shouldn't I come and give you a hand?'

'No, we'll be fine.'

'Tea or coffee.'

'Oh, tea!' she said, from the landing, as though it were obvious. I have a baby now. I want tea of course! 'There, there,' she said to the child, which had stopped writhing for a moment to flinch at the sound of her raised voice. 'Doesn't your dad make a fuss?' She paused and said it again – 'Your dad' – and she felt a rush of excitement, like a girl with a crush. She carried him into Baby's Room.

'Yellow!' she announced, as though the child might pipe up with, 'My colour! How did you know?' And it was yellow – the walls, the ceiling, the glossy furniture – a veritable assault of buttercup yellow.

Kenneth came in with a tray – two cups of tea and a baby-bottle with freshly prepared formula. Sandra stared at the second cup, as though it had somehow betrayed her, then she saw the bottle.

'Oh, Ken!' She started to cry.

He put down the tray and hugged her and therefore his son too.

'Don't crush him,' she said, but there was no harshness in her voice.

'No. I won't. I'll look after mum and baby.'

'Mum,' and she smiled through her tears.

His grey-blue eyes were shining too. 'Have you thought about his name?'

'It's your surname, and as you've only nieces, he'll be the only Gardner.' She liked that fact. She'd never really cared for his older brother and his ability to have children so easily. It didn't seem fair that he'd been immune to factory fumes. After all, he'd grown up in the same house as her husband. But her brother-in-law's offspring had been exclusively female: Sandra could afford to feel magnanimous. 'You choose.'

'Well, I like the name Anthony.'

His wife didn't respond. She glanced down at her son and then back to her husband as though still waiting for him to speak.

He searched around the room, but the colour flooded him, so he shut his eyes and searched around his head. 'James?' He'd had a Jameson's whiskey while he was preparing the tea. A metaphysical sign for his subconscious, James and Son united in one word.

'James,' she said, gazing down at her new baby.

The child didn't seem to object, though maybe that was just his nature. He hadn't objected to the lurid yellow either. Perhaps he simply assumed that this arrangement was only temporary, like everything else had been in his short life. He couldn't have realised that names are for life, and that the effects of a buttercup room can take a lifetime to overcome.

James was reluctant to take to the bottle. He turned up his nose; he turned the other cheek; he tried every evasive manoeuvre a restless baby could muster.

'Maybe he just isn't hungry,' Kenneth proffered.

'Small babies eat between six to eight times in every 24-hour period,' Sandra told him, with textbook authority, 'and he hasn't eaten once yet.'

'Maybe they fed him before we arrived.'

She didn't bother to respond, and placed James in the cot.

'He's stopped squirming,' Kenneth observed.

It was almost too much for her to bear. It had been a long day; a long two years to be precise, and she was overwrought. 'I can see that, for goodness sake!'

Her husband left the room. She stayed.

'I do love you, Ken,' she whispered, while looking at James.

She sat by the cot for an hour or two, watching her son as he slept. And as she sat there, a feeling akin to love began to grow inside her. The next time she picked him up, he was still sleeping. She bounced him till he opened his eyes, and then, before he knew what was happening, she slipped the bottle into his mouth and he was suckling, hungry or not. Instinct had kicked in and she'd tricked him into drinking his first meal at home.

Sandra and Kenneth could have taken turns at feeding James, but she wasn't prepared to give up the privilege. Feeding time is when mothers and sons bond, and bond they would. It was her compensation. She hadn't been tainted by gasworks. Kenneth could have other responsibilities that she'd devise.

During the next somnambulist feed, Ken came into the room and the light that he brought in with him woke James fully. Immediately, he became distracted, stopped his sucking and started squirming. He then projectile-vomited a yellowish bile that perfectly matched the decor.

'Ken!' – his name an expletive. And before he could offer any assistance, Sandra was whispering with full force, 'Please get out! This is your . . . I was doing fine!'

Her husband had proven categorically that his presence was unhelpful. Reluctantly he retreated and took solace in a bottle of his own, his son's namesake.

This became the daily routine. Feeding him was a game of grandmother's footsteps. There was no point in trying when he was fully awake, he resented the intimacy and shook, like a dog on bonfire night, or he became tense and rigid, as though her very touch caused him physical pain. When she put him down he'd jolt, arms outstretched, as though he'd been dropped from a height. Only then would his body finally relax, as he slipped once more into the solace of slumber. He had a seemingly limitless capacity for sleep, perhaps preferring the land of dreams, where dead twins lived and mothers remained.

Kenneth had planned to take some time off work to be with his family; his new, complete family.

'To be honest, Ken, I think it'll be better all round if you go back to the office. You'll only get under our feet. Maybe wait till we've got a routine established . . .'

He was feeling more and more fenced out by this exclusive club of we.

He was not the only one. Grandparents were also excluded entry from the inner sanctum.

'Not just yet,' she'd say, as her husband fielded the incessant calls. 'It's too soon for him.'

Friends were also positively dissuaded. Ken selected the excuse – 'They're both sleeping. It's been a long night' – and he stuck to it. Flowers and cards were restricted to the lounge, and Kenneth was relegated to the spare room, obliged to sleep among the unwanted Christmas presents and clothes for charity.

On his return to work, he played the role of Proud Dad. Everyone wanted to see a photograph of James, but the only picture he possessed was the one from *Be My Parent* magazine and he really didn't want to get that out. He decided to buy a Polaroid camera on his way home.

Sandra stayed in their small, terraced house, devoting her days to motherhood. And after a few weeks, she stopped trying to pick James up all the time. She admitted to herself that this approach wasn't working. She'd have to be patient. Talking. That was her next tack. If coma victims could hear you, then he certainly could. Soon he'd know her by heart, and this little heart of his would open to her, and he would smile.

She talked and talked and he slept and slept. And eventually, visitors had to be permitted . . . grandparents, neighbours, friends. They all trooped in – in pairs – and were met by shiny, radiant parents full of the joys of their perfect baby boy.

'We're so happy,' they told each guest in turn, as they led them into the dimly lit room. 'Now, don't speak when we're in there . . . we've just got him off to sleep,' they'd lie.

They endured endless tales of how lucky they were:

'When we had our Nicholas, our lives turned upside down, it was such a strain on our relationship . . . Wasn't it, Ron? The little so-and-so wouldn't sleep for more than an hour. I swear, *we* only slept for about twenty minutes at a time for the first few years . . . Didn't we Ron? Changing nappies, trying to stop him crying, breastfeeding . . .' adding quickly, 'you know, you're so lucky not having to breastfeed. I swear, my boobs have never recovered, have they, Ron?'

Ron shook his head.

'Thank your lucky stars he's not colicky, like our second one,' confided Margery from along the street. 'The first three months were hell! I had to take sleeping pills. I got addicted. I still take them now.'

'When we had our Susan,' another friend informed them, 'I had to keep going in to check that she was still breathing. I was so afraid she'd died. Are you like that?'

'Yes, yes, I am,' Sandra agreed. It was the first thing she'd heard about a baby that she could confirm she'd experienced at first hand. 'Even when I get to the cot, he still . . . I'm still afraid he's stopped breathing.'

'Well, it does happen – cot-death – you read about it a lot,' her mother, who'd never read anything a lot, considerately told her. 'It's called something like ICD . . . initials, in any case. No one knows what causes it, or how to stop it from happening. One minute they're alive and the next – '

'I don't leave any toys in his cot and I check the temperature isn't too hot all the time!' Sandra blurted, precariously balanced on the brink of hysteria.

'She does,' Ken agreed. 'About once every fifteen minutes.'

'It's strange, but doesn't he look like his daddy?' Ken's mother said, supposedly without guile.

Kenneth looked pleased.

'He's got your bluey-grey eyes, Kenny.'

'All babies are born with blue eyes,' brown-eyed Sandra said. 'They'll probably change.'

They wouldn't change, and the similarity between father and cuckoo son would be commented upon for the rest of their lives.

On and on came the torrent of advice, of sympathy, of congratulations, till, in the end, Sandra thought she'd do something that her baby never did: scream. Her husband decided that it would be best if they had no further visitors until the first month was up.

'I don't think I'm being over-protective, Ken, but the sleeping. It should be sixteen hours at the most, not twenty-four . . .'

'It's an average . . . And he doesn't sleep for twenty four hours.'

'*He* has a name.'

'James then.'

'I think he might be deaf.'

'What?' he said, trying to add an element of humour to the proceedings.

Sandra didn't notice, or at least didn't acknowledge it. 'He doesn't make a sound.'

'Deaf babies can make sounds.'

What she'd meant was that he didn't respond to sounds, but now she was confused and her husband's obtuseness was making her cross. She didn't like being made to feel stupid, not realising that she did all the legwork herself. 'Well, I've made an appointment. I'm going in this afternoon. If you don't care about our son, I do.'

'You know I care, I just think you might be overreacting.'

'Well, I hope you're right.'

Of course he was right, but, as Sandra told him that evening, the doctor had said, 'It was better to be safe than sorry.'

In this pairing, she was Safe and he was Sorry. So she lost no ground.

Sandra continued to use her baby book as her bible, and James seemed to defy every anticipated behavioural change. By his first birthday they should have had a baby who spoke a little and understood a lot; a baby who was able to crawl. He was a baby who could not – or would not – do any of these things.

They had an album full of photographs, but each one looked pretty much the same: a small boy with a big head, no neck, thin shoulders, a belly that jutted, bowed legs and archless feet. There were no pictures revealing his beautiful, big blue eyes, as they were always hooded by long-lashed lids, baby Sleeping Beauty, under a spell. He ate a bit, shat a lot and slept a great deal. It was so uneventful a year that it had to be a cause for concern. The only skill that he had mastered in the space of twelve months – to Sandra's horror – was the ability to rub himself, and there were certainly no Polaroids to commemorate that.

TWO

They decided to mark the occasion of his first birthday with a party, which was really more of a carefully vetted gathering. The idea filled both of his parents with foreboding. Kenneth worried for his wife. Her voice, he noticed, went up an octave every time she mentioned it. She desperately wanted it to go well.

Sandra – who was not a woman given to trusting other people's appetites – would take control through food. She'd provide a spread that she could talk everyone through: curried rice with raisins; vol au vents; a selection of quiches and, of course, a cake . . . she would bake James a birthday cake. She'd dress him up in his best clothes and he would do them proud and sleep through the whole thing. They'd lay him on the sheepskin rug, child-in-a-manger style, and their guests would all come and pay homage to their immaculately conceived son. Kenneth hoped for Sandra's sake that this was how the day would play out.

The guests arrived at an exceedingly tidy house, at 'two for two-thirty', which meant two.

'I don't know how you find time to keep the place looking so nice!'

Sandra had all the time in the world, but instead of admitting this, she said, in a voice that was sterner than she'd intended, 'I don't see why having a baby should mean you let your standards slip. I just do it whenever I get a second,' and as she said this, she removed an invisible piece of dust from the hall table, illustrating that that second was just such a second and she was taking full advantage of it. 'Calm down,' she told herself, 'these people are my friends.'

The afternoon rolled on with small talk and the sipping of sherry brought back from a holiday in Jerez. James's outfit was admired, his beauty appraised and his good nature applauded. The Magi guests gave Sandra and Ken gifts 'For Children Aged 12 Months', which they opened with grateful noises made for the first and last time. The presents would soon sit unnoticed among all the other mobiles and uncuddled toys in his spotless room.

The hour was approaching when couples look at each other and simultaneously decide that they should probably say their goodbyes. All the other hackneyed euphemisms were about to be rolled out, the red carpet of retreat – 'You probably want to feed him', 'We should let you get back to your day', 'We'd better be making tracks' – when all of a sudden, James's eyes snapped open with all the unnatural abruptness of a ventriloquist's doll.

'He's awake!' said Margery, their friend and neighbour with the car. Sandra, Margery knew, would want to be warned.

Sandra turned to her husband. They feared the worst. Would he screw up his legs and turn puce? Would he rub his crotch like a lunatic? What fresh humiliation would he have in store?

But he did something that neither of them anticipated. He smiled. Their baby Sleeping Beauty had awoken from a year-long slumber and this was the first thing he did. It was not one of those standard baby smiles, that happen by mistake, some involuntary muscle experiment; this was a splendid grin that took in the room and all its inhabitants and said, 'I know that you're here and I am happy for you to be so. I permit it.'

Sandra and Ken were spellbound.

'Happy birthday!' they said, to their son. And for all

concerned it suddenly *was* one.

Other parents could brag about how their child could sit or stand, name and strike the dog each time it passed, eat solid food, babble like a loon, but now it didn't matter. He would eat solids and chatter eventually. But – in the meantime – he had this killer smile.

The friends and family were suddenly reluctant to tear themselves away. If they could have, they would have remained, but Sandra the overzealous housekeeper tidied them up and swept them on their way. She wanted this moment all for herself.

'Take a picture, Ken!' she said, and she lay down next to her son, placing her face next to his. She wasn't going to risk picking him up, in case she scared away the smile. She wanted it recorded, and she wanted herself in the picture: the game-hunter posing with its grinning prey.

And so the smile, his first smile, was captured.

James, for a long while, had seemed reluctant to stop being a baby. No one could have accused him of toddling. Then, sometime around September, when he was already two and a half, he made another sudden development: he stood on his own two feet.

On many an occasion Sandra had quit the room leaving him lying on the rug in the hope that he'd make a sound, cry or try to follow her, but he'd never seemed inclined. Then one day, when she came back in, her lungs already heavy with defeat, he was no longer there. Fear rose up inside her, like ivy sliding up her bones, wrapping around her lungs and heart. She stood staring at the space that he'd occupied just moments before. Then she heard a noise from behind her and turned.

There was a boy standing at the glass-panelled door, which led to the small back garden, and he was reaching, fingers finally outstretched, for the handle. For a moment, she didn't think it was James, but someone else's son. She'd never seen him upright, or with his legs extended. He looked too big to be her boy.

'James?' she said, almost in a whisper, but he didn't respond.

To be fair, he'd never responded to his name previously – or, for that matter, to any other word. She moved over to him and knelt down.

'James?' she said again, but he did not look at her; he was entirely absorbed. He wavered and reached, and wavered and reached, determined, it seemed, to get outside.

Sandra didn't know what to do. She wanted to stop him from trying to get out, though she didn't really know why. She circled her arms around his waist. Slowly her son turned to her, and for the first time in over a year the smile completely vanished. He stared at her as though he didn't know her, a look of defiant incomprehension in his eyes. His mother withdrew her hands as though they'd been pricked.

Not knowing what else to do, she left him at the glass door – which she told herself was locked at least – and went to call Kenneth.

'Is everything all right?' He sounded concerned. She rarely called him at work any more.

'He can walk,' she told him.

'What? James? That's amazing. How?'

'With his legs,' she said, flatly.

'But, I mean, how did he learn?'

'I don't know. At night?' she ventured, imagining him as a soldier engaged in nocturnal manoeuvres. She looked at her fingernails. They were cracked.

'That's great though . . . isn't it?' He didn't sound sure. 'I told you there was nothing to worry about.' He'd kept on telling her this, though he'd long since given up believing it.

'I suppose so. But he's stopped smiling. I didn't recognise him.'

'Will she never be happy?' he thought. 'That's what

children do,' he said. 'They grow up and you can't understand where the baby went.'

'Well, he's gone.'

Ken didn't like the way she put this, but he was at the office and other things were pressing in on his thoughts. Her words entered the room, but they were laid out on top of memos and mail and a long list of people he had to telephone to tell them they were not covered by their insurance policies. He made excuses and said he'd be home as soon as he could get away – which over the last two years had been later and later. At work he was needed, he had a role to play, people listened to him, ran things by him, respected his opinion, whereas at home the same could no longer be said.

When she returned to the sitting room James was asleep on the rug once more. It was as though he'd never moved. She sat herself down on the brown sofa, which she'd recently had reupholstered, and watched him.

Ken arrived home around eight. His wife heard him not wipe his feet on the extra square of carpet that served as a doormat, but she didn't even flinch. She was still sitting on the sofa, staring dumbly into where the dust particles danced. She admitted that she was beginning to think she'd made it all up, a phantom mini-perambulation. Her husband assured her that he didn't think she had. If she said that she'd seen him walk, then he'd walked. But looking at the sleeping boy it was hard to believe.

It was about this time that Sandra noticed that random household items had been displaced. Her eyes were always on full alert to change. Everything in her world had a home. She was one of those people who gave life to inanimate objects, a St Francis of domestic miscellanea.

'You know that cup doesn't live there. That's what the mug tree's for. How many times do I have to tell you? Biscuits live in the bottom cupboard' – as though families of Bourbons and

Ginger Nuts had set up a commune in there. To Sandra, the house itself laid down the law and it was a crime to go against it. Certain doors had to be 'ajar' when the heating was on, others closed, and condensation was an inhabitant whose demands came first. Kenneth believed that a man's home was his castle, but he would never have said so to his wife.

Sandra had no room in her head, or her home, for poltergeists, so she could now confirm that James was mobile. And no matter how minor the alterations were, her instincts alerted her immediately. 'That ornament of the dog is further to the left of the fireplace than it was, and it isn't guarding the fire any more but watching it. That small bowl with the scalloped edge, for nuts on special occasions, is no longer on its cork coaster. The wooden magazine stand is no longer strictly parallel to the arm of the sofa.' She felt like a double agent, hunting for clues.

It became a game.

It was also around this time that James allowed his mother to put him in the baby chair. He was happy up-on-high, but he would wriggle and struggle when the time came to lift him out. She often gave up and left him there till he invariably fell asleep, slumping lifelessly over the side, plastic plate in hand. Getting him to eat was still an ordeal. He wouldn't let her spoon-feed him, turning his head away as though distracted by some far more interesting soundbite on the radio. It was a battle of wills she could never win.

She tried everything she could to coerce him, but he became irritable and his chair was the perfect vantage point from which to hurl things. He smiled as he threw the bowl to the floor or sent his cup flying. This, she understood, was normal, this discovery of gravity. But James was not excited by the object itself falling through space. He was no aspiring Newton. It was his mother's slow-motion expression of horror that so engrossed him every time. She tried not to mind, but she couldn't help it. She liked her linoleum clean.

In the end she resorted to turning her back on him, so that all he could see was the involuntary flinch of her shoulders as the plastic Beatrix Potter dishes hit the floor. At least there was one benefit. Sandra discovered that if she didn't face him, he would surreptitiously dangle his fingers into his food and suck upon them. It was a meagre reward.

'Mum is just worried about you, James. You never eat enough. You're still small for your age,' she told him, as though a rational explanation might help. But then she became exasperated, 'You spoil every mealtime!' a phrase that stacked up by the day, like dirty dishes.

It felt like he was deliberately sanding away at her skin, exposing the grain of her nerves. To make matters worse, he'd often let his father feed him, looking innocently up to the heavens with the wide eyes and mouth of a hungry bird.

'I don't see what all the fuss is about,' Ken commented, unwisely.

But James seemed determined to exclude her from his every development, resolute in his desire to govern himself. Sandra felt sure that he'd have changed his own nappy and sterilised his own sippy-cup if he could have. James had evidently decided that if he had to live in the waking world, he would … but on his own terms.

After weeks of waiting and watching, Sandra caught him on his feet again. He was off to the same glass door.

'I knew you could walk!' she said, as she bowled triumphantly back into the room.

Her voice made James jump. He turned quickly, lost his balance and fell onto the unforgiving parquet floor with a slam. There, he started writhing around, a giant fish slapping against stone. Then there was a noise. It was coming from James, a bestial distress call, like the cry of an elephant. His body had never entertained such shocking vibrations before. His eyes strained wide with fear as the wailing grew louder and even more prolonged. His mother ran to his side, but his panic had poisoned all the air in the room and she felt short of breath.

'It's all right,' she lied. 'There, there . . .'

James looked through her blindly, his limbs still flailing, frenzied and wild.

'A baby cries,' the books had insisted, 'because he needs something.'

'What do you want?' she almost screamed.

Children make children of us all.

With all the poise that she could muster, she took herself out of the room and made a telephone call to the social worker. She was crying now, tears of shame and defeat, her eyes threaded with red.

'I just don't know what to do. I can't cope.'

'Don't leave him alone,' the woman told her.

'Easy for you to say,' she sobbed. 'I think I might kill him.'

'Terrible twos.'

If Sandra condoned swearing, at this point she would have cursed like the damned, but swearing was the reserve of those who have a limited vocabulary.

'Take a moment to calm yourself, regulate your breathing, then sit with him. Let him know you're there for him. Do you have a relative you can call?'

She had, but she wouldn't. There was no way she was going to let her mother – or worse, Ken's – come round and see her like this.

'Yes,' she said, and she was immediately more contained. 'I'll be fine.'

'Call again if you need to.'

'Yes.'

'It's normal at this age, tantrums. You may be expecting too much from him.'

Sandra put down the phone. She hadn't called to be patronised; her husband could do that without her running up the phone bill.

She re-entered the room to find James somewhat pacified. He sat on the rug-island, rocking himself, weeping silently. His wheezing breath was broken by sobs, which wracked his body. All the fury had fractured like an eggshell and had fallen away, leaving him exposed and vulnerable. It was hard to believe that this tiny, blinking bird was the same creature she'd witnessed a few minutes before. Her heart went out to him. She reached down tenderly and touched him on the shoulder. He looked up at her and it was as though he saw her for the first time. His eyes filled with disappointment. 'Why can't you help me?'

By the time her husband came home from work – at gone nine – James was asleep again.

Sandra murmured impassively, 'He walked and had a tantrum,' as she cleaned the sitting room with the expertise of an exorcist.

'I seem to miss out on everything.' He said this almost as encouragement, rather than out of self-pity. Gone were the days when he pined for inclusion.

'You missed him making his first sounds as well.'

'Really? Well, I'm sure he'll make them again.'

'I hope not.'

Kenneth decided not to enquire any further. Instead, he went to pour himself a whiskey and see what she'd made him for dinner. Sandra picked up the limp boy and carried him upstairs to his room.

'I waited for you . . . We can eat together,' she called to the kitchen.

Ken felt a wave of disappointment he wasn't expecting. He had grown accustomed to solitary dining.

'I didn't think it was very fair of me, leaving you to eat alone,' Sandra said as she entered the kitchen. 'The least a wife can do is put a meal on the table and eat it with her husband.'

Wife? Suddenly after all this time, Sandra was using the

word wife and not the word *mother*. Ken wasn't sure he wholeheartedly welcomed this about-turn. He'd reverted back to the days of being a bachelor, except that now – aside from the financial security, the matching accessories and the general cleanliness – there were spectral visions that inhabited his space, the apparition of a mother and a ghostly baby, ever present but almost imperceptible.

The newly united husband and wife ate in silence – an overly adventurous fish pie with too many ingredients fighting for supremacy in an excessively creamy sauce.

The awkward peace was broken by a bang that came from upstairs. Not a little relieved, they both rose to investigate.

The bang marked the beginning of James's night wanderings. His parents had never put the sides of his cot fully up, because he'd never shown any inclination to move, not even a muscle. But when they made their speedy ascension upstairs on this particular evening, they discovered that James was not in his room. It was dark and empty. Secretly Sandra was pleased: now her husband would see the pudding-proof of her mobile son, *their* mobile son. He couldn't have gone far – their room, or the bathroom – but what if he had really vanished, what if he'd been chased away like a nightmare when the day swoops in? Then they could start again with a new boy . . . or maybe a girl this time? Sandra had always wanted a girl – someone to go bargain shopping with; someone who'd be amazed by the way she'd matched the Mediterranean peach of the bed-valance with the peach in the curtains. If she'd had a child of her own, she would have had a girl; her body would have made sure of it.

But they did find James. He was in the cramped, predominantly blue bathroom. He'd pulled the dangling light-cord from its ceiling socket and was holding it like a cartoon fuse. He didn't react at all to their intrusion.

'I still think he might be deaf,' Sandra said in a whisper that was surely unnecessary if what she said was true.

As soon as she spoke, their son turned to them and grinned.

'Look at you, standing up,' Kenneth said, instantly feeling foolish for stating the obvious.

'It's past your bedtime,' Sandra said, and she heard the voice of mothers everywhere reverberating around the shiny tiled room. 'You should be asleep.'

Without another word, Ken scooped up his son – who put up no resistance – and carried him back to his room, his wife following close behind. With a helpful flick of her slim wrist she switched on the overhead light. Somehow James had moved all the trinkets and toys, which had so neatly lined the walls, so that they surrounded his bed, a boy-made barricade. The cuddly animals faced out like mongrel guard-dogs, their eyes blank and black.

His parents settled him in his bed, ignoring his recent room renovation, and Ken carefully extricated the light-cord from the little fingers. James's shining blue eyes stared up at them innocently. They said their goodnights-sleep-tights and tiptoed out, turning off the light. That was when the wailing started. Ken's eyes bulged as the noise reached inside him and gave his guts a good squeeze.

'Bloody hell.'

Sandra, now with the air of the seasoned lion-tamer, re-entered the room, with Kenneth in her shadow. They could clearly make out James's upright frame in the gloaming yellow. He was retching air, rasping in and braying out his anguish. They tried to soothe him with sugared words, but he could not hear them. With each of his rhythmical rocks he struck his head hard against the end of the cot. They tried to cushion his blows with a blanket, but he simply moved to where the glowing wood was still exposed.

Ken seemed more concerned than Sandra. 'What's he doing?'

She didn't reply.

He switched on the light and the spell was broken.

'He's afraid of the dark.' Ken was pleased. He had diagnosed and swiftly eased his son's suffering.

'Well, that's a new thing,' Sandra said, sounding a little cross. 'He never used to like the light on!' She was trying to claw back her authority on the subject.

'He does now.'

'It's a waste of electricity leaving it on all night.'

Kenneth didn't reply, but took himself downstairs, the trace of a smile on his lips, and tucked into the rest of his meal.

THREE

James's third birthday came and went, marked only by the immediate family and 'spoilt' by James on two counts: his deplorable table manners and a humdinger of a tantrum. He was now a bad-tempered child; a child who always wanted his own way. He was secretive, furtive, only developing in the dark – like film – when he thought no one was looking. And his fits of rage were building in force.

Getting help now seemed like the only answer. Even though it made them feel like they'd failed as parents, they agreed to see the social worker. Kenneth's mother and father were allowed to babysit for the first time in three years. The proviso was that it was at Sandra's house, which was clean.

Only Ken's mother came.

'Gordon can't travel very far.'

'Good God, Ethel, it's only a short bus ride. I'd have thought he would want to spend time with his *only* grandson.'

Ethel didn't say anything. It wasn't the grandson her husband was avoiding.

Sandra stepped aside, and her mother-in-law moved indoors. 'Take your shoes off, would you?'

'Sorry, Sandra . . . didn't know you'd gone Buddhist!' Ethel remarked with a sarcasm she reserved especially for her daughter-in-law.

'Well, the last time you were here you walked something

in,' Sandra couldn't help but say. Then, before Ethel could respond, she swiped up the maroon slip-ons, shouting 'Ken! Put your mother's shoes on the mat at the back door will you?'

Sandra proceeded to subject her mother-in-law to three readings of the two-pages of instructions she'd written – in capital letters – before she could, in good conscience, leave the house.

'Occasionally he has a bit of a temper tantrum,' she understated. 'It happens when I leave him for too long.'

Ken stayed silent.

'He's just been bathed, so you won't need to. There are two bottles of milk in the fridge and some food for him in the Tupperware boxes. Not the ratatouille – that's for us.'

Ethel, though she was grateful to be included, was becoming taut, like a bin-bag stuffed to splitting point. 'I have had a family of my own, you know.'

Sandra just managed to stop herself from saying, 'And look how they turned out,' saying instead, 'Help yourself to tea and coffee. The milk is in the fridge.'

'Like it would be anywhere else,' muttered her mother-in-law.

As they were halfway out of the door, Sandra was compelled to explain one last time, 'There's a number next to the phone if there are any problems.' The telephone number had no corresponding name, as she did not want Ethel to know where they were going. 'It's none of her business.' It just said, 'EMERGENCY NUMBER!!' Still not appeased, she went back in – just to make sure that her mother-in-law could work a phone. Then, finally, she left the house shouting, 'Come on Ken! We're going to be late!' – unaware that her husband had been waiting on the pavement for some time.

They took a taxi. Sandra pretended that it was so they were on time, but they both knew she just didn't want anyone witnessing them entering the building.

On arriving at the offices, they were told that they wouldn't be seeing the woman that they'd spoken to on the phone, which immediately set Sandra's nerves on edge.

'She's on maternity leave.'

This was more information than Sandra needed, or would have liked. They may as well have said, 'She's fertile.' Their stand-in social worker was called Chandra Muckerjee. Sandra didn't think herself racist. She was not a cruel woman, she never set out to offend, but her beliefs had been accrued slowly like compost.

Where are you from?' was Sandra's first question.

'Preston.'

'No, I mean where are you *from*?'

'That's actually where I was born.'

On the way home, Sandra said to Ken that she didn't see why the woman had taken *that attitude* with her. 'She knew what I meant.'

The woman knew only too well.

Question two: 'Are you married?'

'No.'

'I suppose it'll be arranged for you by your family?'

'No.'

'You don't have any children then?'

'Yes, a little girl.'

Well, that really took the Farley's Rusk. How could someone who wasn't from the same culture, wasn't married, and had a child out of wedlock – a daughter at that – give advice to an English, educated couple with a son? Sandra took her outrage one step further and speculated that the little girl was probably a *half-caste* and although she'd nothing against people falling in love per se, she was certain that that sort of set-up just wasn't fair on the child.

God save the child.

Kenneth did most of the talking from this point on, apart from when Sandra couldn't help herself. For the main part she just sat there, resolutely refusing to take off her coat, her bag attached firmly to her lap, handles clenched, as though in among her lost mints, and her lipsticks, lay her damaged pride. She was all buttoned up, battened down, her pursed lips shut, and she wouldn't even accept tea. She wanted this to be over.

Chandra invited them to open up the proceedings by talking about what was on their minds.

'My wife is concerned, well, we both are . . . that he still isn't saying anything.'

'And how old is he now?'

'You should know that,' Sandra said, as an audible aside.

'I do. It's in my files, but I'd like to hear it from you.'

'He's three,' Kenneth told her.

If Sandra had been talking, she would have said to the day how old he was, but as she wasn't, she didn't.

'That is late,' Chandra conceded. 'But there's no hard and fast rule. Children develop at different stages. I'm sure you've heard this before, but Einstein didn't start speaking until he was four.'

They hadn't heard this before, though neither of them admitted it, but it did come as some solace, and later they would repeat it with pride, only Sandra would invariably say Einstone.

'He's started making sounds though.'

'Screams,' Sandra corrected.

'He throws tantrums.'

'That's normal too. At James's age . . .'

Sandra flinched; she did not like her son's name in this unmarried mother's mouth. She would have preferred it if she'd stuck to the more abstract *he*.

'. . . a child's feelings are a mystery to themselves. He doesn't know how to think ahead yet and his past is all a jumble. Tantrums are . . . they're expressions of negative emotion. It's not personal. He just does what his body tells him to.'

The couple said nothing. Chandra took them both in. She

could see their distress; it flitted around them like flies. People never like to admit that they don't understand their children and, as she *had* read the records, she knew that James was adopted. She waited for the flies to settle.

'It's hard on parents.' She was careful to talk in the abstract. She didn't want to accuse them of anything. 'On the one hand the child is demanding autonomy and on the other he needs constant reassurance.'

Kenneth was appeased. He'd grown accustomed to Sandra talking textbook. 'At the moment he rejects our help. Is that normal too?'

Sandra didn't like this admission. It stung.

'It's difficult to understand, but when a toddler's frustrated, his anger can be directed at you, but really it's just a manifestation of anxiety. The anger itself frightens him even more. It builds up inside him, until only an explosion can release it. In James's case it is probably heightened by the fact that he doesn't express himself verbally . . . yet.'

'Makes sense,' Kenneth assented.

Even Sandra was pacified by what she took to understand from this . . . It wasn't her fault.

'Does he get much exercise?'

'Only when we aren't looking.' Sandra tried to smile.

'Three-to four-year-olds like their privacy. What about out and about? Do you go to mother-and-toddler groups?'

'Not really,' Kenneth admitted.

The mother-and-toddler groups had been abandoned after an incident involving a little boy being pushed down some steps while his father looked on. Sandra was too ashamed to venture to another.

'You should maybe try letting him wear himself out with play. Take him to the park and let him run around. Children seldom go very far and they always come back.'

But each time Sandra had taken him to the park he'd scurried away and she'd had the mortifying job of getting him home without looking like a child-snatcher. When neither Kenneth nor Sandra responded, Chandra understood that they had indeed tried, and failed.

'If things don't change in another few months, you could always try taking him to see a child psychiatrist,' she suggested. 'There are always options.'

Sandra had heard enough. These words frightened her. She pictured ominous, cold-brick hospitals and surgical masks.

'Come on, Kenneth, we should get back.'

'Have you any other questions?'

'No.' Sandra replied for them both, adding, 'Thank you,' fencing her off with formality.

'Would you like a home visit?'

'That's not necessary.' Sandra would have no idea what to bake for an Asian guest. 'Thank you very much for seeing us.' Again, now that she knew their departure was imminent, she could relax her grip on her handbag and soften her edges.

Once outside, all Sandra said was, 'We need to get a car.'

At the ripe age of three and three-quarters, James decided it was finally time to untie his tongue, break his vow of silence – bar the screaming – and say his momentous first word. It was one of two words, but which one it was would never be clear.

Sandra was sitting on the carpet beside her son, who sprawled on the sheepskin rug – which was now referred to as 'his rug', as he always sat on it. She was wearing a purple, ubiquitously seventies polo-neck and her hair was tightly permed. Until they'd adopted James, she'd sported a bob with a soft wave at the bottom. Now, her hair was wound up with short, electrical-fuse curls. Ken was in his armchair quietly trying to mend a radio his wife had been on at him to 'have a look at' for weeks. They were the picture of domesticity, or perhaps this was the picture of domesticity they chose to remember for the occasion.

James stared straight ahead, as was his custom, looking

through his persistent, clucking mother, his fixed smile almost mirroring hers. She was encouraging him to move, tug at the fleece, make a noise, do something – anything. Her newfound patience was implacable . . . anything for her little Einstone. His smile egged her on, told her that any moment now he'd respond. It said that he loved her, understood her and would do everything in his power to oblige . . . just a few minutes more was all he asked. She'd seen it all before, but she was single-minded.

Suddenly, his attention shifted from the place marginally beyond his mother to a place somewhere in the vicinity of the ornamental dog that guarded the fireplace. Then it happened. He made a noise that could not be said to resemble a scream; it was a real sound, a sound that communicated, or tried to communicate, a meaning, a meaning other than distress.

'Day,' he said.

The three of them froze, uncertain that it had really happened. Then it came again, as though it had just crept back up through his still-small-for-his-age frame and leapt, cricket-like, from his lips.

'Day.'

And then once more, this time in the more elongated form of 'Dayda'.

Sandra and Ken snatched a quick glance at each other, before snapping their heads back, like tango dancers. Only when they were certain that that was their lot for the time being, did his mother say, 'That's right. Clever boy!'

'He said "dadda!" He just said "dadda!"' Kenneth was thrilled.

Sandra's lips tightened involuntarily, the draw-string mouth. Competition between parents is common, but she'd previously managed to keep her husband's advances at bay. Now all her efforts seemed lost. She batted away his claim like it was a bluebottle.

'Oh, I don't think it was a word. Unless it was "day".' And she resumed her cooing to stem any further response. 'Clever

James said, "Daya", didn't he?'

Ken said nothing more at the time. He was quietly confident that his son had chosen him, had named him first over anything or anyone else.

After this initial foray into vocalisation, James did not seem inclined to speak another half-word for the next few days, despite the considerable pains taken by both his parents.

'Daddy,' his father mouthed and pronounced.

Sandra didn't compete publicly; she knew that she had all day, every day, to work on him. 'Mummy. Mummy. Mummy!' – an urgent prayer.

The next time he made an utterance – aside from the screaming at night – he was alone with his mother.

'Day.'

'Day!' she repeated.

'Dayad,' he replied. It sounded like a Deep South drawl for dad. Sandra didn't like this.

'Day. Day?' she offered.

'Dayid.'

'David?' his mother asked him. 'Are you saying David?' She thought that perhaps he was referring to David and Goliath from the *Bible Stories for Children* that she'd been reading to him, though he'd never seemed to pay much heed at the time.

'Davad,' he duly responded.

'David.'

And so, either by choice or by persuasion, James's first word became 'David', a word that once mastered, he would say a lot, until in the end even his mother had a change of heart.

'Is he saying "David"?' her friend Margery asked, with evident surprise.

'It does sound like David, but he's trying to say "Dad".'

'David, David,' James corrected, and smiled the smile of the guileless.

The first momentous memory that James would hold on to

was not a conventional one. He did not pick out a place or a colour, nor did he elect either one of his parents or even a favourite toy. Instead, he selected some one, or some thing, rather insubstantial, at least in the physical sense. His preferential memory was of his imaginary friend, whose name – it turned out – was David. Was it David the boy or David the word that came first? Who could say? In either case, James could not remember a time before David. He could not say just when he arrived, or how, just that he had arrived and that he was here to stay. Sometimes he materialised in the form of a question – 'David?'; sometimes the summonsed – 'David!'; sometimes the accused – 'David!! David!! DAVID!!' David, a word to punctuate and puncture any occasion, day or night. David, the constant in James's life.

Unsurprisingly, James's second word was 'James'. It was the linguistic exchange of vows. 'James, David. David, James.' He enjoyed saying his two first words and for several weeks he needed no more; he was content to celebrate their allegiance all day long. 'James-David-James.'

It was Sandra who put one and one together and made the two, James and David. She'd been reading the Bible story that she'd assumed James had requested, and yet he still said, 'David!'

'Oh where, James? Where's David?'

And James pointed. It was his first point and it led to nowhere, to a space opposite him on his rug.

'Is David there?' she asked, pointing to roughly the same area, and James smiled his most winsome smile and said, 'David', like he was introducing him to her.

Kenneth came home late again. Sandra heard his key in the lock and was eager to show off her new finding. She never stood on the formality of waiting for someone to enter a room before she addressed them. If she'd had her own way, she'd have held all her conversations from different parts of the house. So as soon as he was in earshot – which, with her range and pitch, meant as soon as the front door was ajar – she called to him, 'In here,' with the addition of, 'and shut the door please! You're letting all the cold air in!'

Compliantly Kenneth shut the door, masking a muttered swear word. He shuffled towards the disembodied voice, before remembering that he should have taken his shoes off, which he did, returning them to – where he should have left them – the mat.

'What?' He hovered in the doorway.

'Well, come in.'

His wife stared at him standing there, in his raincoat, briefcase in hand. He was only thirty-three, yet already his shoulders were settling into a submissive hunch. She frowned. 'Ask him where David is,' she said, in a whisper.

'I can't hear what you're saying.'

'Ask him where David is!'

'Where's David?'

And James pointed to the back door.

It wasn't as conclusive as Sandra had hoped for. 'He's pointing at David,' she explained.

'He's pointing at the back door.'

'No, it looks like he's pointing at the back door, but he's pointing at David.'

Ken looked perplexed.

'Are you all right?' he asked, quietly.

'Of course I'm all right!' she said, in a tone that added to his supposition that she wasn't. 'James's got an imaginary friend, like Suzy Barnes.'

'Suzy who?'

'Suzy Barnes. She was at school with me.'

'Oh.'

'She died of leukaemia. She had a friend called Clive.'

Ken really thought that she was beginning to rave now. The strain was obviously too much for her.

By the time he understood her ramblings, it was such an

anticlimax he asked what she'd made for dinner.

'Is that all you can say?'

'Is what all I can say?'

'I tell you that David isn't David from David and Goliath after all, that he's James's imaginary friend, and all you can say is, "What's for dinner?" I had waited to eat with you, but now you can eat on your own in the kitchen, you miserable sod, and I'll eat in here with James.'

'And David,' Ken couldn't help but add.

'Yes!' she shouted. 'And David!'

'What's for dinner?'

'Chicken casserole with dumplings, in a white-wine sauce.' Not long after these first words, James started to collect a few more, like apples scrumped from the language tree. Then one day he gave the trunk a good shake and they all broke free. Suddenly, he had at his disposal all the words that his parents had handed out over the years, words of anger, words of chastisement, words of reproach, noticeably few – which he'd remembered – of encouragement. Sometimes he even availed himself of words that they didn't know they'd taught him.

'What's that called?' Sandra asked, holding out a ball.

'Agony,' he said.

James wasn't interested in most of his toys. His only real treasure was his miniature zoo set. It served as a realm he could preside over without parental oppression – only he generously shared his reign with David. Here, they could play at being God together.

James had heard the names of the animals and knew their corresponding sounds, but he didn't decree it necessary to adhere to this outmoded code of practice. Their empire would have its own rules. 'Squeak,' went the wolf. 'Hiss,' went the horse. 'Moo,' went the hippo. At first, Sandra and Ken tried to correct him, but it was futile. They soon allowed the lamb to roar, the tiger to quack, the monkey to oink. Also, under James and David's administration, there was no longer any need to segregate the species, domestic from wild, predator from prey. It was back to biblical times. The wolf would lie down with the lamb, and why not? No wolf that squeaked could possibly strike fear into a lamb that roared.

The lion may have eaten straw like the ox, but James and David ruled their empire with iron fists. Two legs were definitely good and James could be heard disciplining the animals for flouting his laws. 'You are bad. You are a bad zebra!' His father often had to replace a disabled sheep, or a goose, with its neck wrung into a corkscrew.

His parents struggled to tear him – or rather the two of them – away from their play. More often than not, it resulted in a tantrum beaten out on the table. They reassured themselves that he was engaging himself now at least, even if it was exclusively in make-believe. He was imaginative. They had to give him that, though they would try to take it away from him later.

The fits of temper, they'd hoped, would have shown some signs of waning by now, but if anything they were growing in both intensity and regularity. They'd thought that the company of David would have been some comfort, but James's fears seemed to feed off their allegiance. Sometimes James screamed 'David!' as though it was his companion who was the cause of his distress.

When Sandra entered her son's room, first thing, her brown eyes would search his clear blue ones to see if that haunted, glacial glint was there. She learnt to sense the vibrations below the ice, a human seismograph. She monitored the pressure of his fury expanding inside him and knew that eventually it would rupture the surface. When it did, it would be sudden. So, after a few mortifying outbreaks in supermarkets – which cost his mother dearly in damages and dignity – she knew that it was safest for everyone concerned if, on days like these, he was kept indoors.

Once his outburst was underway there was no way of reaching him. He was lost to the world. He screamed as though under persecution and was so physically involved in his terror that anything in his way would be carelessly trashed, or crashed into. Then, after a stint as the whirling dervish, he'd fling himself to the floor, where he'd writhe and kick, wrestling frantically with invisible, wiry demons. He showed no instinct for self-preservation and often cut, or bruised himself, quite severely. If Sandra tried to restrain him, he lashed out at her, biting down on the hand that fed him. It shocked her the strength his rage could muster. Sometimes, too, he said hateful things. Other times he cried out for her, even when she was present. But, more often than not, it was David whom he called for.

When the tantrum had passed his eyes would glaze over, like a porcelain doll's. He'd stare fixedly at one spot and wouldn't be distracted from it. His terror seemed sinister and primitive, and so contagious that his parents could palpably feel his fear. Sometimes, after the fit had loosened its grip, he'd hold his breath, clutching his ribcage so that it couldn't expand. And then, like an opal when a cloud covers the sun, he'd turn a worrying grey colour. But on most occasions his stubborn body would double-cross him by making him throw up, prizing his arms apart, allowing the breath back in. Then, one time, the convulsions were so furious and frenzied that he passed out.

Sandra and Kenneth accepted that it was time to go for more advice; this time from the doctor.

They decided to take James with them. It was safer that way. When Ethel had babysat that first and last time, she'd neglected to put a drop of hot, soapy water in her empty teacup and it had stained the china. She'd also trodden incriminating cake crumbs into the living-room carpet. The doctor in question was their GP and he already knew about their intimate fertility case-history, so Sandra had no problems talking to him. Not trusting her hairdresser, he was her Protestant priest.

When they entered the medical confessional, Dr Hazeldene addressed the husband and wife exclusively, ignoring their son. James didn't mind. He blanked him right back and sat on the moss-green carpet facing the other way, while his parents explained their predicament.

'Perhaps you're being too lenient,' the doctor told them, sagely. 'Only children,' he said, a term that always made Sandra think of lonely children, 'are often a little mollycoddled.'

Both Sandra and Kenneth objected to this implication. They objected to the word 'mollycoddled' almost as much as they objected to the idea.

'I always say, "Cocker thy child and he shall make thee afraid,"' the doctor continued.

Sandra looked nonplussed, picturing happy red spaniels.

'We try to be firm with him,' Ken said, trying to sound firm when he said it.

'*Try* might not be enough. I'm pretty old-fashioned when it comes to discipline. What is it the Germans say? "Better the child should cry than the Father."'

Sandra, who used idioms herself to fill any silence, was now truly bamboozled by his onslaught. A taste of her own medicine.

'He has horrible tantrums,' she confided in a whisper, stealing a glance at her son's dark curls.

'Tantrums?' he repeated, from behind his horn-rimmed spectacles and his well-worn suit. 'And how do you respond to these tantrums?'

'We've tried everything, reading to him . . . singing to him.' Ken looked at Sandra as he said this, to illustrate that he didn't sing to his son, his wife did. 'Nothing seems to help. He refuses to go to bed or to let us turn out the lights.'

'We've even smacked him,' Sandra spurted, and then concealed the lower part of her face with her hand as though to cover a sudden nosebleed.

'I've nothing against giving a child a smack,' the doctor assured her. 'A child is like a tree: if you do not correct the sapling, it will grow a crooked trunk.'

'He's a crybaby,' Ken said. It took some resolve to say this. He didn't like to think that a son of his was of a cowardly disposition, but then James wasn't, in truth, a son of his.

'Have you tried turning out the lights once he's asleep?'

In the corner, James started talking to David. If the adults were having their private conversation, then he could have his. The doctor refrained from looking at the infant. He was as invisible as David. Instead, he crossed one long limb over the other. Sandra noticed that his trousers were an inch too short. If he'd been a normal person, she would have offered to turn down his hems for him, but she liked it somehow. She also forgave him the tuft of hair that always stuck up on the back of his head, like an exclamation mark. It didn't, for some reason, make her want to take a brush to it. Dr Hazeldene corresponded with her expectations about doctors. She couldn't imagine one any other way. It seemed fitting that a man whose job it was to care for others should take so little care of himself.

Ken, battling above James's babble, rubbed his grainy, grey eyes and told the doctor that they'd tried that, but he woke up as soon as the room went black.

'Well, this may sound a bit harsh . . . and you'll find it hard not to break your resolve . . . but I recommend that you let him cry himself to sleep. Only this way will he realise that you won't come running every time he kicks up a fuss.'

James's chatter became louder at this point. It was evident that, though the doctor kept his eyes straight ahead, it was taking all his restraint not to stride over on his ostrich legs and take a swipe at the boy with his long, prehensile fingers.

'He's doing it on purpose!' Sandra wailed.

'Mr Gardner, why don't you take your son outside for a moment?'

Ken complied. He offered James his hand, but his son

ignored it. He stood up of his own accord, and continued his own conversation. As the heavy, white door of the room shut, on its slow-spring hinge, his words slipped through the tiny gap: 'David, he is a bad doctor, a naughty doctor. He made Mummy cry.'

Dr Hazeldene pretended not to catch this.

Sandra flushed and blew her nose on a handkerchief, as though the noise might magic the words away.

'Now, don't be upset, Sandra,' he told her.

'Sometimes he frightens me,' she confessed, before quickly shuffling her words. 'I mean I'm frightened for him. He loses control and hurts himself. No matter how bad it is for me, it must be far worse for him.'

'Don't count on it,' he told her, giving her absolution.

'He's started holding his breath now, till he passes out,' she said, dabbing her eyes.

'Not possible. His body's reflexes would reassert themselves and force the air back into his lungs.'

Despite the fact that she'd seen him pass out, she trusted the doctor and would not dream of refuting what he told her.

'Oh. That's a relief,' she said, and meant it. 'He has an imaginary friend, called David.'

'Just a phase,' he assured her and gave her a prescription for sleeping pills. 'Like I said, put him in his cot, and if you're afraid that he'll do himself some damage, pad the sides, but let him scream till he's blue in the face. Mark my words, he'll change his tune.'

'Thank you, doctor.' She put the holy sacrament in her bag and rejoined her family, who were waiting in the car, a new one, which Ken had dutifully bought.

That evening they would follow the doctor's advice. There was a sense of anticipation during the remainder of the day. They were almost looking forward to it, wishing the hands of the clock on their way to seven. When the time did arrive, and not a moment before – Sandra was scrupulous with instructions

– Ken scooped James up and took him to his bedroom.

'David!' the boy called out, blue eyes wide, arms outstretched, the painted Christ-child reaching for John the Baptist.

Sandra followed her husband, head bowed ritualistically. The altar-cot was already prepared with padding, the cell sides up.

'Now, you be good. Promise me you'll go to sleep,' Sandra said. In truth, just this once, she wanted him to scream, so that they could put their cure to the test.

'David?' he asked.

'Yes, David's here too,' she told him, though she couldn't have known.

Ceremoniously, his mother switched out the light and his father slowly shut the door. They stood on the threshold, expectantly, like Christmas carollers. First came the familiar low moan, then a wail, which rose rapidly, before a crash of the cage sides as he bashed against them. 'David! David! David!'

Sandra and Ken shared a guilty grimace.

Downstairs they turned on and turned up *The Good Life*. This served as a distraction for the next half an hour. Ken, like most men his age, had a thing about Felicity Kendal, and Sandra, like most women her age, fancied that she *was* Felicity Kendal. When it was over, which was all too soon, Sandra asked Ken if he fancied a cup of tea and a slice of homemade cake –

'The one you like, with the coffee and walnuts.' She always said 'the one you like,' or if the person hadn't had it before, she said, 'You'll like it,' as though she'd made it with them in mind. It was her way of making sure people said yes. In this instance, the tea and cake offer was an excuse to hear if James had settled at all. Before she left the room she made a pretence of picking up a bit of fluff from the carpet, holding it dramatically, as she always did, between finger and thumb, before dropping it in the 'convenient' bin in the corner.

As soon as the door was ajar, his cries could be heard.

Sandra winced and then set about her counterfeit objective, closing the door behind her first, to keep the heat in. She poured two cupfuls of water into the kettle, ever heedful of energy preservation, or, more accurately, fiscal preservation. She cut a slice of cake, her hand shaking a little, as though the vibrations from the cacophony upstairs had travelled down each step, across the carpet and up through her conductor-like body. She cut a smaller slice for Ken. 'He shouldn't really be having any,' she said to herself, even though it was her idea. She'd secretly put him on a diet.

In preparation, she wiped the already clean wooden tray – a wedding present – and laid out saucers, cups with milk already in, a small china jug for refills, cake forks and tea cosy. She did this with surgical precision. When she'd completed this task to her satisfaction, she gave the spotless laminated wood-look surfaces another once-over, as though the action would somehow wipe clean her conscience. The muffled cries continued unabated.

Once the teapot was warmed, then filled, then cosy coated, Sandra braced herself for the walk back to the sitting room. Without even a cursory glance up to the source of the fracas, she tapped, with the corner of the tray, on the glass-panelled door. Ken jerked upright, like he'd been snapped out of hypnosis, and went over to open the door, shutting it carefully and quickly behind her. She placed the tray on the coffee table, minding not to scratch the glass. Ken reached out to remove the floral tea cosy.

'It's not brewed yet!' she snapped, and his hand recoiled like it had been struck.

Ken couldn't sit down. He moved fretfully about the room, a tired bird, looking for somewhere safe to settle. The door opened. James's sound waves had travelled back along the hall in Sandra's wake, tracking them down, turning the handle.

'You never shut it properly!' she scolded bitterly, as though he'd deliberately committed some violent assault against her person. As she said this, she whipped off the cosy and poured the tea.

'The latch has lost its tension,' he explained and, to prove this, he crossed to the door and turned the handle a few times, before shutting it properly so that he could hear the 'click'. The howling was shut out. She put the cosy back on.

'Then mend it. And the door into the garage. Go to the hardware shop in the village after work tomorrow. And while you're there, you can take those two films to the chemist's. And we need a new thermos flask. James threw it and the glass shattered.' Sandra was punishing him, inventing chores to eat into his evening.

Kenneth didn't say anything.

His wife was picturing the camera films in the drawer, next to the pens, the tape-measure and the batteries. He'd forget to pick up the film in the morning, she knew it, and she'd be obliged to call him at the office. 'Did you pick up the film?' she'd ask, as the two rolls tapped against each other in her palm. He couldn't be trusted to do anything. And she would have proved it again.

Another excruciating hour passed. Sandra pretended to watch something on TV that she was sure her husband wouldn't want to, while he did the crossword, knowing full well that she liked to do it with him.

'I think I should go up in a bit,' Sandra suggested, her resolve drooping suddenly, like a flag when the wind drops.

'The doctor said we should let him stew,' he reminded her, throwing her tea-fascism back in her face.

'Yes,' she agreed, without much conviction. 'It's for his own good.'

After the news had finished, the couple looked at each other and nodded. Enough time had elapsed. They could now put themselves out of their misery, in the hope that James already had.

Sandra loaded up the tray, picking up a walnut fragment

from the vicinity of Ken's armchair. He opened the door for her, deliberately rattling the handle again to prove it was at fault. Their ears were eager-terrier-erect as they froze to listen. Nothing. No noise. Not a sound. Sandra took the crockery to the kitchen. Ken wouldn't dare go upstairs without her, would he? She hurried back, but found her husband waiting for her on the bottom step. She insisted on ascending before him, as she fancied herself better equipped to map out the quietest route. He followed her, concentrating hard; the strained silence rushed in his ears; the sound of the sea through shingle.

'Turn off the hall light,' she whispered, without looking back, gesturing in the vicinity of the switch. Then together they crept forward. And with trepidation, Sandra inched open the door.

All was quiet, but her intuition cried out. Something wasn't right. She didn't need to look at the cot to know that it was empty. Beside it was an island mound of pale-blue pyjamas, surrounded by a dark and glistening moat.

'Good God!' her voice cracked like bones. 'Turn on the light.'

'What?'

'The light! The light!' she screamed.

James had used the padding as a climber uses a rock-face. He'd scaled the side of the cot and had either fallen – or thrown himself – from it, landing on his head.

'He's dead. We've killed him,' she whimpered, cradling the limp body to her, like she'd never been able to before. His blood emblazoned her clothes and face. 'I told you we should have checked up on him!' Blame launched from her mouth, like a missile. 'Call an ambulance,' she instructed Ken, suddenly calm amidst the crisis. Her husband stood dumbly looking on at this perverse pietà, the prematurely dead Christ and his despairing mother. He broke himself away from the vision, half fell down the stairs and dialled 999.

Only now could Sandra feel the faint, steady heartbeat

in her arms, and her tears of guilty grief were exchanged for those of guilty relief.

'I'm sorry,' she told him. 'I'm sorry.'

She said this to the ambulance-men, and the doctors and nurses, over and over again. 'I'm so sorry.' These words went in the doctor's report, along with the bruises and cuts that were discovered elsewhere on the boy's body.

When James was stitched up and conscious again he was all smiles. 'Hello, Mum. Hello, Dad. Hello, David,' he said, happily.

Sandra was greatly reassured by this. He'd said hello to her. She was expecting to be shunned for ever. But Ken couldn't help but wonder if James hadn't masterminded the whole thing.

FOUR

After this fateful night, James abandoned walking for a few weeks. It seemed he'd simply forgotten that he'd ever done it. When Sandra took him into hospital to have his stitches removed, she told this to a nurse, who went to ask a doctor, who came to have a look at the smiling boy.

'Hello there, I'm Peter,' he said to James cheerfully, from beneath a big mop of sandy hair.

'Say hello, David,' James instructed.

The doctor looked at Sandra quizzically.

'His imaginary friend,' she explained, with a fake laugh.

'David says you look like a farmer.'

Sandra laughed again.

'Does he? Hello, David,' he said to the air, before addressing James again. 'So, I believe you don't fancy walking any more? I feel like that sometimes.'

'I think he's concussed. Maybe it's brain damage?' Sandra speculated, certain that she'd impaired her son for life.

'So you had a fall?' he asked the boy, while inspecting the scar. James's curls nodded, beneath the fingers.

The doctor had mastered the ability to keep two people engaged without excluding either, so as he examined James, he spoke to Sandra.

'I don't think he's concussed . . . an emotional shock can cause regressions in behaviour. But if he doesn't get on his feet again in the next few weeks, then I'd go to your GP and get him checked out.' He then launched into a rendition of 'Jack and Jill went up the hill'. While doing this he simultaneously removed the stitches from James's scalp, an act he completed with surprising dexterity considering the size of his large, gamy fingers.

'There! You're very brave,' he said, handing the discarded sutures to the boy as a gory souvenir. His mother would of course bin them as soon as they left the building. They were an unsightly reminder of the incident and, to her mind, probably not hygienic.

The broken crown healed pretty quickly, but James would carry for ever a memento mark that scored his side-parting like chalk. Sandra continually tried to smooth his hair over it, but it stubbornly refused to be covered up. And a sudden, sideways jerk of James's head was all it took to reveal the skeleton finger scar, which pointed to his parents, reminding them of how they'd failed him.

Sandra was determined to negotiate around his daytime tantrums and get him into a nursery, even if it meant resorting to bribery.

She was well aware that James, like most children, had a penchant for sweets. She'd much rather have opted for the old-fashioned healthy carrot of encouragement, but she'd seen how well her mother, Maude, got on with her grandson and it was by killing with kindness.

'Are you pleased to see your Grandma?'

No reply.

'Give her a cuddle,' Sandra would insist, ordering him to betray his body with a gesture.

If he obliged her, furnishing a kiss on sponge-cake flesh, then he expected a pay-off.

'David would like some sweets, please.'

And when his grandmother fetched the Quality Street tin,

with its array of Topics, Double Deckers and Fox's Glacier Fruits, there was a look on James's face that was close to love. Sandra could settle for this. She harboured no reservations about resorting to a backhander, not if it meant that looks of love were exchanged and a superficial semblance of peace was established.

So a small packet of Chocolate Buttons saw him dressed in the morning, smiling, and to the nursery without any resistance. The initial introductions proved to go without a hitch. The teacher welcomed his mother warmly and seemed quite captivated by her son.

'Well, I'm sure that James will be a lovely addition to our school,' she concluded. 'Is there anything I should know about him?'

'What do you mean?' Sandra asked, not a little flustered.

'I mean . . . does he have any allergies, that sort of thing?'

'Oh.' She was visibly relieved. 'No, he's normal.' Well, it's what everyone had told *her*. 'But he has an imaginary friend,' she admitted, as casually as she could.

'Really? That's nice. What's your friend's name, James?'

'David,' he beamed, and then looked shy and hid behind his mother, something he'd never done before.

'Was he flirting?' Sandra wondered. No. He was far too young.

It was all settled. James would start his attendance the following week and Sandra was invited to sit in the class for an hour or so, while James got acclimatised.

The journey there was fraught. Mother and son had sat in the car, with the passenger door open. They were waiting for David, who wasn't ready yet. Time was getting on. If she couldn't even deliver her son to nursery punctually on his first day, she was going to look really incompetent.

'We're just going to have to go without him,' she told James, but she caught a glimpse of her son in the mirror and something told her that he was about to hold his breath. 'OK!' she quickly added. 'Call him.'

'David!' James shouted, louder than she thought was strictly necessary. And a few minutes later, James leant back to let David clamber over him, before shutting the car door.

'Ready now,' he said, as though addressing a cab driver.

They were ten minutes late.

'So sorry,' she said to Miss Ryan. 'Traffic!' Only a white lie: there had been traffic.

'Not to worry. If you'd like to take a chair over by the wall,' she said, pointing to a garishly orange child's seat. Sandra did as she was bidden, feeling silly and oversized. The room was high-ceilinged and brightly lit and children's paintings and collages covered every available inch of space. There was a corner where the books were stored and above it a sign read 'SHHH! LIBRARY'. Sandra smiled her approval. Maybe this was just what the doctor ordered.

James did not look at his mother once. He took Miss Ryan's soft hand in his small one. Sandra flinched. He may as well have slapped her across her face with it.

'Is David here?' Miss Ryan remembered to ask.

James nodded.

'Well, we've got lots more friends for you to make.' Twelve to be exact. James was told all their names. He smiled at each child in turn, the sort of smile a floor manager gives to his staff.

'Maybe you and David would like to play with Jessica?' Miss Ryan suggested. Compliantly James sat down next to the girl who was serving tea from a red plastic teapot. Miss Ryan and Sandra waited to see if he'd interact or snatch away the teapot for himself. He did neither. He smiled and looked on, though slightly to his left, perhaps to where David sat.

Jessica asked him if he wanted some cake.

'There isn't any.'

'It's pretend cake!' she advised him with an exaggerated

sigh.

'David will have some.'

'Who's David?'

'He's David.'

'Can't see him,' she said with a frown, the law of let's pretend being turned against her.

'I can't see your cake.' Without another word, he took his leave and set off for the SHHH! LIBRARY, while Jessica returned to her play unperturbed.

Sandra reddened, but Miss Ryan smiled.

James couldn't read yet, as such, but he could make it look like he could. He took down a book and sat with it open on his left knee, so that David could see it too. He waited for enough time to pass for him to have read each page before turning to the next. Occasionally he giggled as though he had just read something quite hilarious.

Another lady came in and one of the boys, called Mark, abandoned his building blocks to run over to the woman.

'Mummy, Mummy!' he proudly rejoiced.

It transpired that every day, a different mother volunteered to come into class and read to the children, to give Miss Ryan a break. Only this mother was glamorous, blonde and well dressed and her son's spontaneous elation surged through Sandra, making her melancholy. She quickly made her excuses to the teacher, waved at James and left. He didn't acknowledge her departure. He nonchalantly joined the other children on the floor, in anticipation of the story. But when she was out of sight, his eyes fell to his palms and tears quietly started to fall. The other boys and girls didn't notice, nor did Miss Ryan, who was busy collecting crayons from the childproof carpet. He was left alone.

In the afternoon Sandra came back to collect him. He was holding the teacher's hand again, smiling at her as though they'd just shared a joke. 'A joke about me,' Sandra thought.

'How was he, Miss Ryan?' she asked, ignoring James.

'Good as gold. And it's Sophie.'

'My son has charmed you into our being on first-name terms,' she thought resentfully. 'Good as gold!' Sandra was resolute; she would remain 'Mrs Gardner' to her.

'I don't think he's used to spending much time with children though. He gravitated towards me and Mark's mother. He doesn't have any brothers or sisters, does he?'

'No.'

'I have David,' James reminded Sophie, with a squeeze of her hand.

'Oh yes, I forgot about David.'

Sandra wished that she could.

'Well, I'll see you two tomorrow,' she said to James and the space to his left.

James nodded and beamed. Then, turning to David, he said, 'Shhh!'

The teacher laughed and Sandra tried to force a smile.

'He's adorable,' Sophie confided to his mother, sure that she'd agree.

Sandra reached for James's hand but he withdrew it, using it instead to gently pull the teacher down to his level, before planting a kiss on her cheek. Sophie blushed, and so did Sandra.

'We need to get going,' Sandra said, already on the move, and her son trawled slowly after her.

His teacher watched him with concern. 'Poor little mite,' she thought, 'he's starved of affection.'

His mother opened the car door and he climbed into the back seat. He refused to sit in the front. He preferred to sit with David. He chose David over her every time.

'You're all sweetness and light with your grandma and everyone else. What about me?' she asked him, like he was an adult, her lover.

James didn't respond.

'Did you like it there better than at home?' She was

being petulant. If only she'd looked into his bloodshot blue eyes in the rear-view mirror. They told a very different story, one that she would have liked.

'It's better than being home. But David doesn't like it. He doesn't want to go again.'

'Fine, tomorrow David can stay with me,' she said, fastening her seatbelt with a snap.

James would never let that happen.

Sandra had thought that Sophie would soon realise that her son was not all he seemed, or, rather, that he was more than he seemed. She wanted him to betray himself. Somewhat perversely she longed to hear the words 'I can't take him back. He's too much of a handful for me on my own. I don't know how you cope.' But no, her blue-eyed boy could do no wrong.

James and David were in fact already wreaking their own private havoc, but they used discretion and were never near a child when the tears began to fall. They were mini good-cop, bad-cop. James would say, 'David, do not hurt Jessica!' or Nick, or Amelia, or whoever, and a second later they'd been hurt. Sophie did hear a small bell of suspicion tinkling when, on one occasion, she asked Mark why he was crying and he replied, between sobs, that 'David did it.' But she couldn't very well make David sit in the corner.

It was Sandra who first saw him – or them – at it. It was her turn to come in and read the children a story. She was nervous. Her forceful personality assured her a limelit place in the life around her, but she didn't like performing as such. She sat precariously in the small, children's chair – moulded for a bottom much smaller than her own – and opened the book she'd brought. Pinocchio, one of James and David's favourites, a tale of a piece of wood that tells lies and comes to life.

She'd dressed up specially – a blouse she'd bought from a charity shop, though it *was* Jaeger – and she'd put on some make-up, hoping for a celebratory welcome like Mark's mother had received. But her son wouldn't look at her. He talked loudly to David, arguing about crocodiles and whether or not they could cry.

Self-consciously she started reading, and James settled down with the other children. He did love the story and he would concede to be silent while she read, if she did the voices properly. Sandra felt the eyes of the little audience on her. Those sweet-natured, pretty girls in nice dresses made her want to cry. Her body yearned to leave with one of them. Then she lost her track in the book and spoke Lampwick's line 'Being bad's a lot of fun, ain't it?' in her Jiminy Cricket voice.

'NO!' James shouted.

She looked up, lost somewhere between the page and her thoughts. Sophie was distracted, rearranging paint pots in the store cupboard. James flashed his mother a look of recrimination, before leaning over the boy sitting next to him to slap the puppy-fat face of a little girl.

'Stop it!' Sandra screamed.

A second later, there followed a huge clattering noise. The pitch of Sandra's voice had caused an avalanche in the store cupboard, and the sound made all the children jump. This sent the room into chaos. The little girl who'd been struck started to wail and everyone copied her, in a collapsing house of cards.

Sophie came out of the cupboard to see a room of children all in different stages of distress, an army of clockwork soldiers winding each other up. Sandra was already at the classroom door, holding her son almost off the ground by his arm. He was shouting and flailing like an angry monkey. The teacher didn't have time to ask questions, she had to quell the swell of hysteria that was gaining strength and rising up ready to consume the whole room and everyone in it.

Sandra held James aloft all the way to the car, a lioness carrying her cub in her jaws.

'David!' he yelled. 'David made me do it!'

She set him down and he tried to bolt, but her primitive instincts were on alert, her arm shot out and she caught hold of him by his hair, yanking him back with a helpless yelp.

'I won't have you hitting people!' she barked and, without a trace of irony, gave him a tremendous slap across his face. 'I won't have it!' Slap.

Mother and son were left in the hollow silence, until the noise of the traffic slowly entered at the fringes. At least James had stopped screaming. Sandra too was still, except for her hand, which was shaking violently. The force of the blow had mussed up his hair, exposing the snail-trail white scar, and to complement it a reproachful red welt was rising on the side of his face. His alarming blue eyes had darkened and were fiercely locked on to hers. They spoke unequivocally: I always thought that you never loved me. Now I know.

They stood, locked in this stand-off, for what seemed like a long while. Then his mother slowly released her hand from his hair, which she hadn't realised she was still holding. He did not flinch, or break his stare with a blink. She faltered.

'You made me do it,' she whispered, unconsciously mirroring her son's own alibi.

Sandra looked down at her hands accusingly: her left, the hair-puller; and her right, the face-slapper. She opened the car door in a daze and slumped, quite exhausted, into the driver's seat. She felt defeat and shame sidle in beside her, familiar but unwelcome accomplices. Had her son just smiled as he climbed into the back? She thought she caught a glimpse of it in the mirror, but the red handprint had made her look away.

'David says that we will not be going back there,' her son said, without a trace of intonation.

'Yes, you will! First thing tomorrow! You're going to apologise to Miss Ryan.'

'Do you mean Sophie?'

'You know full well who I mean.'

'What for?'

'If you don't know I'm not going to tell you,' she snapped.

As though to illustrate how ludicrous this sounded, James repeated her phrase, handing it over to David: 'If you don't know, David, I'm not going to tell you.'

After the insult, there was a pause for David's response.

Then followed the injury, 'You'll do as you're told,' capped off with the illogical bonus affront, 'Because I say so!'

His mimicry was merciless and precise.

That evening brought a full-blown tantrum before bed and an episode of night terrors from which he was inconsolable. Sandra felt like letting the playschool thing drop, but Ken was strong on this point.

'He has to learn.'

She had to agree. He did have to learn, and whether they used a hook or a crook was immaterial. He'd thank them in the end, when they'd all go on holiday together to Spain and laugh about how he'd been a bit of a tearaway as a child. They set their eyes to the future and their imaginary, wish-fulfilment son.

James took some bribing to get him into class again, but he finally submitted. Sophie noticed Sandra enter and didn't halt the frown sliding down her forehead.

'Hello,' she said, 'I wasn't sure whether you'd come back.' Sophie was suddenly Miss Ryan again.

'No. Well . . . I wanted James to say he was sorry.'

'You wanted *James* to say sorry?' Miss Ryan shook her head incredulously. Then she pulled her hair back and bent down. 'What are you sorry about, James?' she asked, earnestly.

'David and I are sorry because Mummy said Lampwick's words in her Jiminy Cricket voice.' As he said this, he stared steadily at Sandra, before turning away to give his teacher his full-fat, butter-wouldn't-melt focus.

'I see,' said Miss Ryan, her frown a fixture. 'I don't think you need to be sorry about that.' She stood erect and ruffled his hair and the scar smiled up at her. She took it in and her forehead furrows deepened. 'Why don't you go and play with Richard?'

James nodded, his repentant blue eyes perfectly framed by the curls of his coquettishly long lashes.

'Come on, David,' he said meekly, making his way over to the SHHH! LIBRARY corner.

Miss Ryan followed him with her eyes. Sandra tried to speak, but was silenced by a hand younger than her own. She'd be obliged to wait until James had settled himself. She took Miss Ryan in properly for the first time. Mid-twenties and beautiful – she had to admit – open-faced, full-lipped, with long, fair, wavy hair. She'd always envied naturally curly hair. Miss Ryan was now glaring at her. Sandra opened her mouth to speak, but she'd lost her conviction. In any case, she was not going to be allowed to have her say first.

'Can you shed some light on what happened yesterday? I turned my back for a few minutes and all hell broke loose. I didn't appreciate you leaving me like that . . . on my own . . . to try and calm a class-full of children *you'd* somehow upset.' Her eyes were narrow, defying her. This had better be good, they said.

'Me!' Sandra couldn't believe her ears, which were reddening. 'It wasn't me.' She heard her words ring out into the colourful, cavernous space. Even to her, it sounded like she was telling tales. She gawped at Miss Ryan and at the room, her judge and her jury. 'He h-h-hit a little girl,' she stammered.

'I find that *very* hard to believe. He's such a good-natured boy.'

'He's not all sweetness and light,' Sandra managed to say, her eyes filling with angry tears.

'No child is sweetness and light,' Miss Ryan asserted dispassionately. Witnessing Sandra's distress did not encourage her to soften her tone. She was used to the child who cried wolf. 'We'll forget all about this, but I think it's better if you don't come in to read again. I can't risk another episode like yesterday.'

And that was that, Sandra was cast in the role of troublemaker. There was nothing she could say in her defence. She stood defeated, weighing up what to do next. Should she stop him from going there for good, severing at once this repellent teacher-pupil bond of complicity? She could always try another playschool. No. That was not as easy as it sounded, he'd been asked to leave almost all the others in the local vicinity. If Miss Ryan liked him so much, she could bloody well have him. She'd admit the error in her judgement eventually. Time, not her, would play this out. In the interim, Sandra would have to be content with sitting on her hands and waiting.

'I'll bring him back tomorrow,' she said, and without looking back – a trick she'd learnt from her son, the master of snubs – she dragged James out of the room and bundled him into the back of the Escort. There was no call for her to speak: the erratic way she drove was clearer than conversation. He was surprisingly calm. The victorious can afford to show good grace.

When they arrived home, she jerked on the brakes, sending him lurching forwards, and in a flash she was yanking him out of the car, her hand pinching his thin upper arm like a crab claw. He didn't make a sound, despite the discomfort. His mother marched him through the garage and flung him out into the back garden. After shutting and locking the door behind him she went to the kitchen, where she set about rearranging the freezer compartment.

Everything had a handwritten dated label on it:
Cock-a-Leekie 3/3
Gooseberry Fool 13/9
Chicken Stock 26/4

This way she could establish which items had been in there the longest and therefore needed using up first.

That evening they were to go to Ethel and Gordon's for supper. Ken was to join them there when he'd finished work.

Unfortunately for him, he phoned to see what time he needed to come home.

'You know we're meeting you there!'

'Oh, is that what we decided?' 'We' was used here in its loosest sense.

'Yes. Last week.'

'Oh. OK. How's James?'

She'd succeeded in pushing her son, the exile on the lawn, completely out of her mind. She peered out through the kitchen window but couldn't see him.

'He's fine. I'll see you at your mum's,' she said, and put the phone down. Then she flew through the house and out into the garden.

'James?' An alarmed bird call.

No response.

She rushed round to the side of the house where the laburnum tree flowered. No sign.

Then she spotted him. Her son was sitting up in the boughs of the apple tree, whispering with David. Thankful, but determined not to show it, Sandra walked over, catching her breath.

'Time to get ready.'

He pretended not to hear her.

She was about to give his leg a slap when she saw that it was covered in blood. 'What have you done?'

'Nothing.'

'Come down, now!'

'No.'

She struggled to grab hold of him. It was awkward as he was lodged between a Y of the jutting branches and the blood made him greased-pig slippery. He shoved her off a few times with his sandal but she was not to be dissuaded. Finally she managed to snake her arm around his slim waist and haul him out.

When she set him down, she knelt to look at his leg.

It oozed blood, his familiar blood. James had not thought to cry before, but on seeing the anguish in his mother's face, his own crumpled in compliance. She carried him through the house and set him down on the beige-tiled window ledge in the bathroom. His legs dangled foolishly. After removing one small Jesus sandal, she eased off his long, blood-soaked sock.

The cut was not as bad as it looked, but there was a reservoir gouge, which refilled with blood each time she winced and wiped it.

'How did you do it?' she asked, suddenly in nurse mode.

'I told you. I didn't do anything.'

'This will sting. Be brave,' she said, applying Germoline.

He inhaled sharply.

'Then how did it happen?'

'David did it.'

'Did he now?'

'Yes.'

She put a plaster on with more pressure than was absolutely necessary.

'Ow!'

Now that Sandra had ascertained the cut wasn't deep, her attention quickly transferred itself to the breadcrumb trail of blood he'd dropped across her carpet. Her anxiety metamorphosed into anger once more. She left him stranded on the ledge while she attacked the shagpile.

'David didn't do it,' she told him, as she dabbed hot water onto the dark red stains.

'Did.' He was crying afresh now.

'Stop crying or I'll give you something to cry for.' She could barely believe she'd said this, but she had, and that was that. Her mother, whom she'd always sworn she'd never turn into, had used this line on her time and time again when she was a child. But she couldn't help it. When parental push came to shove, many such well-worn phrases came tumbling out, bags of old clothes she'd forgotten she'd kept.

She'd had her fill of David for the day. She was sick of it. David was testament to a lie. It made her inclined to punish James or, at the very least, catch him out.

'Let me tell you something, young man,' she said, getting up off the carpet, which was going to need something stronger than hot water to get the blood out. 'David isn't real.'

'Yes, he is,' James spluttered through his sobs. He was gulping for breath, drowning in mucus. He was starting to get hysterical.

'No, he isn't. He doesn't exist!' She slapped him. Not hard, just hard enough to shock him.

James's colour drained, his white opal change.

'Don't you dare!' she warned him, but he was deaf to reason. He turned red, then a washed-out grey, then deathly white, before he fell into a faint and slumped off the window ledge. She managed to catch hold of him before he hit the washbasin, but then the two of them fell backwards onto the floor, crushing her breath away.

She lay there, with the weight of him on top of her, and decided that both literally and figuratively she would no longer take this lying down. It was high time that he understood who was boss. She rolled him off her, quickly checked that the plaster wasn't leaking, then purposefully quit the room. 'Let him come round on his own,' she thought, 'then he'll see how much good David is!'

She was still a mother, though, and her austerity was skin thin. She couldn't help but watch over him through the crack in the door, just to make sure that he was all right.

A few moments passed and he came to. He sat up and looked about. 'David?' he said. He rose to his feet and turned round. 'I can see you,' he said.

Sandra didn't know if he was talking to her, or to David, but she moved hastily away.

This was when James understood that his parents didn't think David was real, not in any sense. James had grasped early on the fact that adults couldn't see David, but how could he have known that adults have to see something before they'll believe it exists? He would show them. David had been his private adviser so far; now James was going to make him public.

FIVE

His mother stood impatiently by the front door and jangled her car keys like a baby's rattle. When James was ready, he strode past her without acknowledgement.

'Come along, David,' he said affectionately, and opened the car door so that his friend could clamber in. He didn't bother to close it after them, pretending to be too engrossed in conversation, so Sandra was left to sulkily slam it shut with her hip. She sat heavily in the driving seat and switched on Radio 2. She was determined to drown him out, to hold his busy mouth under the surface of easy-listening sound waves. But her ears betrayed her. They plunged beneath 'Don't It Make My Brown Eyes Blue' to retrieve every word he said. The ears knew that it was for their benefit.

'She says you're not real.'

Pause. Laugh.

'Yes.'

Shorter pause.

'Her. There!'

Pause.

'I don't know.'

Pause.

'I think Dad will get cross.'

Pause.

'Probably not.'

He paused again. Then he spoke in a whisper to spite her fickle ears.

Without realising how transparent her gestures would be – children are not insensible to subtleties – Sandra turned down the radio and adjusted the rear-view mirror so that she could try to read his lips. But her son immediately froze, his lips still parted. Then slowly he met her reflected eyes with his own and they shone brightly. The afternoon sun was trying to take refuge there. James turned to David, then back to her again and he smiled knowingly.

Sandra told herself that she was being silly. She'd been trying to eavesdrop on a two-way conversation that didn't exist, worrying about what David was saying about her when she knew that there wasn't a David there. How could she be anxious about the mischief they were concocting when she could see with her own eyes that there wasn't a 'they'?

When she arrived at Ken's parents' house, she was actually pleased to see his mother, a sensation she'd never experienced before: the women's mutual animosity was an open wound. Ethel didn't know what to do with herself when Sandra gave her a hug.

'Where's Kenny?' she asked from inside the embrace.

'Didn't he tell you? He's coming straight from work.'

'But you've got the car!'

Sandra didn't think this merited a response.

James came rushing up the steps. 'Grandma!' and, in the wake of his mother, he flung his arms around her too. Sandra saw this, but she turned her head away.

'How's my favourite grandson?'

'I'm OK. David hurt my knee,' he said, pointing at the plaster.

'Let me see. Oh, little soldier. Why did he do that?'

'Ask him.'

His grandmother indulged him. 'David, why did you do that?'

James waited a second and then, looking at his mother who was hovering like a battered moth in the hallway, said, 'It was an accident. He didn't mean to do it.'

Sandra asked Ethel where Gordon was. It was a rhetorical question. Gordon was always in the same place: in his sagging armchair.

'In there!' Ethel said, with a hint of exasperation, as though Sandra was a bit simple.

James crouched to take off his shoes.

'What are you doing?' his grandmother asked.

'Mum makes everyone take their shoes off at the door.'

'Well, we're not in your mum's house now,' she said in an audible whisper, and helped him to put them back on again.

'David never takes his shoes off,' he confided.

They entered the sitting room together, to see Sandra vainly trying to make small talk with her resolutely underwhelmed father-in-law.

'You've laid the table.'

'Ethel did it.'

'It looks lovely, Ethel.'

'Well, I know in your house you aren't allowed to eat off trays.'

'I think it's nice to sit around the table at mealtimes.'

'Tray suits me fine,' Gordon said. He couldn't be doing with Sandra and her fancy ways.

Sandra laughed nervously and looked around the room for someone to roll her eyes to. Ethel? James? Even David would have done.

'Grandma, can David and I play in the garden?'

His grandmother gave her blessing and James skipped out, leaving his mother, no longer on the hallowed, hygienic, moral high ground of her own home, to sit on the edge of a settee, searching for something in the room to compliment.

'That's a lovely jumper. Where did you buy that?'

'From a flea market. Got it the other month.'

'Oh. Well, it's nice.' Sandra shuddered involuntarily. She was all for charity shops, you got some quality items there, but flea markets and jumble sales – just the mention of the words made her eyes water.

A little while later, Ken arrived. He let himself in with his own house keys. His parents had always lived there, and for some reason he'd never relinquished his set. He popped his head round the door like an elbow in a baby's bathwater. He expected his reception to be lukewarm.

'Hello,' he said, with faux jollity.

'Hello, Ken,' all three replied, in lacklustred unison.

'Will you move the car?' Sandra asked him, before he could settle. She handed him the keys.

'Where to?'

'Just put it in front of the house where we can keep an eye on it. I parked it round the corner. There were no spaces earlier, but now that it's getting darker, I don't think we should leave it there.'

'Why not?' Ethel asked.

'I don't think it's safe,' Sandra told her, without pausing for thought. Ethel had already picked up on the inference and Ken exited before the inevitable 'we've never had anything stolen in forty years' conversation commenced.

When he came back into the room it was still going on.

'I wasn't saying that, Ethel.' Sandra was busy digging herself a far deeper grave. 'I just thought that maybe you'd . . . you know . . . be friendly with the people around here . . . so they wouldn't steal from you. I mean, the houses are so close together you must – '

'I'm starved,' Ken interrupted, truncating the condescension midway.

His mother immediately stood and knocked on the window pane, waving at James and David to come in.

They all took seats around the dark wooden table with the pull-out extensions. Gordon took his time in order to illustrate how all this fuss over eating at a table wasn't worth the effort.

'Where's David's chair?' James asked.

'Oh!' His grandma stood up to go and fetch a stool from the kitchen.

'No, Ethel, don't encourage him please,' Sandra said with authority.

Ethel looked at her son and he shook his head, so she sat back down again.

'How was your day?' Ken asked James, making a stab at civility.

'Horrible.'

'Why?'

'He cut his knee,' Sandra answered for him.

'No, I didn't. David did, but not on purpose. It was an accident.'

His father made noises he thought corresponded to such news.

'But that's not why it was a horrible day,' James continued, casually.

'No?'

James shook his head, and waited a moment so that everyone was suitably expectant. '*She* hurt my arm and locked me in the garden and she upset David, and now he hates her. That's why it was a horrible day.'

All eyes turned on Sandra, who had been polishing her fork with an out-of-season holly-patterned serviette.

'It's not true,' she said. 'He's making it up. I did no such thing. You know what happened to Pinocchio when he lied?'

'Yes.' Her son paused again to look to his left and they all waited to hear what David had to say. 'David thinks you should cut your nose off for lying.'

'I don't want to hear another word from you, not another word!' Sandra was like a game of Kerplunk. If one more straw was pulled out, the whole thing would come clattering down.

'Liar!' he said again.

'James, that's enough.' Ken could see that his wife was in need of assistance.

The grandparents were dumbstruck by James's audacity. They'd never have let him speak to them like that, but to Sandra . . .

'*Thwack*!'

The noise made them all jump.

Then again, '*Thwack*!'

It was the sound of James's sandal hitting one of the wooden table legs.

'Stop it, James!' his mother warned in her clipped, tears-before-bedtime voice.

'It wasn't me. It was David,' he told her, smiling wide.

'*Crack*!' went his foot again.

'I'm warning you!'

James was overjoyed with his own genius. He knew that it wasn't David, but what had he to lose? His mother didn't believe in David in any case. He gave the table an almighty kick and the whole flap collapsed.

An assortment of chocolate biscuits, cold meats and some very hot tea landslid onto his mother's lap. She was held in suspension for a few seconds, torn between dealing with her son and dealing with her scalded self. Then, deciding that it was circumspect to attend to the burn first, she rushed to the kitchen and from there she directed her husband to see to her son: a voice from the cold tap.

'David spoils everything!' she screamed.

Well, at least she'd admitted that David was involved.

Ethel went to see if she could help.

'Tell James he can sit in the car till we leave,' the cold-tap voice called.

'Does she think it will be safe?' Gordon asked his son dryly. 'Someone might nick him.'

When Sandra returned there was a large wet patch on her skirt. James glanced up but he showed no remorse. He was eating a piece of ham with his fingers. His mother bent down and started to pick up the fallen food and crockery.

'Oh leave that,' Ethel said, lighting a cigarette. Ethel was a woman who could smoke while simultaneously gutting a fish, the paper cylinder turning into a long, ashen finger without ever falling off.

Sandra ignored her and continued to pick up bits of meat and buttered bread from the carpet.

'Kenneth! Will you put him in the car?'

Kenneth, the quiet-lifer, did as he was told and Gordon surreptitiously slipped his grandson a biscuit in a wrapper.

'David says goodbye,' James announced to the room on his exit.

He climbed into the car without any objections.

'I don't think we'll be much longer,' his father told him. 'I'm going to lock the door on you.'

'Like Mum did.'

Ken made no reply. He went back into the house and closed the door behind him.

Alone, all the bravura broke away and slipped off James like defrosting ice. He looked lost for a moment. Then David must have said something to him, as his reverie was broken.

'I'll take you to the zoo,' James said, clambering into the driver's seat. He pretended to fasten the safety belt. Then he settled his hands on the wheel and they were imaginatively off on their journey. It only took a minute to get there.

'Look, a stripy elephant!'

A pause.

'Yes, they do, they have stripes, but you can't see them, only I can. What is the nose called?'

He waited.

'No silly. It's a trunk!' he teased, munching on the chocolate biscuit. 'It's sucking up peas through it. And there's a cow in trousers . . . and a wolf planting vegetables.' And they were safely entrenched in their private world once more, where lions ate straw like the oxen.

His parents didn't leave them in their Eden for long. Sandra could never abide spending much time 'in that house'. And the sound of them unlocking the car door brought James back from his animal adventure all too abruptly. He'd practically forgotten his parents. It was only when he saw the big patch on his mother's skirt that he remembered that he'd put it there, and this was his car-cage punishment.

Their son – the monkey-boy – jumped into the back seat of the car to sit with David. He left behind a small, incriminating piece of chocolate, but fortunately for him, his mother was far too absorbed in being the injured party to spot it, so she sat on it.

'I'll drive,' she said, with a conclusive slam of the door.

Then the two of them – or three of them, depending on whom you asked – were subjected to the silent treatment all the way home. It was meant to be an edifying time, a time for all concerned to consider their behaviour and see the errors of their ways. Inevitably, though, it simply served as a welcome respite from the constant chiding. Ken put on the radio, but it was swiftly turned off with a nifty flick of the wrist. No privileges. The turn of events had somehow become Ken's fault as well. After all, he did have Ethel as a mother, and Sandra couldn't be held to task for that misdemeanour.

'David wants the radio on.' David hadn't in fact mentioned the radio, but James didn't care. He knew that his mother wouldn't believe him either way.

'Tell David that *want* doesn't get,' Sandra said.

Ken was too mature to play child's games so he kept quiet.

Suddenly their son adroitly shot between the narrow valley of the seats – the trap-door spider – and spun the small dial round so that 'Una Paloma Blanca' blistered out. Sandra panicked, struck out at him, missed and hit her husband, who was frantically fumbling with the radio controls. In one of those slow-motion moments, the family became tangled up. The steering wheel slipped to the right and the car, following suit, spun off the road into a signpost, where it finally stopped.

Time and the family untied themselves. The white dove was silenced, with the engine. As their eyes refocused and their ears rebalanced, they took stock of the situation, weighing up what they felt about it. Once it was established that no one had broken any bones, Sandra felt the urge to break some. James was in easy reach. He'd been flung into the front of the car with them, all very cosy. She drew back her hand, but he was too fast for her and his small, frog's-tongue fist flew out, catching her squarely on the nose. Then, as this hit home, he reverted back to the trapdoor arachnid and shot onto the back seat again.

'I'm going to give you such a good hiding!' His father was trying to get his crumpled car door open. It was jammed shut.

James laughed, but it was not the laugh of the brave.

'How could you? How could you hit your own mum?' Sandra asked, still reeling.

'David told me to.' He was clearly panicking. He looked to his left. 'He says he's sorry,' he told her, but David showed no signs of remorse. 'Anyway, Dad taught me how to do it. He said if someone bullied me, I should give them the nose treatment and they'll stop. It works, Dad. She stopped.'

His father was halfway out of the window when James imparted this information. He froze for a second. 'I'm going to teach you another lesson now,' he murmured ominously as he rounded on the passenger door.

James held down the knob while rocking nervously back and forth.

'Open this door!' his father bellowed.

A car pulled alongside them. The driver wound down his window and asked if they needed any help.

'Mind your own bloody business!' Ken snarled, turning his

anger onto the man. The man swore back, but drove off hastily.

James had never seen his father in a rage before, nor had Sandra, not like this, and she too was afraid. It occurred to her that he might kill their son. Ken slammed his palm on the glass, making James almost sick with terror.

'David!' he wailed.

His father was circling the car like a carnivore tasting adrenalin in the air.

'When I've done with you, you'll never dare to raise your hand to your mother or me ever again!'

'You're not my mum and dad! Only my real mum and dad can hurt me. David says you're not allowed.' James glanced at David and caught him smile. David knew that it would do the trick. James saw that his friend's words had worked like magic, but what his parents felt when he spoke them was lost on him.

His father tugged one last time at the door handle and his mother's hand rose to her face like she'd been struck again.

'I'm going to find a phone and call the AA,' Ken said in a shallow voice and he set off along the verge, like the lobotomised. Sandra turned the key in the ignition and the engine flared. She tried to reverse, but the street sign was jammed beneath the car's underbelly and all that happened was a rasping whirr as metal hit metal. She turned off the engine and lowered her forehead onto the steering wheel; a churchgoer folded in prayer, head resting against the pew.

When his un-dead father returned, he sat on the side of the road and watched the cars pass by. His wife wound down her window but didn't try to speak to him and James sat as still as a plaster saint in the back of the car and ignored David's banter.

It grew dark outside and Sandra put on the hazard lights, which flicked and ticked furiously, slicing up time. The AA van arrived. Sandra got out. Nobody spoke. The fault with the car was pretty obvious. The mechanic refrained from asking any questions. He was used to silence and probably preferred it to the tearful catalogues of disastrous day-trips. He towed the car off the sign.

'It's a good job you didn't try to start the engine,' he told Ken. 'The attrition between the metal of the chassis against the road sign could've caused sparks.'

Sandra didn't comment. At that moment if they'd been blown to heaven in tiny fragments of flesh and fuselage she wouldn't have cared in the least. She climbed back into the car and turned the key.

'Would you like me to tow you home?' the man asked, in a job-done kind of way, inviting them to decline his offer.

'No. We'll be fine.' Ken, who didn't think his pride could withstand a climb through the window again, reached into the car, unlocked the back door and slid in beside his son, and David. James looked pale, but his father was lamb meek. Sandra switched on the headlights and they illuminated the sign on the ground. 'Safari Park' it read, and next to the words was a white emblem of an elephant. Only now it had large scratches across it.

'You see,' James whispered to David. 'I told you elephants had stripes.'

James turned five: the year he was to attend primary school. His parents held a birthday party and invited other boys and girls from his playgroup. But the children chose to stay a respectful distance from James, and he didn't encourage them to come closer. He moved among them, the ghost of Banquo only grown-ups could see, accompanied by David, whom only he could see. James didn't consider his contemporaries to be worth his patronage, preferring to donate his attention to the adults. The perfect host, he introduced himself to them, offered them cake, laughed at their jokes – whether he understood them or not – and generally put them at their ease.

When they left, he looked forlorn.

'Do you really have to go?' he asked.

He even had the audacity to take one of the more attractive mothers by the hand and say, 'Please stay.'

The woman stopped for a moment and gazed at James with a dreamy expression. It had clearly been some time since anyone had paid her a compliment like that. It seemed like she might just stay. Then she broke his stirring stare, realising suddenly that she was talking to a little boy.

'He's going to break some hearts when he's older,' she told Sandra, not realising the prophecy in her words.

'Yes,' Sandra agreed. 'He's a fully qualified heart-breaker.'

It looked like a corner was being turned. James had successfully attended the playgroup for many months, without any further upset, and Sandra no longer hoped that he would show his true opalesque colours. She didn't risk venturing into the inner sanctum to collect him though, preferring to wait in the car, her fingernails tapping the plastic steering wheel.

Then one day James fell into another remission. What provoked him to forsake his progress was an announcement that Sophie made to the class: 'For some of you this will be your last week. It's a very exciting time. Lucy, Tracy, Peter, James, Mark, you'll all be starting school in the autumn.'

'What about David?' James eventually asked, trying his hardest not to cry.

'Yes, James, he'll be going as well, if you want to take him with you.'

And that was that. The moment was sliced in two.

James and David sat completely still. What had they done wrong? Why had Sophie singled them out for dismissal? How could she so casually close the doors on them? James couldn't comprehend that it was the way of the world, that he was being excluded by an age bracket. As far as he was concerned, he was a little boy, as little as other little boys, littler than most. Why had they been excused, exempt, chosen for salvation over him? It was inconceivable. After he'd been so nice to her too! Well, he would teach her, his teacher.

James and David rose together to launch their tyrannical rampage. All heads were to roll. No one was to be spared. No pardon granted. They started with stealth. The bear-hug served them well, plus the pinch or nip, excellent covert methods that could be carried out in passing. This way they could be far from their victim by the time the tears ensued. Then, like Good Samaritans, they could return to the crime scene seconds later to dish out consolations.

'There, there, Andrew,' James said, playing the caring adult. 'Don't cry. What's the matter?' leaving the confused Andrew strangely quietened by his recent torturer's tenderness.

Next they built up their onslaught into a tornado of devastation. They destroyed everything in their path. With a furious battle cry the SHHH! LIBRARY corner was demolished. The children's paintings, all the brightly drawn mummies and daddies, were ripped from the walls. Blows were dished out to boys and girls indiscriminately. His father's nose treatment made its return, and he'd picked up a few more manoeuvres as well. The worst weapon in his new arsenal was the bite. The bite hurt feelings as well as flesh.

Miss Ryan was at a loss for what to do. She'd read many tips on how to handle unruly children, but she'd never dreamt of having to put them to the test and each tactic she tried failed miserably. Finally she telephoned James's mother, requesting her presence. Then she called her own, requesting sympathy. She even considered calling the police, but felt too embarrassed. In an attempt to restrain James she suffered a nasty scratch under her eye and a bite on her arm. So she looked on, the defeated queen, as her ill-equipped army fell before her.

By the time Sandra arrived the siege was over. Other outraged parents had already been and quickly gone or were marching out cradling their tearful tots in their arms. Miss Ryan was going to be in trouble over this. It wasn't the first time their children had come home with war wounds. The classroom was destroyed, detritus strewn everywhere: ripped papers, spilt paints and cracked plastic lunch-boxes.

James was sitting on his own – with David – in the centre of the tiled floor, a shipwreck victim, debris all about him. Sandra, mother first, ran straight to his side.

'James, are you all right?'

He flinched away from her hand.

'He's a little devil,' hissed Miss Ryan from a crouch in the decimated SHHH! LIBRARY corner. She was sifting through torn stories, fragments of 'once upon a time' all around her.

'You've changed your tune,' Sandra replied, standing upright.

'I've never seen anything like it.'

'Well, now you have.'

'He bit me.'

Sandra's I-told-you-so moment had finally come. Usually she was a cruel vindicator, but today she decided that silence was her best riposte.

'Come on, James. Let's go home.'

Her son immediately ceased his rocking and accepted his mother's hand to help him up. At the door he stopped for a moment to take in the ruined room.

'Miss Ryan,' he said calmly, 'David says goodbye.'

'Get out!' the teacher screamed, from where she still crouched, collecting fallen alphabet cards. Her body, James noticed, mirrored the shape of the letter 'Z' that lay among the 'O's on the floor.

'ZOO'.

His mother drove him home in silence as she searched for the word to describe what she felt like. It was *pariah*, but she settled on *piranha*.

'You make me feel like a bloody piranha!' she screamed as she parked and pulled her son from the car.

He stared at her blankly.

Sandra spotted her neighbours in their garden and gave them a terse wave while she ushered James indoors. Then she started again. 'What did you do?'

'Can David and I go and play with the zoo?'

'No, you can't.'

He tried to walk away from her. She grabbed his wrist and started slapping his bare legs. Her arms thrashed about and her elbow hit the hall table. 'Ow!' she winced.

James started to laugh. It was not a vindictive laugh. It just struck him as comedic.

'Why did you bite Miss Ryan?'

'I didn't. It was David.'

'I won't have you lie.'

'I'm not.'

Before she entertained another thought she'd grabbed hold of his arm and bitten it. Not too hard, but hard enough. James screamed, his eyes wide with surprise. He stared at her, trying to take in what had just happened, but his overstimulated senses crowded in on him. He saw so much he felt blind and he could smell iron in his nostrils: the smell of blood. With limbs stiffening and jaw jutting, his mouth cracked open and he hissed like a cat. Sandra retreated a few steps, only something told her not to turn her back on him. 'That'll teach you not to bite,' she said, but she didn't sound convinced.

SIX

Unsurprisingly, he didn't make it in for his last week at playgroup, and nor did Miss Ryan. She didn't make it into that school again, jumping before she was pushed.

James's parents had unwittingly succeeded in arming him both physically and verbally. He was fearless, despite his small frame, and cunning to boot. When they scolded him he took to laughing. Only now they were reluctant to raise a hand to him for fear of him raising his to another. They had no emotional or retributive hold whatsoever. Whenever they came too close he simply spat out, 'You can't touch me, you're not my parents,' and they were crushed like invertebrates.

Sandra admitted to herself that it was time to change her mind about seeking advice and she agreed to enlist the help of a child psychiatrist.

'Perhaps his behavioural difficulties are somehow linked to David,' the expert told them. 'Children grow out of their imaginary friends when they make real ones.' As she said this, she ran her hand down her coarse, straight hair. 'Why don't you encourage James to play with other children?'

'But he causes havoc,' Ken told her.

'He upsets them,' Sandra understated.

'Do you not have any neighbours who have youngsters?'

'There are lots of kids on the street,' Sandra conceded. But she'd tried locking James out of the house on numerous occasions, instructing him to play with children his own age.

'But David's my own age,' her son would insist.

'David isn't real.'

James would shake his head. When would they learn?

'Don't worry,' he'd reassure his friend. 'It's like the stripes on an elephant. Most people can't see them.' And he'd sit patiently on the front step, chewing the cud with David, colouring in his zoo animals with felt-tips or biting off their legs and tails. He had an affinity with the damaged.

'Each animal tastes different, David.' The lion tasted of marmalade, the cow of custard, the duck of liquorice.

His father had bought him a football.

'Why don't you ask Mrs Griffin's boy if he wants to play?'

'Why?'

'Because it's fun.'

'David says it's fun for dogs. What's the point?'

What could they say? What they invariably did say, when stumped for something reasonable, was, 'Don't be clever with me,' to which he soon started replying with, 'Should I be stupid with you?' He was too precocious for words.

'Now he's started lying about playing with other kids,' Ken said to the psychiatrist. 'He crawls under the garden gate and hides round the side of the house.'

'In the Judas tree,' his wife added. 'It's flowering at the moment, fuchsia pink blossom. We cut it right back last autumn and it really did the trick.'

The analyst wasn't interested in horticulture. 'Why don't you bring him in so I can meet him?' she asked. She was ready to hear from the accused.

Of course, when she – whom Sandra referred to as the Specialist – met James he was charm personified. His parents were well aware that he preferred the company of adults – other adults to them – so it came as no surprise. James liked to impress grown-ups. He knew how to win them over. He played the young gentleman and flirted with alarming proficiency.

'Hello,' he said to an old lady one day, when he and his mother were walking through a car park.

'Hello, dear.'

'Who was that?' Sandra asked him.

'I don't know, but old people like it if you're nice to them.'

When his parents occasionally had friends over he'd bid them goodnight without a fuss and pretend to ascend heavenwards to his bed. But he'd double back and eavesdrop through the central-heating vent in the wall. 'Grown-up.' 'Articulate.' 'So beautiful.' He liked hearing these epitaphs. It made him smile and David a little jealous.

The Specialist was clearly impressed by his apparent maturity. He sat upright in his chair and took some time aligning the ribs in his elasticised socks. She crouched down in front of him, American diner style, in an attempt to make the psychological set-up conducive. She started by asking him a variety of unthreatening questions to establish and engage his trust, and he proved to be obliging and eloquent – until she brought David into the proceedings.

'So how did you meet your friend?'

James turned to David and smiled. She was in their club. She'd acknowledged he was real.

'He's always been here,' he told her simply, still smiling broadly.

'Where?'

'With me.'

'What about when he isn't with you?'

James looked perplexed. 'He never leaves me for long. I know him. He walks with me. He talks with me. He says I'm his very own.' These strangely archaic words sounded curious coming from a mouth so young. The adults paused for a moment to take stock. When stock had been taken, the Specialist smoothed her hair and asked what David looked like.

'He has a leopard's body and a pig's head,' he told her.

'Really?' She sounded fascinated.

'No, silly.' He laughed and looked at David, who laughed too. 'He looks like a boy.'

She smiled. 'What colour is his hair?'

'Blond.'

David evidently disagreed.

'It is,' James insisted.

'And his eyes?'

'What about them?'

'What colour are they?'

James smirked. 'Brown.'

David really didn't seem to agree, as James raised his voice to reply, 'They are not blue! My eyes are blue! You can't see your eyes, I can!'

'How tall is he?'

'Short and fat!' James said, and rocked with laughter. 'Yes, you are!' he jeered.

No one else was amused.

The Specialist turned to Sandra and Kenneth and said knowingly, 'The opposite of James.'

They nodded their approval, though what it was they approved of they couldn't be certain.

'When's his birthday?'

James had stopped laughing now. He messed up the lines on his socks, clearly tired of order, and raised his eyes at David, who shrugged.

'I don't know, but I pretend it's the same as mine.'

'And where are his parents? Won't they be worried about where he is?'

'He's not got any real parents,' he said, with a glance at his own. 'Anyway, I look after him and he looks after me.'

Ken touched Sandra's arm comfortingly, but she looked down at his hand with irritation and he quickly removed it.

'He must have parents. *Everybody* has parents.' Her tone was accidentally veering towards the condescending.

'That can't be true,' he corrected her calmly. 'I have two I can see, and two others I can't see. If I have four, then someone must have none.'

'You're very clever, aren't you?' she cajoled.

'Mum wants me to be stupid.'

'No, she doesn't, I'm sure she doesn't,' she said, turning to Sandra for confirmation.

Sandra was pretending to read a laminated poster about the benefits of inoculations for children.

'She tells me not to get clever with her.'

The Specialist smoothed down her hair and stole another quick look at Sandra, who was apparently still engrossed in the health warning, despite the fact that she wasn't wearing her reading glasses.

'What your mummy means is "Don't be rude".'

Suddenly his mother broke her silence, betraying her lack of preoccupation with an outburst. 'He knows bloody well what I mean,' she blabbered. 'Do you know he laughs at me when I tell him off? He makes me want to scream!' She half screamed as though to illustrate her point.

The Specialist's voice was the epitome of restraint. 'Yes, an intelligent child can be very frustrating.'

James liked this woman more and more, whereas his mother liked her less and less.

'Will you introduce me to David?'

'Yes. David, this is the lady Dad says is a waste of time and money.'

'He never said that,' Sandra said with a laugh that bordered on the hysterical.

Kenneth said nothing.

'You know what happens when people lie,' James warned his mother, and to demonstrate he moved his finger under from his nose.

The Specialist looked studiously unruffled and smiled at Ken to make him understand that his opinion did not matter to her in the slightest.

'That's OK,' she continued. 'What does David think about me?'

James paused to listen.

'David says that *you* think that your hair is pretty, but really it looks like Lego hair.' He paused again while he studied the woman. 'I don't agree. I think it looks very nice,' he said, and gave her his most candid smile.

The Specialist's expression had frozen; her brain had jarred. But Sandra elbowed the ghost out of her machine with an ejaculation of 'James! Don't talk like that to the Specialist!' He was being sacrilegious about her new-found religion.

James was, if nothing, conscientious. 'It's what he said,' he confirmed, refusing to err from the truth. 'Do you want me to lie again?'

'No,' Sandra said, lying herself.

'Well then.'

The Specialist intervened. 'I don't mind what David says.' She'd had an idea, and an almost imperceptibly thin grin appeared on her lips. 'I'd like to get to know David better.' The smile was allowed to be unveiled in full now. 'I would like it very much if David came to stay with me for a few days . . . for a small holiday.' Her words sounded suddenly very 1920s, as though she was appealing to the boy by adopting his style.

James considered this offer.

'Do you have a zoo?' he asked.

'A zoo?'

'Yes, a place where wild animals are kept,' he explained.

'No,' she faltered.

'Or a farmyard . . . where animals are kept for eating?'

Her mouth exchanged its grin for a grimace. 'No, I don't.' Nor did she want one.

'I didn't think you had,' he told her sadly. He was starting to have his reservations about this lady.

'Maybe you could lend me yours?'

He scoffed at this suggestion. 'What would *I* do then?'

'You could play with other toys?'

James wasn't convinced. He would have to question her further.

'Are you an animal doctor?'

'No . . . but – '

He cut her off, the expert lawyer. 'Then you couldn't look after them properly. A lot of them are in the animal hospital.'

'I know a lot about medicine,' she said, trying to defend her corner. 'I'm sure I could help them.'

He shook his head sceptically, but he'd allow her one last chance to prove herself.

'Do elephants have stripes?'

'No?'

He could see that she wasn't absolutely sure, but he had to take her first answer and it was a no. James couldn't allow himself to leave a sick, striped, trunk-less elephant in her hands. If anything were to happen, he'd never forgive himself.

'Elephants never forgive,' he said and no one thought to correct him.

But James didn't want to hurt this lady's feelings; he would offer her a compromise, let her down gently.

'What about if I come too?' He quite fancied a holiday.

'That would be lovely, but I only have a small house, there wouldn't be room for both of you.'

James shrugged his well-I-did-my-best shrug and admitted that he'd be obliged to decline the generous offer. It sounded like a narrow escape: a small house with no zoo, farmyard or medical facilities.

But the Specialist was a dog with a rubber bone.

'I didn't hear you ask David what he thought.'

James could have taken exception to this approach, and on another day he might have, but today he was in a magnanimous mood, so he decided, for the time being at least, to play along with her. 'It would be nicer if you asked him yourself.' Did she know nothing of manners?

'Yes,' she said, feeling foolish. Was he humiliating her on purpose? Why hadn't she become a sex psychologist after all? She took a breath, smoothed her Lego hair and asked in a saccharin-sweet voice, 'David, would you like to come and stay at my house for a few days?' She addressed her words not to David but into the middle distance.

James couldn't let this go. 'David is standing *there*.'

She tried again but she couldn't bring herself to fix her gaze while waiting for a reply. She looked to James imploringly, a dog raising its paw for a reward.

James almost laughed at David's response, but he suppressed it.
'David says that maybe you should play with someone your own age.'

The Specialist stood abruptly, breaking the subservient 'Hi, I'm Mandy, I'll be your waitress for today' dynamic. She winced as her circulation resumed its natural cycle and then sat heavily in her chair. Her hand rose up to her hair like a serpent but something stopped it, so it stayed suspended in the air, awkward and incongruous.

'I want to speak to your parents, James,' she said. Her honeyed tone had vanished altogether. 'Could you wait in the room outside?'

These words would be said to James over and over again in the course of his life. He'd be perpetually asked to wait outside, while on the inside his fate was measured.

'Would you like David to stay?' he asked, refusing to let his good manners slip, even if she had.

'No!'

James nodded and held out his hand. She physically recoiled. The snake-charmed arm was released from its spell and fell awkwardly onto her head. Then, before she could prevent it, her palm was on her hair, soothing it. His hand remained outstretched, like a challenge.

'Nice to meet you,' and he beamed, the star car-salesman clinching a deal. 'I'm sorry David upset you about your hair. It's very pretty.'

She blushed, either through embarrassment or rage.

'Come on David,' he said, a little boy again. 'David says goodbye.' And with that he quit the room.

The three adults were silent for a second listening to the sound of the traffic beyond the horizontal blinds. Then the Specialist said, 'He's quite something.'

'Yes.' What else could they say? They wanted *her* opinion. They'd formed their own already. They waited, expectantly. And when the psychiatrist realised that the couple still respected her as a professional, she became one again.

'I think,' she mused, settling back in her chair, 'that you need to change your approach.'

'He's listening!' Sandra blurted. 'I can see him in the glass door.'

But before the Specialist could confirm this, James had slipped out of sight. She made a mental note – 'Paranoia evident in the mother,' – before reclining into the safety of her certified objectivity. 'Evidently, denying the existence of David results in his adamant denial . . .'

They were advised to accept David and include him. This way he could no longer serve as a weapon.

'David is somewhere James retreats when he feels threatened and isolated. If David is brought out into the open his usefulness will become obsolete.'

Sandra wasn't quite following. She counted on the fact that Ken would be, and allowed her eyes to drift back to a wall-chart that she couldn't read. The Specialist, realising that she'd lost Sandra, layman's-termed it. 'Set a place at the dinner table for David.'

Bingo. 'Dinner' and 'table'. Sandra was all ears. This was her domain.

'Ask about David all the time. Find David funny. James will get jealous of the attention.'

'So you want us to set up sibling rivalry?' asked Ken, who had been brought up with a brother, so had experienced the sting of exclusion.

'Yes, exactly.' She smiled encouragingly. 'The father is quite intelligent,' she thought.

'But wouldn't that spur him on, if we joined in? We'd be supporting his . . . lies. We'd be as bad as him.'

'Kenneth!' Sandra intervened. 'She knows what she's talking about.' And she looked at the Specialist with teacher's-pet eyes.

'No, no. These are good points.' Unprofessional note to self: 'the husband's attractive.' Then she continued, 'But I think you'll admit that previous approaches have not been successful. And it's not about lying. We must assume that James thinks David is very real. You should also refrain from using the word bad. You just said "we'd be as bad as him", for instance. James will latch on to a word like bad and believe it defines him. Also avoid the word *imaginary* . . .'

Sandra had started writing all this down on the back of a shopping list, which was rather disconcerting. The Specialist didn't appreciate her keen student – note-takers had corroborative evidence if things went *bad*. But she continued, after a brief flirtation with touching her hair, 'Each time you say that David is imaginary, or made up, you're calling James a liar.'

'Yes, I see,' Sandra said.

'He evidently has problems with the word already.' She glanced at the mother, so that it hit the mark. Nobody likes a crawler. 'James is very . . . bright. Perhaps this is why he doesn't like the company of other children. In some ways he's very grown up. However . . . there's no denying that, on some levels, he's delusional. If you'd like to attend regularly . . . I could establish where the root of these problems lies.'

Sandra didn't like the sound of this. She wanted James to be judged independently; in isolation; she didn't want any blame to be traced back to her. She put her shopping list back in her handbag and looked for her car keys. These gestures declared that the session was coming to a close.

In order to remind Sandra that she was dealing with a qualified professional and successfully intimidate her into subscribing to a session a week, the Specialist threw in some more jargon. 'James is not simply expanding the normal field of consciousness . . . he's creating a new one.'

Sandra responded to the only word she understood. 'I told you it wasn't *normal*,' she said to Ken, and abruptly stood up.

Her husband stood too like an automaton.

The Specialist gave Ken her card with an encouraging smile. 'At least let me know how you get on,' she said, showing that she really cared as a fellow human being, not just as a highly paid professional.

'She fancies him,' Sandra thought. 'Do I pay you? Or the girl at reception?' she said, succinctly illustrating just who wore the trousers in their relationship and who held the purse strings.

But Sandra was also determined to extract her money's worth from the advice and intended to follow it immediately and to the letter. As soon as they were all in the car, she said, 'David was right. She does have Lego hair!' And she laughed, alone.

So it was decided: David was there to stay and the long-suffering couple were now forced to adopt a second little boy into the fold of their household – one even more indefinable than the first.

James was thrilled about David's inclusion. His friend was presented with his own chair at the table and Sandra even thought to ask if he'd like to join them in some lunch.

'Yes please, David would like that,' her son replied, on his friend's behalf. But clearly David didn't like that, as James then whispered, 'I know, but we will pretend.' He was reluctant to appear unappreciative of her efforts. He didn't want to deliberately hurt his mother's feelings – even if David did.

When the food arrived, David – as James had anticipated – refused to touch it. He was not going to be won over so easily. He turned up his nose, folded his arms and refused to talk, even to James. So, when Sandra nipped back into the kitchen, James was forced to shovel some of the food off David's plate onto his own. Of course when his mother came back in she immediately spotted what had happened: she was hawk-eyed when it came to the reception of her cooking. It occurred to her that maybe now she could get her compensation after all. She could pile up David's plate with the vegetables that James refused – swede, cauliflower, sprouts – knowing that her son would be compelled to eat them in order to keep up the pretence. Plus, they'd be playing the game of David together. He would be *their* friend, not exclusively James's. And it seemed to be working. Her son was not complaining or causing a scene. He was not even chattering with David.

This might, Sandra thought, go down as their first meal without incident. It was going so well that she became complacent.

'David hasn't eaten very much,' she said, clearing away their plates. 'Didn't he like it?' It seemed that she could feel a culinary snub even when it came from someone she didn't believe existed. But she'd laid herself open.

James looked a little uncomfortable about the news he was about to break. 'He did like it . . .'

His mother was halfway out of the door with the plates when she stopped, waiting for the 'but'. She didn't have to wait for long.

'But he ate earlier.'

'Oh.' She sounded relieved.

'But – ' there was another – 'he says that you're not to make food for him again. He's happy just to sit with us.' James didn't like his mother's cooking at the best of times, so he certainly didn't relish the prospect of eating each meal twice. Lamb stew with splinters of bone lurking in the gravy, times two? No, thank you. Plus, he'd recently formed the belief that if he ate a lot it would kill him, born out of the words *living room* and *dining room*. He was sure that *dining room* was a polite way of saying *dying room*. It made sense.

His mother looked put out.

'He'll eat chocolate sponge, with the sauce,' James offered. It was the only thing that he could think of that he liked himself. It came out of a tin, so Sandra was hardly pacified.

'I wish you were as well behaved as David,' she said, wrapping herself up in a sulk. '*He* never cries at bedtime, or reads after lights out.'

'He does!'

Maybe she'd inadvertently hit upon something here. She could divide and rule. Play one off against the other. '*And* David doesn't wet the bed.'

James was stunned by her accusation. It was too shaming. He wished that she were dead.

'It's not true, I don't wet the bed!' Tears were being drawn up through his body. 'It's not me. It's David. David does it.' He flushed at the lie and couldn't look at his friend. Anyway, it served him right. If David had eaten his mother's food in the first place, none of this would have happened.

'No, he doesn't. David is a good boy.' She'd made a concerted effort to stop telling James that he was bad, but the word was forever skulking hungrily in the shadows waiting for a moment to pounce. So David was now *good* and James was the antonym.

Suddenly, her son started laughing; it was phony and maniacal.

'Stop it!' she sounded afraid and the plates that she was still holding rattled against each other nervously. She couldn't endure another tantrum. 'What are you laughing at?'

'What David said about you!'

'What did he say?'

'He hates you! He hates you!'

The tension in her body shifted and she held the dishes out at an angle, like a surly girl in a greasy spoon café. Then she left the room, clack-clacking her wooden sandals on the lino floor. After she'd dropped her plates in the sink, she slammed shut the door with such force that the glass juddered in its frame. James carried on laughing, louder and louder, the strain showing in his neck. The kitchen cacophony was also building up, until the competing noises rose to a crescendo. Then – '*crash*!' – a missile smashed through the glass of the kitchen door. A tumbler – still intact – skimmed across the floor and, after a slow ice-skater's spin, righted itself proudly.

Sandra connected with James's eye-line through the cartoon-character hole; she opened her mouth, but nothing came out. James, who was still seated at the table, held up a tumbler as evidence. He hadn't thrown *his*, which meant that it must have been David.

'David doesn't like it when you slam things,' he told her, taking a sip of water, before replacing the glass with exaggerated care on the – everything has its place – mat. His mother had a pathological fear of watermarks on wood.

Liking David was going to be difficult.

When Kenneth came home, Sandra informed him that David had broken the door.

James nodded his agreement. 'It was an accident though,' he added, for his friend's benefit.

Ken was finding it more difficult than Sandra to commit to this 'let's pretend'. He felt idiotic addressing the air, and James immediately spotted the opportunity for poking fun and sharing private jokes with David.

'Dad, you are talking to an empty chair.'

'I know.'

'Why?'

'I'm talking to David.' He felt exposed, a sleepwalker waking naked on a traffic island.

'But he's behind you.' The pantomime call.

Another variation was the musical chairs routine.

'Dad, stop! David is sitting there.'

'Is he?'

'Of course he is, Ken.' Sandra would widen her eyes with all the subtlety of Widow Twanky, reminding him to be patient.

Ken would take solace from the pattern on the carpet for a moment before admitting defeat and relinquishing one of his only certain joys, the armchair.

As soon as he started to sit on the settee, James would shout again,

'Nooo! He's there now. He moved for you!'

Somehow, Ken's building resentment was redirected towards his wife, though he wouldn't show it or say it. He'd encountered too many strident geese over the years to start bandying the word boo around now. No, he would store up little parcels of bitterness in different parts of his body. When there was no more room, he'd tap out grains of rage into the furniture with his fingertips, or nail bits of wood together – under the pretext of making something – hammering free the fury from his ample hands. Perhaps, if he hadn't been blessed with the facility to exorcise this build-up, he'd have started to harbour secret, murderous desires; fantasising about releasing this repressed wrath upon his family, until one day he'd act on it: the crime passionnel. Ken worried, what would happen once all the pieces of wood and furniture in the house became rage satiated?

SEVEN

James's behaviour outwardly improved, but he still blamed all the damage and destruction on David.

'How can I say that David is nicer to have around than James?' Sandra asked. 'Today he told me that the bin was on fire because David thought it would be nice to get rid of the rubbish for me.'

Ken, in bed next to her, made no response.

'Ken!'

He was listening – in the ear that she couldn't see – to sport on the radio, another of his certain joys. He, like James and David, wanted to be left alone.

With exaggerated movements his wife rearranged the covers. He wasn't asleep; she knew that. He assumed that she was oblivious to his surreptitious radio listening, but she knew. She had, just a few days before, adjusted the volume, as the tinny noise had been interfering with her Barbara Taylor Bradford novel.

Couldn't she let him be, just this once?

'Ken!?'

Apparently not.

'What?' He spoke just below the wavelength that she'd take exception to.

'James.'

'What about him?'

'You know well enough what about him.'

'Well, *I* don't know what to do. Why don't you go and see the Specialist again?'

'Oh, it's OK for you. You just go off to work. I have him every day!'

'And I have you both every night,' he mused, ruefully. His eyes closed themselves, the bottom lids meeting the top ones in the middle, like an owl's.

Sandra could hear his fingers tapping on the radio casing. Irritated, she rolled over, put down her book and flicked off the lamp switch like she'd seen people do in films. But her life was no Doris Day movie and when the light went out it was not replaced by a mellow-moon luminosity but rather by a cold, steely blackness and a noise quieter than silence for them both to flounder in. They hid from the knowledge that this child, their son – on whom they'd blindly pinned their hopes, like the tail on the donkey – this real little boy, with his mirror-image imaginary one, was opening up a gulf that a whole team of Specialists would struggle to bridge.

In late summer, preparations for school began. Sandra behaved like an expectant mother, planning in advance, but in her case it was not for the arrival of a child but for the removal of two, hopefully one of them for good. She was convinced that school would knock David out of James. She was counting on the cruelty of children. In the meantime she'd continue to indulge him, and even had a little fun in doing so.

She set about buying duplicate pairs of white vests and white underpants, pretending that one set was for James and the other for David. Then, as the school had a regulation uniform, she bought James's shirts, blue and cotton; a pair of shorts, flannel and grey; a tie, striped with green; a V-neck jumper, azure and wool; and the final ubiquitous item, a duffle coat with tooth-like toggles. Then she put out feelers and found a second-hand replica set ostensibly for David. She had little cotton labels made with James Gardner in blue and another pack with David – no surname – in red, and she sewed them both into everything. She then took James into the village to buy a pair of shoes and even allowed David to have his feet measured too – though she wouldn't stretch to getting him a pair, children grew too quickly to be buying two sets of shoes regularly.

'He looks sweet,' the sales assistant cooed as James stomped about the shop in brown Hush Puppies.

'Only when he's asleep.' Sandra always rolled out the same, moth-eaten carpet of a joke.

She told everyone she met that her baby boy was about to start school and repeated all the things that she'd heard other people say: how tearful she was going to be; how empty the house would feel; how this was the first step to him leaving home completely – though perhaps this was wishful thinking. Her days were going to be her own again. She couldn't – if the truth be told – wait. James, too, seemed to get caught up in her wave of enthusiasm and talked excitedly with David about their first day at school.

Kenneth and Sandra knew that it was their duty to make a thorough checklist and answer all the pertinent questions:

Is your child bookish or sporty?

Is he scientific or arty?

Will he relish being a part of a large class or will it overwhelm him?

Is your child a leader or a sheep, industrious or lazy?

Does he have special needs or special needs?

They knew only too well that James was arty, a loner, a lazy leader, a voracious reader and he had one very special need – David. But they had no intention of sending him to an institution that would encourage any of these qualities.

With this transformation in mind they selected the appropriate place for him. It was a school that reminded Sandra of her own: superficially friendly but ultimately controlling. It smelt like school. The headmaster was tall, thin and dark, and, Sandra admitted to female friends – rather handsome. He made *her* feel like a schoolgirl, which seemed appropriate enough.

She'd arranged in advance to accompany James there with another mother and son from down the road, the Arnolds. Sandra didn't like Doreen Arnold very much, she found her 'mannish', but the son, Christian, seemed nice enough and he was also on the small side, so Sandra thought the two boys might hit it off. Of course, she hadn't counted on the third boy.

The four, or five, of them, depending on whom you asked, walked along awkwardly. Fortunately the weather was good, so Sandra could talk about that.

'I think we're going to have an Indian summer.'

'That would be nice.'

'Oh, mind the dog dirt!' she said helpfully, pointing it out on the verge.

But Mrs Arnold turned away and asked Christian if he'd remembered to brush his teeth.

Sandra felt admonished but she rattled on regardless, like a runaway train. 'James says hello to old people, you know . . . He says they like it.'

'Hello!' James said immediately to Mrs Arnold, who couldn't decide whether to look offended or laugh, so she laughed while looking offended.

'I didn't teach him to do that,' Sandra blurted. 'They do the funniest things sometimes!'

James started talking to David.

'He has this imaginary friend.' His mother suffocated a smile and looked nervously at her son. She'd inadvertently used the forbidden word, *imaginary*. But she couldn't have said that he was real to Mrs Arnold – she was a trained accountant.

Christian had lots of energy. He ran ahead, then back again, like an excitable dog. James, on the other hand, walked along stiffly. He was all civility and teacup conversation. He pointed out birds to David – a chaffinch; half a dozen starlings; a female blackbird; a thrush – while his excitable mother twittered on about everything and nothing.

As soon as they arrived at the school Christian darted off to talk to some children he already knew, coming back once more to say goodbye to his mother. James looked up at the school gate and the gable of the building that rose behind it. His mother kissed him on the cheek and when he didn't object, she hugged him tightly; python love. He smiled his dry compassion.

'See you this afternoon.'

'Yes.'

'You be good,' she couldn't help but say. Then she added, 'Goodbye, David.'

She almost felt sentimental. It was as though she were saying goodbye to David for the last time. Would she miss him?

'David says goodbye.'

James walked away bravely, her little soldier. He looked more like a small man than a boy, as though childhood had never really belonged to him. His mother stood sadly looking on as he disappeared through the doors. She knew that he wouldn't look back. She could still feel the empty hug in her arms, aching for something else to hold. She had so much love to give.

Mrs Arnold came over and said that she had some errands to run in the village before going to her office. It sounded like a lie but Sandra was relieved. She didn't want to walk home with Doreen, the man-woman. She knew she'd only say more foolish things. She knew it, but it wouldn't have stopped her from doing it. The women agreed to take turns in walking the boys to school. It seemed silly them both doing it every day. After they'd parted, Sandra slipped through the car park. She also had a list of things to buy in the village, but this way they could go their separate ways immediately.

It wasn't like she'd imagined it. She'd pictured herself bonding with other mothers, going out for coffee and toasted teacakes, capitalising on her new freedom, but she felt hollow, like a Russian doll who'd lost her little ones. Her shopping trip was joyless. Even adding up the prices and questioning the total – the girl had overlooked a reduced sticker – brought her no satisfaction. She took herself home and polished her altar, the dining-room table.

James's class were taken straight into the assembly hall to be introduced to the teachers. The school had a policy of starting the new children a day early so that they could acclimatise. Mr Stewart, the headmaster, played them a Bob Dylan track on a record player. It was meant to relax them in the same way it relaxed him. It was the first-day-at-school welcome that he would have wanted. He didn't say anything while the music played. He shut his eyes and swayed; tall and thin like a poplar tree. The children sat cross-legged on the floor, like baby frogs uncertain which way to jump.

When the song had finished the headmaster paused for a moment so that the last drops of music could be absorbed, then he took the needle off the record and got down to business. He told them who he was and who the rest of the line-up were and said that he hoped they'd all be very happy in his school. But James felt hemmed in. His crystalline blue eyes were saucer wide. It was at this point that the child next to him started to cry. He was a scruffy boy with a dirt-engrained face that no amount of washing would improve.

'There, there,' James said. 'Don't cry,' and he looked up to the row of teachers for assistance. Mrs Hughes, the second-year head of class, came over, took the snotty boy by the hand and led him out. James looked after her gratefully. Now there was room for David to sit down next to him and James patted the empty space encouragingly. Perhaps they were going to like it here after all. His eyes softened and his pupils dilated a little.

Days wormed their parasitic way into weeks. School was a

success. No complaints. No tantrums. The teachers found James delightful and David – who did not, as Sandra had hoped, disappear – was deemed sweet. Their blue-eyed boy saved up all his havoc for home. He started wetting the bed every night and the temper tantrums and night wanderings were once more frequent and brutal. Sandra and Ken would wake early, bleary from fractured sleep.

For some reason James was only calm and constrained once he had donned his uniform. Then he became like a lamb and was willingly led to school. Chaperone duty fell to his mother most mornings now. She'd known this would happen. Mrs Arnold, the man-woman professional, was bound to let her down. James still seemed not to really notice Christian, but it was becoming clear that Christian looked up to him. He was still the terrier running ahead, then back, but now James was the master and a neglectful one at that.

This shift happened one day in the playground. Christian, egged on by a group of boys, had tried to provoke James into fighting. He'd approached wielding an imaginary sword, while the other boys had followed behind like a mean and wretched pack of strays. James held his milk bottle like a grenade but talked on to David seemingly unperturbed. When Christian began to feel foolish in front of his peers, his sword grew in size and acquired a swooshing sound-effect in order to get James's attention. He started circling him – a jackal masquerading as a wolf – before squaring up, brandishing the now enormous sword.

Then suddenly James sent out his cuckoo-clock fist, which cracked Christian on the nose. The boy fell flat on the ground like a cartoon character. For a few seconds he lay there dazzled by a halo of circling stars, the tweet-tweet of birdsong ringing in his ears. The punch had made his eyes water, which told him he was crying, which meant that he was hurt, so Christian committed to his tears. Scrambling up, he scurried off to bury his boohooing in private. The other boys skulked away into cement shadows where, disgruntled, they turned on each other for entertainment. They hadn't known exactly what they'd wanted to see. They just knew that they hadn't seen it.

By the lunch-break Christian had relinquished his alpha-male aspirations – when it came to James – and asked him if he would be his friend. James agreed. It was his first offer of amity, after David's, and it occurred to him that it might be useful to have an ally that everyone could see.

> Make friends, make friends,
> Never, never break friends,
> If you do, you'll catch the flu
> And that will be the end of you.

But Christian's loyalty was only apparent when they were alone together. His insecurity insisted that he hang around with the other boys at school. He knew that his safety lay in the numbers game. James didn't pay any heed to this rule. He was always the plus one. Besides, the mainstay of his attention was firmly focused on the teachers. They were the true power-source, and so his allegiance, he knew, must lie with them.

His own teacher, Mrs McKee, was a freeze-dried, elderly woman with a face like a bird of prey. He didn't really care for her but he was determined that she would care for him. He made a concerted effort to be neat and tidy and effortlessly polite. He washed up all the paintbrushes and fastidiously cleaned the blackboard without bidding. He listened when she talked and laughed when he thought she meant to be funny. It was all it took. And as soon as he knew that she was fond of him, he could pass his own judgement at leisure.

In the end, though, she let him down and there were two injustices that he'd never forgive her for. One day a child wet themselves during break-time, leaving a puddle of betrayal on the floor. Mrs McKee told the class to stand in a line along the wall. She then walked along it, patting each child on the groin until she found the red-faced perpetrator. This humiliation was too much for James. He objected to being touched altogether and resented being grouped in with the other children. Surely she must have known that it wouldn't have been him? The very thought of it made him hot and angry.

The second injustice occurred the day she called him a liar. She'd asked the class to write a poem about whatever subject they liked and James and David had put their heads together and written a piece called 'The Seagull'. James explained to David that poems didn't necessarily have to rhyme and so they decided that theirs wouldn't. The children all queued up in front of Mrs McKee's desk and she read out each poem in turn and then gave her appraisal. James didn't even hear the other poems; he was grinning impatiently, waiting for her to commend his talents. Finally the moment arrived. She read it.

'This is wonderful,' she said.

He feigned surprise.

She fell silent and read it again. 'You didn't write this,' she declared.

James couldn't believe his ears. He flushed crimson. 'I did. David helped me.'

'No, you didn't. You're lying, James. You copied it from somewhere.' She rose from behind her large desk and marched over to his little one. After looking it over, she rifled through his satchel.

'What are you doing?' he asked.

'Empty your pockets.'

When he didn't move she shoved her fingers into the tiny nylon linings but found nothing incriminating, just a trunk-less stripy elephant.

David told him that he should strike her, stop her from touching him, make her take back her words, but somehow he resisted.

The rest of his classmates looked confused but they

understood that James had committed some crime. And he hadn't. He waited for Mrs McKee to admit that she'd wrongly accused him but she chose to continue as though nothing had happened. She returned his book to him – without a gold star – and read the next piece, belonging to a very precious little girl, a prim rhyming poem about a red balloon. The praise that was rightly his overflowed onto her instead. Though he said nothing at the time, like the elephant in his pocket, he wouldn't forgive, not ever.

After school, when James saw his mother waiting in the car with Christian sitting beside her, his anger was released. As soon as he was in the back seat he started tearing off his clothes. David, in unseen solidarity, did the same. Then he started screaming and bashing his forehead against the window.

'I hate her. I hate her!'

People were beginning to notice.

Swiftly, Sandra pulled the car away from the curb, nearly colliding with a milk float, and sped up the road. She dropped Christian at the corner of the cul-de-sac and told him not to tell his mother. At that moment he'd have agreed to anything. He jumped out of the car and hurtled off down the pavement like a rabbit.

When Sandra slowed down again to turn up the driveway, James flung his half-naked body out of the moving car. He landed lupine on all fours and started frenziedly lolloping about the garden, howling like he was in flames. Suddenly he launched himself into the rose bushes. With a torrent of tears and a mouth wet and open, he writhed and struggled and screamed until he was entirely tangled and trapped. There he hung, suspended, like the fairy-tale nightingale, bleeding and limp with thorns tearing into him.

When the fit had passed he was barely conscious. His mother carefully prized him off the spiny, barbarous hooks. He put up no resistance, his lungs were straining and moaning and his mouth dribbled saliva, speckled with blood. She carried him inside and took him upstairs to his bed. She wiped and disinfected his wounds and applied plasters where necessary. Then she went to the car and retrieved the clothes and torn-off buttons. She took out her sewing box from the cupboard under the stairs, put on the television and silently started to sew.

Ken came home late and James was still in an exhausted sleep. Sandra didn't mention the incident. She'd decided that she'd go and speak to his teacher the following morning. There was, she understood, a remedial class, and she accepted that maybe it was time to come clean and admit to the school that her son had a few behavioural problems. Surely they'd already guessed. She also knew that by the morning she'd have decided against this decision but it was her way of tidying James out of her head for a time. For one night she was going to forget all about him and have a nice meal with her husband.

Inevitably, by the time they'd finished their moussaka, she was telling Ken – in her clipped it's-only-going-to-get-louder voice – that she hated how he never had anything to say for himself about his day, about the house, about the food she cooked. He didn't even have anything to say for himself by way of apology or defence. A row would have been fine by her. She longed for a two-way exchange of words. He longed for silence. And he got it, of sorts, for dessert: loud forkfuls of lemon-meringue pie sliced up by a cut-with-a-knife atmosphere.

One benefit born from the superficial acceptance of David was James's newfound love of the outdoors. Sandra no longer had to lock him out. Tired of being the reluctant interpreter, he volunteered. He'd had his fill of 'Does David want to do this?' and 'What does David think about that?' Nowhere was safe. They were even denied peace in their private plastic nature reserve. So they were forced to take their studies outside, to the real thing. They were allowed to go as far as the nearby fields, as these could be reached without having to cross any roads – the semi-rural was not perceived to be a hotbed of threat. Cars were a worry, not people.

On their expeditions James went armed with an illustrated wildlife handbook, a notepad and pencil, a toy gun and a packed lunch, which invariably went to the birds. And if anyone had seen him – the below-the-knee blue shorts, the T-shirt with its rows of apples, and the Jesus sandals – he would have looked just like any other boy. There were only two things that marked him out. He possessed a remarkable air of confidence as he strode along, his stiff little limbs striking the air with all the zeal of a grand marshal at the head of a marching band. And if you looked closely, you'd see his mouth moving in conversation, when he was evidently alone.

Together the two boys explored the hedgerows and, with the aid of the trusty wildlife guide, they soon learnt to distinguish between the woody and the deadly nightshade, the dock-leaf and the nettle, the rook and the raven, and one of Nature's other, more rudimentary, laws: the living and the dead.

On one of their many field trips they'd not been wandering long when they encountered a sheep in distress. Its head was caught fast in a barbed-wire fence, perhaps while straining to get some of the greener grass from the pasture beyond. When they drew nearer it struggled to pull itself free. But, clearly exhausted from previous attempts, after a few pathetic jerks it collapsed with the exertion. To its side a lamb stood awkwardly, its tail thrashing and jerking like a live cable. James wanted to pick up the lamb and hold it close to him, feel its warm breath and newly curling wool against his skin. David recommended stealth but James disregarded his friend's advice and made a sudden lurch. The lamb darted away from him with a bleating plea for clemency, making the protective ewe thrash about again but to no avail.

James then tried a different tack. He laid his bundle and stick on the grass and sat himself down beside the fretting mother.

'There, there,' he said, stroking her, putting his face next to hers, his eyes all the while fixed on the lamb. He thought that this way he might trick it into thinking he was a trusted comrade come to save the day. Two uncertain steps it advanced . . . then another two. He lunged again but the lamb was not sweet-talked so swiftly and it sprang out of his way.

David laughed.

'You made it do that!'

David shrugged.

James untied his bundle and took out his gun. First he pointed it at the lamb.

'Come here!' he commanded, but the lamb wouldn't obey.

'Shoot its mother,' David whispered.

James put the gun to the ewe's head. 'I'll shoot,' he threatened.

'Do it!' David mouthed.

Instead, James pointed the gun at David. David backed away, a mixture of confusion and malice on his face. Then he laughed and in order to turn it back into a game he put his own head through the barbed wire and pretended to be the struggling ewe.

For a moment James's eyes were unyielding, then suddenly they softened. He giggled the moment away and joined in, taking the part of the lamb. On his hands and knees he jolted this way and that, his bottom thrust up into the air. Then he stood stock-still with wide helpless eyes. After they'd tired of this game David suggested that they go and tell the farmer.

'Tell the farmer what?'

'About the sheep with its head stuck.'

'But the farmer did it,' James explained.

'Did what?'

'Put him there on purpose to teach him a lesson.'

'It's a her,' David corrected.

'Well, her then.'

David didn't look convinced, so James elaborated.

'Sheep are supposed to have three bags of wool. You know that!'

'Yes.'

'Well, sometimes they lose a bag.'

'Oh.'

'So this is punishment. The farmer will be cross if we put our noses in where they're not wanted.' This was a phrase of Sandra's. He enjoyed patronising David with his mother's words. 'But we can come back every day and visit and then the lamb will think that we're its parents and we can adopt it.'

'Can it be our dog?' David asked.

'If you like,' James said, humouring him.

David said goodbye to the sheep and the lamb and then ran after James, who'd already packed up his stick and bundle and had set off towards T Woods.

T Woods was their favourite find. Neither of them knew why they called it that. It was not in the shape of the letter 'T', nor did it have an aroma of tea. T Woods simply happened to be its name. The forest sat, fenced in, on the top of a hill. It was the archetypical English woodland, with bluebells, brambles, ferns and grassy glades between tall trees. It was not huge but to James and David it was as big as a country. They never felt like they'd explored it in its entirety. Impenetrable thorns guarded some spots and others seemed to mysteriously uproot and migrate between visits. The boys killed hours and hours in the wood. James made notes of all the birds and animals they saw: jays, thrushes, rabbits, finches, wagtails and voles.

The day after they discovered the sheep the weather was downcast and neither of the boys felt inclined to go out. Then James had a temper tantrum, tripped and banged his head. He was put to bed, where he buried away from the daylight into a long and woozy sleep. When the sun rose again the following morning the boys were raring to go out, and Sandra was only too happy to see the back of them.

They set off early for the woods, and just as they were crossing the fields they remembered the lost sheep and their plans to parent the surrogate lamb-dog.

'Get down,' David instructed.

James followed his order and they crawled cautiously up the slope; no mean feat when you're carrying a stick and bundle. When they reached the top they could see the wire fence. The mother and infant were surprisingly still there.

'We need to approach them from behind,' David whispered.

James nodded, but signalled that he'd lead the party. He couldn't trust David. He knew that he'd bungle the operation.

They moved further off so that they could squeeze between the wires without being spotted. Then they crawled back, trying to avoid the rain-sodden cowpats and molehill landmines. James put his hand on a thistle and winced but made no sound. The two animals had their backs to them. When the boys were about five feet away, with a gesture from James, they stopped. He'd gauged the distance carefully. He'd estimated that with one spring and one lunge he could easily travel as far as the lamb.

One. Two. Three. He pounced. The lamb didn't try to lurch away and his outstretched fingers fastened on the small ribcage with ease. He lifted it up, the great game-hunter with his quarry, and the movement made a cloud of flies fill the air like a rank spray of perfume. James panicked. He could feel the flies in his mouth, nose and eyes. He was forced to retreat a few steps, shaking his head and crumpling up his face. When he was sure that his body was fly-free, he opened his eyes to take in his prize. His mouth fell slack. All the lamb's resistance had vanished. Its head and legs dangled limply like a puppet without a master. James shook it gently and it released a feeble bleat.

He could feel its lungs straining to inflate its ribcage. He was holding it too tightly. Releasing his grip a little he held the body out at arm's length. Not sure what to do next, he turned to David, who was kneeling by the ewe.

'It's *deaded*,' he told James, without turning.

James stepped closer – still holding out the lamb like a Christmas present he didn't want – and stared down at the lifeless heap at David's feet. The flies had settled again, a living veil of iridescent blue, shrouding the ewe's head. Its eyes stared out, uncaring, as the sequin bluebottles drank their fill. James felt sick. The air stank. He started to cry.

'I'm frightened,' he told the back of his friend, who seemed unperturbed by the flies and the stench.

'The farmer must have been really angry,' David whispered. 'To make it die.'

'I want to go home.'

A handful of crows landed nearby. They were boldly strutting back and forth, crash-victim voyeurs craning to get a glimpse of roadkill.

'Take some wool,' David told James, solemnly.

'I don't want to.'

'Do it.'

Reluctantly James gently placed down the lamb. It bleated weakly as though even the touch of the grass caused it pain. The tears still falling, he put one hand over his mouth, while with the other he pulled out a clump of oily grey wool. His first memento mori.

'Our dog looks sick.' David sounded dispassionate.

'It's our fault,' James said, stuffing the wool into his pocket.

'It's its mother's fault. She lost the bag of wool.'

James had made up that part, but now he had to swallow his own invention. 'That's true.'

David stood up and kicked the carcass, making the flies burst into the air again like miniature fireworks. James knelt down where David had been. He picked up the lamb and cradled it like a baby. It had small gashes all over its body and its eyes were open sores. He brought his hands together over the lamb.

'What are you doing?' David wanted to know.

'Praying for the dead sheep so that he goes to heaven.'

'She,' David corrected.

'She,' James conceded, bringing his praying hands up to his face. When he raised his head again there was a smear of lamb's blood gleaming on his brow.

'Shall we take the dog home?'

'Stupid! Mum would cook it and make us eat it. Anyway, it's a lamb.'

'But you said . . .'

'Shut your face. We'll take it to the farmer-man.'

'Sheep don't go to heaven,' David told him coolly.

James stood up, ignoring him. He would only talk to the lamb. He picked up his bundle and set off, and David followed, like a sulking shadow.

EIGHT

They walked for some time but didn't come across any buildings. They took a break and the moment they stopped the big black birds, which had been stalking them, descended. James shouted to try and frighten them away, but they were unabashed. They cackled shamelessly and began to slowly circle them, ominously, closing rank. James tried to feed the lamb a stick of celery filled with cream cheese, but it didn't fancy it any more than he did. It turned its blind eyes away. He rose again and placed the lamb around his neck.

'You look like Jesus Christ,' David jeered.

They crossed the fields in silence until they spotted a lane leading to some farm buildings. There was a wooden gate at the perimeter. They climbed over it and entered a cobblestone yard dotted with muddy potholes where some of the rocks had become dislodged. Suddenly a couple of black sheepdogs came hurtling from round a corner towards them, tongues lolling. They tumbled over each other in their excitement, like hungry waves. David froze but James walked stoically on. The dogs jumped up at him to inspect the lamb and in the process knocked his stick and bundle to the ground, nearly toppling him over.

The first building that he came to had a Dutch stable door. The top half of it was open.

'Hello!' James shouted, his wavering voice betraying his

anxiety. 'Mr Farmer?' Tears were welling again. When he peered over the door he gasped. Row upon row of beady amber eyes were bearing down on him, as hundreds of battery chickens craned from cages that stretched back bleakly in a hall of mirrors' infinity. He couldn't breathe, the wheezing lamb was around his neck, the dogs were under his heels and the thousand cold eyes were boring into him.

Then a coarse disembodied voice said, 'Come away,' and the black dogs sank down in immediate submission, struck by some invisible hand. James wrenched his eyes away from the threadbare hens and struggled on. He turned the corner to his right and then stopped in his tracks.

'What have you got there?'

In front of the boy was an elderly lady in a wheelchair; her thick bifocals blinded him with sunlight. She sat in the door frame of a porch that brimmed with plants and flowers. He was stunned. What he saw was a woman whose lower-half was constructed out of steel and rubber.

'Let's go,' David said from his side, but James held his ground.

The old woman rolled towards them.

James flinched. 'I've got a lamb,' he told her. It sounded like a threat.

'Where did you find it?'

'In a field. Its mother is dead, but I didn't do it. And the lamb's hurt and its eyes . . .'

'Give it here,' she said, wheeling closer still.

He lifted the lamb from around his shoulders and handed it to her carefully. There was blood on his T-shirt, splashes of red merging with the rosy-apple print.

'Poor dear.' She held the lamb up as though looking for a price on a vase. 'They've pecked out his eyes.'

James inhaled with a gulp. 'Who?' He wanted to bolt. He looked round for David but he was nowhere to be seen.

'The crows.'

'But why?'

'Once they've blinded it they can separate it from its mother and . . .' She stopped.

James felt sick again.

'Nature red in tooth and claw,' she said to herself.

James was starting to panic. He wanted to draw his toy gun but it was in his dropped bundle. He looked about for David but he still couldn't see him.

'Have you lost something?' she asked.

'David.'

'A friend of yours?'

James nodded.

'I'm going to call my son. It's probably one of his. You'd better come in and wash off the blood.' She reversed her wheelchair back into the porch, where she placed the lamb between some terracotta plant-pots on a compost bag. Then, in order to enter the house, she slickly turned her wheels ninety degrees. James was compelled to follow. He averted his eyes from the lamb. Now that he knew it was blind he couldn't bring himself look at it.

The kitchen was large with a high ceiling. The light was almost brown, a stark contrast to the brightness of the foliage-filled porch. The tiled floor was dirty. Spoiled feathers lay amidst shards of sawdust and eggshell. Sticky-looking stains and muddy footprints formed what could have been mistaken for a pattern. The smell was overpowering, a heady blend of butter, manure and eggs. Looking up, James saw yellow ribbons of flypaper hanging down from the ceiling like macabre bunting. He watched the bluebottles that were still alive furiously trying to prize themselves free. The woman wheeled herself over to a red telephone and rang her son.

'You're going to have to put him out of his misery,' James heard her say.

'Who?' he thought. 'Me?'

This half-woman and her son, human spiders, catching

things and letting them die – sheep, lambs, hens, flies, boys? He tried to work out what to do. Should he punch her on the nose? She was wearing glasses. Frantically, he looked about the room for something with which to defend himself: a chair . . . too heavy; a big mixing-bowl . . . too cumbersome; scissors . . . large metal scissors . . . they would do nicely.

She put down the receiver.

'What's your name?' she asked.

'David,' he lied.

'I thought that was your friend's name?'

'It is . . . too . . .'

'Oh. Well, David, you'd better wash your face and hands.'

She's going to cook me, he thought, and feed me to her children.

'Does your s-s-son have wheels t-t-too?' he stammered.

'No,' she said with a laugh, revealing teeth the same colour as the flypaper. 'He has big strong legs.'

'Eight of them,' he told himself, 'hairy like a spider.'

She wheeled herself forwards and he shrank back, so she rolled past him into the porch and inspected the lamb – but really, James knew, it was to block his exit. While he weighed up his options he did as he was told and washed his hands with the rough, strong-smelling soap. There were two other doors leading from the kitchen. One room had the same tiles on the floor, but it was dark and could have been a dead-end larder. The other opened into a large old-fashioned sitting room. It was adorned with heavy-looking furniture, and led off to another room beyond. Where was David? Like Jesus, James had been forsaken in his hour of need.

Then suddenly he spotted his friend, a shape at the kitchen window. He was gesturing urgently at the scissors on the table. James nodded and edged towards them, keeping his eyes fixed on the back of the wheeled woman. He reached out and his fingers grasped the cold metal. He slid the scissors slowly from the table and concealed them behind his back. Then he looked at David and he knew what he had to do next.

He approached the old woman stealthily. He'd stick the scissors in her. Not in her heart – you killed people through the heart and he didn't want her to die – he'd lodge them in her head or neck. Then he'd make a run for it. First he'd have to lure her away from the door. He looked about himself for a diversion.

'What's that?' he asked.

'Sorry, dear?'

He pointed. A dangling drop of water on the tip of his outstretched finger fell in slow motion and landed on an oily feather, where it rocked like a diamond.

'It's called an Aga,' she was saying, but he couldn't hear her words. He just heard the noise of metal and wheels as she drew near. His nails dug into his flesh around the steel. Breathing in, he shut his eyes.

Then he heard a churning, rumbling noise, growing louder by the second. At first he thought that the sound was coming from inside him and that maybe he was having a fit. But when he opened his eyes a Land Rover was rolling up the driveway. The big black dogs were barking. A cold hand of indecision seized him. Then instinct took over. He rushed for the door but his moment of hesitation cost him a clear run. He collided with the trunk of a man, framed by two Hades dog-heads that leered at him menacingly.

'Where's the fire?' he asked James.

James said nothing. He still had the scissors behind his back.

'What's the rush?'

'I've lost my friend, David.'

'And found a lamb.'

'Yes. I didn't hurt it . . . Is there a fire?'

'No.'

'Oh.' James didn't understand why he'd mentioned one then.

'You shouldn't be in those fields, you know.' The farmer

picked up the lamb, which had started to wheeze again like an asthmatic.

'No harm done,' his mother said.

'Not this time, but if you set foot in the pine wood, you're likely to get shot at.'

James couldn't have made a response even if he'd felt so inclined. While the lamb's tongue lolled, his was stuck fast to the inside of his mouth.

'Did you hear me?'

James nodded vigorously, staring up at the wide face and the coal-black curling hair. The farmer looked at him quizzically. He seemed to have forgotten the lamb, which he dangled inches above the mouths of the drooling dogs.

'Hadn't you better bugger off and find your friend?'

'I can't.'

'Why not?'

'*You* are in my way,' James told him.

'Ah.' And the man moved aside.

James squeezed past, receiving a smearing of dog saliva in the process.

When he'd backed a safe distance away, he asked, 'What will you do with the lamb?'

The farmer started to say something but his mother rolled into the porch and cut him off. 'We'll stop it feeling poorly.'

He could see her fleshy fingers reaching up to her son's arm. And she gave him a wide-eyed look, magnified even more by her glasses. James knew that she was lying. He turned and ran.

Round the corner he collided with David, who was casually inspecting something on the ground – the cane and bundle. The farmer had driven over them. James, still brimful of adrenalin, dropped down onto his knees and, with his scissor-free hand, scrabbled to rescue his belongings – the torn headscarf, his badly mangled nature guide and his gun, which he slipped into his waistband. He'd leave his sandwiches in the muddy hollow to curl up on themselves like fortune fish. As he stood he picked up the cane; the tyres had broken it and the two halves hung together by a thin bamboo strip.

'Where were you?' he asked David as he marched away.

'There.'

'No, you weren't.'

'It was the woman . . . she could see me.'

'Liar,' James hissed. 'They wanted to kill me and they would have too . . .' – James was emboldened now that David was back by his side – 'if I hadn't stuck these scissors into her,' and he brandished them, shutting the blades with a snap near David's Pinocchio nose.

David jerked back but he looked impressed. 'Did you really?'

James didn't reply. Instead he stopped, turned round and started back towards the farmhouse.

'What are you doing?' David's voice was shrill with alarm.

As James approached the redbrick building he slowed down so that he could peep around its corner. Reluctantly, David followed. What they then witnessed made their shoulders hunch and their eyes freeze over with horror.

The farmer had one hand on the lamb's head and the other round its neck. The dogs sat beside him, their tails sweeping the cobbles in encouragement. With a violent jerk the man twisted his hands in opposite directions. A final, strangulated breath escaped from the lamb's mouth before its neck snapped with a loud crack. James dropped the scissors and they hit the stones with a clatter.

'Hey!' the farmer shouted, looking in their direction.

'Run for your life!' James said, his voice all bunched up, snagging in his throat like a spool of spoiled cassette tape. They fled from the farm into the fields, scratching and stinging their legs on the reaching nettles and thistles. As they tore along they could picture the farmer's boots pummelling the ground behind them. So they kept running, like frightened little piggies, wee-wee-wee, all the way home.

James hit the doorbell urgently. He longed to see his mother. For once, he craved her contact, her hug of reassurance. He was breathing heavily, his eyes fixed on the drive, anticipating the farmer's approach.

A hand grabbed him by the T-shirt.

'What time do you call this?' his mother said, pulling him inside. 'Your dad's going to be so cross when he gets home.'

James was speechless.

Sandra looked him up and down and shook him. 'Look at the state of you! What's this?' She was holding on to the bloodstained top so fiercely that he was almost lifted off the floor.

'Lamb's blood,' he explained through the neck of his T-shirt.

'Don't you lie to me!'

'I am not.'

She slapped his legs and the sound rang out.

'Shoot her,' David whispered.

James dropped his bundle, pulled the gun out and held it close to her face. He pulled the trigger twice and two little red caps exploded with white flashes.

'Bang! Bang!' He shouted the sound too, to give it extra force.

Sandra screamed.

'You're dead,' he said calmly. Then he laughed, but it was the hollow laugh of a jaded old actor.

David clapped his hands with glee.

'Get out of my sight!'

'I hate you,' James said and kicked his mother on the shin.

She yelped but managed to grimace out her threat: 'You just wait till your dad gets home.'

All his fear, exasperation and relief welled up and he started crying.

'Get to your room or I'll give you something to cry for.' She contorted her body like a tightly wrung dishcloth. 'And give me that top!'

He tore it off and threw it at her. 'I hate you,' he spluttered again between sobs. 'Come . . . David.'

Sandra listened to him ascend the wooden stairs, slamming his Jesus sandals down hard on each step.

'I hate you. I hate you. I hate you.'

Not able to bear it any longer, she slammed the kitchen door and felt the newly repaired glass panel vibrate like a tuning fork.

'I hope you die!' he screamed.

'I hope you die too,' she whispered, before she could abort the thought.

Then she immediately started lining up all her cups on the pine-look kitchen worktop before filling them with hot water and a false-teeth cleaning agent – one of her housewife's tricks for removing tea-stains. When her husband came home she decanted all of her guilt and anger into him. Without a word he about-turned and exited the way he'd come in, leaving the defeated Sandra to sit and sob to the sound of his reversing car. 'He's driven over the corner of the flowerbed again.'

Kenneth had indeed – quite deliberately – driven over the flowerbed, a little victory for a big man. He was so tired of throwing eggshells in his path before he took a step. He was obliged to kowtow all day at work and then when he got home as well. His rebellious gesture would now mean that he'd have to spend the night at his parents' house. And, in order to stave off the 'I told you, you never should have married her' reproaches, he'd be obliged to lie about the whys and wherefores. He knew that he wouldn't get a wink's sleep. He'd lie in his musty old room – the heavy, umber-coloured blankets pressing him to the bed like a stuck insect – while he worried away the hours thinking about the car getting scratched or stolen.

Slowly, Sandra moved to the oven. She took out one portion of their dinner for three. The following day she'd reheat some for lunch and then maybe give the rest to the old lady a few doors down whose family never visited.

'Another meal spoilt,' she said to the fridge – braised beef in Guinness with pickled walnuts, St Delia's recipe.

The table had been laid in the dining room but she wouldn't sit in there on her own, so she took her supper into the lounge to eat guiltily in front of the TV.

Upstairs James hid the gun he'd shot his mother with under his pillow. Then he pulled off the rest of his clothes and sat on the carpet, next to David.

'Look at your hands.'

James held them out for inspection. His fate line, life line, and heart line were bloodstained rivulets both on his right palm and his left – destiny and reality perfectly mirrored.

'Take off your clothes too,' he told David, as he licked his hands clean.

Then he began to set out their zoo.

'This is the sheep,' he said, holding one out. He didn't possess any in the lying position, so he bit the legs off the plastic replica . . . one, two, three, four . . . Then he forced its white head between the slats of one of the fences. He took a kneeling lamb, clamped its neck between his milk teeth and twisted it, almost to breaking point, so that its head hung limp. This he placed beside the sheep. He took a black pen from his bedside table. With it he dotted their bodies with flies. Then he inked over the white cuffs and collars of the sheepdogs and turned the white doves into crows.

David wanted to know why black things lingered around dead white ones. 'Dogs, crows, spiders, flies . . .'

'And vicars,' James added.

'And vicars,' David agreed.

'It's so that we know not to go near them.'

'Why don't farmers wear black?'

'They do. They wear black clothes underneath. I saw them. It's a disguise to trick and trap people.' Wolves dressed in sheep's clothing.

'What do you think they did with the lamb?'

'Shared it out with their black dogs and the crows. They'll eat it up off the floor with flies for pepper.'

James looked down at his graven image of the lamb. It resembled a floret of cauliflower – which he hated – but he picked it up and swallowed it whole. He could feel it scraping his insides as it went down, making him gag, but he wasn't sick. He couldn't face eating the sheep, so he buried it in the soil of a pot-plant in his room, a sickly wispy fern. David knelt down and shut his eyes.

'You're not praying, are you?' James asked, as he began to wee in little patches on the carpet, like a tomcat marking out his territory.

'No.'

James peed on him to make him open his eyes.

'Stop it!'

'I'm baptising you, like they do to babies, because you're a baby.'

David turned his back on him in a sulk, so James climbed into bed and hid under the covers. He read *Alice in Wonderland*, David's second favourite book, and laughed out loud when the baby turned into a pig, just to let his friend know what he was missing out on.

When James heard the door open he assumed that it was David taking his huff somewhere else. That would be no fun. He threw back the covers and saw his mother standing there. She wanted to forgive him, absolve him. She wanted company that was not a fridge. In the same instant, mother and son realised that he was naked. David laughed at his expression – young Adam, ashamed. Then, with a flurry of sound and movement, like a large bird taking off, the hardbacked Alice was flying across the room and James was following, fists and voice raised in attack. Sandra was out of the door and racing down the stairs in seconds. She could palpably feel her sanity escaping, oozing out through the pores of her skin.

Around this time James's grandparents became a bigger feature. Both of his grandmothers were still alive but only one grandfather – the other had died before he was born. He'd overheard Sandra say, 'My mother killed my father, you know. She worked him to death.'

Naturally James had taken her at her word. He had a murderess as a grandmother.

It didn't take the boy long to learn that the way to one grandmother's heart was to verbally dissect the other's.

'I much prefer seeing you to my other grandma. Her house smells . . . And she won't let me eat sweets.' Cue the sound of the Quality Street tin being opened or the paper bag being extracted, and every time James affected surprise and delight. From then on in, he became braver and greedier and as the crimes of the other grandmother escalated, so did the spoils. His best ever reward was a kitten from the murderess.

He'd spent some time – over several visits – peppering conversations with his love of animals, and cats in particular. He told tales of how poor his other grandmother was and how paltry her presents were, which – rather unimaginatively – were restricted to Christmas and birthdays. The rest of the year, he implied, the measure of her love was uncertain. And she didn't believe in bestowing anything upon one grandchild without doing the same for the others, which James thought illustrated a rather underdeveloped character. He wanted her to choose a favourite and for it to be him.

'It's David's birthday next Saturday,' he told Grandma Maude, the murderess. The date also happened to coincide with their next visit.

'It isn't,' David said.

James paid him no heed.

'I want to buy him a present, but I haven't any money.' His saucer blue eyes fell to the earth, full of feigned resignation.

'What do you want to get him? Or is it a surprise?'

'No. Well, yes, it is a surprise, but he is in the garden, so he can't hear me.' He knew that his grandmother could not see David.

'I'm not in the garden.'

'I want to buy him a cat.'

'A cat?'

'Yes, a black one. All black, without any white on it.' He couldn't face colouring in a cat with a felt-tip.

David could now see where this was going. He would make no further interruptions.

'What does your mother think?'

'I've only told you. But I don't think she likes cats very much.'

His grandmother smiled. She wasn't that keen on her daughter. She'd always preferred her boys.

That following Saturday the murderess presented James with a black kitten to give to David for his birthday. Sandra was furious. A row ensued that shook the plastic polka-dot beakers in the kitchen.

'Stop fussing. It'll be good for him . . . to care for something.'

'You should have asked me first.'

'Can't I buy a present for my own grandson?'

'Not one I'll have to look after!'

Soon the sounds became an unintelligible cacophony.

Meanwhile, James and David sat on the sheepskin rug – identical to the one at home – deciding on a name for the cat. Of course, it was James who chose it, though it was purportedly David's present.

'Cifer,' he declared.

'What?'

'Cifer. Do you get it?'

David nodded that he did, but he clearly didn't.

'C for cat. Cfor. Cifer,' James explained slowly.

'What about Figaro?'

'From *Pinocchio*?'

'Yes.'

'No, that's a boy's name and she's a she.'

David knew that he wouldn't come up with anything as original, so he conceded that Cifer was indeed a good name.

Shortly afterwards the boys were ushered hastily into the car. James cried to be let out but his mother's fury made her efficient.

'This is a trial,' she said to the back seat. 'If you look after it properly . . . then I *might* let you keep it. If not, I'm going to get rid of it.'

James clutched Cifer defensively and she mewed, blinking her apple-green eyes. Sandra saw this in the mirror. Maybe having a cat *would* help him. Maybe the cat would replace David. David. David. David. It hurts when your child prefers another to you, but coming second is far worse when the first doesn't exist. 'At least a cat is real,' she thought, though it tore at her heart to watch him cuddle the tiny creature.

James did not give his mother any excuse to get rid of Cifer. But sometimes, when her discontent made her burn with spite, she used the kitten as leverage.

'You'll eat everything on your plate or the cat goes back.'

It worked, but she saw the hatred simmer in his eyes.

Since the day he'd come home all bloody, Sandra could feel him retreating ever further away from her and she hadn't realised that that was possible. So she decided that if James could have David and Cifer, then she too deserved an ally. She would buy herself a dog. Dogs were constantly pleased to see you, even after just a moment's separation. When it came down to it, she would settle for amnesiac love.

'Would you like a surprise?' Sandra asked the boys.

'David would like a surprise.'

That would have to do.

'Well, shut your eyes.'

'David has. I'll have to lead him.'

That would also have to do. Sandra steered her son into the dining room. From there, he could make out a grey, spectral shape through the glass of the kitchen door.

'What's that?' James asked.

'It's your surprise,' and, with a lady mayoral flourish, his mother swung open the door. A small white dog rushed out and jumped up at her excitedly. It was veritable calendar fodder: tongue out, ears erect, eyes bright and pedigree dumb.

'Hello . . . did you miss me?' she asked.

'Oh dear, it's white,' James said sadly and, sidestepping them both, entered the kitchen. 'Cifer?' he called.

'Yes, *she's* white.'

Sandra had insisted on getting a bitch. They were far more faithful and the idea of an animal that tried to dry-hump your leg made her flush with mortification. 'You're adorable. Aren't you? Yes, you are, you are! Say hello to James,' she told the busy dog. 'She's so good-natured,' she assured the room. 'Pat her,' she instructed. 'She won't bite you.'

'You can open your eyes now,' James told David.

David evidently said something, as James shook his head gravely.

When the dog eventually turned its attention to the boys, its attitude visibly changed. James immediately moved forwards like the Tin Man, his legs stiff with resistance. He leant in. The dog growled. He leant out. It stopped. He leant in again. The teeth were unveiled with a warning snarl. Out, and they were concealed once more. James turned to David and they giggled – a new game.

'Now, don't growl,' Sandra chastised, without much verve. 'I don't know what's up with her. This is James. You have to smile and say something nice.'

James wasn't listening. He was still absorbed in antagonising the animal. The clock cuckoo, he sprang forward then leapt back to timber-lodge safety. Finally, he pushed the dog to its – all bark – limit and it snapped its jaws centimetres away from his retreating nose.

'Now look what you've done!' Sandra scolded.

'What? I didn't try to bite him!' he said, blinking wide. Then he sniggered. 'David says I *should* bite him. Fair's fair,' and he bared his teeth and barked, which riled the dog even further.

'It's a *she*,' Sandra said.

'What do you want to name her?' Ken said, his usual cue. He'd been hovering the whole time in the door frame, like a TV bit part. Now he was trying to diffuse the situation, while simultaneously pouring himself a healthy-sized whiskey.

James shrugged.

'What about David? What does he think is a good name?' His father was utilising all his skills as negotiator.

'Woe,' James relayed.

'Woe?' Sandra laughed, though clearly not amused. 'You can't call a dog Woe,' she said, trying to calm her still bewildered animal.

'David did.'

'Do you know what the word means?' his father asked him. James shook his head.

'It's just a pretty sounding word. David made it up. Where's Cifer?'

'Outside,' Sandra said, before quickly adding, 'just while the dog settles in . . . I think we should call her Whitie,' she announced, summoning all her flair and originality. 'Do you like that, Whitie? Yes, you do, don't you? Who's a good girl?'

'I'm going to call it Lamb Chop,' James decreed.

His mother elected not to hear him.

James, David and Kenneth left the woman and her dog together in their mutual appreciation. Ken was going to have another whiskey after this one. Maybe two. Fuck it, he might even get drunk. In the marital game of snakes and ladders he had slipped away from his wife again. She hated his apathy and evasion. As far as she was concerned if her husband couldn't commit to loving her, then he could at least make some effort and hate her. He'd agreed to her buying a dog without any argument. All that he'd suggested was that she chose a medium-sized one, as he didn't relish the prospect of being seen walking a small dog. But in this, as in all things, he'd been easily overruled. Sandra had set her heart on a West Highland Terrier. Whitie the Westie.

NINE

Whitie was discussed with the second Specialist.

'What is it you don't like about her?' she asked James.

'Who? Mum?' he replied, knowing only too well who she meant.

'No. Your dog.'

'He is not my dog.'

'She,' Sandra corrected. 'She's a bitch,' she said to Specialist 2, almost inhaling the final word. She needed the woman to know that she understood the correct terminology for a female dog.

'*He's* white,' James stubbornly continued.

'And what's wrong with being white?'

'I don't like the colour,' he said, with a hint of condescension.

Ken was tempted to say that white wasn't strictly a colour, but he held off. He didn't want to expose his pedantic streak in front of Specialist 2.

'What does white mean to you?'

'Sheep.'

'That's nice.'

'Dying.'

'Oh . . . Will you explain that to me?'

'White things die.'

'Do they? Tell me, how do they die?'

'Slowly.'

The Specialist 2 seemed intrigued. His parents weren't. It was getting macabre. They didn't want to understand the machinations of his mind. They wanted to change them. There was something about their son that unnerved them, something nebulous and intangible, something that shifted and moved. Sandra much preferred to have life laid out before her plainly like a yard of cloth. She needed to see it, needed to be able to put her finger on it.

'What makes them die?'

'Black things.'

'Like what, for instance?'

'Like black dogs, or birds, or farmers, or flies, or vicars, or David, or me, or Cifer . . .' it sounded like he could go on for ever.

'What is a Cifer?'

'We've already told you,' he sighed. His patience was being scraped away. 'You're not very good at remembering things.'

'No. Sometimes I'm not.'

'She doesn't mean it,' David warned him.

'I know,' James said.

The woman thought he was talking to her. She went on in her defence. 'When you get older, your memory's not as good.'

'Then maybe I should have your job and you should go back to school.'

She laughed. 'Maybe I should.' She glanced at Sandra and Ken, inviting them to laugh too.

They laughed too.

'But explain to me why you think that you're black . . .'

'Just because you can't see something, it doesn't mean it isn't there.'

'That's very true,' she said soberly. She looked at his parents again and raised her eyebrows, acknowledging that she was impressed – if not encouraged – by the remark. She then half turned back to James but her eyes rested on the empty chair that she'd allocated for David. She was deliberating which approach to use next. Ethically she was torn. Should she stitch up her patient now or should she bury deeper and delve for something more malignant? Was she up to the job, or should *she* get a second opinion? She resolved to perform some more superficial tests.

'Tell me, James, why do black things kill white things?'

'Kill?'

'Yes, kill.'

'Because they can?' He didn't sound certain.

'But why?' Specialist 2 suddenly realised that the pupil and pedagogue had reversed positions. Was he more qualified to do her job? She righted herself, the competent canoeist. 'What makes the black things do it?'

'Something inside.' The boy was growing flushed.

Sandra gestured to Ken. She knew the signs.

'Inside?'

'They need to be taught a lesson.'

'What if you were white and not black?' the psychiatrist asked, trying to maintain her balance. 'Would you need to be taught a lesson?'

James looked scared. He flicked his eyes nervously at his parents, then at David.

This was good. She thought that she was back on course.

Then, without warning, James lunged, crying out as though in pain. Specialist 2 slipped off her chair in surprise, landing on her rump. Ken stood and Sandra shrieked, 'James!' He paid his parents no regard. The therapist was saying, 'I'm fine. Really . . . I'm . . .' as James with a sudden butterfly stroke sent her in-tray flying one way, her out-tray the other. The woman covered her head with her hands. His emotional tide was flooding the room. He launched himself up onto the raft of her desk and raised his arms, but before he could make his next move his father had snatched him up and manhandled him outside.

The boys' interest in animals and their demise were not restricted exclusively to white creatures. Their approach was more haphazard. James would capture any insect that he could lay his hands on, which amounted to a good many – he had fast fingers and the reflexes of a snake. He caught crickets and butterflies, beetles and bees, wasps and spiders. Few of them survived or were fit for release. He loved the feel of a butterfly kiss in his cupped hands, but he wasn't aware that when 'flutterbys' (as he still childishly called them) drunkenly left the ballroom of his palms – with their patterns faded and their dusty dresses torn – that they'd never recover from their dance. He didn't know that a mayfly only lived for one day and he didn't understand – at first – that when a bee parted with its sting, this tiny stripy cupid with its single hara-kiri arrow also parted with its life.

Wasps were quite another matter. The boys had no respect for them. Wasps were merely soldiers, all primed and trained up, gagging for a bit of action, with no war in sight. David and he caught battalions of them, keeping them captives in communal, jam-jar holding cells. These despotic jailers would then vigorously shake their quarry, vexing their prisoners to the point where they'd flex their barbed abdomens and open fire indiscriminately on each other. And when the wasps were at their most incensed, the boys would woo Whitie out into the garden with a biscuit incentive. Then they'd whip off the lid to unleash their swarming weapon into the atmosphere, before beating a hasty retreat to the sun lounge to watch it take effect. Their army, still in the clutches of civil war, would stumble and brawl their way out of the jar, before regrouping to focus their fury on their seeming enemy. Once their victim established that there was no bunker to run to, she'd hold her ground and face the enemy, valiantly snapping together her jaws on the dive-bombers.

More than once Sandra, in Fay Wray mode, was stung as she rushed to the aid of her helpless beast. On one such occasion the dog nearly died. She'd simultaneously chewed up three or four wasps, which had stung her repeatedly on the tongue, making it swell up so much that she could barely breathe. She would have been a Pavlov reject. She never seemed to learn, and her perpetual mistrust of James and David was always forgotten when a biscuit was produced.

Thus far in his short life James had already witnessed – or had been the cause of – the fatalities of many fauna. He'd seen that moment when a living being had stopped; stopped being alive. And in each case the creatures had been cut off in their prime – countless wasps, butterflies, beetles, spiders and two sheep. Not one had died naturally.

But to this point he'd had never been confronted with the death of a fellow human. Of course he'd encountered countless deaths in the world of fiction, but all these unfortunate characters had come to their end by a murderous shot to the head or a knife through the heart. He also had some comprehension that very, very old people died, but he hadn't for a moment imagined a slow drift into death. Old people simply vanished in alphabetical order, or if they'd breathed a million breaths that was them – gone – in a cloud of vapour. And people couldn't possibly live beyond the age of a hundred, as they'd never be able to summon up the breath to blow out that many candles.

James's grandfather was by no means a centenarian, though he'd certainly breathed a great many breaths, but it was this man who was marked out as the first person the boy would see die.

Gradually James had grown fond of his grandfather and was not afraid of him as everyone else seemed to be. He was the only member of the family who could make him laugh. He'd mimic the old man by plucking bobbles off his jumper and then pushing them up his nostrils, so that they mirrored the tendril tufts of nasal hair that protruded from his cavernous nose. James could also prize his grandfather out of his armchair – a feat few others had mastered – and into the corner shop, where he'd be coerced into buying nature magazines. This was another breakthrough in itself: parting the man from his money.

Grandad Gordon was treated by Grandma Ethel – and so by the rest of the family – like an invalid. He was not in fact an invalid but he wasn't about to correct them. He sat like a hippo in his exfoliating armchair, while his oxpecker wife hopped about him, preening him, cleaning him, taking what nourishment she could from him. He would say little but punctuated every conversation with his hacking cough, spitting phlegm into pieces of the *Daily Express* torn into careful squares by Ethel. He smoked Golden Virginia roll-ups, which he magicked up in his silver rolling tin, a trick that never ceased to amaze his grandson.

'Do it again!' James would say as his grandfather shut the lid and the little white cylinder appeared on the top.

Gordon indulged him and David too. He'd never said anything about David one way or the other, so James trusted that he'd accepted him into the family. Perhaps the man's lenience was due to the fact that James was the sole remaining male to shoulder the name of Gardner, even if it was only nominally. And perhaps the boy's approbation was born out of him being the only grandfather he had left.

The grandparents spent alternate Christmases with the family. They'd tried having both at once but it really wasn't constructive to the continuum of peace on earth. This particular Christmas it was Ken's parents' turn, though Gordon nearly cancelled because of the snow. He refused to take the bus in case he slipped, so Ken was compelled to pick them up, much to Sandra's chagrin.

'The least they could do is take a taxi. We're doing

everything else. There's nothing wrong with the man, except that he's bone idle.'

The snow certainly was unusually deep. Everywhere was a symphony in white, so the boys had a presentiment that something was going to die. Neither of them really cared much for Christmas, aside from the pagan vestiges of Santa Claus and the tree, and the prospect of the grandparents' coming to stay didn't excite the boys either, as Sandra grew stiffer and stiffer as the tick-tock of their arrival approached.

However, James knew his part by heart. When the car rolled up the drive he swiftly assumed an animated air and a veil of charm descended over his features. Then he opened the front door and hugged them both tightly like they'd just been rescued from certain death.

'Let me take your coats,' he said, the ingratiating butler in miniature.

'Shoes!' Sandra involuntarily ejaculated and pointed down at them, as though all present might have momentarily forgotten what shoes were.

'If you don't mind . . . I'll just get my coat off,' Ethel responded frostily. 'I can't do both at once.'

'It's bitter out, isn't it?' Sandra offered.

'Yes!' Ken was still standing in the snow, as the coat and shoe removal ritual was being carried out on the threshold.

Ethel helped her husband into the lounge, lowering the bulky man into Kenneth's armchair before taking a seat herself with a sigh.

James and David stood by, the humble servants.

'Would you like Dad to make you a nip?' James asked Gordon, not knowing exactly what a nip was, but remembering that that was what he always discreetly requested.

'That's a good lad,' his grandfather said, speaking for the first time. He smiled for an instant before his mouth spread into a cough. 'Don't tell your mother though.'

James nodded his complicity and left the room.

He took his grandmother her 'nice' cup of tea (not in the best china, she wouldn't appreciate it) and his grandfather his 'nip' as secretly concocted by Ken (one fingerbreadth of whiskey to two fingers of water). He handed the tumbler over. The old man's unsteady hands nearly let it slip through them. He concentrated his efforts.

'I'd rather see a church fall down than spill a drink.'

'Mum says you should make your way to the dining room, Grandad . . . because it takes you a while.'

Sandra hadn't planned for him to repeat the last part, but she really wouldn't have cared that he had. The day was to be run to a strict schedule: arrival of parents-in-law; post-journey tea; a light-lunch, consisting of a cold spread of her speciality dishes – curried rice, Waldorf salad and quiche Lorraine; some television-watching while grazing on Roses chocolates and mixed nuts; dinner – beef casserole – which was already well underway; more television and polite chat and more chocolates; a mince pie or a slice of Christmas cake, and another tea, or a sherry, before an early night in preparation for the next exciting instalment.

His grandmother rose to her feet in order to help her husband out of his chair, but James relieved her of the task.

'You drink your tea, Grandma. We'll take him. David, you go to his other arm.'

The old man huffed and puffed his way through to the dining room, an outmoded steam engine. James pulled out a chair for him so that he could ease himself down after the exertion.

'Don't tell your mother,' the man said, for a second time, as he shoved a large slice of cold lamb into his mouth.

James looked on, not a little disgusted – a rat's tail of fatty skin was dangling from the old man's wide mouth. He was trying to swallow the slab down in one but it was too substantial. This rodent was reluctant to go into its hole. It became lodged halfway. His grandfather tried to cough but it was stuck and would not allow any air to pass in or out. This hulking mass of flesh started to panic and its fat arms flailed about like they were underwater. The top row of his false teeth fell out and clattered onto his pre-set Christmas plate, followed by a thick trail of saliva. James had never seen false teeth before and assumed that they were real. His grandfather then threw back his head and opened his mouth wide.

'He *is* a hippo,' David whispered.

James looked at David. David looked back.

'Don't tell your mother!' David reminded him.

Now the hippo-man was gripping wildly at his throat and turning puce like a huge, newborn baby. Then he jerked forward again and the bottom set of teeth fell out.

James was horrified but transfixed by this strange metamorphosis from grandfather to gargoyle: his eyes bulged, his tongue lolled and his throat gurgled like a rainspout. Time dragged and almost stopped. Then it was as though the light changed. Time had caught up. Everything had returned to normal. The only difference was that his grandfather was dead.

The kitchen door opened and there were sudden flashes of movement, screaming, telephone calls, tears and recriminations. James started to fit. He slipped off his chair and onto the carpet under the table. There he lay, unobserved and shaking. An ambulance arrived. Sandra, suddenly on hostess autopilot, rallied and raised herself above the mayhem. She fussed around the ambulance-men, apologising about getting them out on Christmas Eve, and trying to get them to take mince pies or at least a slice of the Christmas cake that she was so proud of.

One of the men spotted James quietly convulsing on the carpet. He'd almost wedged himself under the sideboard. The man knelt down and eased him out. When he'd established that the boy was not in any danger, he carried him – under Sandra's directions – to his room. And James could remember nothing more.

When he came to, he was in bed beside David and his father was perched by his feet. He handed him an eggcup containing hot-chocolate powder with crushed-up tablets in it and watched as his son dabbed at the bittersweet dust with his finger before licking it away.

'Do you understand that your grandad is dead?'

'Why is he dead?'

'He choked.'

'Because he was in the dying room?'

'No. He had a bad heart.'

'He had a bad heart,' James repeated. 'Do I have a bad heart?'

'Of course not.'

'Where has he gone?'

'To God.'

James didn't look convinced.

'Why didn't you fetch me or your mum, when you saw that your grandad was poorly?'

'He told me not to.'

'What? I don't believe . . . that. What do you . . .?'

'It's true . . . You can ask David.'

'What did he say?'

'David?'

'No, your grandad.'

'He said, "Don't tell your mother."'

'What else?'

'Nothing. He had a bad heart, so he died.'

Ken shuddered. James was explaining back to him with his own words.

'Did he struggle?'

James gazed at his father blankly and licked more chocolate residue off his finger.

'Did he look poorly for long?'

'Yes. Why do your teeth fall out when you die?'

'They don't.'

'His did.'

'He had false teeth.'

'He had false eyes too,' David whispered.

'Errr!'

'What happened, James? What did he do?'

'He waved his arms, like this, and he turned red. And his eyes popped.'

His father went as grey as his irises for a moment, unable to speak.

'And you didn't do anything?'

'Yes, I did. I did as I was told.'

They were silent for a few moments. James dabbed up the last particles of his powder.

'Will Father Christmas still come?'

'I imagine so.'

'I should put out my letter.'

'I'll do it.'

'And the carrot, and the drink . . . and the mince pie?'

'Yes. Are you hungry?'

'No.' James didn't want any real food, ever again, if he could manage it. 'David says goodnight,' James said, handing back the empty eggcup. The discussion was over.

His father turned off the light and left the room, shutting the door behind him. James tried to close his eyes, but each time he did he saw an image of his grandfather, gummy and glaring through big blood-red eyes. David tried his best to soothe him but it was no good.

Christmas Day came and went without any good cheer. Even less of the turkey was touched than Sandra had anticipated, as there were fewer people alive to eat it, and no one could face the lamb now that it had committed manslaughter.

James did not see his grandmother again until the funeral, and when he walked into the church he was emotionally zipped up.

His mother had, on some unacknowledged level, desired to cause a rift between grandmother and grandson, so she'd intimated that Ethel held James somewhat accountable for her husband's death. But to James's great relief his grandmother seemed to bear him no malice. She seemed smaller than he'd remembered her, and her hard pointy jaw seemed softer, rounder. He hugged her and she started to cry.

'Don't you look handsome?' she said to him.

James was dressed in a small black jacket, his charcoal-grey school trousers and a black tie of his father's, which was far too long for him. The mini-butler turned mini-undertaker. He copied the mingling adults and shook hands with people. He wasn't sure what to say, so he asked them questions.

'If they bury the body, what do they do with the head?'

'They bury that too,' a woman told him, trying to suppress a smile.

'On its own?'

'No, with the body.'

And James imagined a toothless head under his grandfather's arm, like the armour-suited ghosts.

During the service he tried to make himself cry, but he couldn't. He hadn't mastered grief. He didn't have the equipment to anticipate it, nor the ability to empathise with it. But he couldn't stop obsessing about the corpse and his eyes were pinned to the coffin. People had been discussing the wake, and James had assumed that that was why they were all whispering, so that they wouldn't rouse his grandfather too early. Would he wake now or when he was in the ground? Sandra saw her son suddenly turn pale and his breathing become irregular, and decided that it was high time to whisk him away.

But she was too late. He'd started to wail. The congregation turned as one and even the vicar broke from his recital.

'Ken, we're leaving,' Sandra hissed to her husband as she pulled James from the pew. She paused to try to apologise to her mother-in-law, but unsurprisingly her advances were shrugged away. So she dragged her howling child outside, hiding her face from the mourners under the pretence of searching for her car keys in her bag. They were already in her hand, pressing white into the flesh of her palm.

Once they were outdoors James wormed free and threw himself down onto the white gravel, shearing the skin off his hands, smearing the pale chalk red. Kenneth, who'd followed them out, scooped his son up in one fluid movement and shoved him unceremoniously into the back seat of the car. The child-locks were always on. James was in floods of tears. He hit his skinned palms against the windows, smearing grease and blood, his face crumpled up with anger and anxiety. Ken was standing beside the car, exhaling heavily.

'He's a devil,' he told her.

Sandra's blushes were cooling now that they were away from the church. 'Oh, it'll be OK. The man's dead after all.'

'That's my dad you're talking about.'

'You never liked him.'

'No,' he corrected her, biting down on his patience. '*You* never liked him.'

'I haven't seen you cry once about it.'

'What? What did you just say?'

'I'm going to take James home. You go back to your family if you care about them so much.' She clambered into the car and slammed the door. As she drove off she wound down the window, saying, 'You make sure you bring those bloody flan dishes back from your mother's. They're in matching perspex.'

And Ken was left in a cloud of white dust listening to the sound of the tyres as they churned up the driveway. Then he looked back at the church. His fellow mourners, he knew, would dole out sausage rolls and pitying looks, blaming the incident entirely on his absent spouse.

James was withdrawn and morose for the remainder of the

day, and Sandra left him and David to their own devices. She took the dog for a long walk to numb her brain. The snow had started to thaw and it was bitterly cold, but she had waterproofs and a dog-coat for Whitie so they could face the elements together.

Kenneth came home late. James had already gone to bed before he'd even been asked. Sandra heard the key in the door. It was taking her husband too long to come in. She half stood to go and investigate. Then she decided against it and sat back down, smoothing the cushion to her side as she did so. She was still in a mood and he would bear the brunt of it.

'Good girl,' she said to the dog that sat smugly behind her legs. Her husband was in, she heard him shutting the door with too much force.

'He's drunk,' she thought.

He came into the lounge. He was a little unsteady on his feet but his grey eyes were steely bright.

'Whitie!' he called.

'I've already taken her for a walk,' Sandra told him without looking his way.

'Whitie!' he said again, more firmly, and the animal meandered over to him and out of the room. He closed the door and for once it stayed shut. Sandra pretended to watch the television. The dog scratched to be let back in, but Ken ignored it. He moved into the room and crossed over to his wife, leaning in to kiss her.

'You reek of alcohol,' she said, pushing his face away. 'You should've stayed the night at your mother's.'

'I wanted to come home.'

'You drove drunk.'

'Maybe I did.' He was holding her jaw.

'I bet you didn't remember to pick up the flan dishes did you?'

'No.'

'Oh Kenneth, I – ' he cut her off with a hard kiss that was

not going to be diverted from its target. He had buried his father. Now he was going to sleep with his wife. The fecundity of death. She put up some resistance, but secretly she craved his advances. She wanted him to be more assertive. She'd told him time and time again: 'Be more *assertive*, Ken!'

That night the supposedly sterile couple conceived a child. And Life and Death sprinted on, relentlessly passing a baton between them.

TEN

Sandra didn't unearth the miracle of her pregnancy for several weeks. Her period was late, then very late. She threw up once or twice. She felt nauseous. She had a weak bladder. She felt fatigued. She put it down to a stubborn tummy-bug. Eventually she went to see Dr Hazeldene. When he suggested that she was exhibiting the symptoms of pregnancy, she laughed. Then she looked severe. That had been insensitive of him. He knew their circumstances. Was he suggesting that she'd had an affair? And for a split second she scanned her brain to make certain that she'd not, feeling that sensation of guilt that arose whenever she saw a policeman at close quarters. No, she'd not had an affair. She was again affronted by the implication.

'Well, sometimes the body surprises even the medical profession,' he told her, as he ran his finger around a hole in his jacket sleeve.

Finally Sandra obliged him by taking a pregnancy test but she was certain it would be negative and couldn't accept it when it wasn't. She made him check again, so he gave her a blood test, though he assured her that he was right. He was right.

Then she cried.

'I've got a child already,' she sobbed.

'Well, now you'll have two.'

'I am so happy,' she said, through her tears. 'Are you

absolutely positive?'

'Absolutely.'

She couldn't contain herself. She rushed round the desk, threw her arms about the seated professional and kissed him on the cheek, almost pulling a muscle in his neck in the process. He tried to medicate the emotional outburst, separating their physical proximity with words.

'Though of course during the first three months there is always some risk and I'd like to ask you some more questions about any illnesses that run in the family . . .'

'Run in the family,' she repeated reverentially, and walked back round the desk to the appropriately distanced chair.

James was at school. Mrs Arnold would have to pick him up for once. Sandra was going straight home to call her husband. She was so agitated that she nearly crashed the car several times on the way. She rubbed her belly encouragingly, still barely able to believe that there was something in there, something growing; a human, her own human.

Kenneth was in a meeting. She didn't leave a message. Then, unable to control herself, she phoned again and told his secretary that it was an emergency.

'Why didn't you say so a second ago?' the woman asked.

Normally Sandra would have been sharp with her, telling her that it was absolutely none of her business, but today she could make allowances for anyone.

'I should have, I'm sorry, but it's really very – '

The secretary had cut her off, but put her through.

'Hello . . . I was just in the middle of a meeting with – '

'I know.'

'Well, this – '

'I went to see Dr Hazeldene.'

A pause.

'Are you OK?'

'Yes.'

'Good. That's OK then. Look I'll – '

'I'm going to have a baby.'

'A what?'

'A baby.'

'Are you sure you're OK?'

'I'm fine. I don't have a tummy-bug. I'm pregnant.'

'I'm coming home,' he said, and hung up. He rubbed his grey eyes and looked not out of the window but at the window, as though it were another wall. Naturally he was sure that James had finally tipped her over the edge, that these were the initial stages of a complete mental breakdown.

When he arrived she seemed fine, better than fine, happy, but there was a worrying glaze over her eyes, and she hugged and kissed him like a girl, which was certainly out of character.

'Call the doctor if you don't believe me,' she said.

Previously he wouldn't have dared take her up on such an offer, but this time he simply had to. The doctor – when he eventually came to the phone – confirmed the news. He was going to be a father, properly, for the first time. Then he remembered his son; born first, but not their first-born.

'What about James?' he asked, still holding the dead telephone.

'Give me a hug,' his wife urged, putting the receiver back in its cradle, so she could embrace him.

'What about James?' he asked again.

She'd had plenty of time to consider this, time to scour away any traces of her own instinctive apprehension.

'What about him? He's still our son.'

'Yes.'

'What?'

'He's not here, is he?'

'Of course not, he's at school.'

Ken looked visibly relieved.

'Well?' Sandra was in full possession of her well-maintained moral high ground and even though she'd had the same thought processes, she wasn't going to forgive him *his* so easily. 'What do you mean?'

'Nothing. I just . . . How will we tell him?'

It was a good question. They'd explained to James that they couldn't have children of their own – that he was special, that they'd chosen him. This looked like an act of betrayal, like they'd lied, like they were trying to replace him.

They opted not to tell him for a good while, but James and David sensed something was awry the minute they saw that Mrs Arnold was there to pick them up from school. Then when they arrived home and pressed the bell his mother opened the front door and beamed at him. Was there a twinkle in her eye?

'I've made your favourite for dinner,' she said, as he stepped inside.

He had no idea what that would be, he didn't think that he had a favourite, and he was instantly suspicious. The house felt different too, like there was more room somehow. The hall looked cavernous and made him feel like he'd shrunk. Whitie pranced up to greet him, which was always a bad sign. To test the waters further he made a dummy lunge at the dog and it responded with a growl, but his mother ignored it, moving her head away like an owl.

'Hello, son,' his father said from the lounge.

Son? And what was his father doing back from work? He turned to David. He seemed none the wiser. It was as though they'd come home to a different family. It all looked the same, but something infinitesimal had been altered.

That night James wet the bed again for the first time in months. Sandra noticed before she took him to school, but she wasn't going to make a fuss. She didn't want to acknowledge to herself that it could be meaningful. He seemed to be going through a good patch. There was no room for regression now. She put the idea from her mind. Today she was too happy to consider anything that did not correspond with her mood.

The day would be spent looking at photo albums. Suddenly

her family tree seemed relevant and she scanned the faces of great-aunts and-uncles, picking out their best features for her unborn child. It would be a girl. She was certain. What she'd always wanted, a little girl to give the childhood to that she'd craved for herself. Boys were more difficult than girls. James slipped into her head. She wouldn't forget about him, couldn't forget about him. But now she was girl within woman; she was all femininity, miracle worker, Earth Mother. The life within her may have been tiny, but she felt its presence, her presence. She already had a pet name for her: Amy. She wasn't sure where it came from, though it half rhymed with tummy. Amy was her secret name. It was for their private mother-daughter chats. And now, suddenly, David – the unseen – did not seem so ridiculous. Sandra had her very own concealed child and she too felt the urge to talk to her, encourage her, collude with her and cut out the rest of the world.

News of the pregnancy was finally broken to James when his mother was four months, five days and eleven hours pregnant – there was no disputing the hour of the conception. James was off school with tummy ache and as his mother was due for her check-up, she was compelled to take him with her. Dr Hazeldene came out to meet them.

'Hello, James.'

'David says hello,' James replied in a bored tone.

'Oh, is David still here?'

It didn't merit a response.

'Are you coming in with your mum?'

'No,' Sandra replied for him. She told James to sit quietly in the waiting room and play with the toys. Her son grimaced over at the toys and, with David's help, selected a magazine.

Beyond the wall his mother heard her baby's heartbeat for the first time. She knew already that it was there behind her abdomen wall; she'd felt her daughter shift and kick, but hearing the reassuring tick . . . tick . . . tick . . . made her want to cry out with delight.

'How did James take the news about having a baby brother or sister?' the doctor asked, with a slight furrowing of the brow. He was clearly anticipating the answer: not well.

'Oh, he hasn't noticed.'

Dr Hazeldene looked perplexed. 'You haven't told him? You're really starting to show now. How will you explain – '

'Explain?' Sandra cut in. 'I'm sick of explaining. It's all I seem to do. *Ah, but why?* this, and *why can't I?* that.' She stopped herself. 'I'm afraid he'll take it badly,' she admitted.

'Why don't you let him hear the sound of the heartbeat? That generally interests children.'

Sandra conceded that with his help, it might be easier. At least he could restrain James if things got out of hand. Above everything, she wanted to safeguard her hidden child.

The doctor asked a nurse to bring in the boy. He entered clutching the waiting-room magazine and was reluctant to give them his attention. The doctor took command of the situation. He put the stethoscope on Sandra's heart and asked her if she could hear it beating. She said that she could.

James was naturally intrigued.

'David wants to know what she can hear.'

'She can hear her heart. Do you want to listen?'

'No. But David does.'

The doctor held out the earpieces. Then he tried to place the diaphragm onto James's chest. The boy backed away.

'What are you doing?'

'I was going to let you listen to your heart.'

'To see if it's bad?'

'No.' The doctor shook his head like a friendly horse. David laughed.

'OK.' James moved closer again. His eyes widened as he listened to the noise coming from the core of his body, coiling out of him before looping back in through his ears.

Then Dr Hazeldene put the stethoscope on Sandra's

abdomen. 'Listen again.'

James complied and then held it out for David to listen. 'Now what did you hear?'

'A clock. Mum has swallowed a big clock like the crocodile in *Peter Pan*. That's why she's fat.'

'No. That's not a clock, it's another heartbeat.'

James looked terrified.

'Inside your mummy's tummy, a baby is growing.'

'David says, "Get it out,"' he said, looking around the room.

'We have to wait till it has grown some more.'

'*She*,' Sandra thought.

'Why isn't it dead?'

'What do you mean?' the doctor asked.

'Aren't we dead . . . before . . . before we're born?' His voice was wavering with panic.

'No.'

'David says we are.' James imagined the baby inside his mother. It horrified him. He thought of maggots in apples. What if it hurt her? What if it had a bad heart too? It might make her die.

'Who will look after David and me if you die?' he asked.

The doctor told him that she was not going to die, and his mother launched into a list of poorly rehearsed reassurances.

'Your dad and I love you so much we wanted to have another child. We won't love you less. We'll all love each other and when the baby's born, I'll need your help. It'll be our baby. It'll belong to all three of us.' She came to a halt with her final phrase. 'It'll be nice for you to have a little sister to play with.'

'Or brother,' the doctor added.

James was entirely bewildered by this barrage of guarantees. 'I don't want anyone else to play with. I have David and Cifer. I don't want a baby.' He started pulling at his hair.

'Well, I'm having one whether *you* like it or not!!'

James fled the room and the nurse followed.

'Do you want to know the sex?' the doctor asked, trying to defuse Sandra.

'I do already.'

'Yes. Women often think they – '

'I don't think, I know.'

He nodded indulgently. 'Well, there are no abnormalities.'

She was given a blurry black-and-white photo of her daughter. To anyone else it wouldn't have looked like a baby, but to her it was blindingly obvious. Amy. Her daughter. The picture of health. She kept it in her purse. James was in there as well but now he was out of sight, obscured by his baby sister.

This prolonged pause of pregnancy segregated Sandra from James. He didn't mention the baby again. He pretended to have no knowledge of it and whenever his parents tried to entice him into conversation about having a sibling, he talked to David till they let the matter drop. Sandra wasn't concerned: a bubble protected her from her son's indifference, her own amniotic sac of security.

Eventually James – who'd previously always craved his privacy, his seclusion with David – started to miss the attention, even if it came in the form of anger. His mother's blissful nonchalance made him fume. He wanted to flick her, pinch her, shake her – get a response. On numerous occasions acid words were poured over her. 'You're not my mum. I hate you. I wish you were dead.' Only nowadays she barely flinched. He turned once more into the stroboscope child, unpredictably shifting colour and focus, fragmenting light into dark. Incident followed incident and Sandra carelessly shrugged them all away.

Their house was now a place of transformation, both psychologically and physically. Obviously Sandra, like her baby, was putting on weight fast. But James was changing too. He was still the late developer, but he was gradually gaining in height; his button nose was becoming sharper; his round face, more oval, and his jaw was changing, lengthening, like a werewolf, as he became ready to shed his milk teeth. Now his little toothy-pegs began to look absurdly small and one by one they started to wobble. Tooth fairy time.

When the first one fell out he showed it to his father.

'You're growing up.' This was meant to be encouraging, but it upset James.

'Why don't David's teeth fall out?' he asked, trying not to cry.

'Maybe they do.'

James shook his head. 'If I have to grow up, you have to make David grow up too.'

'He will. Everybody grows up.'

'What about dead people?'

'No . . . they . . . Put your tooth under your pillow and the tooth fairy might come tonight and leave you some money.'

This distracted James from his line of questioning. 'Will the tooth fairy leave money for David too?' he asked, his mercenary side shining.

'You said that his teeth didn't fall out.'

'Ah, but I meant how will the tooth fairy know? What if she can't see them?'

'If they're there she'll be able to see them, don't you worry.'

The next morning he found a shiny ten-pence piece under his pillow and could talk of nothing else. He bragged to David about how rich he was and how when all his teeth had fallen out he'd go away on holiday without him. He didn't mean it, but David often tormented him so he liked to exact his revenge.

'He won't come again now that you said that,' David jeered.

'Will! And fairies are shes, not hes, stupid.'

David was right, though. James pulled and waggled his teeth furiously, enjoying the pleasure of pain, until eventually another came free with a pop. He showed it to David but didn't bother to tell his parents. That night he wrapped it in cotton wool, because it was sharp and he wanted to be considerate, and slipped it under his pillow. The next morning it was still there and he wept bitterly.

'Told you,' David taunted. 'It's because of your bad heart and because you made your grandad die.'

'I didn't. It was you.'

'And the sheep.'

'I didn't, I did not!' He began to cry and ran downstairs to seek refuge in a place he never normally sought it: his mother.

Nowadays whenever he ran into a room she put out her arms defensively.

'Don't run!'

Her son moved closer to hug her, but she was too unnerved. She wanted him away from her and she shifted her bulk to one side. James was stung by her rebuff but he persisted. He tried to hide his streaming face in the folds of her maternity dress, one that she was proud of, as she'd made it herself. His mother touched his hair uncertainly. She wasn't convinced that this wasn't some kind of trick.

'What? What is it? Don't cry. Have you had a wash yet?'

'The tooth fairy didn't come.'

'Yes, she did . . . Kenneth! She gave you ten pence.'

'No, she didn't, not this time.' He held out the tooth in its cotton-wool shroud. 'Look!'

'Ken! Well, your Dad will give you ten pence.'

'But it's not the same. I want it from the tooth fairy.'

'He'll get it from the tooth fairy.'

'That's a lie. He doesn't know the fairy.'

'He does.'

'Is it because I'm bad?'

'You're not bad. Kenneth!'

Her husband was in the shower, and couldn't hear her call

to arms.

'I am. You told me I was bad.'

'No. No. I didn't mean it. Now you be . . . good and go and have a wash, you'll be late for school. Dry those tears. Come on, handsome.' The warmness in her voice made him cry even harder.

'I don't want you to die,' he said, the sobs coming from deep inside. He felt nauseous and light-headed.

'I'm not going to die. James, come on, don't squeeze me so tightly.'

'But the tooth fairy . . .'

Sandra was beginning to fret. 'The tooth fairy isn't real, James. Stop it now. You'll hurt your baby sister.'

He released his hold immediately and spotted David standing at the door, grinning at his indignity. He turned back, raised his hand and brought it down hard on his mother's belly, before running from the room.

Sandra wasn't hurt but she was badly shaken and anxious that she'd miscarry. She sat back on the settee, smoothing her stomach and whispering desperate assurances to Amy. When her husband heard what had happened he knew that his role was to go and reprimand his son, but James was so distracted there was little point. He wouldn't have understood what his father's anger was for. Instead he dressed his son and bundled him off to school, but the boy was soon home again. His teacher explained that he'd climbed up a tree in the playground and, one way or another, had fallen out.

'He said he was pushed, but I don't know how he could've been, there were no other children with him.'

'Is he OK?'

His arm was fractured.

'Fractures are common at his age. They've outgrown their own strength.'

When Kenneth collected his son he was phantom pale and on arriving home went straight upstairs to see his mother.

'David says that he is sorry.' He spoke to her from the door frame.

Sandra didn't invite him any closer and her hands involuntarily splayed over her bulge like a web of armour.

'What about you? Are you sorry?' She noticed his arm in a sling and thought about saying something sympathetic but decided not to. There was a silence both of them expected the other to break. Then he stared at her for a moment – like a man seeing his lover for the last time – before leaving the room. He shut the door behind him.

As the pregnancy came towards its close Sandra spent prolonged periods in bed. One reason was her aching back, but primarily she was paranoid that the slightest thing might make her lose her child. Part of her wanted to keep Amy in there, safely tucked away from prying eyes and pincer fingers. Her husband pandered slavishly to her whims and even took time off work to be at her disposal. He surrounded the bed with everything she needed, which, it transpired, included the dog.

'Will you bring Whitie's basket up?'

'What for?'

'I want her here with me.'

'Is that a good idea? You always said it was unhygienic to–'

'I won't let her on the bed,' she lied. 'I've seen her downstairs with her head on the bottom rung. She's pining for me.'

'But she'll get into the habit.'

'No, she won't. She can't climb the stairs on her own. She slips on the varnish. You'll have to carry her up and down.'

His heart sank. He didn't like dealing with the dog at the best of times. Now he'd be obliged to carry it about like a lonely old woman or, even worse, some mincing queer.

Sandra's other essentials included her pregnancy guides for reference and a notepad. In this she wrote every new sensation – her hypochondriac's handbook – constantly comparing and contrasting the most minor changes, ensuring that nothing even slightly detrimental could be overlooked. Each day she completed the Cardiff Count, noting the precise times that Amy moved. She had her husband buy a foetal stethoscope – which was really nothing more than a small trumpet – so that she could reassure herself, with increasing regularity, that her baby's heart was still beating. The radio was also on the bed, so that, if she wasn't talking to her daughter, Radio 2 could serenade her with unthreateningly sentimental ballads. Sandra wanted Amy to be like her, right down to her taste in music.

There were so many things that she considered bedside crucial that there was no room in the bed for her husband. It came as no surprise to Kenneth, who uncomplainingly decamped to the downstairs sofa. Sandra was pleased that she hadn't had to ask. Her own sleep was broken enough already by the constant movement inside her, without him interrupting it further with snores or faint radio mumblings.

Hers was a self-appointed quarantine.

'I need to be stress-free,' she explained. 'If anyone makes me upset then the upset hormones in my blood will go into her.'

Maude, the murderess, and Ethel, her now widowed mother-in-law, were once again kept at bay. Friends could call, by appointment, but were not invited to linger, and her son and his imaginary devil were to be denied entry whenever possible.

Kenneth became his wife's lady's maid, more hired help than husband. She had him pack her suitcase for hospital: two front-opening pink nighties – she fully intended to breastfeed; a matching dressing gown and slippers; the prettiest yet functional romper suits, all in size 'Coo coo' zero; the Polaroid camera and the checklist of everything that the midwife had recommended.

There was also a second case, which Kenneth was to take in when his wife was ready to come home. It contained another assortment of baby clothes, a couple of maternity dresses and a few loose-fitting frocks, in case – as she hoped – she lost a lot of weight immediately. He was also instructed – by the back-seat driver in the bed – to assemble the cot and disinfect more than once all the surfaces in the room. As he worked Sandra talked to her daughter – always careful not to use her name – or she educated her husband about her body.

'Her head's engaged now. That means that it's between my pelvic bones ready for the EDD.' She said this on purpose to see if he was paying attention.

'The EDD?' Full marks.

'The expected delivery date.'

'Ah.'

'She will have shut her eyes now. Ready for . . .'

'Blast-off.'

'. . . her four-inch journey into the world.'

It made her feel less worried if she reminded herself that Amy only had to travel four inches. What could possibly go wrong in such a short distance? 'It'll be her who decides when to come out. It's very clever. She'll release more of a hormone called excitin.' She meant oxytocin. 'Do you know what I am doing now?' she asked.

When he didn't respond – he was trying to decipher the cot instructions – she told him: 'I'm exercising my uterine muscles.'

He hadn't heard the context but he still shuddered at the words, which somehow managed to inveigle their way into his brain.

When labour day was a week away, James was sent to stay with the neighbours opposite – a retired policeman, also called James, and his wife Joan. Sandra had arranged it. It was Ken's job to deliver the news to their son.

'Pack up a suitcase for him,' Sandra told him. 'I've made a list for you, and there's a note for Joan explaining everything they – '

'But he's only going across the – '

'Yes, but I don't want him coming over all the time ringing the doorbell and disturbing me.'

It would be the first time that James had ever stayed away from home, but he took the news like a well-seasoned traveller.

'David is coming too.'

'Fine.'

'And Cifer?'

'No.'

And that was that.

He even helped his father gather together his things, including his gun and his runaway's bundle.

Joan came over to collect him and his little case.

'Thanks for this,' Kenneth said. 'Oh, and this is from Sandra.' He handed her an envelope, making it sound like he didn't know that it contained a meticulous set of instructions and some money. His wife was adamant that they shouldn't be out of pocket in any way.

'David wants to know if you have any animals,' James said.

'We've some butterflies but they're not alive, they're under glass.'

James said, 'Good.' It was unclear whether he was pleased that she had butterflies or pleased that they were dead.

Ken shut the front door after them and the sound seemed to echo. Then the dog trotted through the hall and sat at the foot of the stairs looking up at him expectantly.

Across the road the boys were shown their new room. James checked it over, opening cupboards and drawers, all the while nodding his satisfaction. He looked so au fait with the situation that had he had a wad of notes on him, he may well have slipped the woman some money and said, 'It all seems fine. That'll be all for now, thank you.' Instead he fixed a smile and after refusing a glass of orange juice, Joan took the hint and said she'd leave him to settle in. He closed his door discreetly behind her and carefully opened his case. Cifer mewed crossly.

Last minute he'd exchanged her for his clothes, salvaging just his gun, his bundle and a book.

'Welcome to your new home!' he announced.

In his head, he'd rearranged the facts. Now it was he, the fairy-tale boy, who'd heroically made his escape from the hands of his gargantuan captors, while valiantly rescuing his faithful band of followers. They were safe for a time.

Then there was a knock at the front door and he froze, listening. It was opened. There was a dialogue. It was shut again. A knock at his door. Cifer was swiftly secreted under the bed.

'Come in.'

'Your dad just came over with your clothes. Have you got the cat?'

'No.'

'Oh. Well . . . I have her food and her water bowl. So if you do find her, she might want to eat something.'

'I know where she is, but I don't have her.' Always the politician.

'Where is she?'

'I think she might be under the bed with David. David, is Cifer with you? Oh, yes, he says that she is.'

The neighbour nodded and left the room.

Joan knew all about David. James's mother had sobbed openly about him on more than one occasion. She'd also been a witness to Sandra's shameless screaming and railing at her son. It had come as a shock, seeing this behaviour close up. Joan hadn't experienced, or been exposed, to such extremes. She understood the strains of parenthood, but still, she could not relate to this. And of course James proved to be the expert, enchanting house guest. He complimented the food, cleared the table, looked attentive – even when his mind was engaged elsewhere – took full responsibility for the cat, went to school on time and to bed when bidden. They had no complaints, which of course made them question the behaviour of his mother even further.

A week passed and no baby came.

Then eventually, after ten days, Sandra explained to Ken that she was showing. 'That means that I've found bloodstains in my panties and – '

'I know,' Ken interrupted, though he didn't.

A few days after that the contractions started.

'Shouldn't I take you into hospital?'

'No!' Sandra screamed. 'It's just my cervix stretching!'

'Are you sure?'

'Yes! I'm not going into hospital until I need to. Make me some toast.'

Thirteen hours after that her waters broke.

Ken, in his panic, took the leaving-hospital suitcase rather than the arriving-at-hospital suitcase.

'Go back and get the right one!' Sandra shouted from the hospital bed. 'Bloody hell, Ken, after everything I told you.'

'Won't this one do?'

She looked at him and he knew that it wouldn't.

'I brought some trifle.'

'What?'

'You said you hated hospital food.'

Sandra screamed.

Her husband hurried away, trifle in hand.

While Ken was stuck in traffic, Amy – it was a girl – was born.

By the time he returned to the hospital the suitcase was immaterial. The nurse said that the birth had been amazingly easy, that Sandra had been very brave and that his daughter, Amy – he'd never heard the name until now – was a healthy seven and a half pounds.

Sandra was in the maternity ward with Amy wrapped up tightly in her arms. Kenneth thought she would be cross. He was wrong. She smiled at him and there was a softness in her hazel eyes that he hadn't seen for years. His guilt was replaced by anger. Why had she made him go back? How bloody ridiculous! Why hadn't he ignored her for once?

'Ken, she's so beautiful.'

'Well, let me see.'

Sandra tilted their daughter very slightly in his direction.

'What shall we call her?' he asked, well aware that she'd already decided.

'I don't know. I was thinking Amy.'

'Were you?'

'Yes, don't you think she looks like an Amy?'

He could barely see enough of her to decide if she even looked like a baby, but what he could see – the small patch of skin raised at the nose – made his heart beat fast and he didn't care what she was called. Amy would do just fine.

'Amy it is then.' He sat on the bed and put his arm around his wife and she let him.

On the third day Sandra rang Kenneth from the hospital demanding that he bring the leaving-hospital case and get her out of there. When he arrived the nurse told him that his wife had been exhibiting signs of acute paranoia. She'd accused one of the nurses of trying to harm their daughter and refused to be separated from the baby even for a moment.

'Is she allowed to come home?'

'We wouldn't have recommended it. But she's persuaded the head-nurse, so we can't stop her.'

Sandra, Amy and the two suitcases left the building.

ELEVEN

Amy's parents couldn't help but compare this new baby with their adopted one, and the most dramatic distinction was the crying. This baby cried, and cried a lot.

At the same time their absent son was becoming more and more silent. He was still behaving himself and superficially he seemed to be fine, but his polite interest had grown more subdued. Even David and he seemed to have less to say to one another. Joan and James-the-older knew that the baby had been born, but they were forced to maintain the pretence that they didn't.

'It seems a strange carry-on to me,' James said to his wife, when the boys had gone to bed.

'I know,' she nodded, as she put some holiday slides back in their little plastic house. 'You brought Tim into the hospital the day Sarah was born.'

'Mmm.' He was rolling up the projection screen.

'It's like he's being punished,' Joan said, holding the slide of a white-throated bird up to the standard lamp. '*Sylvia communis*,' she murmured to herself. 'It'll be a shock for him when he does go home.'

'And when will that be?'

She shook her head sadly. She didn't want to have a conversation about James overstaying his welcome, about how they'd finally got the house free of their own children and didn't really want the burden of someone else's. She shifted the focus back onto the boy. 'He must feel like he's been deserted.'

James, who was listening with David at the door, suddenly did feel deserted, and shocked, and punished. He realised that this holiday from home had not been his idea after all.

On the evening of Amy's seventh day in the world Sandra conceded that they couldn't expect their neighbours to look after James any longer. Ken was dispatched to collect him. And, courteous to the end, James thanked his hosts and, in his customary fashion, left his farewells to David.

Sandra had a smile rehearsed, but it fell slowly like a late leaf when Ken entered alone.

'Where is he?'

'In his room.'

She frowned.

Ken knew that this would somehow be his fault.

When he went to let James know that he'd cooked him some fish fingers, his son was already in bed with the lights out.

'I've made you some food.'

No answer.

He wanted to tell his son that it was OK, that he would sit with him if he wanted, that he'd missed him, but he anticipated and feared rejection just as much as James did. Instead, he went downstairs and sat in the dimly lit kitchen, sharing fish fingers with the cat, making do with capricious company.

James lay in his bed with David, trying to blink away the darkness of the room. His mother had lined the yellow curtains and it was now so pitch that he couldn't be sure where his body ended and the darkness began. Then there was a noise beyond the door – the wooden stairs alerting James to Ken's approach.

The boy willed his father to cross the corridor again and admit some light into his orbiting room. In preparation, he hung himself half out of the bed and felt the blood rush to his already spinning head. There he lay limply. He knew that he often ended up in this position when he slept, as he'd occasionally opened his eyes, like a slow aperture camera, when his parents carted him out of the room. He'd see snatches of an upside-down house, and felt that flying sensation, as they carried him to the toilet in an attempt to prevent his bed-wetting.

The door did eventually open and his father slipped in, his shadow stretching out in front of him. James shut his eyes tightly and felt the large hands slide under his neck and legs; there was comfort in the contact.

'James? James?'

Ken gently scooped him up, colluding in the pretence that he was asleep. His wife, he knew, wanted to get it over with and see James before the night was out. As he carried the boy one of his thin arms trailed and bobbed beside him as though drained of blood.

His father entered the marital bedroom and placed his son, like a sacrificial offering, on the bed. Tenderly Sandra returned her sleeping baby to the cot. Ken kindly nudged James until he obliged him by opening his clenched eyes. He looked about, blinking grainy innocence, and asked for David.

'He's here too,' his father promised.

'Hello, James! How's my favourite son? Did you miss me?'

James rolled onto his face and curled into himself, a hedgehog stirred too early from hibernation.

'Don't you want to meet your sister?'

A sleepy groan.

'James?!' His mother's tone was suddenly sharp.

He sat bolt upright. His saucer eyes looked black; all the blue had bled away.

Sandra struggled on. 'There's something for you in there,' and she gestured to the cot.

This was not the yellow-painted, second-hand crib that

he'd slept in, hit against and fallen from. This was a virginal white, shiny-new affair.

'   Go on, have a look. It's your baby sister, Amy.'

Not able to sustain his indifference, he crawled across the bed and tentatively peered over the rail. Then he looked up at his mother, his black eyes returning to their native blue.

'David says, "Hello, Amy."' He redirected his gaze back down to his sister and gave her one of his broadest grimace smiles. 'No, you cannot pick it up, David. You will drop it. Tell him, Mummy.'

'Yes. She's too small to be picked up by little boys. Promise me you won't pick her up?'

'Promise.'

'And David? Did he promise too?' she asked, wanting to cover all eventualities.

'Yes,' James lied, and then he giggled, for at that moment David was pulling down his pants to give his mother a mooney.

Kenneth pointed to the cot. 'There's something else in there.'

James peeked in again and spotted a polar bear figurine and two cubs. He picked up the larger animal and left the babies where they were.

'Is this for me?'

'Yes. They're from Amy. A mum and two children; one is you, and one is Amy.'

'What about David?' he asked, taking one of the cubs from the cot.

Sandra wasn't going to acknowledge this. 'You have to love your baby sister and help me look after her.'

He'd heard it all before. He stared down at the white cub and the white child, with its halo of white plastic, and he felt like he might be sick. He didn't think that he could love her. 'Love' meant as much to him as 'for ever': nothing at all. He stole a glance at David, who knew what he was thinking.

'Can you send it back?'

'No, we can't send her back and we don't want to. You wouldn't like it if we sent you back, would you?'

His cheeks flushed. Now he understood that they must never find out what he really felt about the pale maggot in the cot; they would hate him even more.

'Nice baby sister,' he said.

And then there were two.

Around this time James began to experience strange episodes of a new order, which primarily manifested in the form of nightmares. The dreams grew stronger and stronger, and eventually no longer needed the portal of sleep to break into his brain. They consisted of simple but vivid blobs of colour, which resembled huge purple peas and giant red grapefruits. These splodges would then dance towards him at different conveyor-belt speeds to the accompaniment of a jarring mulch of noise. The effect was terrifying and it felt to James like his nightmares had grown legs and were now free to trample over the contours of his waking brain.

Before they took hold of him, he could sense their imminence and he'd rush around trying to absorb himself in the mundane: he'd turn on the radio, the television; anything that he thought would cancel out the noises that escalated with every panicky in-breath – but none of it was any use. He was at the uncompromising mercy of the subterranean world of his subconscious. Desperate to compete with the clamour within, he'd vomit up a prolonged scream, which would send his father flying in to try to soothe his spirit. James couldn't even see him. The man simply became an indistinguishable part of the nightmares that played on a loop in his head. At these times, even David became indistinct. James had never felt so alone.

Dr Hazeldene prescribed mild sedatives, but the boy was certain that his parents were trying to poison him. He became suspicious of everything. He was tempted, and taken in, one last time, by the tablet crumbled into chocolate powder, but this mixture tasted different than before and it made him sleep. And sleep was the last thing he wanted to do.

When James was at home, Sandra wouldn't let Amy out of her sight. She'd already had one fright, when she noticed a white bear-cub gripped in her tiny fist – a choking hazard if ever there was one. Since then, she'd found a few bouncy balls, a dog chew and a plastic goose in the cot, so she'd insisted that Ken invested in a cat net to catch these accidental missiles. James, of course, could never account for the arrival of these little offerings, leaving David to pick up the insinuated blame.

Despite these incidents, it appeared that James liked his sister. He always said nice things to her and David had no end of praise for her little nose and ears and her dark brown eyes. But Sandra grew more sceptical one day when she heard James saying, 'Nice Amy. Little sister, she is funny.' He was gently stroking her head. Then suddenly she was screaming.

'Silly Amy,' he was saying. 'Why are you crying? Poor thing. Mummy, Amy is crying.'

His mother already knew that her daughter was in distress; the noise she made was like a rope around her windpipe. And when she rushed to console her, she clearly saw teeth marks on her arm. James must have bitten her, through the netting. With a gasp, she tore away the gauze and seized up her child, cradling her tightly, and before she could help herself, she slapped James hard across the face.

'What was that for, you bloody cow?' His cheek smarting, his eyes darkening.

'For biting your sister, you little bastard,' she said, and slapped him again for swearing, but more than that for making her swear.

Sandra was vigilant over her child, but there are always times when a mother has to turn her back for a moment and occasionally she found odd scratches on her daughter's skin that she couldn't account for. In general though, Amy – unlike her brother – was the epitome of a normal, healthy baby. She liked nothing more than to be held, and Sandra liked nothing more than to hold her. She enjoyed her milk. She slept peacefully and woke often, wanting a feed or to be rocked. She lost the surplus fluid in the first week and put on weight by the second. Her umbilical stump came away with ease and the skin healed in no time. Whenever she heard her mother's voice or Radio 2, she wriggled with delight then lay still like she was listening. As a rule she was placid and gazed about with trusting eyes, and only when James and David were close did she begin to blink rapidly. Eventually, as her little girl became sturdier on a daily basis, even Sandra had to concede that her initial anxiety had been a little overzealous.

By the beginning of her seventh week – the age James was when they collected him from the Adoption Society – Amy had started to smile. It was unsteady and cautious at first, but it quickly grew in confidence. She'd gurgle and grin and coo at her mother, her wrinkled face opening up like a daisy under the encouraging gaze of the sun. Sandra knew that this love was mutual. Everything would be all right now. James would change and transmute: the dark, ugly duckling inevitably becomes the stately white swan. He couldn't be a troubled child for ever.

But this optimism – like her daughter – was short-lived. By the end of the seventh week, Amy was dead.

'SIDS,' the doctor told them, 'Sudden Infant Death Syndrome.' The post-mortem could come up with nothing more satisfactory and concluded that it was indeed part of SUDI, Sudden Unexpected Deaths in Infancy. 'We don't know why' was all this meant to the distraught parents.

They'd woken to the sound of James screaming – which was nothing out of the ordinary – and Ken climbed out of bed to investigate. He ambled out of the room and along the corridor, like a drugged bear, while Sandra switched on the bedside light. Already she knew in the pit of her stomach that something was wrong, really wrong.

Her instinct led her over to the cot but Amy looked like she was asleep. She was lying on her back, her head turned to one side. There was nothing covering her face and the room was not too hot, so there shouldn't have been any danger, but Sandra just knew. Then she noticed that the net was not secured at one end and there were incriminating cat hairs in the cot. Cifer, however, who was not allowed upstairs under any circumstances, was nowhere to be seen.

Her husband was in James's room trying to catch hold of his son, who darted about squealing like a piglet. Unlike his wife, he had no sixth sense about his daughter's demise. His son went ricocheting down the corridor – a furious champagne cork shooting from a shaken bottle – and his father lurched after him, trying to grab hold of his shoulder before he reached the top of the stairs. But his grab became a shove and he watched, open-mouthed, as the boy lost his balance, wavered for a moment and then slowly toppled backwards. The skinny body bounced like a hewn branch off each bough of the wooden stairs, until it came to rest inert on the half landing. Blood spouted from his son's mouth, and despite himself, Ken suddenly thought how cross his wife would be if it stained the small square of carpet.

'God! James!' he cried, jumping down to where the boy lay. 'Sandra!' he called, suddenly a child himself.

She came to the doorway of their bedroom and looked down at her naked husband and unconscious son. She'd never felt less like a human being and more like an animal. All she wanted to do was crawl on the earth, curl up with her baby and nuzzle her cooling flesh back to life.

'She's dead,' she said, without any trace of emotion.

'What?'

'Amy's dead.'

He couldn't access that information, so he shelved it. 'I think I pushed him. What do we do?'

Sandra returned to their bedroom and stood looking into

the crib.

Her husband carried his wilting boy into the room and started throwing on clothes.

'Sandra, will you help me? I have to get him to hospital . . . I think he might have broken something. Sandra? Fucking hell, Sandra!' he felt like giving her a smack.

'Your daughter is dead.'

He froze, slicing time with incomprehension. 'What?'

You heard me.'

He pulled on his jumper, went to the cot and picked up the baby. She was limp. 'She's not breathing,' he said, almost in a whisper. 'Isn't she breathing? Why aren't you doing anything? We have to get to hospital.'

'*He* did it. He killed her. Was the bedroom door open?'

'You're fucking insane, woman. Snap out of it. Get some clothes on.'

Sandra took her baby off him. 'It's too late,' she said, wiping traces of foam away from her infant's mouth.

'Get downstairs! And get in the car!' He picked up James, who was coming around but was clearly in a lot of pain. 'Get downstairs *now*!'

Sandra, who'd always asked her husband to be assertive, would have swallowed every glass word if it meant that her daughter was still alive. She picked up the bed-rug to wrap Amy in. Then she did as she was instructed. She was still in her nightdress and had nothing on her feet but she didn't seem to notice. Kenneth put James on the back seat and Sandra climbed into the front, placing the baby on her lap.

'Sandra, let me drive.'

She started the ignition.

'You can't drive. You've got no shoes on,' Ken said, as he scrambled into the passenger seat.

She pulled out onto the road.

'Fasten your seatbelt and give Amy to me!'

'Why? Are you worried I might hurt her?'

Her husband started to cry. He just wanted to wake up again to a day when this hadn't happened. He tried to take the child off her lap, but Sandra's hand flew out and caught him under the eye.

At the hospital Amy was pronounced dead.

James had bruised – but not broken – his ribs, but the fall had forced his remaining milk teeth back into his gums. His parents were in a state of trauma. Sandra was impassive and Ken could not stop crying.

It looked suspicious – a dead baby, a damaged boy and a husband with a red welt on his face – hardly the stuff of Happy Families. Why hadn't they called an ambulance? Why had they come by car? Why did she drive and with the baby on her lap? Naively Ken had let this slip. It was like the adoption process all over again, tier after tier of officials: the coroner, the pathologist, the GP, the health visitor, the social worker. The police took away the bed-blanket and came round to photograph the cot. They went to James's school and made enquiries about his behaviour and temperament. His mother and father endured all the indignity of interrogation in a daze. James, on the other hand, made a speedy recovery. His nightmares stopped altogether and he finally slept soundly again.

The official reports concluded, with regards to James, that there was enough documented evidence of his eccentricities to explain away the incident. And when it came to Amy, the Uniformed Division simply accepted the doctor's diagnosis. There was no real evidence to distinguish between natural and unnatural death, cot death or smothering – any infant mortality seems unnatural – so SIDS was officially blamed. The case would not be passed on to the Criminal Investigation Division. Privately, Sandra felt certain that Cifer had been the instrument and James the hand, but Ken would not hear of this, wouldn't believe it to be true. He told her categorically never to repeat it to anyone, ever.

'David wants to know where Amy is,' James hissed, in the hospital, through tombstone teeth.

'She's gone back to heaven,' his father told him.

'With Grandad?'

'Yes.'

'Is it because of me?'

'Did your mum tell you that?'

James paused to take this in. Then he swallowed his grief, like a large mouthful of fizzy lemonade, shook his head and pointed at David. 'Why do children die?' he asked, and pulled up his gown to inspect the black bruise that was spreading like an oil slick up his ribcage.

'I don't know,' his father said, breaking down. He felt the hammering of a heavy rainfall of guilt. He'd hurt his son, and his daughter was dead.

Sandra wouldn't speak to James, nor would she have him near her. Nothing could comfort her, and she didn't want it to. She could still hear Amy crying in the night and her breasts wept milky empathy. Her heart ached and her arms yearned for a heartbeat to hold. Ken wanted to dismantle the cot but she wouldn't have it. Instead, she put fresh bedding in and secured the cat net over the top. She told her husband that under no circumstances was James allowed at the funeral.

All the extended family attended, though not one of them had had the chance to meet Amy. The last time that Sandra had seen any of Kenneth's side of the family was at Gordon's funeral. Now she felt their eyes on her, accusing her of infanticide. Her husband wept like a baby, but she maintained her frozen despair. She kept her fellow mourners at a distance so that they'd pour their pity onto her weeping husband. In their hearts they were all pleased that it had not happened to them, and in the church they prayed that it never would.

When they arrived home from the burial, Sandra made two requests: to leave James with Joan for a few hours longer and to take Whitie for a walk. Her husband was relieved to leave her. They'd barely talked or touched since Amy died. Their daughter had been the fusion of their separate selves, their separate cells, but now she'd gone the link was irretrievably broken.

After Sandra heard the click of the front door, she moved from room to room, trying to locate the cat. She found it stretched out on the rug, black belly up, in front of the fire. Picking it up by the scruff of its neck she carried it into the kitchen. She switched on the gas cooker, without igniting it, and swung the animal into the spotless black box. Then she slammed shut the door, trapping the creature inside. This done, she sat impassively on a wooden kitchen stool and listened to the pathetic, plaintive scraping and mewing, until it stopped.

About half an hour passed and she'd not shifted in her chair. Then she moved to the cooker, turned the dial to off and took out the dead cat. The room filled with gas but Sandra didn't flinch. Carrying the body by its tail she threw it in the black bin-bag that hung against the garage wall.

When Ken came back he smelt the lingering trace of gas but wouldn't have thought anything of it had Whitie not started barking at the bin-bag, refusing to be pulled away. He felt like snapping the yapping dog's neck, but he half-heartedly peered inside the rubbish bin, expecting to find nothing more extraordinary than a chicken carcass. Even when he saw the dead cat he didn't make any connections. His brain was wrestling with enough demons already.

'In a plastic bag?' was all he thought. It went against all Sandra's sanitary obsessions. If she'd lost cleanliness, then maybe Godliness had gone too.

When he entered the kitchen and the gas was even more pungent, his next thought was that his wife was killing herself. He searched the house and found the bathroom door locked.

'Sandra! Sandra?'

She didn't reply.

He banged on it and the dog joined him, scratching at the

paintwork. He went to the telephone and was about to call for an ambulance, when the door opened and the dog slipped in. It was about to shut again but he forced it open.

'The cat?'

His wife stood with a towel wrapped around her, her skin glistening like it was crying. 'Is dead,' she said and her voice was brittle like kindling.

'I know. I found her. I don't . . .'

She shut the door. 'Hello, Whitie, have you missed me?' she asked, her soft words soaking through the wooden panel.

When James was retrieved from the neighbours Kenneth hugged him and Sandra said, 'Cifer had an accident.'

James looked to David, then to both of his parents, and Whitie jumped up warmly to greet him. As usual he shoved her away and was rewarded with a growl.

'She got hit by a car,' his father lied, for the sake of something to say.

James held his silence for several minutes. He looked like he was listening, absorbing the room, compiling and assembling his thoughts like a collage.

'You did it!' he yelled suddenly, his assimilation complete, and his eyes glowing like coals. 'David saw you!'

'Well, if David saw what happened to Cifer, he must've seen what happened to Amy too.' Sandra was calm and her tone was sympathetic. 'Ask him what he saw.'

'Sandra . . .' Ken didn't like this at all.

'What did David see, James?'

'Nothing. He didn't see anything. Why are you doing this to us?' he whispered, his body rigid with horror. His mother didn't respond.

'Come on, David,' he choked out between tears, and ran upstairs to slam his bedroom door.

'Come on, Whitie,' Sandra said. 'Let's make dinner.' She walked into the kitchen with the dog at her heels. The door clicked shut.

Kenneth had a lot to contend with, what with a son inconsolable over the death of his cat and a wife on the brink of suicide over the death of her daughter. Not to speak of his own grief, which he'd buried even deeper than the tiny coffin. He wanted to help, to be a human Band-Aid. He was unable to replace the baby, nothing could do that, but he could at least buy a substitute cat. Without consulting his wife, he used his initiative and found a black and white one at the local RSPCA. He even made sure that it was house-trained. Sandra would be proud of him. She was always on at him to think for himself, be his own man.

When he walked into the bedroom she screamed, first at the cat, and then at him, so he made a hot-tin-roof retreat to see if he'd fare any better with his son. James had deliberately kept his distance from his father since the accident on the stairs and applied thumbscrews of guilt by flinching dramatically whenever he approached. But the gift of the cat appeased the boy immediately and even merited a hug.

'Look, David, look! Cifer the Second.'

'But she's got lots of white on her fur.' David was resolutely unimpressed.

'Don't be ungrateful,' James said, for the benefit of his father, in his father's words.

'What?' Ken said.

'I was talking to David. Thank you, Dad.' James smiled, before frowning. 'I will not forget Cifer the First though.'

And they all sat still for a moment, as though in remembrance.

James was willing to absolve his father for shoving him down the stairs but his begrudging body wasn't. The bruises stubbornly refused to fade and his teeth turned custard-yellow and fell out, one by one. Again no tooth fairy came. James felt now, more than ever, that he had no one he could trust, no one other than David. And sometimes even David frightened him.

TWELVE

Life stood still as time ticked off the years, leaving the family encased in their loneliness like flies in amber. James's growing body pressed against the confines of the house until he could no longer remain in isolation. He'd have to learn to run with the pack.

With their combined active imaginations, James and David came up with a plan. They'd infiltrate the neighbourhood gang. First, they'd have to ascertain who was in charge. James found boys easier to manipulate than girls. Boys were, in the main, more forgiving and, usually, more forgetful.

There was, of course, Christian, his school travelling companion, but he was too easily led to be constant and there was his prissy sister, Tara, who was bright but too moody. Then there was Rebecca and Paul. Sandra thought – and therefore Sandra said – that they were 'common'. The sister was assertive and well aware of her budding sexuality and the brother was all rough and tumble, a boy who'd bare his bottom for a penny chew.

Matthew who lived along the road also had a sister, but she, rather exotically, lived somewhere else with her father. Matthew was the joker, willing to take the fall. He always announced his arrival by sounding his bike horn with its medley of different settings. Graham was the eldest by several years but the most immature and had a handsome but gormless face. He too had a sister – it was a town of two by two – but she was quite a few years older. She liked men, men who owned cars, so she wouldn't deign to acknowledge her brother let alone his friends. The real leader was another girl called Rebecca – Rebecca the First. No one knew if she had siblings, but she seemed like the sort who'd have lots of brothers. James realised that Rebecca as the one he needed to work on.

One of their endless summer holidays had just begun, a perfect time to put their plan into action. James invested in a bag of pear drops, as to him sweets still remained a symbol of demonstrative affection. Then he hunted down Rebecca the First. She was loitering with the other children in the cul-de-sac. Walking straight up to her, James offered her a sweet. He was careful not to look her in the eye. To take one sweet would have looked like patronage, so she snatched the entire bag with her long, skinny fingers and put it in her dungaree pocket. Everyone understood that it was one of the spoils of her status. She then strolled away to talk to Matthew and Rebecca the Second, leaving James on the opposite pavement with his invisible friend. He didn't mind. He was willing to let a few humiliations pass in order to get his own way. So, with the first move of his operation executed, he headed home to play with David.

'Spastic!' Rebecca called after him. She'd never spoken to him at all before, so it was a start.

The next time Rebecca spotted James, she stamped hard on his foot and before he could check himself his kangaroo reactions sent his fist flying out. It connected neatly with her thin but prominent nose. Blood started to trickle out like sap from a spindly tree. With a wail, she turned and sprinted off on her long thin legs and James listened to her sandals as they slapped out her retreat rhythmically on the paving stones.

'You can't hit girls,' Tara explained with the voice of a tired barmaid.

'I just have.'

'Well, you can't.'

'Who says?'

'Everyone.'

'And who is everyone?'

'You know what you are? You're a disciple of the devil.' Tara hoped to overawe him with her cleverness.

'The devil makes work for idle hands,' he threw back at her, not knowing where he'd found the phrase. He flexed his fingers. 'Would you like me to use them on you?' And he outstretched his arms, his hands like crab claws, reaching for her neck.

'Chris, tell him,' she said, backing away.

Christian, James knew, would not tell him anything.

'Shut up, sis, you spoilsport.'

Tara immediately turned like a majorette and strutted off to tell tales.

The others all watched James expectantly, waiting for his next move, but he'd already achieved enough for the day.

'Climb on, David!' There was room on his horse-nosed bike seat for two. 'Let's go to the Disciple of the Devil Den!' And he cycled away, leaving his words behind to hover.

The next morning was Saturday and the doorbell rang, which was unusual for the Gardner household. It was Rebecca the First, asking if James wanted to come out to play. Kenneth was thrilled. It was the first time that anyone had called round to call for his son of their own volition. Maybe things were looking up. It was a girl but it was a start. Before he knew it, James would be kicking a ball around, just like other boys his own age. But Sandra was less buoyant. Nowadays she reserved her optimism for the weather and tapped the barometer like it was a crystal ball. She looked outside. It'd been cloudy but she had to admit it was slightly clearing up.

'There's someone here to see you.'

James descended the stairs slowly. 'Hello, Rebecca,' he

said, with a dignified nod of acknowledgement.

'Do you want to come out with us?'

David whispered that it was a trap, but James was pretty confident that it wasn't, and didn't really care if it was.

'I'll fetch my bike.'

Rebecca smiled up at his parents, then stepped out of the porch to wait for him on the drive.

The garage door opened like a clamshell and James wheeled out his bike.

'You're going to show us where the den is,' Rebecca instructed him.

He clearly wasn't second in command yet, but he'd been conscripted. The mention of the den, he knew, would arouse their interest.

'OK,' he said, hopping onto his orange bicycle.

The rest of the gang were already assembled on the corner, with the exception of Graham. He'd been grounded. He'd been caught peeing into the kitchen sink while his sister took her time in the bathroom. Tara had also threatened not to come, but when her brother hadn't offered to drop out as well, she was compelled to swallow her words and resort instead to an impressively chilly sulk. Paul was excitable and feverishly rubbed his knees to charge himself up; Rebecca the Second was playing with her hair, teaching herself the guile of girls; and Matthew, who was doing wheelies, sounded his siren to herald their approach.

James was not a particularly strong bike rider, so he didn't stop to say his hellos. Instead he rode his orange charger off along the street expecting them to follow – another subliminal nudge in the direction of dictator. Not wanting to miss out, they all clambered on their racers and gave chase. Rebecca, who could feel her power-base slipping, caught up with him, her breath in the soles of her feet.

'Where is it?'

'What?'

'The den.'

'Ask David,' he told her, sitting upright, like a bygone professor on a boneshaker bike.

'Don't be bloody stupid!'

They knew about David. And they understood.

'I can't explain where Devil Den is. It's far too complicated,' he lied. 'I will show you.' He spoke without once turning in her direction.

He was beginning to enjoy himself. He'd never really committed to a two-way interaction with his contemporaries before. David, on the other hand, was less than thrilled. He didn't relish this back-seat role and was starting to feel a little resentful. James pretended not to notice.

At his own Pied Piper pace he delivered them to the barn, which he'd re-Christened Devil Den. He'd chosen an unnecessarily convoluted route so that the others would have trouble finding it again without him. He made sure not to go anywhere near T Woods. He'd introduce that to them later, if he felt so inclined. Everyone was out of breath when they came to a stop outside the barn, but they were fairly impressed.

'It's huge!' Paul said, dropping his bike so that he could be the first to explore.

'Wait!' His sister harpooned him with her words and he jerked to a standstill. She didn't like the other Rebecca, Rebecca the First, but she understood the pecking order and if she enforced it on her inferiors, she could maintain her own status near the top. James held back and let the team leader go in first, though he knew that in reality she was second. David, who didn't feel inclined to observe protocol, had gone in before her.

Everyone else then piled in. Rebecca the First had already climbed up the haystacks to re-establish her position at the top of the hierarchy. Rebecca the Second lounged on a bale and chewed her hair. Matthew, Paul and Christian ran around, throwing each other to the dry and prickly floor, while James and David looked on.

'Why don't we have a high-jump competition?' James suggested.

Tara and Rebecca the Second looked underwhelmed but the giddy-goat boys were raring to have a go. Christian, who couldn't for a moment forget that he was small for his age, had the most to prove. He immediately started practising, trying to intimidate the others with his bulldog determination.

'Shall I make a start line?' James asked.

'Yes,' Rebecca the First agreed. 'No one can go in front of the mark . . . or they're disqualified.'

James dragged his foot through the dirt, making a dusty scar.

The decision of who was to go first came next. Quickly bored by the heel-digging debate, Rebecca the Second agreed to start the proceedings. She wasn't enthused by the game but at least if you went first everyone watched you with interest. The others cleared a space. David, who knew that he wouldn't be invited to participate, quietly climbed to the top of the bale-stairwell to share Rebecca the First's King of the Castle vantage point.

Rebecca the Second was getting ready to make the jump. Milking the moment, she pulled up her skirt and looked down, drawing their attention to her legs.

'Your knees are bruised,' Tara pointed out, matter-of-factly.

'You've got a nose like a pig,' Rebecca sneered, unashamedly resorting to a cruel non-sequitur.

Tara flushed and would have started to cry had Rebecca the First not said, 'On your marks . . . Get set . . . Go!' and the focus of their attention shifted away from her and her undeniably porcine nose.

Rebecca the Second took a run up but it was all for show. When she reached the line, she stopped and threw herself onto the first tier, where she gracefully reclined, head in hands, the rustic pin-up girl.

The boys all clapped, including James, much to David's chagrin.

'You've got to take it seriously!' Rebecca the First reminded them. 'Otherwise you won't win the prize.'

'What's the prize?' Paul wanted to know. There'd been no mention of one till this point.

Rebecca the First hadn't thought this through. She looked to James, which he duly noted. Little steps.

'We're all to give ten pence to the winner. Is that what you said?' James proffered.

'Yes.' Rebecca the First confirmed, but she saw that she needed to reclaim the reins. 'You go next, James.'

'I can't.'

'Why?'

'Because my head might split."

'Scaredy cat!' Paul piped in.

'You have to,' Rebecca commanded. 'Those are the rules.'

James knew that words wouldn't be as effective as evidence. He knelt down and shook his head until his hair fell into two distinct pages, with a shiny scar for a spine. He opened his mouth as well to expose his tombstone teeth and make the effect more grotesque. A collective gasp came from the group. These were war wounds indeed. Rebecca the Second forgot her pose and stood up, her hand already outstretched to touch his skull, but he shook his head again and the spell was broken. Her hand fell.

'You still have to pay the winner,' Rebecca the First announced. She would subjugate him yet.

'I will. So will David.'

David said that he would do no such thing, but James winked at him. He knew that if David contributed no one would say that he didn't exist.

'But what happened?' Tara asked.

'What?'

'To your head.'

Her beady eyes made him rebellious. 'I killed my sister and God punished me.'

Tara stepped back.

Matthew started laughing, making light of the moment, and one by one the others saw that it was a joke. David laughed the loudest but only James could hear that and, when he did, he softened and joined in.

'Chris, I want to go home.' Tara was not so easily distracted.

'Shut up, Tar!' Christian wasn't going anywhere till he'd jumped. He needed to win.

'I'll tell Mummy.'

Her brother despised her blackmailer's streak. It was one of the few things that made him fratricidal. 'Tell her. See if I care!'

'I will!'

He lowered his head as though he might butt her, but she turned on her well-greased tap of tears just in time and he was immediately contrite.

'Don't cry. Stay and play. We'll go home when I've . . . when the game's over.'

'I'll go next. Drum roll please!' Matthew said.

Paul obliged, beating one out on his backside. Matthew was asthmatic, so he was not playing to win, he was playing to play. First he did a roly-poly to get momentum and then a handstand. When he jumped, he did so backwards and landed in a sitting position on the first bale. As he touched down, Paul – the perfect comedy second – made a well-practised fart noise under his armpit. Tara looked appalled but the others fell about.

James was delighted. He was really laughing, right from the bottom of his belly, like he'd never laughed before. His blue eyes sparkled like washed turquoise. David, meanwhile, frowned down from on high like a forgotten deity. Paul took his turn next. He wanted to show off, but possessing neither the polish that

Matthew had, nor the wit, he bungled it and stumbled over the start line.

'Disqualified!' Rebecca the First announced, raising her hand.

Tara refused to take her go and, to her disappointment, no one tried to sway her. So it was Christian and Rebecca who were left, the only real contenders.

'You can go first if you want,' Rebecca offered.

Christian was meant to decline, but when it came to competition he'd willingly flout the rules.

'OK.'

The others fell silent. He focused on the line, determined not to make the same mistake as Paul, and then he stared hard at the third bale, his objective. His eyes narrowed with a wilful concentration that James spitefully wanted to break. Rebecca the First clearly felt the same way, as she jumped down one bale, harrumphing as she did so. Paul, Rebecca the Second, Matthew and Tara were all willing him to win. They held their breaths in anticipation.

Christian took a deep inhalation, ran and jumped. He looked like he was going to make it. James's heart skipped a beat. No, he hit the third level but on the corner and he slid onto the second, where he lay, defeated.

'He was on the third!' Tara spurted.

'Yeah! He was on it,' Paul agreed.

The others said nothing. Christian looked up at Rebecca the First, but he was not hopeful.

She shook her head, thumbs down. 'Second step. It's where he landed. Me now.'

Christian stepped down to receive a runners-up consolation pat on the shoulder from Matthew.

Rebecca the First, looking even taller than normal, took the floor. She tucked her lank brown hair behind her ears and, without any of Christian's ceremony, took two long leaps and then sprang, clearing the second bale with ease, landing on the third. Then she screamed, following it with a long drawn-out wail. She looked at her side and all eyes followed hers. There was blood spreading across her dungarees.

'Oh my God!' Tara said, her face the colour of moss. 'I knew we shouldn't be in here.'

Rebecca the First, who'd come first, was crying. Her body rose and fell like a plastic bag in a wind-trap.

'You won,' James said, the party-host trying to salvage a desperate evening. 'We owe you . . . seventy pence.'

He clambered up alongside her. He tried not to notice the blood, but the dark stain on her denim compelled him. It was then that he saw the spike of metal sticking out of her side. He felt nauseous and could hear the first hoof tremors of his advancing day-mares. He looked up to David, but his friend was unmoved.

'She's landed on something metal,' he told the others, not even certain that it was himself speaking. The words sounded like they came from outside of him. 'I'll go and get help.' The noises in his head subsided for a moment and the room came into sharp focus. He'd assumed control. It was that easy. Everyone nodded, relieved that someone had the situation in hand.

'Don't move,' Tara told Rebecca, gradually recovering her own composure. 'Keep still.'

'How do you know?' Paul asked.

'It's basic first aid!'

David was already climbing down. He wasn't going to stay there. He'd rather be ignored by James than unseen by the rest.

'You did it!' James hissed, as he climbed onto his bike.

Tara, who'd followed him out to get a few gulps of fresh air, had not only a pig's nose but also large ears and a long tongue.

James the rescuer, the hero, tried to cycle fast over the fields. He was pleased to be out of the barn and he pedalled for all he was worth. They came out of the fields onto the country lane and eventually reached a cottage with wisteria growing in the garden. He put his feet down, to assist the rather weak brakes, and they scuffed along the tarmac, spitting out stones.

'Go on then,' David goaded. 'Get help if you're going to.'

'I will.'

'I think we should leave her to be killed.'

'To die! God, you are so stupid!' He had never shouted at David like that before.

It took the woman, who was middle-aged and suspicious, a long while to answer the door. When she did, James launched into an unnecessarily in-depth explanation. She gleaned what was necessary and called for an ambulance. James was given a cup of tea for the shock. He didn't have the heart to tell her that he wasn't shocked or that he'd much rather have juice. The ambulance arrived and James and David got in, bike in tow. It was exciting, as they got to sit up front. They came to a halt, under James's instructions, at the barn. The ambulance-men took out a stretcher and James and David led them inside. Rebecca was quieter now and greyer.

'You've been ages,' Tara told him, as though she thought he'd deliberately dawdled.

The ambulance-men worked quickly. They were going to try to leave the spike in, but they discovered that it belonged to a pitchfork, which was wedged down between the bales, so they had to slide her off it instead. Once outside James muscled his way through the others, who were bustling around the stretcher like nervous hens.

'We'll go with her,' James told one of the men, referring to himself and David.

'Only one of you can come.'

'OK.' He climbed in next to where Rebecca the First lay and nodded to David so that he knew to sneak in too.

'Take my bike home, Christian.'

The ambulance pulled away and James looked out of the back window at the collage of concerned faces.

'Is she going to die?' he asked.

'No. Don't worry, she isn't going to die.'

David looked disappointed.

'Is she in *a lot* of pain?'

'She is, but the doctors will take good care of her.'

James fell back into silence and so did the man.

At the hospital, Rebecca the First was sedated and stitched up; the prong had somehow missed all her vital organs. She'd need rest while the wound healed, but she'd make a full recovery. James telephoned home.

'Mum, I'm in hospital.'

'Oh James, are you all right?' For the first time since his sister's death, his mother wanted to know if *he* was OK. 'Only your bike is here, we were worried about you. James?'

He paused, stretching her anxiety, plucking it like a violin string. 'I am fine. Rebecca the first had an accident.'

'Rebecca? The girl who came to call?'

'Yes.'

It was her turn to pause.

'What happened?'

'Can you come and pick me up please?'

She sent her husband to collect him.

The following morning James pulled out another yellow tooth at the side. He held it up so that the neglectful tooth fairy could see what she was missing and gave himself a gash of a smile in the mirror.

After breakfast he stole twenty pence from his mother's purse. He'd decided to become the self-elected deputy, and cycled round to everyone's houses to collect Rebecca the First's prize money. Then the two boys headed for the local newsagent's where they bought pear drops – to remind Rebecca of their first meeting and highlight the reversal of fortunes – and lots of chewy cola bottles. He also bought a packet of fake cigarette sweets for himself.

His parents, he was well aware, would never have let him cycle to the hospital on his own – had he bothered to ask for their consent – so he explained to the lady in the shop that he needed directions.

'You see, my best friend is dying.'

David looked askance, but James knew how to tug at the heartstrings.

'Would you draw me a map, please?'

The woman took pity on the little pilgrim and went upstairs to get a street plan. While she was away he helped himself to some of the strawberry laces that lay sweating in a tub by the till. Equipped with sweets and instructions, they set off, James with a candy cigarette hanging from his mouth.

They found the hospital with ease, and James dropped his bike in front of the main entrance. At the reception desk he asked the girl, who sported a birthmark the size of a pebble on her forehead, if he could see Rebecca. He didn't know her surname. He doubted it was 'the First'. Eventually, and not without a good deal of huffing and puffing, she managed to locate the ward and asked a nurse to take him there.

Rebecca looked surprised to see him, and not altogether pleased.

'What are you doing here?'

'I came to bring you your prize,' he said, handing her the two bags of sweets.

She opened one of them and peered in. 'Thanks.'

He exchanged a glance with David. She didn't seem happy with his choices. 'How are you?' he asked, trying to look like a concerned adult.

She turned a comic face down on her bed and flicked her hair back. 'Bored.'

He was tempted to say that only boring people got bored,

but only because he'd heard it so many times from his mother's lips. Instead, he affected distraction and turned the comic face up again.

'David, look!' He giggled. 'It's a little girl's comic!'

'My auntie bought it.' She moved it onto the bedside table. 'I don't read it.'

'Oh, I see.' He giggled again. 'Can I see the hole?'

'No. It's bandaged up.'

'Oh. Does it really hurt?'

'No, it itches.'

David whispered in his ear. James followed his suggestion and gave her side a prod.

'Ow!'

'You said it didn't hurt.'

'Well, it does if you touch it, you bloody dildo.'

James didn't know what a dildo was, but the word conjured up an image of an instrument you might use to measure the depth of a swimming pool. 'Sorry,' he said, and took a cigarette out of the packet and stuck it between his lips. He stood up.

'Are you going?'

'David says goodbye,' he said over his shoulder, without bothering to look back as he left the room.

Retracing his route, he called in again at each of the gang members' houses. 'Rebecca the First', he informed them, 'has a bad heart and is in a lot of pain. Under no circumstances,' he advised, 'does she want visitors.'

None of them had even thought of visiting, but they were adept at faking disappointment.

'When will she be coming home?' Rebecca the Second enquired, donning the unlikely air of a vicar's wife.

'Not for a very long time,' James said, nodding gravely to corroborate this fiction. 'If ever . . .'

He predicted their moves. Tara would be governess to Christian. Paul would look to Matthew for patronage and Rebecca the Second – now elevated to just Rebecca – would lie bikini-clad in the garden, encouraging a tan to creep up her skin and cover her bruises. The iron would never be hotter and James was set to strike.

Devil Den, James knew, would now be out of bounds, so he'd have to relinquish T Woods. But he was feeling optimistic. He was now prepared to give some ground, secure in the knowledge that he was set to conquer an even larger terrain. The deposed Rebecca the First would have turned in her hospital bed had she known what he was up to. And David was dead against it. The woods were sacrosanct. He didn't want the gang's sacrilegious imprints sullying their territory. He felt that they'd forfeited enough already.

'You'll let them play with the zoo next!'

'Never!'

The contours of the woods were engraved on the boys' minds: the open glade with its secretive circle of trees; the nocturnal playgrounds of the badger sets; the rabbit-warren boltholes and the furtive fox dens. Then the man-made elements: the empty Tennent's Lager cans; the sheets of corrugated metal; the dirty pots and pans; and the porn, pages and pages of porn, which curled up like cup fungus. It was as though the God of Anatomical Instruction distributed the magazines weekly to woods and railway sidings, gory but edifying pamphlets for the unenlightened.

All that the pictures made James feel was slightly clammy and sick, like he was seeing the insides of his mother. James could not yet equate his butterfly desire for Rebecca the Second with the caterpillar grub-lust for a woman. But he understood that he could use the magazines to lure the others. And in order to seal the deal, he told each of them in turn that the rest were already on board.

James had not been introduced to Graham yet, but he knew where he lived, and he thought it prudent to include him. The boy's sister opened the door and loomed her blondeness over him. Before he could speak, she turned, flicked her fringe and stalked off, shouting, 'Graham . . . door!' as she disappeared out of sight. There was a three-stairs-at-a-time descent, then a crash as two feet hit the hall floor. Graham loped along the corridor.

'Hello.'

'Hello, I'm James.'

This was the first time that he neglected to introduce David. It did occur to him, but he knew that Graham was already at big school, so he thought it shrewd not to allude to him yet. David, as could only be expected, was deeply offended by the exclusion.

'We are going to T Woods tomorrow,' James informed Graham with a fleeting but inclusive glance at his friend.

'Where?'

'Do you want to come too?'

'Who else is going?' Graham rubbed the side of his head slowly.

'Paul, Christian, Matthew and maybe Rebecca.'

'Rebecca?'

'Paul's sister, Rebecca.' James was formal but friendly, a doorstop politician canvassing votes. 'The other Rebecca is in hospital. She might die.'

'Yeah, I was told . . .' It was as though there was a time lapse between Graham hearing words and making sense of them. 'Why would I want to go to some woods?'

'There are some pictures there you might want to see.'

'What kind of pictures?'

'Pictures of girls.'

'I've got enough stuff of my own.' Graham had a habit of lying. And, as all his playmates were younger than him, he assumed that they'd unquestioningly swallow everything he said.

James had been taught to respect his elders, but it certainly didn't mean that he had to believe them. 'Oh, I see. Are you not allowed out?'

'Yes. I'm twelve.'

'I'm ten. I'm just not very tall. Come to my house with Paul in the morning.'

'OK.'

'Bring a knife.'

'OK.'

James almost said 'David says goodbye', but David didn't and James didn't think it wise to confuse matters. Instead he clambered back onto his bike and, after an awkward nine-point turn, trundled out of the drive to cycle home.

THIRTEEN

When James opened the front door he found the entire assembly waiting on the driveway. Rebecca the Second wasn't there but he made no comment.

'So we're going to see the magazines?' Paul hissed.

The other boys looked at him, their guilty expressions shifting like steam.

James smiled at David.

'Have you got your weapons?'

The boys gave a collective nod and took them out for inspection. Graham had a Swiss Army knife in the signature pillar-box red, with more attachments than were strictly necessary for a twelve-year-old. He prized open each feature until it resembled a strange metal sea urchin.

'What do soldiers want with a nail file?' Matthew sniggered.

'Not for their nails, you wally! It's for making keys fit in doors.' What Graham didn't know, he made up.

'There aren't any doors on a battlefield,' Christian said.

'Switzerland doesn't have an army,' James told them.

'It does. You can ask my dad,' was all Graham could say in his defence.

'I don't know your dad.'

'So? Ask him.'

'Is he from Switzerland?'

'Er . . . No.'

James looked at David and then at the other boys. He had rested his proverbial case and Graham knew it. One by one, Graham put the blades back in their slots, while James resumed the inspection.

Matthew had a bright silver cowboy gun.

'Do you have any caps?' James asked.

'No. I've run out.'

Paul had stolen a small wooden-handled kitchen knife from home – an accident that couldn't wait to happen – and Christian self-consciously held out a pea-shooter. 'My mum won't buy me a gun.'

David slipped onto the back of the bike seat and James climbed on the front. His mother was peering at him through the blinds in the lounge. Without deigning to look her way, he gave her a wave, slickly swung his satchel over his shoulder and set off.

When they came to the crown of a steep hill they let out a prolonged whoop of delight as they freewheeled – legs capital 'A' akimbo – all the way down, adrenalin spinning in their stomachs.

'This way!' James shouted as the others hared off down a wrong turning. They all put out their feet to brake and turn, some more gracefully than others, and then followed him down the gravel track. When they came to the gate, James and David stopped and dismounted. The others did the same, and lay, tired and happy like post-chase bloodhounds, panting on the grass.

'Jesus!' Matthew wheezed, taking a gasp on his inhaler.

Paul couldn't even speak; he just nodded his head vigorously like a woodpecker.

'Leave your bikes here. We are going ahead on foot. Paul, give me your knife,' James commanded.

'Why?' Paul asked, sliding it out recklessly from his waistband. 'Ouch.' He rubbed at where the blade had shaved off a sliver of skin.

'That's why.' James rolled his eyes at David and slipped the knife into his satchel, but David was resolutely unresponsive. He kicked his heels and looked bored.

Paul ran ahead to the hawthorn hedgerow that surrounded T Woods. Then there came another yelp as he caught his leg on barbed wire while trying to squeeze through the fence.

'Bad sheep,' David whispered.

James frowned. 'Are you hurt?'

'No. I'm bleeding though.'

'OK. This way!'

James led them alongside the hedge to a wooden stile. Christian vaulted it, Graham barely needed it and Matthew commando-rolled off it and sprawled among clusters of white flowers that looked like little old ladies' swimming hats.

'Err! It smells.'

'Garlic,' David said and James repeated.

Paul could now be heard crashing through the undergrowth like a wild boar, squealing and grunting as the supple summer branches whipped at his bare legs and arms. He broke into the clearing and spat on one hand to smear the stings and blood. In the other hand he proudly held up a magazine page, a naked woman in a position that looked like it might be difficult to hold for long.

'Porn!' He grinned triumphantly.

For the next week or so, things went from strength to strength. The children moved about as a pack, sometimes with Rebecca and occasionally with Tara. They didn't really know what to do with the porn. Graham said that he did, but no one believed him. All they knew was that it was somehow illicit and that in itself gave them a thrill. There was the occasional indulgence in some furtive trouser rubbing and a few bravado comments flew about, but it was all pretty primitive.

'How many holes does a girl have?' Paul asked.

James laughed as though he knew, but he looked to each of them in turn expectantly to see who could enlighten him.

'It's three. I know,' Graham insisted.

'How?'

'How do you think?'

Paul sniggered at the inference. 'You've had it off?'

'Yes.'

'You told me you'd only fingered a girl,' Christian said, and then froze, fearing for a second that Tara was there. She wasn't.

'Anyway I've got a sister.'

'You've had it off with your sister?' Matthew asked quickly.

'Yes,' Graham said with conviction.

Everyone laughed and mimed vomiting.

'I mean, no,' Graham said with as much conviction.

They laughed again, Paul so violently that he toppled backwards off the tree trunk he was sitting on.

'Shall I ask your dad?' James said, and the others roared even more. He liked this feeling, being in a gang, making people laugh. He gave a smile to David and even received one back. At last he was part of a large and harmonious surrogate family.

It was shortly after this time that James met David, another David, a 'real' David.

Then things changed, irretrievably.

Sandra, with her extensive curtain twitching and barometer-tapping ticks, had ascertained that a family were about to move in at the end of the street. She spotted the removal van as soon as it pulled up and decided that Whitie could do with a walk and there was never any time like the present.

When she drew close to the house, she saw a woman with brown shoulder-length hair and rather pale, drab features. Sandra, who was the queen of snap judgements, decided to overlook her first impressions and give the woman the benefit of the doubt.

'Are you moving in?' she asked, rather pointlessly, taking refuge in the safety of small talk.

'Yes,' the woman replied, with a smile.

To Sandra's mind the smile didn't really do any favours in enhancing her demeanour, but she decided to let this go too, like a helium balloon.

'I'm Sandra and this is Whitie.' The dog always broke the ice.

'I'm Doreen.'

'Oh, there's another Doreen down the road!' Sandra said, as though they should know each other. 'She's got a boy my son's age.'

Doreen came closer. 'How old?'

'Ten.'

'Oh, my boy's ten.'

'What a small world!' Two Doreens and three ten-year-olds! Sandra then busied herself forgiving the woman for the blandness of her blouse, before asking, 'What's your boy called?' Now that they were firm friends she could get down to the important details like names.

'David.'

'Oh.' Her mask dropped for a second and she bent down to stroke the dog while she picked it up again. 'Isn't that funny?'

'Why?'

'My son James has an imaginary friend called David.'

'My daughter has a make-believe friend.'

'You have a daughter?' Sandra swallowed a wave of pain that shot up through her ribcage like a blade. She had to ask: 'How old?'

'Two and three months.'

This was about the age her own daughter would have been. 'Oh, how sweet.' She bent down in order to stop the searing knife's trajectory a second time and patted the now restless dog. 'What's she called?'

'Sally.'

That was something – at least she wasn't called Amy. This small world would have engulfed her whole if this woman's daughter had shared that sacred name.

She stood again and was relieved to see that there was some debate going on between the pot-bellied Tweedle Dumb and Dee removal men over how to unload a dressing table. 'I should let you get on,' she said, nodding over at the dispute.

'Oh . . . yes.'

'But you should come over for coffee and our sons can make friends.'

'Thank you.'

'We live at number seven.'

'Number seven,' Doreen repeated, in order to illustrate that she was committing this to memory. 'OK.'

This was not enough for Sandra. 'Call over tomorrow.'

'All right. Thanks, Sandra.'

She would tie her down more than that. 'Bring David too . . . And let's say eleven thirty. It'll be the weekend and besides, you'll need a break by then.'

'I'm sure I will. Thanks again, Sandra.'

It pleased her, these words in combination, 'thanks' and 'Sandra'. 'Say goodbye, Whitie,' Sandra said, mirroring her son's parting catchphrase.

That had gone well, she thought, as she headed back home. There'd been a few tricky moments, but she'd made a friend for her son, one for herself – even if she was a little dowdy and had a living daughter – and she'd done a neighbourly good deed. 'Thanks, Sandra,' she repeated to herself. It was *her* pleasure.

When James rose the next morning he was raring to go out with the gang, but his mother needed to keep him indoors in order to make her introductions.

'I want you to stay in till lunchtime. I've got a surprise for

David.'

'Then I can go out and David can stay.'

'It's a surprise for you too.'

'Is Grandma coming over?' James was suspicious.

'No.'

'But I want to go out.'

'You go if you want . . . but the surprise won't be here when you get back.' His mother was taking a risk here. If he called her bluff she'd feel very foolish when Doreen 2 and her son David 2 called round.

'OK, we'll wait.'

At ten minutes past eleven the family arrived, all four of them. Sandra opened the door.

'You're early,' she announced, unable to hide her irritation. 'And you're all here, I haven't cut enough cake.'

'Would it be better if we . . .?' Doreen 2 looked a little shaken by this bluntness.

'No. You're here now. Come in. Could you take your shoes off at the door?'

This business with footwear would take some time, so Doreen decided to start introducing her family.

'This is Mike – ' she got out before Sandra interrupted.

'James! Kenneth! We've got visitors.'

Ken arrived first and shook hands with Mike and Doreen 2 and then said hello to the children.

'James!' Sandra barked.

James was taking his time. It was already clear to him that he'd been duped. The 'surprise' was simply strangers in his house.

'Ken, where is he?' Sandra asked sharply, while ogling the little girl with the hungry eyes of a latent abductor.

At that moment James – with Cifer the Second in his arms – glided into the room like a ghost.

'There you are,' she said, the tension in her voice sliding

away by the word *are*. 'This is David. He's just moved in down the road.'

Later, James would believe that as soon as the word *David* was pronounced, his own David immediately became more indistinct, as though his silhouette had softened, a lens slipping out of focus. David smiled weakly, shyly. James didn't; he just held out his hand and waited for the boy to shake it.

'Shake his hand, David,' Doreen told her son in an encouraging voice.

David complied. David, the real David, was a polar opposite to James. He was blond with brown eyes and fair skin. He was neither beautiful nor plain. He looked like a memory of childhood. His air was imbued with innocence, but at the same time he seemed distinctly serious.

'This is David,' James said, remembering his old friend.

'James has an imaginary . . . an invisible friend who's also called David,' Ken explained.

'My sister Sally has one called Panther.'

'Is it a boy or a girl?' James wanted to know.

'It's a panther.' David spoke quietly and sincerely, the low and reassuring hum of a beehive.

James looked doubtful. He wondered if this was some sort of joke. 'I can't see it.'

'I've never seen it either. It lives in her ear.'

'Ah.' James was satisfied. Plus, panthers were black.

Sally, James noticed, was staring at the spot where his 'invisible' David stood. Could she see him too? Then she pointed at the cat. There was no way he was going to let Cifer the Second near her, not when there was a panther in the vicinity.

'Lamb chop!' he called, offering up a substitute sacrifice for the ear predator.

'Go into the lounge. I'll bring in the tea and cut some more cake,' Sandra was saying, arranging her guests like a girl with a doll's house. 'Ken, you go in and keep them company. James, you take David into your playroom.'

'Which David?'

'Both.'

The three boys were left to stand awkwardly in the hall, like ill-acquainted gentlemen obliged to retire to a smoking room.

'It is in here,' James said, after a long pause, and he led the way. The first thing that he did was take David around his library of books, and David was impressed by how many of them he'd read. He then permitted him to play with his Red Indian string puppet, while he operated – with a satisfying skill – his Pinocchio marionette. For a time the two boys were silently absorbed in their industry, while David the First sat, overlooked, stroking Cifer the Second on the beanbag. It was pleasing to James, this quiet recreation. David the Second was different from the other children he'd met. Paul had played with the puppet once and all the strings had become desperately tangled. Matthew and Christian became listless the minute they were inside, much preferring a kick-about outdoors. Graham had the annoying habit of always wanting to play with the toy that James was employed with. Rebecca the Second could never keep her limbs still long enough to play a gentle game, and Tara . . . well, Tara's presence just annoyed him altogether. For the first time he was in control and at ease simultaneously. He'd only ever achieved that with David the First before.

James became so relaxed that he even went so far as to approach the drawer where his zoo animals hibernated. As he reached for the handle he turned and saw that the old David was glowering at him, goading him into this act of betrayal. He decided against it and took his microscope box off the top shelf instead.

'Look at this,' he said.

Carefully, David placed down the puppet and came to stand beside him, and he watched – without touching – as James laid out all the components. He showed him, one by one, each of the slides: the butterfly antennas, the bee stings, the wasp wings – his miniature private collection. Ignoring David the First's shaking head, he then lifted a tray from the box to reveal what he called his 'treasure'. This consisted of items unearthed while digging round the side of the house or discovered in the nearby fields and hedgerows. David crouched to admire the various bits of porcelain, the old penny pieces – which James insisted were Roman – the nettle flowers and, his jewel in the crown, an ink bottle brimming with deadly nightshade berries.

'These can kill,' James said, solemnly.

David immediately stood up so that he didn't get too near them. James smiled at David the First and David the First smiled back, the only moment of complicity since this second David's arrival. They could sense that this real David was scared.

'I am going to call you David the Second,' James told him.

'Oh.'

'You see . . . I already have a David the First.' He smiled at his David, who seemed happy to be David the First. 'I hope you don't mind,' he said, diplomatically addressing the new David again.

'No.'

'Good. We did have a Rebecca the First and Second.'

'I see.'

'First does not always mean best,' he added, in a hushed tone, hoping that he wouldn't be overheard.

By lunchtime James had invited David the Second to join them in their trip to T Woods. But being a good boy first and foremost, David went straight to his mother to ask permission. At first she was reticent.

'He's diabetic,' she explained to Sandra.

This meant as little to Sandra as it did to James, so she nodded vaguely, in a way that said diabetes was either a very good or a very bad thing. Mike was more optimistic than his wife. He said that David was responsible and as long as he came home for lunch first and then only went out for a few hours, he didn't see why it would be a problem. David the First did not approve of this hasty baptism, nor would he be alone in this view.

When James and David the First and Second met up with the rest of the gang in the cul-de-sac, the mood perceptibly shifted. Christian was immediately unsettled. It knocked his equilibrium off balance, and when insecure he turned aggressive. Within a few minutes he was wrestling with Paul, which ended abruptly with Christian winding him, making him cry. Matthew played all the tunes on his bike horn in a quick and repeated succession, turning the screw on everyone's nerves. Graham started bragging about anything that he could think of. Rebecca did handstands on the Arnold's front lawn and Tara looked on, like a governess, from the lounge window.

David the Second was evidently overawed by this circus freak-show being performed for his benefit, but James was amused. He saw that this boy could serve as his second in command, his trusted right-hand man. Of course, the other David would still be there, to his left, but his new friend was made of flesh and blood, a real boy that his Pinocchio pal could only dream of becoming.

Over the next month each sun-blurred, over-exposed day of summer seemed to last for a year. David the Second accompanied James and the original David almost everywhere they went.

The boys also spent a fair amount of time with the rest of the gang playing games in T Woods. There, acts of violence were played out, either mimed or actual, but with no adults present the repercussions and recriminations were soon forgotten. But aggression did remain an integral part of their play and a war wound was deemed a highly prized accolade.

'Get out your dangerous things.' James insisted that they always remember their weapons.

They did so.

'I have something for you, David,' he said, opening his bag.

David the First looked excited. He'd seen – the increasingly private – James whittling away at something and he'd been told he mustn't peek or it would spoil the surprise.

'It's a catapult,' James said with a satisfied smile.

David the First held out his hand but instead of presenting it to him, James handed it to the new, prodigal David instead. 'I carved it, from my *Hundreds of Things a Boy Can Make* book. Now you can knock down giants like David did Goliath.'

David the Second was thrilled but the others resented and envied this special treatment, though they chewed their tongues to conceal it. David the First was not so proud. He stormed off into the undergrowth, where he sulked and spat for the rest of the day. James pretended not to notice and none of the others could have.

There was a particular order to the proceedings. First of all the gang delivered up their dangerous things into James's bag. Then, with great pomp, James would empty them into the special tree stump. It was a tree that had been sundered by lightning or destroyed by disease and was truncated about three feet from the ground. It stood awkwardly in the clearing, like a huge elephant's foot, its rotting insides exposed to the elements.

The children were then ordered to turn their backs. Unbeknownst to them, David the First was excluded from this rule. James needed him to invigilate and ensure that no one cheated. Then, one at a time, they'd about-face and solemnly walk up to the stump. There they'd stretch their arms down into the guts of the tree to hurriedly select their pot-luck weapon.

This day the arsenal was dropped as usual, like communion coins, into James's bag before being emptied into the trunk. Only today, as David had sulkily quit the arena, there was no one to report back on the proceedings. James wouldn't know if one of his flock had swapped their weapon after their initial draw. Nobody wanted the short-straw pea-shooter.

The game of choice was Cowboys and Indians and, after much debate, two teams were established. The proud Indian was the part that most of them tried to avoid. Everyone knew that Indians were shot much more than cowboys were scalped. Graham complained so much about being relegated to the role of Indian that, as compensation, he was permitted to choose his weapon first. He walked up to the stump and although his nerve failed him for a second, he knew he couldn't take much time or the others would call him a coward. In a get-it-over-quick fashion he thrust his lucky-dip fingers into the hole and seized upon something. Then, with a sharp cry, he withdrew his hand.

'I've been bitten!' he screamed.

They all turned to look. He had blood running down his hand, which he waved in the air like an eager pupil.

They huddled round him.

'What by?' Paul wanted to know, his eyes wide, his dirty palms smoothing down his oily brown hair.

'I don't know.'

'I bet it was a rat,' Christian said.

'No. It was slimy,' Graham lied, with a melodramatic shudder, his hand still aloft.

'I bet it was just Paul's knife and you grabbed the blade,' Tara said. She'd tagged along for once, just to tarnish their fun.

'Shut up, Tara.' James knew that invention engaged the imagination much more than the mere truth. And the result was always more interesting.

'I bet . . . it was a . . . little devil.'

'Or a troll?' Paul suggested.

'Trolls don't exist.' Rebecca was keen to correct her brother. 'Anyway, they're big.'

'Maybe it was David,' Matthew said.

'No. It wasn't me,' said David the Second.

'Not you . . . The other one.'

Initially they all laughed, but then they looked to James.

'He's hiding somewhere,' he said, before raising his voice so that his David would hear. 'He's in a mood because I didn't make him the catapult!' He paused for a response, but none came. 'It could have been him,' he admitted.

The others looked a little unsettled. Most of them weren't sure if they believed in David the First or not, but none of them liked the idea that he might be out to get them, especially when they couldn't see him.

Graham sucked at his cut and felt the attention draining away from him.

'It definitely had teeth. Look!' and he held out his finger for inspection. They watched as the white wound flooded with blood.

Christian could not resist jabbing the cut, making Graham yelp and retreat back.

'Don't be wet,' he said, holding up his blood-daubed finger. 'Now I'm your blood brother.'

'No, you're not,' James corrected him. He knew about such things. 'You have to have a cut too and then you mix up your blood.'

'Urgh!' Rebecca squirmed.

Not deliberating for a second, James walked over to the stump, put his arm in and with a look of concentration on his tilted face he felt around. The others held their collective breath and waited, imagining the whole arm being ripped out at the socket. When he pulled out the Swiss Army knife, they breathed out. Only Christian looked disappointed to see the arm intact. James opened one of the small-sized blades and then he made a slice at the base of his palm, in the crease of his life line. A few drops of blood oozed out. His head spun for a second at the sight of it, but as leader he couldn't let it show.

'Place your finger on here,' he told Graham.

Graham did as instructed. The others were church-quiet. Slowly, James slid Graham's bloody finger over his cut.

'*Now* we are blood brothers. Who's next?'

'I'm not doing it,' Tara said, expecting others to back her up.

No one did.

'Then you can't be in the gang,' James said.

'Who says? It's not your gang! Who said it was your gang?' Again she expected support. Again none came.

James said nothing. He smiled at her, revealing his gappy teeth.

'You can't make me. I'm going to stay anyway.'

James shook his head and lowered his eyes, as though he were truly sorry.

'I am!' she insisted. 'You can't make me!'

'You know I had a sister once,' James said quietly to Christian.

'Did you?'

'Yes.' He turned to Tara. 'But she is dead now.'

Tara stared at him defiantly but he held her gaze, his eyes darkening with malice.

'I'm going home . . .' she said eventually, looking away. 'Chris?'

Christian, who was a boy of action over words, took the penknife off James and pushed the tip of the blade into his finger's end, squeezing at the knife-prick until a few drops of blood rose forth.

Tara turned and half walked, half ran to the stile, which she traversed with ease, despite usually insisting that her brother help her over it. Then she was gone.

The initiation ceremony continued without a murmur. James took it upon himself to be Master of Ceremonies and inflict the other incisions. He could feel David the First spying on him from the bushes. His friend was never far away. Rebecca volunteered next, wanting to prove that she was as brave as any boy and not in any way like Tara. Then Paul came forward, followed by Matthew, and the children busied themselves smearing blood on each other's cuts. David the Second appeared reluctant.

'I don't think I should.'

The others stopped their activity at once. James didn't say anything. He stared at the shiny red knife handle and waited.

'I've got diabetes.'

'Urgh. He's got a disease,' Paul taunted. 'Lurgy! Lurgy!'

Christian, Paul and Graham were quick to join in the chant. Matthew, the asthmatic, said nothing.

'I'm not being a blood brother with him,' Rebecca announced firmly. 'I don't want to catch his lurgy.'

'Nor me!' Paul said. 'But Becca, wouldn't you be a blood sister?'

'You can't catch it,' David whispered, his eyes on his feet, his cheeks crimson.

'You *can* catch it,' Graham argued. 'I know someone who did.'

'You can't.'

James held out his hand for David's. 'I will be your blood brother.'

David was torn. He had to decide: either be cut and accept James's offer of fraternity or be dismissed from the gang. Slowly he offered up his hand. Not able to look, he turned away as the blade slid into his submissive finger, perhaps a little further than was strictly necessary. The released blood flowed steadily and James squeezed at his own cut to open up his already meshing vessels. Once he had dabbed David's Doubting Thomas finger into his cut he asked, 'Anyone else?'

They all shook their heads.

'No way!' Paul said. 'Not with lurgy boy.'

'Then I am your only blood brother.'

David nodded, and followed the descent of a blood droplet as it dripped onto a blackberry leaf.

James turned sharply and saw the other indistinct David darting behind a tree. He smiled. He knew that his act would irritate him. It served him right for being so childish.

'What shall we call ourselves?'

The group appeared nonplussed.

'Our gang . . . We need a name.'

Graham, who was mid-assertion that his cut was the most serious, suggested the Little Devils. This way they'd remember how it all started with him being bitten by something in the tree.

'Agreed,' James said before there could be any debate. Deciding it was wise to pay homage to the creature in the tree, he offered up a prayer to it, asking for it not to bite them now that they were all Little Devils too. He then dropped in the knife which had drawn the blood from each of the members. The moment had been marked. The children all implicitly understood and respected an act of ritual.

Now the Little Devils could return to the game of Cowboys and Indians, which was played out in various parts of the wood. Cries of alarm or attack flew up from the undergrowth, sending shivers of excitement or dread down the necks of those who were still frantically hiding or hunting. The rules were that the captor could either take their victim prisoner, which was often the preference, or make them into a member of their own team. This, of course, made their sport more thrilling, because you might think you were approaching a friendly Indian when they'd actually become a cowboy convert.

The contest was supposedly won when everyone was either on the same team or held prisoner by the opposition, but of course invariably it never played out that far. Often, one of them had to go home for dinner, or the game ended abruptly because of an injury of varying magnitude. When this was the case, 'Truce! Truce! Truce!' would be shouted. If you said it three times you meant it. Saying it four times was another trick-tactic, the fourth 'truce' being cried on the attack.

On this occasion it was Paul's screams that made them all halt in their tracks. It was no ordinary cry. Fingers of ice slid over their faces, stripping them of blood and colour, and their hearts careered into their ribcages as they tried to escape. All at once the children started calling for each other, adding to the confusion and making it impossible to establish where the enervating noise had originated. Then, in ones and twos, they assembled at the sacred trunk, where they automatically deposited their weapons.

Paul was already there, just by the clearing. He'd been tied to a tree. It was evident that he was the source of the bloodcurdling cries. He was breathing heavily, his head to one side, his forehead glistening with sweat.

'What happened?' James asked, the last to step into the circle.

The rest of the gang stared at him, dumbstruck, then back at Paul. James immediately approached his friend and tried to unfasten the knots, but blood was pouring down the boy's arm, collecting on the surface of the twine and making it slippery.

'He's struggled too much. It's too tight.'

Paul's sister rushed forwards to help. 'Oh God, he's bleeding,' she whimpered.

'Stop it. You're only making it worse. Who has the knife?'

No one said anything.

'Who has the knife?'

'It must be in the tree,' David the Second said.

'Then get it!' James had taken control of another bloody situation.

Christian was there in a flash, but he was too short to search the insides quickly, so Graham took over.

'Which one? Which one do you want?'

'Either!!'

Graham pulled out the kitchen knife, ran to James's side and handed it to him, as he'd been taught, handle first.

'Be careful of his fingers,' Rebecca pleaded.

James moved the knife round the side of the tree and cut the cord where it didn't touch Paul. When he was finally free, he looked like he might bolt, a spooked colt, but the circle of children hemmed him in.

'Let me see your arm,' James commanded.

The boy was trying to catch his breath, gulping the air, but he held out his bloody arm compliantly.

'A tissue?'

Graham produced one, sculpted by use.

'Here.' James handed it to Paul. 'Wipe the wound clean.'

Paul spat on it and started to rub at the blood.

'Now sit down.'

Paul complied and sat heavily, where he was, at the base of the tree. His breathing was still laboured but he was starting to calm down.

'Who did it?' Rebecca wanted to know.

'Christian tied me up . . .' he began.

An angry swarm of eyes turned on Christian.

'So what?' he contended, looking at each of them defensively. 'I caught him, he was an Indian.'

'Yes, but Indians tie cowboys to trees, not the other way round, and you were a cowboy!' Graham said, feeling very clever indeed.

Rebecca rose to her feet. She was all set to attack Christian, no more questions asked. Her eyes darted to where the bloodied kitchen knife lay on the grass.

'Sit down, Rebecca!' James ordered.

She didn't sit, but she didn't advance either. She had to be content, for the moment, to loom.

'Then what happened?'

'He left me.'

'There, you see!' Christian cried out triumphantly. 'I left him! I told you – '

'And I tried to get myself free but I couldn't, so I was waiting for another Indian to rescue me. And then . . .' he broke off, his eyes welling, his breathing losing its depth again.

'Then . . .?' James pushed.

'Then . . . Then I felt something on my arm, jabbing, and

I thought it was a wasp . . . so I tried to get it off, but it kept coming back. Then I knew there was someone there . . . but they were behind the tree, so I couldn't see them, so I asked who it was . . . but they wouldn't say. Then I could feel that I'd been cut . . . it was hurting and I got frightened and started shouting. And then you came . . .' he trailed off, and began licking his arm like a cat. 'Blood tastes like metal smells,' he added, as though suddenly embarrassed by the fuss he'd made.

'Who did it?' Rebecca demanded, returning to her question. 'Who hurt my brother?'

'He's the brother of all of us now,' Graham said.

'Don't be such a retard, Graham. Who had the knife?'

They were all mute. No one was going to own up.

'There are two knives,' James pointed out.

'Well, one will have blood on.'

'Both will have blood on.' James was looking at the blade on the ground. 'We used the other knife to be blood brothers, remember?'

'You!' she turned on James. 'When you caught me, you said you had a knife.'

'Yes,' he admitted calmly, 'I said that I had a knife.'

'So it could have been you.'

'No. I said that I had a knife but it was a threat, so that you'd give up. I lied.'

'You said – '

'Yes I *said*. But did you see it?'

'Yes.'

'Now *you* are lying.'

'Well, who had it then?'

'Maybe it was the little devil?' Matthew suggested.

'We're all Little Devils now.'

Paul was frowning. 'Was it your David, do you think?' he asked, his face about to pucker again.

James shrugged. 'It could have been. He's not here now.'

A magpie in a tree above them began its machine-gun

laugh.

They all looked up, a circle of Chicken Littles.

'The cut . . .' Matthew said, breaking their sky-falling reverie. He was pointing at Paul's arm. 'It's in a funny shape.'

'It looks like a snake,' Graham said.

'A tadpole . . .' Matthew corrected, 'its head's too big for a snake.'

'It looks a bit like a tattoo,' Paul said, cheering up.

'It does,' Christian acknowledged, a little enviously.

'Maybe we should all bring plasters tomorrow?' James suggested, which could have been a joke, but everyone readily agreed, so it wasn't.

As the blood clotted the drama evaporated, and in no time, the children had packed up and were on their bikes again, careening down the country lanes. Paul weaved in and out as usual, all his worries behind him and a serpent tattoo as a trophy.

FOURTEEN

Other similar incidents occurred. One of the gang would discover that they'd been scratched or cut in the shape of a snake or tadpole. Often it happened in the melee of rough play or when someone succeeded with a ruse –

'What's that thing called that holds up the wires?'

'A pylon.'

To which the response was 'Pile-on!' and everybody did.

There were conflicting whispers as to who, or what, caused the mysterious mutilations. Matthew told them that he'd witnessed Graham branding himself and they all agreed that this was either because he felt excluded, as he hadn't been cut yet, or because he was the attacker and wanted to avert their suspicion.

Graham thought that the culprit was Matthew, mainly because Matthew told jokes that he didn't understand and were at his expense. Christian said it was the new David, as he wasn't strictly their blood brother. Rebecca still fancied it was Christian because in the first assault he'd been the one who had tied up Paul. But Paul still feared that it was the David the First, because the more he looked at his scab, the more it looked like the letter 'd'. No one openly agreed with this verdict, but this was ostensibly because they didn't want it to be true. The invisible enemy is infinitely more intimidating than the open foe.

Later, after adult intervention, their concept of, and belief in, the unseen David would be erased and replaced altogether. They'd learn that he was pure imagination – a fabrication, a fiction – and the actions of David the First would become synonymous with the actions of James.

The relationship between James and David the First was becoming increasingly fraught. David the Second took up more and more of James's time, and even though he knew that it hurt his old ally he persisted, sometimes with deliberate callousness, to flaunt his blossoming friendship. David the Second was bright but entirely bereft of craft or guile, and James found this both amusing and endearing. James also learnt things from his new friend, facts, whereas the old David mostly told him things that he already knew.

Previously the two of them had experienced everything together. They had a shared history, a shared consciousness, and, like an old married couple, conversation had become entirely unnecessary and occasionally irksome. All David could do was forever reflect back James's own fault-lines.

'You make bad things happen,' James would snipe.

'*We* do.'

'No. It's you. I don't do anything.'

'You do. You make things die. Everything . . . everything you touch.'

'That is you! You hurt people because you're jealous.'

'Not me, I don't.'

Clouds of accusations spiralled around the boys until neither one of them could remember who stood as the accused and who the accuser. Tongue-tied and locked in an angry embrace, they overlooked a sheer drop to nothingness, Jesus and the Fallen Angel battling in the wilderness, only in this case neither knew who was who.

David the Second taught James how to fish. They'd lounge idly for hours at a time beside the baked muddy banks of the many local ponds, watching their floats bob aimlessly on the murky water. When they were together James tried not to speak to the other unseen David. Their old banter now seemed silly in the presence of David the Second's seriousness.

What James could not have known was that the boy's gravitas was connected to his malady. From birth he'd been shackled to an awareness of his own frailty, something that other children of his age had no concept of. David the Second, who had to inject himself to stay alive, understood that a thin metal vein separated life from death. James had lost a twin brother, a sister and a grandfather, but it had not made him think about his own death. He understood that other things must stop living, but he had no doubt that he wouldn't, not ever.

While the two boys silently stared at the water, the neglected David would try to amuse himself but he was never very good at that. He took to wandering off on his own. In the past this was something that he'd do to make a point, but he'd never let James out of his sight. Now it was different. It came as a surprise and unsettled James when he remembered his old David and observed that he was not by his side. He would try to make light of it, though, and when his friend materialised again he'd say quietly, 'Been off to look at pictures of ladies?'

David would shake his head. Having fallen out of the habit of conversing, he'd say nothing and sit by James, staring at the stupid brightly painted floats as they ducked pointlessly in the fishless pond.

Then another incident irrevocably bonded the two boys and further excluded the other. One morning, when James cycled down the road to collect David the Second he found him lying in a large cluster of irises in a neighbouring garden.

'David?'

He didn't respond, and James saw that he was shaking all over.

'He's deaded,' David the First hissed in his ear.

Immediately James dropped his bike and, with a strength

that came from nowhere, carried the convulsing boy to his home.

Doreen the Second answered the door.

'It's David,' James said, rather obviously. 'I found him in a bush.'

She gathered her son tenderly but firmly into her arms and took him indoors. James followed partway but then lingered on the threshold.

'What is the matter with him?' he called to her retreating back.

'He's in a coma. He needs sugar,' she said. 'Thanks, James.'

He took this as his cue to leave.

The fishing trip was cancelled out of respect. He would loiter round the side of the house with the other David and then call to see how his friend was later that afternoon.

'What is a coma?' he asked his mother.

Not hearing him come in, she knocked her head on the cupboard under the sink, which she was busy cleaning. 'I thought you'd gone out.'

'I had. What is a coma?'

'It's like a sleep.'

'David's having one.'

'David?'

'The one from down the road.'

'Did you do it?' An automatic response.

'No. I found him like that.'

'Oh dear, I'll ring his mum. But don't think *you're* playing inside on a day like this!'

James picked up the cat, kicked the dog and went out again.

From then on, James was David the Second's trusted friend. Doreen thanked him profusely and gave him a bag of sugar lumps to carry around in case David went into a coma again. He didn't really understand, but he knew that this was important, so he carried them with pride. He was David's protector.

'You should have left him,' David the First said openly.

James flushed with anger and embarrassment, before he remembered that no one else could hear him.

The Little Devils also begrudged the privileged treatment that the new David continued to receive. James was always inventing new rules that penalised them and never David the Second. They were forbidden from visiting T Woods without him, so when he went fishing, the children were left to kick each other's heels. James didn't anticipate a rebellion, but childhood is a hotbed where everything germinates quickly.

'How come he makes all the rules?' Tara wanted to know.

'Because he's the leader,' Christian replied, dully.

'We never made him leader.' His sister's words always went in. They had a direct flight-path to his subconscious.

'He found T Woods.'

'Yes, but he doesn't own it.'

Matthew and Rebecca were James's strongest defendants but even they had to concede that this was true.

'OK then, why don't we find another wood? One of our own ...' Christian was getting into his stride, but he'd made a fatal slip: instead of making a declaration he'd asked a question. He was not at heart a leader and was better suited to being the heavy – the guard-dog, the strong second. James understood that leaders compel, they instruct, and they never open-end a suggestion.

Unbeknownst to James, Rebecca the First was now firmly on the mend. And the scars on her side spoke to her. They wanted to blame someone for their ugly conception and the name they cried was 'James'. Tara, the shrewd politician, made up her mind to call at Rebecca the First's house and find out if she was dead. It didn't seem like an unreasonable question to ask.

Rebecca the First's older brother answered the door and before Tara had a chance to ask her question the teenager, assuming that she'd come to visit his sister, escorted her inside. The house was a bungalow. Tara's nose wriggled at the smell of new carpets and cheap leather upholstery.

'She's in there,' the young lad muttered, scratching himself through his tracksuit bottoms.

Tara curled her lip in disgust.

The door he gestured to had a sticker on it saying 'Keep out or else!' He left her there and ambled off into another room. Did you tap on the door of someone who was dead? She didn't know the etiquette. She decided to knock, not knowing whether she hoped for a reply or not.

'What?'

'It's Tara.'

'Oh . . . Come in.'

Tara did as she was invited and edged open the door. Rebecca was sitting up in bed. It all looked remarkably normal.

'You're not dead,' Tara said, almost making her statement into a question just to be on the safe side.

'You spastic. Do I look dead?'

'No,' seemed like the best response. Though she did look rather pale, plus her hair was in desperate need of a trim and Tara knew that people's hair grew really long after they'd died. She paused to consolidate her thoughts. 'James said that you'd died.'

'Did he?' Rebecca laughed, despite herself. 'The little turd!'

'Can't you leave the house?'

'I've got to wait till the stitches are out,' Rebecca told her proudly, before adding, 'I could really, but everyone's doing everything for me, and I like it.'

Before Rebecca the First had been usurped Tara had never liked her, but now that James was at the helm she preferred to re-remember the past and carefully remould it. And

Tara now recognised her opportunity. She was Rebecca's only link to the outside world. She sat on the girl's bed, without being asked, something she'd never have done before, and talked to her like they were best friends, intent on worming herself into this old enemy's affections. This way, once she'd gained the other girl's trust, she'd be able to drip-feed her own spleen into her and transfer her vitriol: the worker-bee feeding and fattening up her queen.

James was entirely oblivious. As far as he was concerned, he was the epicentre of his universe and no one existed when they were not with him. For the first time, he seemed balanced. His manner had changed altogether. At home he prattled on excitedly, like any other child, about his daily exploits and adventures. Sandra was gradually beginning to lift the blame for the death of his sister from his slender shoulders. This new, reformed, sugar-frosted son was convincing her that perhaps she'd deluded herself all along. He was just a child. If anything, she'd acted unnaturally as a mother. And it seemed that James had also forgiven her for . . . whatever it was that he'd begrudged her in the past. Perhaps this was because it had been his mother who'd given him his surprise gift – he saw now that it was a good surprise – of the real David. Sandra and Ken no longer had any cause to flinch when their son said, 'David and I did X or Y.' Now they could safely assume that it was a corporeal boy he was referring to – even when it wasn't. James was even talking positively about returning to school after the holidays.

When James felt inclined to spend time exclusively with David the First and Second, he wrote a note to his followers, and even when he could see them through the lounge window he pushed it through Rebecca and Paul's letter box. It was Rebecca who then – relishing the role of go-between – broke the news to the rest the gang the following morning.

On one such day she made her announcement:

'James is spending time with the Davids.'

'Good,' Christian stated petulantly.

The rest of the Little Devils yawned and grumbled and tried to come up with a plan, with the exception of Tara. She skulked quietly away. She had a surprise up her sleeve.

An hour or so later, while the rest of the gang were fooling around in the cul-de-sac, Rebecca the First stepped out of the ginnel and into their midst. Initially they gave her the same glance as they would anyone passing through the assembly, but then they looked again and remembered.

'Rebecca,' Matthew said, 'you're alive.'

None of them seemed as surprised by this Lazarus resurrection as Tara had hoped. She'd wanted to be the magician's assistant heralding the show's highlight to a wowed audience, but they barely batted a collective eyelid.

Christian was the first to her side, hands in pockets, head down, eyes up, the lapsed lapdog.

'Hello, Chris.'

Christian nodded. He didn't want to seem too sycophantic and lose his cool. 'James said – '

'Yeah, I know . . .'

'You better?'

Without a word she whipped up her T-shirt. And the others, who'd been waiting to see what sort of reception Christian received, surged forward like running ducks. They were filled with admiration: these angry, shiny scars far outshone their tadpole scratches or blood-brethren blemishes.

Christian and Tara, a team once more, invited the gang – the old gang – into their back garden for a drink of squash. There they sat on the lawn like pensioners, reminiscing about the good old days. It didn't take them long to start talking about, and then pulling apart, the new regime.

'James is a bully,' Tara said, only too happy to throw the first stone. Rebecca understood that she'd have to work fast and use few words.

'*Him* a bully?'

'Yes,' Tara replied, looking about her. She'd decided that she was clearly the most mature, despite her age, and so took it upon herself to chair the meeting. 'He cut them all with a knife, except me.' She'd known all along that her moment would come, that she'd be rewarded for her resolution. 'I wouldn't let him. I didn't want to be part of his gang.'

'*His* gang?' Rebecca was happy to listen and repeat, dipping each word first in acid incredulity.

Now it was Christian's turn. 'Yes, he just decided it was his gang.'

'I named it,' Graham asserted. 'The Little Devils.'

Tara laughed scornfully, to impress upon Rebecca how silly she thought the name.

'I never liked it,' Paul said.

'Nor me!' agreed Christian.

'But you let him cut you,' Tara reminded them quickly, eager to preserve the mainstay of the glory for herself.

Rebecca the First wearily shook her head; such unruliness would never have been permitted under her administration. 'Are we talking about the same James, with funny teeth and the imaginary friend called . . .?' She pretended to forget his name, to illustrate just how inconsequential it all was.

'David,' Paul said, helpfully.

'He has two Davids now,' Rebecca the Second said, addressing her erstwhile rival for the first time.

'Two?'

'The old one and a new one,' Paul explained.

'Are they both made up?'

'Well, you can see one of them.'

'David's a wimp,' Christian said rather bitterly. 'He's only James's blood brother . . . he's not ours.'

Then they explained the ritual, and after that the mysterious letter 'd' cuts. This time, rather predictably, the consensus seemed to be that it was either one of the Davids or James who'd executed them. To be fair, these were the only theories that could be freely expounded upon, as the other suspects were all in attendance.

'Shall we take her to the wood?' Christian asked.

'Let's find a new one,' Rebecca the First decreed. She knew to command rather than entreat. And they all agreed that that was a much better idea.

Christian was about to whine that he'd already made this suggestion, but he decided against it.

'I should go and get my knife.' To Paul a trip to the woods meant being armed.

'No,' said Tara. 'We don't need to take dangerous things with us any more, do we, Rebecca?'

But Rebecca the First thought it wise to work out James's laws before abolishing them and imposing a new set. 'Yes. Get your knife.'

'I've got mine,' Graham told her. 'It's a Swiss Army knife. I always carry it.'

'Let me see.'

Graham dug it out of his trouser pocket. He was older, so he wore trousers, even in the summer, simply because he could. 'James always made me put it in his bag and then we got a different weapon each time. But I didn't think that was fair. It's my knife.'

'I'll look after that for you,' she said, and unashamedly slipped it into her own pocket. 'Paul, you can get him something else from home,' she said matter-of-factly, inviting no response. The gang noticed this, but having only just jumped ships they were in no mood for a fresh revolution.

When Paul returned with his knife, he handed a potato peeler to Graham. 'Sorry, it's all I could get.'

Then, somewhat guiltily, the children climbed onto their bikes and cycled off to the narrow lanes. For once, Paul refrained from his weaving and they were silent, except for shouting 'Car!' when one approached.

Unbeknownst to them, they rode past a clump of trees just

beyond a hedge that grew in front of an opaque pond where James and the Davids fished for no fish. Then they ascended the usual track and left their bikes at the border of the field, as James had always insisted.

'We go on . . . on foot. That's T Woods,' Christian relayed to Rebecca, like a tour guide.

Rebecca the First nodded but looked unimpressed.

'There's another wood on the other side.'

'Yes, but James said that that was an evil wood,' Paul whispered, as though the wood might hear him.

'An evil wood?'

That's what James told us,' Rebecca the Second said, backing up her brother. 'It smells of death and David warned him never to go in there.'

'Which David?'

'The invisible one.'

'How old are you, Rebecca?' Rebecca the First asked, knowing the answer.

'Eleven.'

'You're going to big school soon . . . and you still believe in invisible people and evil woods?'

'I'm just telling you what he said, that's all. You weren't here, so you can't know.' Rebecca the Second had liked James until he'd started devoting all his attention to the new David. He was mean sometimes but at least he was a boy, and she wasn't about to relinquish all her favours without a fight.

The other Rebecca laughed derisively and Tara joined her. Paul, showing solidarity to his sister, ran to her side so they could walk along together. But she didn't want or need a younger brother's sympathy. She did a handstand, which neither of the other girls could do, and was appeased by the sensation of blood rushing to her head.

The troop passed along the side of T Woods and felt the other wood leering at them ominously. This wood was of a very different character. The trees were pines, all tall and dense.

They'd obviously been planted deliberately, unlike those in T Woods, which had shambolically struggled and fought for their natural but haphazard existence. The smell, as the children grew closer, was overpoweringly pungent – acrid waxy needles with nothing but their own company to help them decay.

'It pongs . . . like cat's piss!' said Matthew, who knew because he had a Manx cat.

'Pooh. What a stink! It smells like Graham!' Paul said, barely managing to get out his gag between his own guffaws. Graham punched him on the arm.

This wood was not welcoming. As soon as they'd clambered under the hedgerow, the children felt gloomy. The air was thick and stifling.

'I prefer T Woods,' Rebecca the Second murmured, clearly implying, 'I prefer James.'

'But I think we should explore,' Christian suggested, with strained jollity.

'Why don't we just walk around the edge?' Tara asked, with her innate inclination to stick to the fringes of anything alien.

Rebecca the First had Graham's penknife out and was already using it, rather ineffectually, as a mini-machete to break through the first rank of regimented trees. The others followed her, muttering about the smell and the lack of sunlight. It took some effort to fight their way through each column, and even when they did, the view was just the same: a dark, low path, parallel to the previous one.

'What's this?' Tara had picked up a plastic cylinder. 'They're everywhere.'

'It's a gun cartridge,' Christian told her.

'A gun what?'

'It's an empty bullet.'

Tara dropped her empty bullet and looked accusingly at the others that littered the ground like lurid red lipstick containers.

Christian and Rebecca the First pushed their way through another row of trees and then another, the branches bouncing back like saloon doors and hitting the other children before obscuring them from sight.

'Wait for us!' Tara pleaded. 'Chris . . .? Christian . . .!'

The second party struggled on and found themselves at a wide track with deep tyre grooves in the mud. Christian and Rebecca were a little way off, staring down a drop of some kind.

'Why didn't you answer?' Tara chastised as she drew up to her brother, but she stopped dead when she saw what they were looking at. Graham, Rebecca the Second, Paul and Matthew all followed suit.

Below them was a large pit full of grey and bloodied bodies, a mass grave. Of what it took them a few seconds to establish: pigs, dead pigs. Several decaying heads and snouts tilted up towards them as though they'd nosed their approach and knew that they were there. There was a gust of wind and the stench rose up and smeared their faces.

'I feel sick.' Tara turned away.

But the others were mesmerised. They couldn't stop staring at the carnage. It seemed to speak to them, to the very essence of them, to something they hadn't even known was there.

Suddenly there was a movement below and Graham screamed. A rat scurried across the carcasses before burying itself again between them. They laughed, but the noise was devoid of mirth. Flies were everywhere, but these children were meagre dishes compared with the banquet below.

'David told James it was a place where things died!' Rebecca the Second reiterated. 'He was right.'

'Why did they die?' Tara wanted to know.

'Maybe they were ill?' Matthew offered, hopefully.

'I think someone killed them,' Graham contributed.

'I think we should go.' Tara was looking about herself.

'What if the people who shot the pigs come and find us here?'

'You don't shoot pigs,' Christian told her. 'Pigs aren't wild animals. The bullets must have been for something else.'

The group simultaneously conjured up just who the something else might be. As one they turned and in white panic ran along the dried mud path, stumbling and tripping over the hardened furrows of Land Rover tracks.

Once they were out in the open again, they knew they were safe and could now enjoy their terror. Adrenalin kept them tearing and screaming across the fields all the way back to their bikes.

'That was exciting!' Christian said, while he leant panting against the fence.

No one could disagree. There was nothing like fear to make them feel alive.

'That's our wood now,' Paul said. 'Pig Wood.'

'Do we need a wood?' Tara asked.

'And David told James he shouldn't go in there . . .' Rebecca the First was concocting a plan. 'Wouldn't it be fun if we made him?'

'What?'

'Tricked him. He tricked you. He told you I was dead.'

'He lied to us.' Tara wanted to impress on them how James had mistreated and beguiled them from the beginning.

'Maybe he did think you were dead,' Rebecca the Second offered.

'He came to see me in hospital.'

It was a good point.

'What'll we do?'

'I'll think of something,' Rebecca the First assured them. Children, like wolves, can always find the unprotected underbelly. 'All you have to do is get him to the pit.'

'Easy,' Graham said, trying to be macho. 'I'll tie him up if I have to.'

'You and whose army?' sneered Christian.

'We should go home for dinner. Mum'll kill us if we're late again.' Rebecca the Second didn't want to know the details, but also didn't want her gang membership revoked by stating as much.

'Can I have the potato peeler back?' Paul asked Graham and suddenly the conspirators became children again.

FIFTEEN

Rebecca the Second sat in the lounge with her mother and brother for an evening of TV with meals on trays, on laps. She was not devoting her full attention to *Family Fortunes*. She was willing a note to come through the letter box; a note telling them – but primarily her – that James and the Davids would never be available to come and play again, as they were going around the world . . . on safari. Something in her soul, though she didn't know what, sang to her of imminent sorrow, and no amount of standing on her head would drown out this intimation.

The longed-for note did not arrive.

When she woke in the morning, the feeling was still there, hunkering down in her guts, but the sun was smiling blithely and it promised that nothing too calamitous would occur under its carefree watch. She and Paul trooped along to the Close. Tara was sitting on the wall, coolly looking on, but the boys were already brewing trouble. An elderly neighbour was staring at them from his front window. He did this every time they played in the cul-de-sac and usually they ignored him, but today they were excitable and Matthew was unable to resist the temptation. He winked at the gang. Then he threw the ball so that it struck the glass right in front of the old face. The man fell backwards and the children fell about laughing.

In a few moments he was out on the lawn, admonishing them with all his might, but his impotent rage ran off the feathers of the fledglings before him. And Matthew's words of sniggered apology only undermined his fury and highlighted how silly he sounded. Defeated, and swearing, mainly at himself, the man retreated into his house to take up his watch again.

'Who rattled his cage?' Graham asked, repeating the words of his older, more sardonic sister. The others giggled and shrugged off the incident.

Rebecca the Second asked where Rebecca the First was.

'Don't talk about her.' Tara was fizzing, like sherbet.

'Why not?' Rebecca wasn't going to be told what to do by this stuck-up pig-girl. 'I can if I want.'

'You can if you want, but you'll spoil the joke.'

'What joke?'

'You'll see.' Tara couldn't stop the advance of an 'I know something you don't know' smirk from sailing smugly through the valley of her lips.

When James and the two Davids arrived, plans were made like it was any other day. The unanimous decision was T Woods for Cops and Robbers.

When they arrived at the foot of the hill, the gang dropped their bikes in the usual place and clambered over the fence. James didn't notice, but each one of them cast a furtive glance in the direction of their newly discovered Pig Wood with its hidden horrors. They all felt that the trees were spying on them, listening to their thoughts.

Christian started to sing, 'If you go into the woods today, be sure of a big surprise,' which made Graham and Tara titter like a pair of old women on Brighton Pier. 'If you go into the woods today, you'd better go in disguise . . .'

'Shut up, Christian,' James said abruptly.

Christian met his gaze and held it defiantly. He stopped singing but then starting humming the melody instead.

His sister snorted her applause.

'Where do you think you're going, Miss Piggy?' James said to her as she made to climb over the stile. She'd tagged along without asking permission and he'd let it go so far, but now she was crossing the line.

'Don't worry, I'm not going to play,' she said, with crystal-cut derision. 'I'm just going to sit and read.' She pulled out a book and brandished it. And not caring what someone like Tara read, James didn't even bother to check its title.

'Don't let her,' David the First hissed.

'You can stay.' He was feeling tolerant and wanted to prove that he didn't always need, or heed, his friend's advice. 'If no one else minds . . .?'

No one said that they did.

'OK, Little Devils . . .' James began when they were collected in the clearing. He was oblivious to their embarrassment when he used the old gang name. 'Your dangerous things.'

'I've not got my Swiss Army knife,' Graham informed him rather glumly.

'Then you must have the pea-shooter . . . Christian?'

Christian handed Graham his paltry weapon with a nudge.

'The last one up can use a stick as big or small as they want.'

There then ensued the usual wrangling as to the order of the collection. Next came the debate as to who was a cop and who a robber. Even though cops were synonymous with winners – and robbers, like Indians, were invariably defeated – the role of robber was more appealing than that of cop. Being an outlaw had its own glory. Christian normally wanted to be a robber and would try any tactic to ensure that he was, but today he was all baby-oil charm and golden altruism.

'It's OK . . . I'll be a cop. James, you can be a robber if you like,' he said.

'Something's up,' David the First whispered into James's ear. 'He'd kill his sister to be a robber.'

James frowned. He would not be coerced. 'Do you want

to be a robber?' he asked David the Second.

David nodded with his blond hair. 'Thanks, James.'

All the while Tara sat, pretending to read her book, knitting bad luck.

They chose their secret weapons and disappeared into the wood. Normally, David the First would stay some distance from James, pretending to be absorbed in a plant or gnarl of wood, but today he stuck by his side. James had the catapult and he was hunting about for conkers or oak-apple galls – insect cannonballs – which were perfect as missiles.

'It's very quiet,' James whispered.

David didn't reply. He was too busy straining all his suspicious senses.

A magpie sniggered and a jay flew across their path. Something stirred in the brambles, though there was no discernable human movement. It was eerie, the moment before a car crash. A cool breeze brushed past James but he couldn't feel it, his blood was pumping so loudly he was hot with the noise.

'Where is everyone?'

As though in reply to his question, he heard a cry of attack followed by a cry of alarm from the far side of the wood. Against David's better judgement, James immediately set off in the direction of the noise.

The next thing he knew, his name was being called in a restrained, stage whisper. David was frightened. This was not how the game played out. Keeping close to the ground they moved towards the voice and spotted Rebecca the Second, turning in slow, low circles like a sycamore blade's descent.

'What is it?' James asked from behind a tree.

'James?'

He stepped into view. She moved towards him but he backed away, not sure if this was some new mode of attack. 'Stay there.'

'It's David,' she said. She was pale and short of breath,

and her greasy hair hung about her shoulders like a dirty wedding veil.

James looked to David. 'But he's here.'

'The other David.'

'Is he hurt? Is he having a coma?'

'No. I don't think so.'

'He's a digestive,' he said, having confused the word with diabetic. 'I have some sugar lumps. I can help him.'

'They've taken him to Pig Wood.'

'Where?' He moved closer to her.

'Tara said . . .'

James clearly wasn't catching on.

'The other wood, over there.' She pointed.

'Death Wood,' David advised him.

'Why?'

'I don't know . . . They might throw him in the pit.'

James didn't know what she was talking about, but he understood that this was some kind of emergency.

'Come on, David,' he said, heading for the wood's boundary.

'Wait . . .!' Rebecca called, but he was too fast for her.

If David the Second needed rescuing, he was the boy for the job. James was his only blood brother. He wouldn't let him down. There was no time to head for the stile, so he tore his way through the clawing hawthorn and out into the field. The breeze was still racing about like a mustang, but James was focused and made straight for the woods. David kept apace, all the time pleading with him not to go on.

The rank stench of the trees rushed out to meet the boys, slowing their advancement.

'It smells,' James said, covering his mouth and nose.

'Of dead things.'

They both shuddered as the breeze caught up.

'You are such a scaredy cat.' David's fear was enough

encouragement to goad James on, and he tunnelled his way under the fence, snapping branches and tearing skin. 'Come on!' he whispered from the other side, trying not to be dispirited by the long-fingered gloom.

David compliantly fought his way through, but he was resentful and wary. Legion upon legion of trees barred their way, but the boys squeezed between them at the base of the trunks, one rank after another.

'David?' There was no point trying to be stealthy; the trees would proclaim their approach.

'J-a-m-e-s?' David the Second's voice was so high and tense that the noise helter-skeltered down James's body.

They pushed on and on, towards the voice, fighting against the sea of trees, breaker after breaker. Eventually they came out gasping into the air of the pathway. When their eyes had adjusted to the light, they spotted David a few yards away. He was standing on his own, blindfolded, his hands tied behind his back, his chin resting on his chest. He was the condemned man, waiting while the firing squad finished their cards, downed their brandies, stubbed out their cigarettes and raised their weapons. A low forsaken whimper dripped from his lips like drool.

'David,' James said gently, warning him of his presence.

'They said . . . if I move I'll fall into a pig pit.' His voice was so full of tears and saliva it sounded like he was made of water.

James now saw that David was standing next to a drop of some kind. 'I am coming to help. Stay still.'

David the First tried to pull him back, but he broke free from his grip and boldly walked towards his friend in need. When James touched the knots that bound David's wrists, he felt him flinch.

'It's OK,' he said calmly, but in the corner of his eye he'd caught the greying flesh that lay in the bottom of the pit. He freed his friend's hands and the boy immediately tore off the blindfold, unable to endure the darkness for a second longer. James stood before him proudly, wearing once more the mantle of a boy in shining armour.

But before there was time for back-patting gratitude and explanations, David gasped and pointed. 'Who's . . .?'

'What?' James turned and saw Rebecca the First approaching, all Hammer Horror, her face sheet-white, a knife in her outstretched hand. 'Rebecca!' James said, trying to compose himself and seem pleased. 'You're better!'

Rebecca scoffed. 'No. I'm dead, remember?'

'Not . . . not really.'

'Yes.'

'I saw you . . .'

'After that I died.'

James forced a laugh and heard his David telling him to run, but he stood his ground.

'It's . . . a trick,' he stammered.

'No. I'm dead. You killed me . . .' Rebecca kept on approaching, her ghostly face and blood-red lips leering at him. 'Like you killed your sister and your grandpa.'

'That's not true.'

'Yes, it is. They told me. They're here too.'

He looked from one David and to the other, a cornered fox.

'It's not true!' he shouted.

Then, from somewhere beyond the tree line, Christian began chanting, 'If you go into the woods today, be sure of a big surprise.'

Other voices joined in, and the vibrations sent sound waves of panic shooting up James's body.

Blinding tears shimmered in his eyes like splinters of glass. The approaching form of Rebecca grew blurred and the silver of the flashing blade ate up the only ray of light that penetrated the pines. Frantically he wiped his eyes and looked again from one David to the other – the old to his left, the new to his right. The ghost of Rebecca was a few feet in front of him now. The chanting was all around him, the blade inching closer and closer. He knew that he was going to fall backwards into the pit, unless . . . He felt the point of the blade touch his chest and he stepped back.

'David!' he shouted and reached to his right. He chose the flesh and blood friend. There was a flurry of movement to his left and no arms had reached out to save him. He was falling. He caught onto the earth and dug his fingers in, his legs dangling beneath him. 'David!'

'Stand on his hands!' Rebecca said.

He looked up, but he couldn't see through his tears or the thick noise of singing.

'Do it!' she said.

He thought he heard the word *sorry* Will-o'-the-Wisping its way towards him. As he tried to establish who'd said it, David or David, he felt pressure on his fingers, more and more, until pain dictated that he pull them free and continue falling.

His body scraped the walls of the pit before hitting hit the putrid pig flesh with a slap. He sank into it. Now he was bellowing, a sound that was so primeval it came from beyond him, from beneath him, from the bellies of the slaughtered pigs. And this bestial cry, emanating from his plundered grave of a mouth, brought the chorus to an abrupt stop. Then there was laughter, smothered and nervy, then the word *Run!* whispered in relay, scattering before the sound of retreating feet and swishing branches. He lay shaking among the rotting tissue, insensible to his surroundings; the gladiator butchered to make a Roman holiday. In the distance he heard a series of whoops like exotic bird calls.

'David?' he whimpered. 'David?'

No reply.

David had neglected to say his last goodbye.

James passed out. His unconscious body quickly acclimatised

to the fetid heat, his nose grew accustomed to the stench and his mind became acquainted with the intimacy of death. When his eyes opened they were wide and dark, eyes that said they'd lost all trust.

'David?' he said once more, in case his old friend had crept back while he'd dozed among the dead.

Nothing.

James had had company in the womb and David's company ever since. Now, for the first time in his life, he was truly alone.

Flies sucked at his grazed body and a few drops of his blood commingled with that of the pigs.

The wood was even more ominous at dusk, but he was now numb to its intimidation. He lay there mustering enough energy to climb out of the pit. After several thwarted attempts, which sent him sliding back into the grinning mouths of the pigs, he managed to claw his way to the surface by seizing the severed root-fingers that dangled down from the muddy walls.

Back on terra firma he lay for a moment breathing in the acidic earth before crawling forwards on all fours. The catapult was in front of him in a tyre-track. One of its arms had been snapped off. He rose falteringly to his feet and stepped on it without malice, making the other arm break off cleanly with a crack.

Then he stumbled off through the wood, unaware of the pines lashing his face and body. He crossed the fields of no man's land, tripping over the molehill mounds, until he reached the perimeter fence and his bike. All the while there was a gaping hole at his side, which David should have filled. Instead of riding his Chopper, feeling the invigorating rush of the air blowing the curls of his brown hair, he limped alongside it, the walking wounded.

Night was falling all around him. The breeze had grown

wings and a sharp beak.

On arriving home the garage door was up, announcing his late arrival, telling him that dinner was ruined. He put his bike inside and opened the door into the kitchen. The dog ran to him and jumped up cheerfully, sniffing the scent of blood. James didn't even kick out at her contrary mood, but moved on. The door to the dining room was shut, another indication that he was late. Slowly he turned the handle and his eyes met with his mother's. She'd deliberately positioned herself in his chair so that when he entered he couldn't avoid coming face to face with her wrath. She presented her suspended motion 'You are in so much trouble' face, but when she saw his appearance, it dropped with her jaw.

'Oh my God,' she said, standing up.

James looked, appropriately enough, like he'd seen a ghost. His blue eyes, which were still darkly hued, were wide and vacant. His body was cut and grimy and his clothes were dyed the ugly brown of dried blood.

'What happened?' his father asked, his voice powdery with concern.

Sandra knew that this was no time for questions and was on her son in a second, half carrying, half marching him to the bathroom. She ran the bath and undressed him at the same time.

Passively James allowed his mother strip him, uncomplaining even when the T-shirt tore at his ears. The body-conscious boy had no shame and stood naked before her freely. His legs wobbled like a newborn foal's, unsteady, unready and overawed by the new world that filled his mind.

'Help me, Ken!'

Together they lifted him into the bathtub.

All Sandra's mothering impulses rose within her; she would have licked him clean if she could, disinfecting his cuts with her saliva. She was crying, quietly. This cruel world kept attacking her cubs and she was too powerless to prevent it.

'Who did this to you?' she asked as she sponged down his skin.

'A ghost,' he weakly confided, his eyes shutting her and the soapsuds out.

She fought back the urge to scold him for his fabrication. It could wait.

'Make him a hot chocolate, Ken.'

She washed his hair, more gently than normal, and when he was immersed in the water he gave himself up to it and his shaking finally subsided. His mother noticed his shorts and T-shirt tan-lines and she didn't know why but it nearly broke her heart. She helped him out and towelled him dry, her rag-doll son. The scratches and cuts were many but not deep, and she applied her panacea, Germoline, with its reassuring pungency. Then she put him in his pyjamas, enjoying the chance to be close to him, and hugged his drooping body tightly. No words could convey what she wanted to communicate, so she resorted to what she knew best.

'Your dinner is still in the oven.' A meal for every occasion. He didn't respond.

'Did you eat your sandwiches? Where's your lunch-box?'

It was still in his satchel, swinging from a tree in T Woods.

She couldn't reach him. Her son was far away, lost and alone.

'Ken! Please can you carry him upstairs?'

When he was in bed, she read to him from a book that he'd long since outgrown, but he was paralysed and her words travelled over his body like a centipede. At least it soothed her own spirits. She was the image of a bookplate Edwardian lady reading to a bed-ridden orphan. She finished the story and slowly closed the back cover, like all good readers do, careful not to let the magic escape. It was impossible to tell if he was asleep or not. His eyes were shut, but too tightly, and his brow creased into furrows too deep for a boy of his age. There was nothing more for her to do. She left the room. And the hot chocolate, which sat untouched at his bedside, formed a skin the colour of congealed blood.

While he lay there, his waking nightmares crept back. Faces were projected onto a screen in his brain – tormented, distorted faces: his sister, his grandfather, the ghost of Rebecca and both of the Davids, one turning into the other. A soundtrack rang in his ears: the chanting of the children, growing louder and louder. And he was prone, defenceless against the onslaught, buried alive in the uncaring grave of his body.

Guilt and regret would now continually cloud his light blue eyes, but suicide quickly turns to homicide. And James decided that it might just be possible to entice his old David back, if somehow the new David was made to go away.

After he'd dressed, he took himself downstairs to see Cifer the Second. He'd neglected her of late. Today he would give her the loving attention that he craved for himself. He found her in the dining room, but her pawned affection was not so easily bought back and, using her tail as an insult, she strutted away like a saloon floozy and flirted with his father instead. In the kitchen the red, unbreakable breakfast bowls were laid out. There wasn't one for him.

'Oh,' his mother said when she saw him. Her impulse was to hug him again, but she checked it – a feral creature can never be truly tamed and advances made by night are erased by day. Her heavy heart could not endure the humiliation of fresh rejection. James needed a hug now, more than ever before, but he'd never mastered the language to ask.

'I was going to let you sleep in,' she said, explaining the table setting. 'Do you want some Coco Pops?'

'No, thank you.'

'Does David?' she was trying to indulge him, a moment of mollycoddling.

'David has gone.' James looked down at his feet, as though he wasn't sure they'd still be there either.

'Gone?' She tried to hide the elation in her voice and the word staggered out over two octaves. 'Gone where?' She tried to affect sympathy.

'Away.' His eyes were bright blue again, varnished with tears.

Sandra turned her back on him and put on some Marigold gloves, plunging them into the sufficiently bubbly water. Washing-up liquid lasted much longer when used moderately.

'Do you want to talk about what happened last night?' If she wasn't looking at him, she figured that he might feel more inclined to open up – the comfort of the confessional. She heard the door into the garage open.

Evidently not.

'Are you going out?' she called over her shoulder, water dripping from the tips of her suspended gloves. 'I thought you might not want to today.' She could hear him wheeling his bike to the garage door. She hoped he didn't scratch the car with it. 'I don't want you going out without any breakfast . . . you didn't have anything last night. James...? Breakfast is the most important – ' the sliding door eclipsed the end off her sentence, but she finished it anyway ' – meal of the day!' She took solace from the idiom.

The sun was too bright, so he shielded his grainy eyes and pushed his bike to David's house. He pictured the silhouette of his friend lying where he'd found him once, among the irises. Then he imagined the other David in the same spot. He'd never had to imagine the imaginary David before. Doreen seemed surprised to see him. In her arms she carried her daughter. James craned to look into the girl's ear, to get a glimpse of her panther, but he couldn't see it.

'David's already gone out. I thought you were with them.' She sounded concerned. James was, after all, her son's guardian of the sugar lumps.

'Well, I'm not.' Her words should have felt like a further blow, but he absorbed them with the studied calmness of a contract killer.

'I don't know where they went.'

'Never mind.' He climbed onto his bike and cycled off without any form of goodbye.

The gang would be at T Woods, he felt certain. He prayed that they wouldn't be in Death Wood. He didn't want to go in there again, not ever. He rode at a steady pace and didn't notice autumn curling up the edges of summer; he ignored the ominous grey cloud that hovered like a collection of cremation ashes and he was oblivious to the rabbit, stunned by a car, hopping about in its own blood by the roadside. On a normal day, David and he would have stopped to investigate, carrying the animal home to witness its demise or recovery. Today, he was alone and his vision was blinkered and bleak.

As he expected, the bikes were all lying on the ground near the gate, bar Tara's, which was propped primly on its stand. David's bike, which was even more dated than James's, lay with the others. This proximity filled him with rage and his eyes changed colour. He kicked the rusty metal and a sliver of red paint came away. Picking up the bike he threw it over the gate, making it land with a clatter, one wheel spinning.

'I'll hide it,' he told himself, adding rather archaically, 'as a prank.'

He clambered over the gate and carried the bike further along the hedgerow and then dropped it into the ditch, being careful not to tread down any of the long grass. Then he hid his own bike as well. This way, if the others returned first, they wouldn't know it'd been him. He'd not considered what he was going to do, or say, when he confronted David and the gang, or even if he would. But he didn't intend to be seen at least until he'd assessed the situation, so he took the precaution of using a more covert route to the top hat of trees. The last stretch he crawled, picturing his old friend David creeping along behind him.

'Coming, ready or not!' he heard Christian holler from somewhere inside the wood.

James's face flushed. It was *his* wood. *He'd* found it. They were trespassing on *his* territory, the last Indian in a land of cowboys. He caught a sudden glimpse of Tara, comedy-running about like a panicked coot, so he decided to stalk her from his side of the fence. She ran into the clearing near the stile. There, he spotted his bag hanging from a tree. The bird-girl hurried off again into the wood and he consented to let her go while he retrieved his belongings. Checking that no one was about, he made a dash for the bag, and snatched it, like a fox would a chicken, before darting back over the fence again. Inside was his lunch-box, the gun – which had been returned by someone – his animal book and his blindfold.

Rather than enter the wood itself, he stuck to the perimeter, where he could see without being seen. Graham, who was hiding – very inadequately – in some brambles, was easily spotted. Further along was Matthew, who'd done a better job of concealing himself among the ferns. His head popped up for a second, like a hare's, and then it was gone again. About two-thirds of the way round James recognised a flash of blond. David the Second.

There was a secret hideaway in the wood, and when James had been caught up in the crush of his new friendship with David, he'd rashly shown it to him. It was a shallow dugout, two feet deep, three feet wide and four feet long, with a makeshift roof of corrugated metal that was half concealed by moss and lichen. The boys had speculated, at great length, that it belonged to the village vampire.

James observed David the Second as he removed a plastic bag from the den to make room for himself. The bag, James knew, contained a sharp knife with a broken handle, a fork, a tin mug, a can opener and a large box of matches. Together they'd inspected the contents countless times, but they'd never dared to remove them. This was brave, James thought: not only was David getting into the lair, but he had also displaced the possessions of its bloodthirsty inhabitant. He watched, breath held, as David climbed in.

As the hidey-hole coffin lid was slid shut over the boy, a window of opportunity opened and James spotted it.

SIXTEEN

Skulking along the hedge he found a gap in the barbed wire and after squirming through, he dragged his bag after him. Then he rose to his feet and inched slowly forwards towards the dugout. A young tree had fallen on the far side of it. He knew what he must do. Habit made him look back to warn the other David to be cautious, but there was no David there.

With each step he lifted his foot up high from the knee like his Pinocchio puppet, before bringing it down tentatively. He managed to pass the corrugated metal cover without disturbing it and reached the toppled tree. Before he did anything else, he carefully tore away at the surrounding plants and lifted one end of the tree in situ, to ensure that it wasn't attached to the earth. Then he braced himself and with all the strength and speed he could muster, he dragged the trunk until it lay on top of the roof, trapping the boy beneath it.

David must have been aware of the noise, but he couldn't have suspected what had happened. Other sounds were coming from the wood. James guessed that, bar David, the rest of the gang had been unearthed. Like a bounty hunter, he took out his gun and sat himself down to wait.

'David?' he heard Christian call, from some way off. 'David, you can come out now . . . We're . . . not playing any more.' Christian, who'd never admit that he'd been beaten, was avoiding the words 'We give up.'

'Come out, come out, wherever you are!' Tara sang.

There was a thwarted rattle as David tried to remove his ceiling.

Silence fell for a second . . . then there was a grunt of exertion.

The roof was raised a few inches before dropping again.

'Hello?' David said. 'Is someone there?'

James's eyes were burning but his voice was still.

'Hello?' David tried to lift the sheet again. He was beginning to fret. 'Is this a joke?' His voice was getting louder.

James had to take action. He couldn't let the others hear him. 'No,' he hissed. 'It's not a joke. You are trapped. You are my prisoner.'

'Who's there?'

'Have you forgotten me? Already?'

'Who is it?' His captive was in no state to assess voice tones.

'James.'

There was a moment of stillness as the situation sank into the ground like rain.

'Oh. Then let me out.'

'Daaaavid!' came a bored elongated cry from Graham in the distance.

James anticipated that David would respond, so he darted forwards and slipped his gun under a gap between the metal and the ground. 'Don't you dare make a sound' – his mother's phrase.

David saw the gun and flinched backwards. Then he realised.

'It's not a real gun,' he said, but it came out like a question.

James lay down and tried to peer into the darkness. He waved the gun left and right as a threat, but David, whose only advantage was that he could see out, made a grab for his wrist. James pulled the trigger and an imagined bullet flew out and into David's heart, but as there wasn't a real one David wasn't wounded and instead he managed to prize the gun out of James's hand.

'Chris!' David shouted.

This humiliation further inflamed James. David had called out to Christian in his hour of need. Christian, who'd never shown *him* any charity? Christian, who'd refused to be his blood brother? Christian, who'd left him tied and blindfolded before the pig pit? Without pausing to think, James reached out for the vampire's bag of utensils and rummaged around in it until he found the broken handle of the knife.

'Chris!!' David called again.

More than anything else, James wanted this noise to stop. He wanted quiet, to think. He plunged the knife into the hole and when it made contact he pulled it out again. David groaned.

'You hit me,' he murmured, shocked by this act of violence.

'No, I cut you,' James corrected him, his eyes black with anger.

There was a fumbling noise. The boy discovered the wet, warm blood and whimpered feebly, 'Why did you . . . do that?'

'Where did I get you?' James asked, looking at the smeared centimetre of blood on the tip of the blade.

'My leg. You hurt my leg,' he sobbed.

'Where is David?'

'I'm David.'

'My David. What happened to my David?'

'I . . . I don't know.'

'Yes, you do.'

'No.' The boy was bewildered.

'You killed him.'

'I didn't. I couldn't have.'

'How come?'

'He isn't real. You can't kill someone . . . who isn't . . .'

It was as though David had stabbed him back. 'You don't

mean that.'

'I do! You made him up.'

James's head was reeling. He'd thought that he knew this boy, that they'd been friends, but all along David had thought him a liar.

'Say that again and you're dead meat.'

'But it's true.' Three times he denied him.

'I mean it. I will stab you in the heart.'

'You wouldn't.'

'I killed my sister and my grandad and Rebecca. I'll kill you too.'

'Rebecca's not dead.'

'Yes, she is. I saw her ghost.' James was confused. 'You saw it too.'

'It was a trick. She had face paint on. Please, let me out.'

James shook his head. *This* was a trick.

'David, we're going!' Matthew shouted.

The knife appeared in the hole again, warning David to hold his tongue or have it cut out.

'Stop crying,' James snarled. He was trying to listen to the woods, to hear if the others were leaving. The sobs continued, grew louder even. 'Stop crying or I'll give you something to cry for!' The sound halved in volume as David covered his mouth, sending the waves of anxiety back down, making him hiccup and choke.

'They'll see my bike. They'll know I'm still here. They won't go without me.'

James felt a jolt of concern. Then he remembered that he'd hidden David's bike. 'Yes, they will.'

Even as he said this, he heard the gang giggling and shouting as they crossed the field. They'd notice that the bike was missing and simply assume that David had already gone home.

The clouds of pressure lifted. Now James had space to think.

Retracting his arm and the knife, he reached for his bag and removed yesterday's packed lunch: corned beef and raw onions in wholemeal bread. Normally he'd have ditched them, given them up as an offering to the little devil in the tree stump, but he'd not eaten since the morning before and his empty stomach assured him that they'd taste just fine. He sat quietly on the log, eating his sandwiches, a macabre tribute to rustic innocence, the young shepherd boy.

'Do you want half?' he asked David, not wanting to be rude.

Understandably, David didn't reply.

When he'd finished the food, he started picking the scabs off his cuts. He was so absorbed that David assumed he'd gone. The boy pushed at the metal again and shouted for help.

Though the trunk alone would have prevented the boy's escape, James stamped hard on the corrugated sheet and felt the weight of David's back beneath it. With a yelp, the boy slumped down and the ceiling was back on. It was illogical, but it enraged James that David didn't trust him and wanted to get away. He snatched up the plastic bag again and took out the fork and the matches. He jabbed the fork down the hole, making David cry out. Something in his head told him that if he hurt this David, the hidden David would return. Surely it would appease him that he and the real boy were no longer friends? He was proving that now. Plus, David the First was bound to be intrigued by his stratagem. James looked around quickly to try and catch his friend ducking out of sight, but he didn't spot him.

Maybe if he took the game up a notch? He started striking matches, dropping them into the den from different places so that David couldn't determine where the next one would come from. Each time the boy saw or felt another flame he yelped and frantically tried to bat it out before it burnt him or set his clothes alight. After this, James alternated between the matches and sticking him with the fork. Then he started heating up the fork prongs, pressing the hot metal onto the boy's legs or outstretched arms. The knife he barely needed to use, just a flirtatious flash of the blade was enough to start him screaming. David was half paralysed by claustrophobia and fear, but James was unmoved. The happy executioner, he whistled while he worked.

'If you let me out, I'll help you find David.'

'Ah, but you said David isn't real.'

David the Second paused, searching for a way out through the treacherous maze of words. 'It's what Christian said. I knew he was real.'

'Why did you say *was*?'

'I . . . erm . . . What do you mean?' At least James had stopped dropping matches for a moment.

'I mean, you said that he *was* real and not *is* real.'

'I don't know why I . . .'

'*Was* means *not any more*, doesn't it?'

Silence.

'Am I right?'

'Yes.'

'So if you hadn't killed him, then you'd have said he is real. Am I right?'

'Yes . . . I mean . . . No.'

David heard James strike another match and thought his body might implode with terror. To heighten the suspense, as he wriggled around, searching for the anticipated flash of fire, James let the match burn out between his fingers. Instead, he stabbed him with the blade again without any warning. This time it was not a clean jab. A spasm of rage took hold of James and he jerked the knife like a jagged bolt of lightening.

'I think I'd better leave you to think about what you've done,' he said, using adult words to corroborate his cruelty, but he winced as he wiped the blood off the blade. It collected on the bile-yellow lichen that had spread across the log, and glistened like berries.

'I'll come back when you have learnt your lesson.' The lips

of his parents and all parents everywhere mouthed the words with him, bolstering his belief that he had justice on his side.

'No! James! Please! I'm sorry. James?'

James stayed where he was for a moment, listening to David listening. Then he picked up his bag and, without a word, slipped away like a spectre.

After he had dragged his bike out of the ditch, he sat and carefully plucked away the strands of flowers and ferns from it, like hair from a brush. Then he cycled home with a solitary buttercup spinning in the spokes of his wheel. Unwittingly, he rode over the – now unrecognisable – rabbit, which had been rollered into the road.

Away from the confines of the wood he felt vulnerable. As long as he was close to nature he was invested with its infinite powers. But once he was back in the village he was just a boy, innocuous and small. Images of David interred in the earth slotted into his brain, but he reminded himself that David deserved it. He was teaching him a lesson for his own good. James was simply fighting to get his old friend back, the only way he knew how. And it would only be a matter of time before one of the Davids broke.

'It's a good job you're here,' his mother said, when he entered the garage. 'Your dad would've been cross if you'd been out when he got home. I was supposed to keep you inside today.'

'You used to lock me outside,' he reminded her.

'About yesterday . . .' his mother began, uncertainly. 'There was a lot of blood on you. Was it . . . all yours?'

'No, it was from pigs.'

'Don't be cheeky,' she snapped, assuming that this was some form of sarcasm.

He couldn't hear her. The noises had started in his head again. He was being dragged backwards, sucked into a long insulated tunnel. He frowned and dug his nails into his palms to try and keep focused. It was no good; the waking terrors were taking hold of him. He held his breath.

'I give up.' Sandra turned away from him to busy herself with dinner. 'If you won't give me a straight answer, then I wash my hands–'

There was a clatter as James collapsed into a faint, knocking the pine kitchen stools over like skittles.

When he came to, he was in bed and the doorbell was ringing, but he was so tired that he only had time to take in the glare of the buttercup-yellow walls before drifting off again.

The next time he woke, it was with a bolt at around 6 a.m. Instinctively he looked for David before remembering that he'd gone. Then he thought of the other David, David the Second, whom he'd left in the woods, like an animal in a snare. Within minutes he was dressed and creeping along the landing. The wooden stairs were complicit for once and kept their moaning to a minimum. The dog, of course, barked as he inched open the kitchen door. He silenced it with a chocolate-covered digestive biscuit, and put a couple in his bag for David the Second. If anything could restore him after a night in the woods, they could. After all, a digestive was his illness's namesake.

He released the garage door to edge out his bike and, not wanting to make more noise than was necessary, he left it open. Outside it was only half light and the air was chilled. He cycled as fast as his sleepy legs could manage and tore through the lanes, not giving a thought to oncoming cars. Once he'd arrived unscathed at the wooden gate he unceremoniously flung down his bike, scrambled over the hedge and ran up the sloping field. The woods made a different noise at this still early hour. They were bleached, waiting for the sun, which like a child with a colouring book would apply layers of light and shade into the silhouettes, careful not to bleed over the lines.

As he walked along the perimeter pathway, he tried to regulate his breathing. He hoped to see David the First kneeling by the dugout. He prayed that he'd not been forsaken for good.

The scene that met his eyes was still and innocuous, just a fallen trunk and a discarded plastic bag. James almost convinced himself that he'd made it all up, imagined it. Then he saw a hand, David's grimy hand, resting in the gap.

On closer inspection he could see that David had tried to dig himself out.

'He must have fallen asleep . . .' James crouched down and prodded the upturned palm with his finger. It was cold to the touch.

'David? Wake up.'

No answer.

He dropped his bag and tried to move the trunk. The previous day, anger had made him strong, but today he could only drag it one foot at a time before pausing to catch his breath. Then he lifted up the trap-door roof.

The boy before him looked quite altered. His blond hair was dirty. His face was scratched and swollen. His clothes and body were scorched. Angry-looking fork marks speckled his flesh and accusatory knife gashes gaped on his leg and stomach. The boy had also been sick several times. The sight of him shocked James so much that he let the corrugated metal drop from his fingers and heaving, staggered into the brambles and threw up himself. Had the local vampire attacked David during the night? He couldn't believe that he'd inflicted those wounds. He started to panic. What had he done?

'David. David! David!' he wailed, not knowing which boy he was calling upon. He ran in circles, weeping and dribbling, hitting his head with his hand. 'He is just in a coma sleep,' he told himself. He considered carrying David home, being the hero, the saviour again, but how would he explain the cuts, the state he was in, and what would David say when he woke up? If he told tales to his mother, Doreen the Second, she would tell his parents. They'd certainly disown him then. They'd send him to an orphanage.

'My dad will kill me,' he cried.

There was no one there to advise him, no David to discuss it with. In his desperation he tried to imagine his old pal talking to him: 'Tell the police.'

And he replied out loud, 'No, that would never work, don't be so silly! They'd put me in jail!' It was no use. James knew that there was nobody there.

He couldn't think what to do. The only viable action was inaction. He placed the digestive biscuits in David's hand, which, he now noticed, was trembling and left a pile of sugar lumps beside it. When the boy woke from his coma, he could eat them and go home. Maybe he wouldn't remember what had happened. He hadn't seen him, he didn't think, so he could pretend it was someone else, the little devil, or the other David perhaps? Hurriedly he left again without saying goodbye.

His eyes still streaming, his stomach aching from sobbing, he cycled home. As soon as he pulled his bike up alongside the curb his father rushed down the drive and smacked him hard across the top of his head. He sprawled onto the road, his bike falling on top of him.

'You bloody nuisance,' his father growled. 'I'm late for work now. What have you done?'

James couldn't believe that they knew. How could they have known?

'Why did you do it?'

'I . . .'

'Where is she?'

'She?'

'Whitie.'

James lay where he was on the road, snivelling and baffled, too defeated to even pick himself up. The loose stones from the tarmac were digging into his skin.

'What have you done to her?'

'Nothing. I've not done anything to her.'

His father leant over him menacingly before dragging him

up by his arm.

'Ow, you're hurting!'

Just then Sandra appeared at the end of the road, the dog in her arms.

'Thank Christ!' Ken said, with loud relief. 'If something had happened to that bloody dog you'd have had hell to pay!'

The kitchen door had somehow become unlatched and the dog had gone walk-about, but their wolf-crying boy could never convince them that this was simply an unhappy accident.

James ran to his playroom and turned all his toy animals out onto the carpet. After segregating the pigs, he started stamping over the rest. The wild cats would no longer lie with the lamb, nor would they eat straw. They could all go to hell. But the plastic figures were resilient and would not be easily crushed, so he took a lighter from the kitchen drawer and started to melt and stretch them. The air was fouled by toxic clouds as he dislocated and distended their limbs.

When they were all disfigured beyond recognition, he gathered them up and took them to a patch of earth at the side of the house. It would serve as a mass grave for his animal mutants. He kicked soil over the deformed creatures and ground them into the dry soil, but their grotesque heads and outlandishly twisted necks, tails and limbs stuck out stubbornly. Soon enough he grew weary of his symbolic vengeance and left the creatures half buried. He returned to his room to wreck his microscope and potions – everything he owned which reminded him of the Davids, which was in effect everything that he owned. With his faith lost, his memories infected and his religion destroyed, he would finally desecrate the temple.

The dog barked at the kerfuffle, betraying him to the world of adults. His father had gone to work nursing a martyr's bitterness, so it was his mother who came to see what all the noise was about. She opened the door without knocking and there she froze, on the threshold, neither daring nor caring to enter the bedlam within. The dog stayed by her side, the white witch's familiar.

'You ungrateful little . . .!' She stopped herself. 'We spent good money . . .'

James flashed his eyes up at her, a wolf disturbed while gorging on its kill. This lycanthropic boy looked capable of lunging clean from where he crouched to the throat of his mother.

She continued to address him. 'That's it! We won't be buying you anything else to play with. You can bloody well go without. And you can clear this mess up yourself, because I certainly won't.' She stepped backwards as she spoke, mirrored by her dog, and the door slammed shut. James's frenzy continued unabated until the room was in ruins. Then he lay in the centre of the carnage, panting and spent. With nothing left to break but himself, he decided to do just that. He rose to his feet and ran full force into the wall, splitting open his lip and making his nose rush with blood. Now he would slump down again and wait eagerly to die.

Sandra discovered him an hour or so later and, afraid of the further damage he might inflict on himself or her, she called for the doctor. Not wanting to suffer the shame of taking her son in, she insisted on a house call. In the meantime she put some Dettol in a bowl of hot water and mopped him and the blood up as best she could. James lay lifelessly on the carpet, playing dead. He hoped that if he kept it up for long enough, he might even con Death into thinking he'd already slipped out of this world. Maybe they'd bury him and never know he was only pretending. Pleased that he was not struggling at least, his mother made no attempt to rouse him.

When she left the room James opened his eyes a fraction. He was half expecting his body to be semi-transparent, caught somewhere between this lonely existence and the next. But he was still all there. He adjusted his position slightly so that it was more comfortable to sustain. Then he shut his eyes again and concentrated on the pain in his head, pain as a portal to oblivion. The next thing he was aware of was his mother talking over him like he wasn't there.

This was promising.

'I don't know how he got all those cuts. It looks terrible, like we beat him or something.' Sandra always thought it best to second-guess, pre-emptively uprooting any speculation, but she only ever succeeded in planting suspicion where otherwise it might not have grown.

'No, of course not,' Dr Hazeldene said with as much conviction as he could gather. He knelt down and inspected the cuts and bruises.

James focused all his energy on not giving the game away by flinching.

'How are you finding the anti-depressants I prescribed?'

'Oh, fine,' Sandra told him in her best 1950s housewife voice.

'You were meant to come in for a review, weren't you?'

'Was I? Oh, I must have forgotten. That's not like me . . . I know how much time gets wasted by people not turning up for appointments.' His line of questioning was making Sandra angry. She'd changed her mind about her doctor over the years. Now she wanted to tell him that his hair was sticking up and his jumper needed darning and his trousers were too short, but she didn't. 'There must have been crossed wires, I'll look in my diary and call that girl Sarah at the desk . . .' Implying that if anyone was to blame, it was a lowly receptionist who could be referred to without any call for a surname.

'But have they had any side effects?'

'Oh no! I was thinking about coming off them. I'm fine again now. It was just while I . . .' She couldn't mention her daughter without immediately betraying her true state of mind. She had in fact self-prescribed of late and upped her dose, telling Sarah an overly elaborate lie about losing a box of tablets on a bus.

'Well, you should still make another appointment, so I can keep your records up to date.'

'I will,' she said, sliding straight into, 'Would you like a cup of tea or a slice of cake?'

'No, thanks.'

'I can wrap up a piece for you to take home?' Sandra knew that he wasn't married, and he didn't look like the sort of man who cooked. What sort of example was he setting, a doctor who couldn't look after himself properly? She was tempted to roll out the 'physician, heal thyself' adage.

'Thanks, but I don't have a sweet tooth.'

'That's why you're so thin!' she said triumphantly, like she'd found the cure for cancer.

'Mmm. Has he been behaving erratically again?'

'It was all going really well . . . Too well, I suppose. He was playing out with other kids and eating and going to bed without a row . . .'

'And when did this stop?'

'The other day. He came home in a right state and he's been bad since then.'

'Bad?'

'Badly behaved, won't eat, sleeps too much. I mean, I know that one hour before midnight is worth two after . . . He's so moody . . . Look at all these toys he smashed up. They weren't cheap . . .'

'Volatile and unpredictable mood swings?' The doctor was trying to get her back on track.

'Yes! I said moody!' she snapped crossly, not knowing exactly what *volatile* meant.

'Do you have any idea what brought it on?'

'No.' Sandra had started moving bits of broken toy to one side of the room.

'Nothing has happened that could have triggered a relapse?'

'No.' There were splinters of glass from the microscope

slides and she carefully collected them in her palm. She spent her whole life picking up the pieces, forever saying it was for the last time.

'What about David?'

James suddenly had to split his energy between inertia and acute listening.

'Oh,' his mother said, abandoning the tidying she swore she wouldn't do. 'Yes. The other morning he said that David was gone.'

'Did he?'

'Yes, just like that. He didn't explain, but he said he'd gone. I thought thank God – I mean, he's ten years old!'

'But when he was told . . . or realised that David wasn't real, it must have been quite a shock, especially – '

'Yes, of course.'

'Especially,' he repeated, 'because he believed in him for so long. I imagine it was, well . . . a traumatic revelation. He must be feeling very vulnerable.'

'But it's for his own . . . You can't have an imaginary friend by the time you get to secondary school.'

James could maintain his feigned death no longer.

'He was *not* imaginary.'

'Oh, you're awake, young man,' the doctor said, standing in case the boy decided to do something irregular.

'How is David?' James asked, referring now to David the Second.

'He's fine,' the doctor said, patting his forehead with a falsehood.

When he'd established that James was docile, he asked him to sit on the beanbag where he checked his eyes and did a few tests to make sure he wasn't concussed. Then Sandra escorted him out. He prescribed some mild sedatives for James but suggested that it may be time for him to go and see yet another child psychiatrist. He also said he might send someone round to do a proper check-up. What he really meant was social services, and Sandra felt that she'd failed again.

'And do come in for a review,' he said. 'I'll get Sally at the surgery to call you.'

'Damn!' Sandra thought as she closed the door. Sally, not Sarah. Why hadn't she remembered that? Doreen's daughter was called Sally too. In any case, she'd no intention of going for a review, nor was she going to entertain the idea of consulting another *shrink*. She'd had enough dealings with them now to use this slightly derogatory slang. They'd not helped, not one of them. All they'd done was make her feel like *she* was to blame. James would be fine, once he came to terms with the fact that David had gone the same way as Father Christmas, the Easter Bunny and the Man in the Moon.

Then she remembered the other David, Doreen's son David. It had all but slipped her mind, what with Whitie going missing and James, and then this awful scene. Doreen had called round the night before while James had been asleep, asking if David was there. She'd said that her son had been with the other children for the day without James, but she wanted to know if he'd called round after that.

'The thing is, he's not come home yet,' she'd said, 'and it's well past his dinnertime . . . and it's just not like him.'

Sandra told her that she was sorry, but she hadn't seen him and that James had gone to bed very early. 'He's probably just lost track of time, Doreen. I don't know . . . they do worry us, don't they? Sometimes I wonder why we have kids,' she admitted, with a tired smile. 'I'm sure he'll turn up . . . with some excuse.'

Doreen agreed but didn't look convinced.

'Do you want a cup of tea and some carrot cake?'

'No thanks, Sandra. Mike is going to drive around in the car and I should wait at home. Will you ask James if he's seen him?'

'Yes. If he knows where he is, I'll call you.'

She hadn't asked James and now it wouldn't matter.

David would have gone home long ago. Whitie suddenly barked at her and the memory was tidied away again. 'Oh, it's time for you to have some food, isn't it? Aren't you clever reminding me?'

SEVENTEEN

Dinner was eaten that evening in flinty silence. James was melancholy but amenable. He finished everything on his plate. He put on his pyjamas and sat in the lounge with his parents and together they watched the television like a regular dysfunctional family. Half an hour later his mother gave him a glass of milk with the sedatives in. Half an hour after that he was drooping. As far as her husband was concerned, his family could be doped up to the eyeballs if it meant a modicum of peace. He carried his son upstairs, which was not as easy now that he was ten, and tucked him into his bed.

James moaned a little and his father ran his hand over his curls, nostalgic for a time he'd never had. He headed downstairs and was making the executive decision to swing by the drinks cabinet for a dose of his own anaesthetic to the world when the doorbell rang. The dog barked and Ken cursed, muttering his favourite long-suffering lament, 'No rest for the wicked.'

Whitie continued her barking and above it he heard his wife in a high-pitched voice saying, 'Ken! Don't let anyone in here. I've got my curlers in!'

He opened the front door. There was a silhouette of a man against the glass of the porch. Kenneth didn't have his shoes on, so he gestured at the shadow to come in, hoping to avoid walking on the cold marble floor. But it didn't move, so Ken was obliged to go towards it. He opened the door.

'Hello?'

'Hello. Sorry to bother you.'

Ken clearly didn't remember the man on the threshold. 'It's Mike . . . David's dad.'

For a horrible moment Ken mistook him for the father of the imaginary David. 'God, I must be tired', he thought, and grimaced apologetically, relieved that this man, Mike, could not read his mind.

'Yes. From down the road . . . I remember. Sorry. Erm, come in.'

'No. I won't intrude . . .' Evidently he'd overheard Sandra's command. 'It's about David.'

Again Ken thought of the make-believe boy, then pushed the idea from his head and tried to replace it with a picture of what the real David looked like, but he couldn't find one.

'Yes.'

'He's still missing.'

'David's . . . missing? You said *still* missing? I didn't know . . . You'd better come in . . .' On closer inspection Mike looked terrible, his face drained of colour, but he seemed wired, like a greyhound that had just lost a pointless race chasing a mechanical rabbit.

'Thank you.'

'Come through.'

As he opened the door into the lounge there came the inevitable squawk from his wife. 'Kenneth! I told you not to . . . Hello, Mike, you'll have to excuse me I've got . . .'

'Sandra, David's missing,' Ken cut in.

Suddenly Mike started to cry, and Sandra's compromising hair was no longer a concern. Other people's pain was a welcome distraction. She took up the reins of the situation and Ken was all too ready to relinquish them. Women's tears paralyse men, but the tears of other men petrify them.

'I'll get us both a whiskey,' Kenneth mumbled, unable to

recoil from the room quick enough.

Sandra sat Mike down, applying words like ointment and patting his back till he baby-sicked up his narrative. David, he told her, had been missing since the previous night, and she felt a stab of guilt at her false assurances to Doreen. Mike talked over her silent remorse, explaining that it was especially dangerous for a diabetic as he needed his insulin.

'He'll go into a coma,' Sandra said, so that he knew that she'd picked up a few facts about the illness.

He stopped sobbing. 'No. You see, a diabetic coma is when he's had too much insulin and not enough carbohydrates.'

Sandra did not see.

'He'll become ketoacidotic.' Somehow if he dealt with dry facts for a moment he could keep his tears at bay and his mind clear. 'This is when the body needs insulin. The body produces sugar all the time and a diabetic has no hormones that can break it down.'

Sandra was doing her level best to follow, but he wasn't paying attention to her now in any case.

'What happens is that ketones form in the blood . . . Ketones are crystals.' He spoke with no inflection as though reciting a psalm. 'The symptoms are an unquenchable thirst and when they – ' he was skirting around the word *he* – '*do* drink, the body tries to rid itself of the sugar by vomiting.'

'Oh,' Sandra said, grasping for a glimmer of hope, a flash of gold in the pan, 'so they can get it out?'

Mike looked at her for a second, remembering that she was there. 'No. When the body is sick, it becomes weak, and so it produces more sugar . . . and in a diabetic's case . . . more crystals.'

'Oh,' she said again, only this time more despondently. She was wading about in her shallow word-pool searching for a sentence. 'How long can David . . . survive?'

Mike's eyes filled up and his brain went cloudy again. 'He could be critical already.'

Unable to dwell on this reality, Mike stepped backwards in time to when they'd last seen their son and what they knew about his movements since then. It had been a morning like any other. The family had had breakfast together. David had had his injection. He, Mike, had then gone to work. David had helped his mother give Sally a bath. Then around ten o'clock some children had called round to ask if their son could come out to play. Doreen and he had been pleased that he'd made friends so quickly, as it would make it less frightening for him when he started school. They were overprotective, because of his diabetes, but they wanted him to have as normal a childhood as possible. David and the others had gone off, he said, to some nearby woods. James hadn't been with them – both his wife and the other children had said so. Sandra was greatly relieved to hear this for the second time. After all, James had come home caked in blood, blood that was probably not all his own. Now that she knew for certain it was not the same day, she could disregard the gruesome image.

The children, Mike told her, had been playing a game of hide and seek and David had left for some reason and must have cycled off. The others assumed that he'd gone home. But he never arrived. And he hadn't been seen since. The police were doing everything they could. 'Have they come here yet?'

Sandra shook her head.

'Oh . . . Well I'm sure they will . . . I just have to keep busy, turn over every stone. I can't sit at home, knowing he's . . .' His narrative stopped; he'd arrived back in the present, in a room with a woman he barely knew and the reason he'd come: he wanted Sandra to ask James if he'd heard from David since his disappearance.

'Of course I will, Mike, but I'm sure he doesn't know anything . . . He was at home.' She was the mother impulsively providing an alibi for her child; filled by a desire to cover up before anything could be uncovered.

'I'm sure you're right, but if you'd talk to him, I'd

appreciate it.'

'He's asleep now,' she told him flatly, hoping he'd let the matter drop till the morning. She didn't want to admit that she'd resorted to tranquillising her son like he was a dangerous animal.

'Is he? Look . . . I'd be so grateful if you woke him up . . . just for a minute. It's only that as every hour passes, we're losing hope of finding him.'

This was enough for her. She didn't need to hear the word *alive*. Thoughts of Amy were already swimming in her brain. She would oblige this poor man and send him and his grief away. She had her own misery to keep house for.

Ken returned with the whiskeys. It was his second.

'There you go . . .' He'd forgotten Mike's name.

'I'm just going to have a word with James,' Sandra said, rising stoically, the crown of curlers long forgotten on her head.

Mike rose, whiskey glass in hand, and Sandra thought for a moment that he was going to raise a toast, before realising that he planned to accompany her.

'I think it'd be best if I go on my own. He's asleep,' she explained, 'I don't want to frighten him.'

'Of course,' Mike said, and sat down again heavily. 'If he knows anything at all . . . Anywhere he might be . . .'

Wearily Sandra ascended the stairs, stopping briefly on the half-landing as though battling altitude sickness. When she reached her son's room the first thing that struck her was that her husband had neglected to turn off the bedside light – he was careless with electricity. James was in a deep sleep. She shook him gently and eventually, with the momentum of her body, she managed to rock his eyes open like a doll's. She sat him upright but he wobbled dopily.

'James . . . have you seen David?'

'No,' he slurred.

'When was the last time you saw him?'

'With . . . the pigs.'

'James!' she shook him again and his eyes opened fully on main beam for a second before shutting off again.

'David Fielding. Have you seen David Fielding?'

'David has gone.'

'I know David's gone . . . But your other friend David. His parents don't know where he is. Have you seen him?'

James fought to stay awake. It was important. There was something he wanted to convey, to say, something he needed to tell her, but it slipped through his fingers and caught in an eddy. Then he was swirled away by a current of sleep that he could not fight and Sandra couldn't rouse him again.

Back downstairs she told Mike that it was as she'd expected, James hadn't seen David all that day. She admitted that James was half-asleep, but she promised to press him further, first thing in the morning. Mike finished his whiskey but didn't move.

'Would you like ano – ' was all Ken could get out before his wife intervened.

'You'd better get back to Doreen and try to get some sleep. I'm sure he's fine, you know.' She wasn't sure at all, but it seemed a helpful thing to say and she wanted him to go away now.

The man with his half-broken hope took his cue, said thank you and left. Ken walked him to the door with no words to hand him for comfort. He watched as Mike hunched away, an almost visible hand of pain hooked under the bones of his vertebrae.

When James woke he was groggy and confused. His eyes were open, he was sure, but he still couldn't see. He felt like he was standing a great distance behind his pupils and had to lean forwards in order to peer out of them. Had he dreamed his mother's bedside visitation? David . . . something about David? The last two days had passed like a vivid and ghoulish hallucination. Still in his pyjamas, he made his way leadenfootedly down the stairs. With each step he become more aware of a void inside his body that he did not know how to fill.

'How do you feel today?' his mother asked as he padded into the kitchen.

'Empty,' he told her, the nihilistic philosopher.

'I'll make you some porridge. That'll fill you up.'

'OK.' He had no energy to explain.

Nothing more was said while she boiled the oats in two-thirds water, one-third milk, so that the milk went further. When she felt compelled to speak – as she did by necessity, like a whale spouting water from its blowhole – she talked to Whitie about what she was going to have for lunch.

'What will they do to the person who killed David?' James asked, seemingly out of nowhere, making Sandra's vertebrae lock.

'Don't say that, James. We don't know that he's dead yet.' She'd inadvertently added the *yet*. But he'd said what she herself feared. 'And we don't know that anyone else was involved. He might just have had an accident.' She was no more aware of her word *just*, which had slotted itself into her sentence, casually marginalising manslaughter. In any case, she didn't really believe it was an accident. She expected the worst: a man in a car, armed with sweets and unnatural intentions, a sexually depraved Pied Piper.

'What sort of accident?'

'A car crash,' she said, before she could remember to edit her thoughts. She was still picturing the molester with the car . . . an orange hatchback with flag stickers of different countries on the rear window.

'But he doesn't have a car, he has a bike.'

'Oh, I don't know, James! There's probably some perfectly innocent explanation.'

'Maybe Christian murdered him.'

'Why do you say that? That's a terrible thing to say.'

James shrugged.

'You wouldn't like it if Chris went round spreading rumours like that about you.'

Saying things make them true.

At that moment Christian was telling the police that James had bragged about killing his sister and his grandfather and that Tara had heard him admit he'd set out to hurt Rebecca . . . so it made sense that he'd done something to David too. Tara corroborated this story with an unhealthy enthusiasm. The police noted it all down, but they were sceptical. A child serial killer? They were with Sandra on this: a man with a plan and a car.

The television was full of it. Pictures of David – blond hair, brown eyes, rosy cheeks – splattered on every news channel. Had anyone see him on the day in question? Did anyone know his whereabouts? Anyone with information should come forward. To James it sounded like David the Second was an outlaw with a ransom on his head. There was a tearful plea from David's mother, which was repeated so often it seemed like she was on a loop – motherhood on a monument, clinging tightly to her remaining child. Mike also said a few words, his voice an emotional flat-line. He begged that if anyone had his son or knew where he was, please, please would they take him to a hospital. His boy, he explained, had diabetes. 'He'll be in a critical condition already . . . He needs insulin urgently . . . or . . .' And everyone heard the words he could not say.

James was already convinced that David was dead. Why hadn't he just eaten the sugar or the biscuits? He told himself that the local vampire had come back and drained the rest of his blood away while he slept. But whatever had happened, James had a presentiment that he was probably going to get it in the neck.

'Mum, I'm going out.'

'No, you're not.'

'I am.'

'No, you're not. That's final.'

'Why?'

'The police station rang up. Someone will be calling round today to get a statement.'

'What's a statement?'

'They'll want you to tell them when you last saw David.'

'My David?'

'Yes . . . No . . . David Fielding . . . You saw him the day before...' she prompted.

'The day before what?'

The question was left to hang. Sandra was grating some lemon rind into a cake mix and she shaved off a sliver of knuckle.

'Blood and sand!' she cried. 'Now look what you've made me do!'

He'd done it. It was always him. He couldn't even blame David any more.

'I'm going out,' he said again.

His mother moved him out of her way as she rummaged in the second drawer down for a bandage. 'You'll do as I tell you! There's a madman on the loose,' she spat, as she tried to tear open a plaster wrapper with her blood-free hand. 'I'm not letting you out of my sight till he's caught.'

'You can't stop me.'

It turned out she could stop him. His bike had a chain on it. The doors were locked from the inside and the keys were missing. He prowled the house checking the windows, but none of the downstairs ones opened wide enough and the drop from upstairs was too great, though he considered it several times. And so house arrest removed the option of revisiting the vampire's lair.

That evening he was allowed out, a special pass to attend confirmation class. Normally Sandra dropped James off halfway to the village, letting him walk the rest of the journey. Tonight, however, he'd have the luxury of door-to-door delivery. Confirmation class was the only thing he – religiously –

attended. Normally, his two Davids and Christian accompanied him. And Christian invariably entertained them by drawing pictures of the vicar with ladies' underwear on . . . or not, depending on how risqué he was feeling.

Sandra attended church most Sundays, but she was not loyal to any particular diocese and would shift allegiance without any qualms. She didn't like her sermons served up with too much religion, preferring the services to lie somewhere between stand-up comedy and Delia Smith philosophy. On one occasion she'd informed her husband that they'd be taking their prayers – and their collection money – to a neighbouring parish, as their new vicar was insisting that the congregation shake hands with each other. One may be obliged to love thy neighbour but it was taking things too far if you had to touch them as well. Hers was a lip-sync Christianity. Church was a place strictly for hats and hymns.

'But what happened to Mr Mackenzie?' Kenneth had asked.

'He ran off – ' she paused and added in an in-breath, without any trace of humour, 'with another man.'

'I *thought* he was a pansy.'

'He has a wife and children in the vicarage,' Sandra said, still in hushed tones.

'Not for much longer . . . They'll be turfed out.'

'He will be missed,' she said, all childlike solemnity.

'He's not dead,' Kenneth reminded her.

'No.' She shook her head sadly as though death was indeed a better fate than homosexuality.

'Anyway, you know I don't believe in God.' Ken had a healthy scepticism for religion. In fact, he had healthy scepticism for anything enigmatic.

'What's that got to do with it?'

'It's funny, I thought it had.' He stopped his mouth with desert. He knew better than to go any further down that line of reasoning, when reason was not even present at the proceedings. 'I go quite enough already' – a teenage masticated mumble.

'Not much you don't. I have to drag you there for the special occasions.' The special occasions were the Birth and the Death of Christ, Harvest Festival and Mothering Sunday. 'You've got lemon meringue pie on your jumper.' And the conversation was closed for business.

James and David the First had believed in ghosts and werewolves and God and vampires and Jesus and the devil. They were all cut from the same cloth of their combined imaginations. And James would hang upon the vicar's every word, thinking that he had a direct link to God. He'd been determined to collect all the crumbs of divine knowledge that were inadvertently dropped from the altar table.

This particular evening the class took on an even greater significance. Now he'd lost his faith he craved it even more. This was his last chance to find answers and restore his conviction. He was to be confirmed that coming Sunday.

Christian was there but he didn't say hello or come to talk to him. Instead he sat across the aisle whispering and passing notes to the other boys and girls. Occasionally, James caught them casting furtive glances in his direction, but when he met their eyes, they looked away with gleeful fear. James had no idea why they were behaving like this, but he rather liked it.

The vicar said nothing of significance that evening. He delivered up no truths, no divine messages, but he did mention David the Second and asked them all to close their eyes and join him in prayer. He handed out a few choice words, asking for David to be delivered safely back to his parents. And in that instant James understood that the vicar could teach him nothing, that he was a fraud, a con artist, a charlatan. If he were a real vicar, God would have told him that David was dead. James opened his eyes and let them play in the cusps and foils of the stained glass. Then he stared up at the ornate gothic roofcorbels and the series of vacuous saintly faces that looked down on him. There was nothing for him here – no answers, no salvation.

He stood up to leave before the prayer was over.

'James?' the vicar said, stopping mid-sentence.

'Yes?' James was expectant, hopeful. Maybe the man did know the truth and simply hadn't wanted to frighten the other children.

'Have you practised the reading for church on Sunday?'

'Oh. Yes,' James replied, impassively, and left without a goodbye or a glance towards Christian and his flock.

After class it was the children's habit – under James's auspices – to linger in the churchyard playing among the headstones. But tonight there was no time for heathenism. James could already make out the shape of his father at the lichgate, like Charon by the River Styx, waiting to ferry him home to Hades. They walked through the village square and James came to a standstill before the wooden stocks that crouched submissively beneath the proud memorial cross.

'What do you have to do to get put in there?' James asked. He'd passed the stocks on numerous occasions. He'd even slipped his narrow child's wrists into the holes, but he'd never before imagined a person properly restrained there – a criminal, a thief, a murderer.

'Something very wrong.' His father was in no mood for questions and answers and continued walking in an attempt to fend them off.

For a moment James remained staring at the wormholes on the weighty wooden slats. He could see himself there with people jeering, pelting him with rotten eggs, tomatoes . . . and stones. He peered up towards the church, which sat smugly on its glacial mound, and saw heading his way a children's crusade led by Christian. It seemed to him that they were advancing with purpose, the angry mob with vengeance as an alibi. He ran to catch up with his father and in his mind's eye they surged after him, whispering 'Dead meat', cajoled by collective encouragement. He put his hand in his father's and the spell was broken; the approaching throng became a flock of God-fearing children once more, who peacefully dispersed – thwarted but innocent – to their respective homes.

Another sleepless night was fretted away. Another housebound day passed. The police hadn't kept their word. They'd not come round. Sandra wasn't about to point out their discourtesy. She didn't relish the prospect of a house call. James was getting under his mother's feet, another first. He was pensive, polite and more personable than he'd ever been. Without the imaginary David there was no one else for him to talk to, no one to gang up with, no one to whisper and giggle with in corners. The household was made up of just a little boy, a mother and father, a cat and a dog. Only now that his mother had his full attention, something she'd always craved, she wasn't sure she wanted it. She didn't know what to do with it. Her son had so many questions and she had so few answers. At intervals, she had to ask him to play in his room for a while, so that she could gather up her scattered thoughts like a deck of cards and try to regroup them in their proper numerical order.

'Why do people die?'

'It's nature.'

'But why does *nature* do it?'

'To make room for new people.'

'Because the new ones are better?'

'No . . . Not better . . .'

'Will you die before me?'

'Oh, well, yes . . . of course.'

'Who will look after me then?'

'James, you're too old to be asking me questions like this. When I die, you'll be grown up.'

'But how can you be sure?'

The following day David Fielding was found dead.

No one was surprised. But only James wasn't surprised about where he was discovered: in the woody palm of nature. David had been in the lion's den and there he had lain, mauled and torn, and there he had, with little advances and retreats, fallen into the maws of death.

The television stations showed footage of the perimeter of T Woods. It looked like a round brown fruitcake tied in red and white police-tape and it had feverish blue-uniformed flies crawling all over it. It was strange for James to see such a familiar view in his parent's lounge.

When Sandra heard the news on the kitchen radio she rushed to the playroom – the ever-willing bearer of bad news – wanting to be the first to break it to her son. He was not there. She found him in the living room, sitting cross-legged in front of the TV. His mother immediately fell into a half-kneeling embrace, pressing his head awkwardly into her shoulder.

'Thank God you weren't there,' she said, releasing a burst vein of maternal tears.

'Why?'

'It could have been you,' she cried, and experienced a fresh surge of guilt as she empathised with – and condemned – her projected self for having lost another child. 'Poor Davy,' she murmured, having quickly picked up and adopted the name the tabloids were using. David was a boy, so the diminutive, 'Davy', would be his press persona.

'David is OK.'

'No, James, he's been killed,' Sandra explained. Her son couldn't have comprehended the magnitude or the irrevocability of the situation.

'Then he'll not feel anything, will he? Unless, he is a vampire . . . then he's not really dead.' He was crying as well. He had a lot to cry for.

'Oh, James!' she wailed, both envying and pitying the ignorance of innocence.

'Shall I go round and tell Mr and Mrs Fielding that I am sorry?'

'That's a lovely idea,' she said. 'But I don't think they'll want visitors just yet' – meaning that she couldn't face going herself. 'I'll get them a nice card and you can write something in that.' A nice card . . . Was there a card, she wondered, that catered for a family that had had one of its offspring murdered?

'Can I go to the woods and see David?'

'James!' she said, ejecting him from her arms. 'I don't think you understand. He's dead.'

'Yes. I know. I want to see him.'

'Well, you can't,' she said, shoving mental snapshots of the lifeless boy from her brain. 'I'm not letting you out of my sight till the man who hurt him is found.'

The next morning James was to be confirmed into the church. He dressed himself in the outfit that he'd worn for his grandfather's funeral. Sandra had taken down the hems of the trousers, leaving two almost imperceptible creases. His hair was slicked to one side to cover his scar and if he didn't smile and expose the remaining gaps then he looked like a proper little prince.

His parents had invited selected friends and family over for a sherry before the service, but the prevailing mood was unsurprisingly rather restrained. Talk of the murder was rising in everyone's gullets, but they struggled to keep it down for Sandra's sake, afraid to spoil her day. They went through the motions, just as they would later when they took communion. They presented James with gifts: a small white leather Bible with silver gilded pages; a cruciform silver-plated bookmark; a silver St Christopher pendant and chain – a veritable symphony in silver; plus a smattering of book tokens. He looked uncomfortable and it was not just the scratchy wool of his trousers next to his skin. But his parents put it down to nerves about delivering the reading and made him rehearse again and again in the car on the way to the service.

In the church Sandra and Kenneth sat with their guests among the other proud parents. James was beside his fellow novices: the scrubbed, slick-downed boys and the glowing girls in their starched, overly pretty white frocks. Children dressed up as children, children as parodies of adults. James sucked on his St Christopher pendant and ignored his companions in Christ. When his time came, he rose and walked solemnly to the eagle lectern, stood on the prayer stool and unfolded his piece of paper.

'Defend, O Lord, this thy child with thy heavenly grace,
that he may continue thine for ever;
and daily increase in thy holy Spirit,
more and more,
until he come into thy everlasting Kingdom.'

He sounded like he meant it.

He read beautifully. His voice rang out clear and pure, soothing all who heard him, turning the rough walls smooth. The words tripped off his tongue without a slip or hesitation. And Sandra's spine rose an extra inch towards heaven.

'Wonderful annunciation,' she whispered to her friend. And under church circumstances her mistake was excusable.

The service had many a parent in tears, as did the potent address that the vicar had penned about David. He talked about how the boy should have been there, among the other children, becoming, with them, a full member of the church. He talked of the loss, of the evil in the world, and quoted St Matthew, Chapter 18, verse 5: 'Whoso shall receive one such little child in my name receiveth me. But whoso shall offend one of these little ones, which believe in me, it were better for him that a millstone were hanged about his neck and that he were drowned in the depth of the sea.'

As he finished speaking two bovine policemen were

approaching the church's threshold. They dared not enter the sanctified grounds and as the puzzled parents and children trooped out, they lowered their gaze awkwardly. The vicar sailed directly over to them and like lowly cattle the men dropped their heads and explained that they regretted their intrusion but they'd come to take James Gardner to the station. The news rushed through the throng like a wind through a wheat-field. James and his parents exited the church to an expectant hush. They didn't know what was happening. All eyes were on them and there was not a smile in sight. Had they forgotten to put their offertory money in the smooth wooden bowl?

One of the two-by-two policemen broke the tableau to tentatively explain their presence and their intention. Unlike James, he was not a natural public speaker. When he'd finally stopped his lowing and his message had sunk in, Sandra linked her hands in front of James's heart. She hoped that if she froze, the moment would go on without her and her only, lonely child. It did not.

Ken had to intervene. He extricated his son from Sandra's clutches. If his wife was not embarrassed by the situation, he certainly was. He wanted to get away from this scrutiny and as quickly as possible.

'There's been some mistake!' Sandra spoke suddenly, a statue of the Virgin Mother brought to life.

The policemen were leading her child away, Christ with the soldiers. The onlookers crammed round, craning to get a glimpse of the boy and gauge his reaction, but James looked to the ground in silent resignation and watched the tombstone flags retreat beneath his feet. His father held back like St Paul and Christian smiled at his sister.

EIGHTEEN

Sandra accompanied James in the car, all the time telling him – but really herself and the police escorts – that it was all a mix-up and that as soon as they got to the station, which was just around the corner, it would be sorted out.

'We just want to ask him some questions to help with the ongoing investigation,' one of the interchangeable cow-like men said from the front seat.

'Will you put on the siren?' James asked.

They obliged his childish fancy.

'Matthew's got one of these on his bike,' he told them, as though they should know who Matthew was. In fact they did. They'd already had him in for questioning. Matthew was one of the reasons that James was with them now. 'This siren's much better, though.'

'Turn it off. Please!' Sandra spoke louder than was necessary to emphasise how deafening it was. People were looking and she didn't want anyone to peer in and recognise her.

The car came to a standstill at a pedestrian crossing. It seemed to Sandra that they were doing it on purpose, deliberately prolonging her agony. She screened her eyes. James's hair, she noticed, was starting to spring up around his crown. She licked her fingers and smoothed it down, a cat preening its kitten.

'Where is Dad?'

His mother had all but forgotten about her husband. 'Oh, he'll have taken the car home and seen off your relatives,' she told him distractedly. 'The parking facilities in the village are terrible. You should do something about that!' she said, to the policemen.

They didn't respond.

'Did you hear me?' There was no possible way that they hadn't: she was almost shouting.

'Yes, Mrs Gardner, but that's a council matter, it's not in our jurisdiction.'

She resented this policeman, a young one at that, fobbing her off with big words like *jurisdiction*.

'Well, it's about time it was, rather than spending your time harassing children!'

When they arrived at the station Sandra filled in some forms.

'We need to take your fingerprints,' the desk sergeant told James.

'For good?' James asked.

He laughed. 'No, no . . . just a copy of them . . . you can keep the real things.'

They also took a blood sample. This was for keeps.

'Just a formality,' they assured Sandra. The other boys and girls they'd interviewed had received the same treatment. She was relieved that other children had been questioned. It made *her* feel less like a victim.

They were shown into a room and offered tea.

'No, thank you, we're supposed to be having tea at the church hall.' Sandra was prepared to cut off her nose to spite her flushed face. She could have murdered a cup of crisis tea. 'Couldn't this have waited till this afternoon?'

'May I remind you that a boy has been killed, Mrs Gardner?'

'Well, a couple of hours really aren't going to make any difference,' she said, regretting it immediately. 'My husband and

I are close friends with the ex-chief inspector, you know,' she added.

'It's not very nicely decorated in here, is it?' James said.

'No. It isn't supposed to be.'

'Why not?'

'Because people aren't supposed to enjoy being here,' Sandra told him, ironing the creases out of her skirt with her hand.

'That is silly,' he said, walking around the perimeter of the featureless room. 'The police have to be here all the time. It should be nice for them, shouldn't it? Also, the bad people would feel more at home . . . if there was a picture or a plant. They might accidentally say things that they wanted to keep a secret.'

A little while later one of the policemen from the car and another man entered the room. The first man was young and a little bulky, with large freckles across his nose. The second was tall and wiry like an old wolfhound. His greying hair looked like it was making a bid to escape from his body, reaching out from his head, both ears and nostrils. The blood vessels on his nose were visible and purple and he had pores that looked large enough for James to put his fingers in.

'Hello. I'm sorry to have kept you waiting and to drag you away from an occasion like that. I'm Detective Inspector Brian Richards and this is Detective Constable Andrew Chapman, who I believe you've already met.'

Sandra didn't say anything but her silence was verbose.

James smiled his most accommodating smile.

The DI advised them that he was going to record the interview and that he was just going to ask some informal questions but they were entitled to have a lawyer present if they so wished.

Sandra pooh-poohed the idea. A lawyer, to her mind, would be tantamount to the admission of guilt.

The detective asked James his name and address and what

school he attended, and James told him without hesitation, like he wanted to please the man. The policeman then moved on to likes and dislikes, trying to establish some camaraderie – all boys together.

'Do you like sport?'

'No. Not really.'

'Not even football?' This was going to be more difficult than he thought. Surely all boys liked football.

'No. My dad likes it though,' he offered as compensation.

'So what hobbies do you have?'

'Answering back and giving cheek.'

'Is that a joke?'

'No, that's what Mum says my favourite hobbies are.'

'I see.'

Sandra looked like she was going to explain or intervene, so the DI made it very clear that he wanted her to keep out of the proceedings. Part of her was grateful. She didn't want her voice to be recorded. For one thing, she never liked how it sounded, all sharp and nasal, not her voice at all. And, if she didn't have to speak, then on some level she wasn't involved.

'So, what do you like to play with?'

'My zoo.'

The DI thought that the boy was too old for such a pastime, but he wasn't about to say so. Softly, softly, catchee … 'You like animals then?'

'Some of them.'

'Do you like playing out?'

'I used to.'

'Why don't you any more?'

'I am not allowed to any more until the killer-man is caught, and I don't want to now anyway because David is gone.'

'David Fielding.'

'No.' James looked at him as though he were a bit dense. 'My David.'

At this point Sandra was obliged to interject to explain

that he used to have an imaginary friend called David who he didn't have any more.

'And when did your David leave?'

'Before the other one. Is he here?'

'Who?'

'David.'

'No, he's at the hospital.'

'Is he? Can I see him? What's the matter with him?'

Realising they were at cross purposes, the DI suggested that to minimise further confusion about the Davids they would refer to them from now on as David and David F.

James agreed that this was probably for the best.

'Do you know why you're here?'

'To help.'

'Good. Have you been taught about God?'

'Oh yes.' James knew all about God.

'Do you believe in God?'

'I have been confirmed . . . today, and I gave a reading in church without making a mistake.' James had read about the witch trials and how the accused women were forced to recite the Lord's Prayer. Any slip they made betrayed their guilt.

'That's good. And the Bible talks about truth.'

'Does it?'

'Yes. And you know what the truth is?'

'Yes.'

'We want *you* to tell the truth to us. Do you understand?'

'Yes, but first can I see what it says in the Bible about truth?'

'Not just now.' James had grasped from an early age that this meant no.

'Will you promise to tell us the truth?'

'Not just now.' James smiled, indicating that this was a joke, but the DI understood that he was illustrating just how far he was prepared to play along.

'I'm going to show you something,' the detective told

him. 'I am showing James a plastic gun,' he said, for the benefit of the tape. 'Is this your gun?'

James shrugged.

'James is shrugging. So you don't know if it's your gun?'

'No . . . Or yes?'

'*I* don't know, you tell me. Which do you mean?'

'I mean yes, I don't know if it's my gun, and no, I don't know if it's my gun. You see, I'm trying not to lie, Brian. You asked me to tell the truth.'

The veins on the DI's nose were throbbing with blood. This kid had the audacity to address him by his first name.

'Christian Arnold and Tara Arnold and your other friends said that it was.'

'They are not my friends.'

'No?'

He reminded James of an angry bison, with its nostrils flaring. 'You're ugly when you are cross,' James advised him coolly.

The DI ignored this statement, flashing his eyes at the cassette player as though he wanted to take his anger out on that. He could almost hear the laughter of his officers in the locker room joking about how a child had got the better of him.

'Friends or not, they said it was your gun.'

'It looks like my gun, but the people who made it probably made more than one, don't you think? So it could be someone else's, couldn't it?'

'Yes, my lad, it could.' He could see that he had a clever one here. 'Tell me, have you still got your gun?'

'Not on me. Like I told you, I was getting confirmed. I wouldn't take a gun to church.'

'Where is it then?'

'I think I must have lost it.'

'Then this might be it?'

'It might be, but I think Christian or Tara might have my gun.'

'Why do you say that?'

'Because we shared our dangerous things. I think that Christian had it last. I had the catapult.'

'I see . . . He said the gun had been put back in your bag.'

'I see . . . But I think I've lost my bag as well as my gun.'

The DI felt like he was being patronised.

'Do you know why the gun is important?'

'Did Christian kill David with it?'

'No. You can't kill someone with a toy gun.'

'I didn't think you could. So how can it be important?'

'Because it was found with David F's body.'

'Why is it in a plastic bag?' James asked, ignoring the mention of the body.

'So that it doesn't get any new fingerprints on it. That's why we took your fingerprints – to see if they match the ones on the gun.'

For the first time James cast a glance at his mother. 'Well, of course my fingerprints will be on it, if it is my gun.'

Sandra nodded her agreement.

'Perhaps,' the detective said, pausing to pretend he was still working things through in his mind, 'but if Christian had it last, then his prints will be on it.'

'Can you tell the order that people put their prints on things? And if I held it most, if it is my gun, then there would be more of mine, wouldn't there?' This was the first obvious sign of anxiety he showed, unless he was simply wrestling with a new concept. 'Will I have gun prints on my hand?'

'No, you won't have prints on your hand, but the specialists will be able to get a lot of information from the gun.'

'Then you had better let them have it, hadn't you?'

'Yes. I will.'

'Why do you wear black?'

'What?'

'Why do you wear – '

'It's our uniform.'

'Is that because you see a lot of dead people? Are you in mourning?'

'No. It's just so – '

'What do you wear underneath?'

'James!' Sandra cut into the exchange.

He turned to her. 'Will you buy me a new gun . . . if that one's not mine?'

She didn't know whether it was seemly to say yes or no, under the circumstances, so she frowned and gestured his attention back to the detective.

'I am going home now,' James declared, standing.

'You can't go home yet.'

'I'm going to see if I can find my gun.' He tried the door but couldn't open it.

'But you said that you'd lost it, James.'

'Yes, but maybe I lost it at home. Will you open the door please, Brian?'

'You can't go home yet,' the DI said again, not rising from his chair. 'I've some more questions I want to ask you.'

James saw that he was momentarily trounced and sat back down. 'OK, but please be quick, I want to change out of these trousers, they itch my legs.' And to illustrate this he suspended himself out of the chair seat by his arms so that his legs were no longer touching the plastic or each other.

'Can you tell me what you were doing last Wednesday?'

'No.' James was concentrating on his slender calves, which he was trying to scissor like a ballet dancer.

'I want you to think very hard.'

James sprang onto his feet again. The strain in his arms was too great. 'I can't remember.' He sounded tired, and impatient. 'Can you remember where you were?'

'Yes. I can.'

'Where?'

'I'm asking you the questions.'

'You can't remember, can you?'

'Yes, I can.' The DI was sounding like a petulant child himself. 'I was here, at the station.'

'Yes, but you're here all year. I'm a boy and I am on my school holidays. I do different things every day.'

This was hard to refute.

'Will you please sit in your chair?'

'I can't, my trousers are killing me!'

'You chose them!' his mother snapped.

'I think we should bring the interview to a close for today,' the DI said, accepting defeat. As he talked, he tried to inject some of his hallmark measured authority back into his voice. 'We'll send the gun and James's fingerprints in for tests. If you could come back tomorrow afternoon and maybe put him in some more comfortable trousers?'

Sandra felt reprimanded.

'DC Chapman will drive you home, and I'll send a car round to collect you as well.'

'No. There's no need. Myself or his dad will bring him in and we'll walk home.' Now that the interview was concluded for the day, Sandra was all crisp civility again. 'I need some fresh air.' She couldn't bear the idea of a police car pulling up outside their house.

'Very well. Let's say two o'clock.'

'I do know Mr Dowden, the ex-chief inspector for the whole area. He's a close family friend.'

'Oh, Jeremy, yes. Send him my best.' Curtly, he showed them out.

The dimly lit station had conned Sandra into thinking it would be dark outside, allowing them to slip away unnoticed into the shadows, but it was broad daylight. A leonine sun beamed down on them, highlighting Sandra's blushes and forcing her unaccustomed eyes to narrow. She was holding James's elbow aloft, offsetting his balance, and he kept colliding into her.

'Pick your feet up!'

Her son didn't reply. He was turning puce. His primary

concern was his trousers. He wanted to take them off there and then and throw them onto the hot tarmac.

As soon as she spotted a telephone box, Sandra ushered him inside, pressing him against the cold metal of the machine as she squeezed herself in after him. The door slowly swung to and the last breath of fresh air was sucked out. They stood enveloped in the smell of stale beer and urine that was so thick they could almost taste it. James held his nose and pushed at her to let him out. Sandra started crying now that she was safely out of the public eye. She called her husband and instructed him to pick them up. She had no intention of stepping outside the booth until the car was at the pavement. She was using the phonebook ledge to support her sobbing body, but in order to keep up some semblance of normality she still clutched the receiver to her ear.

When Kenneth drove up she made a dash for the car door. James took his time to climb into the back seat. Sandra wiped at her puffy eyes and scolded her husband for abandoning her to such a humiliating situation. He knew better than to argue. Instead he tried to establish what it was the police had wanted from James, but from what he could gather it was all about his wife – *her* shame, *her* anger, *her* pain. Their son was almost incidental.

'They took my fingerprints and some of my blood,' James informed him from the back of the car. 'They said that it wouldn't hurt, but it did . . . I have to go back tomorrow when they have done tests.'

'And you can take him. I'm not going through that again,' Sandra told her husband, adding, 'I bet you haven't fed the dog!'

Again the family ate their evening meal like mutes, and again they moved to the safety of the living room, where they could bury their thoughts under the security blanket of canned laughter. James took himself off to bed at nine with a cursory nod. Afraid of his dreams, he sat upright with the light on and read and read until it was almost morning. His mother and father went to bed at different times so that they didn't have to exchange words as they carried out their ablutions. When Ken climbed into bed, Sandra feigned sleep and for once she was pleased to hear the muffled hum of the radio beside her. They could not bring themselves to think about their son's involvement. They would rely on the police do that for them.

Under Sandra's instructions, father and son were fifteen minutes early. She wanted them to make a good impression. In the reception they met Christian, Tara and their father, Geoff. They were just leaving. The two men said hello and exchanged awkward euphemisms about how awful the whole thing was. James and the two siblings were in a silent stand-off. Tara was the first to speak.

'You horrible murderer!' she said, relishing each syllable as she bit into it.

In a flash James had his hand around her throat and, for the first time, Christian stepped in to her aid. Bravery is easily mastered in a police station. Within seconds other hands came in to assist him, older, stronger, official hands, and James was prized off the child betrayers and hurriedly bundled into the room from the day before. Kenneth lingered to make apologies but nothing was really going to suffice and Geoff left, shaking his head, trying to stroke away his son's agitation and his daughter's distress.

When the DI entered the room a different police officer accompanied him, a woman. His tack was different from their previous encounter. He wasn't a pal today. He was a professional poker-player. But you can't kid a kid. He introduced himself and the WPC to Kenneth, but not to his son.

'Hello, I am James,' he said, extending his hand and a smile to the woman, before flicking a reproachful glance to the ill-mannered detective.

'Hello, I'm Jenny,' she said, and her eyes caught the sparkle in his like a magpie.

The tape was turned on.

'So, James, how are we today? Did you sleep well last night?'

James physically winced at the man's tone, a honeyed purr that sank into the pores of his skin, making him feel queasy.

'I slept like a baby.' Other people's words to keep the man at arm's length, and he wasn't lying. He was thinking of his sister Amy and she, as though to make the most of her short life, had barely slept at all.

'You look tired,' he said with oily sympathy.

'You look old.'

'That's not very funny.'

James was gauging Jenny's reaction and her eyes told him that it was.

The DI had planned to explain how he'd now gathered statements from the other children and that once Christian had pointed the Judas finger, the others had been all too happy to follow suit, tripping over themselves in their eagerness to tell tales. He was going to lay all these accusations out in front of James like a stallholder would his wares. But this insolent boy needed a short, sharp shock to snap him out of his complacency. The kid gloves were coming off.

'Did you kill your sister?' he asked, a fork of lightning thrown through a cloudless sky.

James looked stunned.

'And your grandfather? I've been told you killed your grandfather too. What do you say to that?'

Ken tried to laugh at the ludicrousness of the proposition, but it caught in his throat as the slab of meat had caught in his father's and he coughed instead.

'I couldn't do that, could I? That's silly. They were my pretend family . . . Why would I . . .?'

The man's eyes had gone cold, but his mouth was open, encouraging the boy to keep his own tongue wagging, letting words tumble out, one after another. James could almost hear the sound those teeth would make when they snapped shut on the sentence they wanted, were waiting for. He was not inclined to oblige the teeth or their owner, so he stopped his justifications abruptly by sucking in his lips. Slowly the DI's jaw closed too, deprived of a meal.

'Pretend family?' Jenny said, quite by mistake. It was not her place to comment.

'Yes,' James explained, 'I am an adopted boy. I have a pretend family and a real one. I've never met my real family, except David. He was my real family. I mean David the First, not David F. Do you see?'

Jenny nodded, though she didn't see at all. Then she turned to the DI apologetically for derailing his line of questioning.

James implicitly understood the situation and immediately righted the train for her benefit.

'Who told you that?' James enquired steadily. 'Who said that I hurt my family?'

'Who do you think?'

'David?' James wanted to appear collected. He hid his trembling hands under his T-shirt in the sockets of his armpits and suppressed an urge to make Paul's farting noise.

'No.'

'A ghost?' He looked at Jenny. He could trust her. She would tell him. A slight shake of her head.

The DI caught the movement like a frog a fly, and frowned before admitting, 'No, a real person.'

James visibly relaxed. 'Oh! Tara.'

'Yes, and one or two others. They said you bragged about it.'

'Yes.' James was composed again now. He pointed his toes and tilted his head to one side while inspecting his gym pumps.

'Why did you do that?'

'Why did I do what?' He curled up his toes into a question

mark.

'Why did you tell them that?'

'You *said* why. I was bragging.'

'Is it true?'

'Of course not. It was a brag! Everyone knows that brags are not true. Durr!' he said, sticking his tongue under his bottom lip. He snatched a quick coy glance up at the WPC to make sure that she was paying attention. She was.

'Then why did you say it?'

'I don't know, do I? I was bored. It was something to say.'

'Something to say?! That you'd killed people?'

'Yes. I wanted to frighten her.' A grain of truth had slipped out, like salt, and another followed. 'They would have picked on me, if I'd not scared them . . . sometimes.' Then he checked the flow. 'She is such a spoilsport. She's as stuck up as her nose!' He pushed up the tip of his own to illustrate.

Jenny looked down at her lap and James gained confidence. She agreed with him, he was certain.

'Why do you believe Tara and not me? Is she your girlfriend?' and he broke into loud, abrasive laughter, freeing into the room all the butterflies that had been floundering in his stomach.

'James!' Ken shouted. 'That's enough!' He wanted this man to know that he disciplined his son.

'It's OK, Mr Gardner,' the DI said, raising his hairy wide hand. Then, in a quieter tone he added, 'Let him laugh now, if he wants to,' and his words cracked ominously like a glacier.

James and his butterflies settled. He positioned himself cross-legged on the chair and gently clapped the soles of his shoes against each other like soft cymbals.

'So what do you think made them die?'

'Maybe it was David,' he replied casually, without looking up.

'David Fielding killed them?'

'No. If I meant him, I would have said David F, wouldn't I?'

'So you mean your David.'

'Yes!'

'And why would he do that?'

'Because he made things happen.' He glanced up from his pumps and levelled his eyes at the detective.

Was he making a threat? the detective wondered. 'What things?'

'Bad things.' James's voice crackled like he was trying to tune himself into a different frequency.

'Like what?'

James shrugged.

'What sort of things?'

'I would like . . . to go to use the toilet,' James said languidly, a holidaymaker suggesting a stroll along the beach.

They took a break. They were obliged to let James go to the toilet and the DI wanted a cigarette.

In the next interview session no more headway was made. James continued to avoid answering anything directly. He turned questions back on his questioner, making the interviewer the interviewee, until the card-shark was all out of bluff. In the end they had to let him go, on the condition that his parents were to bring him back the next day, and the next, until he started to co-operate.

NINETEEN

It was Sandra's turn to accompany James to the station so that her husband could go back to work. Their son was uncomplaining. He was almost looking forward to playing more word games. On the way there he talked about how pretty Jenny was and speculated that when she let her hair down it was long and golden. He asked if he could take her some flowers, but his mother said no, the police didn't like flowers, which struck James as rather sad.

Jenny was not present at the interview, however, which dampened the boy's spirits immediately.

'Where is she?'

'Who?'

'Jenny.'

'She isn't here.'

'I can see that.'

'She asked to do something else today,' the DI lied. In fact, he'd requested PC Chapman instead, saying that Jenny's presence had been too distracting.

James was hurt, but he maintained his poise. 'Hello, Andrew,' he said, making the man's freckles crease into a smile. He was touched that the boy had remembered his name.

'Hello.'

'Today I want to get to the bottom of this gang of yours.'

'I don't have a gang.'

'I've been told that you were the gang leader.'

'These walls need painting.'

'Who was in the gang?'

'Green.'

'What?'

'Green. I have some sunglasses and they are green. The man in the shop said that it soothes the eyes.' He liked the word soothe. 'You should paint the walls green.'

'James, will you just answer the man? I have to get some shopping done today,' his mother said, wanting to draw a line through 'police interrogation' on her internal tick-list.

'Paul, Rebecca the Second, David the First, David F, me, Matthew, Graham and Christian.' He discarded the names like used tissues. 'Christian' was the only word that was over-articulated.

'Not Tara?'

'No way!'

'Who's Rebecca the Second?'

'Paul's sister.'

'Who's the first Rebecca then?'

'The one . . . the other one.'

'Rebecca Clove?'

'I don't know her surname, only her Christian name. Have you found out if it's my gun yet?'

'No. What did you call your gang?'

'We called our gang the Little Devils.'

Graham had, in his interview, quickly handed over the honour of naming the gang to James. It was what the others had said and it seemed that it was what the detective had wanted him to say, so he'd agreed. The press would latch onto this. Out of all the hoops they'd throw at James's head – beast, bad-seed, fiend, freak – The Little Devil was the prize-winner, the one that would land and hang around his neck. It made sense. He'd chosen it – the self-confessed Little Devil. What could be more deliciously ironic?

'Tara wasn't allowed to be in the Little Devils because she wouldn't let you cut her. Isn't that right?'

'I don't know what you mean.'

'She wouldn't be your blood brother.'

'Sister. And I didn't want her to be. She ruins everything.'

'Did you make cuts on the other children with a knife, James?'

'A Swiss Army knife.' He was accurate about details. 'They wanted me to.'

'Is that what they said?'

'Yes.'

'Well, that's not what they told me.'

'Then that makes them liars.'

'All of them?'

'Yes.' James dipped between one wave of thought and the next like a swallow. 'When will you know if it's my gun?'

'We should know later on today.'

'Good. I would like it back if it is mine.'

'You won't be allowed to have it back, it'll be needed as evidence in court.' This was the first time the DI had mentioned the reality of a court case.

'Will I be allowed to go to court?'

'That depends.'

'On what?'

'On whether you are called on as a witness . . . or if you're accused.'

'Accused of what?'

'Of murder.'

'Just a minute,' Sandra said, looking from the DI to the DC. 'Are you saying that he's a suspect?'

'We're not ruling anything out.'

'It is OK, Mum,' James said, roles reversing on the turn of a coin. 'Don't get upset. He is only trying to frighten me.'

'No. I'm trying to find out the truth, remember?'

Sandra fished for a tissue in her handbag. She needed to

add them to her list: tissues. If she kept her thoughts mundane then she wouldn't become unhinged. 'Tissues and some mints,' she said, out loud. 'Sorry. I need to buy some.'

'I can't tell you what happened if I wasn't there though, can I? That would be lying.' James had switched direction again. 'Did Rebecca the Second say that I made her be cut too?'

'They all did. Why?'

This wasn't true. Rebecca the Second had freely admitted that she'd let James do it, but the DI's angle was stronger if the boy believed they were all against him.

'I just wondered.'

'They also said that you branded them.'

'What does branded mean?'

'Put marks on them . . . in the shape of the letter "d".'

'Like in biro? A tattoo?'

'No, with something sharp, like a knife.'

'Why would I do that?'

'I don't know.'

'If I was going to brand them I would brand them with a "j" ... wouldn't I?'

Brian intended to leave this question unanswered, swinging in the air like a lantern.

'Let's start with the day before David F went missing. Can you remember what you were doing?'

'No. Why would I hurt David F? I was his only blood brother. I bet Christian didn't tell you that. None of them would touch his blood because they said he had the lurgy. Did he tell you that?'

'Can you answer my question?

'Can you answer mine first?'

The detective felt an urge to clout the boy, but he put a lid on his simmering blood and continued, 'Let me remind you. You were in the woods near the Howells' farm.'

'Was I?'

'Yes.'

'David F's a digestive, you know.'

'He means a diabolic,' his mother said, incorrectly correcting him with a thin smile.

'So, you were in the woods . . .'

'Are you sure I was there that day?'

'Yes. That was the day you fell into a pit.'

'I didn't fall, I was pushed.'

'All right then, the day you were pushed – '

'Is that the day you came back covered in blood? It is, isn't it? Who did that to you?' His mother was still on the verge of tears, waiting for something to nudge her over.

James didn't have time for that. 'Are you sure that David F is dead?'

'Yes.' The DI tried to keep focused, keep his objective in sight, but it was hard, James was quick-witted.

'How do you know?'

'The body was found.'

'Who by?'

'That isn't important.'

The dead boy had been discovered by a man walking his dog. James had guessed as much. Bodies, he knew, were found either by people out with their dogs or by men fishing in rivers.

'I bet it was important to the man who found him.'

'I didn't say it was a man.'

'So you don't think it's important if it was a man or a lady?'

'Yes, I do . . . I think it's . . .'

'Make your mind up! Anyway, how do you know that it's David F who the lady found?'

Brian wanted to correct James and say that it hadn't been a woman, but then he would have fallen into his trap.

'His parents identified . . . said it was him.'

'What does he look like?'

'You know what he looks like.'

'Not dead I don't.'

The DC shifted uneasily in his seat, moving his weight

from one buttock to the other.

The DI remained impassive. 'He didn't look very well.'

'But like he might look better?'

'No.'

'David will come back and tell you it was not me. David F, I mean.'

'From where?'

'From the hospital. That's where you said he is. Unless you were lying?'

'No, I don't lie.'

James sniggered his incredulity but it gave him no relief. 'Is there a tombstone with David F's name on it yet?'

'Why?'

'Shouldn't someone reserve a space for him . . . like in a car park? Will they make sure it has railings round it?'

'Round what?'

'The grave, silly.'

'That depends. Probably not.'

'Then will he get out and haunt me?'

This sounded promising. The DI hadn't managed to trip the boy up yet, but he was bound to fall on his own and he'd be there to catch him when he did. 'Why would he haunt you if you didn't do anything to him?'

James paused to think about this and everyone breathed, enjoying the break in the quick-fire exchange.

'He will haunt me because I didn't do anything. Rebecca haunted me and I didn't kill her. Maybe David F will come back to life like she did.'

Suddenly the DI was reminded of his own children when they were little, and despite himself his indulgent let-me-explain voice crept out. 'Rebecca didn't come back to life, James. They played a trick on you.' It sounded like he was apologising for their cruelty.

'Ah, then David F could be playing a trick on you.'

'No, James, he can't. David F is dead. Dead people can't

play tricks. When someone is dead, it means that they can't come back.'

James shook his head.

Another tape came to its end and so did another session. The DI couldn't work the boy out. Was he naive, cunning or mad?

The television reports said that a man who'd been sleeping rough in the woods had been questioned, cleared and released and that now the police were allegedly focusing their investigation on the dead boy's friends.

'Is that me?' James asked, animatedly.

'Yes,' his father said.

Sandra wouldn't watch the news any more. 'Aren't you nice and white and clean?' She was busy brushing the already tangle-free dog.

After another night of fitful sleep and waking nightmares, James was wan and feeble, washed up on the shore of another day. Until this point he'd been good at sticking to his story or circumventing it altogether. But incriminating evidence was coming to light and slowly he became more caught up in his own cleverness. The grains of truth turned into Hansel and Gretel pebbles, and each one led the DI closer to the crime scene. Eventually James would trap himself there like he'd trapped his friend.

The same people were present as the previous day. There was no sign of Jenny. The cassette recorder was switched on.

'How do you feel today, James?' the DI asked cheerfully.

James was in no mood for chit-chat. He was sliding his silver St Christopher along the chain around his neck. His mother was attempting a crossword.

'The fingerprint analysis has come back and it is your gun.' The DI paused for a response but none came. 'There were a few other prints on it too, but there are two main sets.' Nothing. 'Yours and David Fielding's.' Still nothing. 'What do you have to say to that?'

'We have talked about this already.' James had grown weary of this court jester with his hackneyed turns.

'Of course, yes. It's your gun, so it's bound to have your prints on it.' He nodded to himself like he'd just remembered but would continue for his own clarification. 'It's interesting, where the prints are. Your prints are on the handle and David's are on the barrel . . . the end.'

'I think you mean David F, not David.'

This satisfied the DI that the boy was following. 'I do, don't I? What's interesting about that is . . . it implies that you were pointing the gun and David grabbed it off you.'

The art of lying: easy to acquire the tools; hard to make them work for you; impossible to master them completely.

'There was also some sick found near David's body.'

'Urgh!'

The DI thought that would get his attention.

'David F's sick?'

'Yes. And you remember that we took some of your blood?'

James nodded.

'Well, it's been analysed . . . tested, and some of the sick they found is yours.'

'Sick and blood are not the same,' James explained.

'No but they are both produced by the same body.'

'My body?'

'Yes.'

Sandra stopped not being able to do the crossword and looked at James. He looked back. Neither spoke.

'And there were some other things . . . found nearby . . . things that also have your fingerprints on them . . . things that were used to hurt David with.'

Sandra thought *she* might be sick. She looked in her handbag before remembering that she was out of mints. She'd bought tissues but had forgotten the mints – not like her. They were still on her list.

There was a long silence. The waiting game.

James was the first to break it. 'Oh. You mean the knife and fork?'

'You used them to hurt David?'

'No. No. I just know that they're there. I have played with them before.'

'Where?'

'There.'

'Do you mean where they found David?'

James was sucking the silver pendant now. It tasted like blood. He tipped it out of his mouth with his tongue and it dropped like a coin from a penny-arcade game, making a wet imprint on his T-shirt. He was playing for time.

'I mean in the woods. If they're where they used to be, then I know where the man found David F.'

'What man?'

'The man walking his dog.'

'I never mentioned a man with a dog.'

This needed no further explaining as far as James was concerned. He raised his eyebrows and sighed.

'What colour is your bike?'

'Orange. It's a Chopper.'

'They're quite unusual nowadays, aren't they?'

'Yes.' It pleased him, the word *unusual*.

'What we are collecting is called circumstantial evidence, James. You see, we can connect you with the crime scene. Your fingerprints are on the gun, on the knife and fork, and there's some of your sick nearby.'

Another silence ensued.

'The murderer must have been wearing gloves then?'

The cassette player made a slight shift in sound, rising by an octave, and they knew that the tape was about to run out. The DI bit his lip in frustration. He wasn't allowed to continue a session longer than the length of the cassette. They all watched as the play and record buttons flicked themselves up like fingers, a surreptitious 'fuck you'.

As Brian led them from the room he told Sandra that a couple of policemen would need to accompany them home in order to take some of James's clothes in for analysis.

'They're all clean,' she said, hoping that they were. In her mind's eye she was busy sorting through the colours at the bottom of the washing basket, hoping that none of them were James's. Her son a murder suspect? A ten-year-old? It was too monstrous. Many times she'd put her son on an imaginative trial for the death of her daughter, but each time she'd acquitted him.

'Can you use an unmarked car?'

'I think that can be arranged.' Brian understood that this must be hard on her and above all he wanted her assistance. A mother is a tough and resilient adversary when she thinks her child is in peril. So far she'd not asked for legal representation and he wanted it to stay that way, at least until he had wheedled a confession out of the boy. He was certain of his guilt, though it chilled him almost as much as it did Sandra. His instincts told him that confirmation of the child's culpability was just around the corner.

The policemen came to the house and took away a pair of sandals, some tennis shoes, a pair of navy Bermuda shorts and three T-shirts. All of them were dirty. Sandra asked naively if she could wash them and then bring them in.

'No,' she was told, 'it's best we take them like this.'

James wouldn't eat any lunch, so his mother left him at the table and went instead to spend some time apologising to Whitie for how little attention she'd been paying her, promising to take her for a long walk that evening.

The afternoon interview session was the most successful yet. Another man with a dog had come forward to make a statement saying that he'd seen a dark-haired boy on the day that David Fielding went missing. The boy had been riding an orange bike, wearing a white T-shirt with something on the front, a picture of some kind. They'd already established that

James's bike was orange and now they had in their possession a white T-shirt with short red sleeves and a racing car on the front.

'You know you mentioned a man with a dog earlier?'

'Yes. Do I have to go over everything again every time?'

'I'm afraid you do, son.'

'I am not your son,' James informed him, his jaw muscles tautening.

'No.' The detective sighed, relieved that he wasn't. 'Well, a man walking his dog near the Howells' farm told us that he saw a boy who fits your description . . . looks like you . . . on the day that David F went missing.'

'I didn't see him,' James snapped.

'So you admit that you were near the farm that day.'

James's eyes glided over to his mother like a pair of iridescent blue dragonflies, landed on her for a second and hovered away again. 'No. I didn't say that, did I? I didn't see him, because I was at home and there wasn't a man and a dog in my playroom. Mum, tell him I was at home.'

His mother nodded but they both knew that he'd not been there all day.

In any case, the detective was not paying any attention to her and neglected to say 'Mrs Gardner is nodding' to the tape recorder, so there was no tangible evidence of her body's white lie.

'So you remember now, do you? You remember what you were doing the day that David F went missing?'

'Maybe he saw me the next day.'

'So you went to the woods the following day?'

'Yes. I think so.'

'If you know when the *next* day was, then you should also know when . . .' The DI couldn't stop the bubbles of triumph from effervescing through his words.

James spotted this at once and studied the man in silence.

The detective didn't like it. He'd wanted to crowd out any

space for thought, but it was too late.

'Do you know there is a woodpecker in the wood? It is a green one. And a cuckoo, I have not seen it, but you can hear it. "Cuckoo! Cuckoo!"' he mimicked. 'Cuckoos lay their eggs in other bird's nests. The chicks look really silly. I've seen them in books . . . a big baby bird and a really small one trying to feed it. They have to catch even more worms than ever. The mother bird's babies die. They get pushed from the nest . . . Is that murder or is it an accident?' He was serious, his brow gathered in concentration.

'It depends on whether the bird did it on purpose or not.'

'Which bird?'

'The cuckoo.'

'But the baby cuckoo didn't choose the nest, did it?'

'No.' Despite himself, the detective was seriously deliberating this ethical dilemma. Then he caught himself and tried to refocus. 'I suppose it's just nature.'

'Yes. That's what I thought.' James seemed satisfied. He folded his arms and viewed the room with fresh eyes.

'What were you doing at the woods?'

'I was looking for David.'

'David Fielding.'

'No! You're not very clever, are you?'

'No, James, I'm not. That's why I need you to explain everything to me very carefully.'

'I see. I'll try, but it is very boring – '

'James, you know what I say – ' Sandra cut in, like a doll with a drawstring, only equipped to repeat the same tired phrases.

'Yes, I know. Only boring people get bored. I'm bored with you saying that too!' He could see the different shades of his temper dangling above him like a mobile. He was so tired.

'Did you discover . . . find David?'

'No.' His eyes glistened with frustration.

'Did you find the other David . . . David F?'

'Yes, I did. I found him in the den and he was dead. It wasn't me. He was dead when I found him.'

'James, why didn't you tell me?' His mother found herself standing up.

'Because you would say it was me.'

'No one's said that, James.'

Sandra sat down but turned her chair so that she faced her son. The protector turned prosecutor. She wanted an explanation.

'You want it to be me. It's *always* me! It's always my fault!'

The DI resumed his questioning. 'Tell us how you found him.'

'He was under the roof, under a log.'

'How did you know he was there?'

'I saw his hand.'

'But what were you doing there?'

'I told you, looking for David.'

'But why there?'

James wouldn't reply.

'How did you know that David F was dead, James?'

'Because his lips were purple and his skin was white and bluey and he had been sick and a vampire had been at him.'

'Why do you say that?'

'Because he had fang marks on him. That is what made me sick.'

'Those marks were made by a fork.'

Sandra gasped. Had she remembered to buy mints, one would have lodged in her oesophagus.

'I tried to help him. I gave him some digestives and some sugar lumps.'

'Why did you do that, James?'

'Because it's how you save a digestive. I saved his life before. I carried him home. Ask his mum.'

'But if he was dead already, then how could you help him?'

314

'In case he wasn't. In case he was in a coma sleep.'

The tape ran out. They hadn't heard its warning sound. The DI hoped they'd caught James's last two sentences. He wished he could carry on, but he had to play it by the book when it concerned a juvenile. He told them that they'd be having another session that evening. Sandra broke down. Kenneth would have to do it. She couldn't face any more, didn't want to hear any more. James was crying but his mother couldn't bring herself to console him, she was too confused. She said that he'd have to wait there and that she'd send for his father. 'I promised the dog a long walk,' she told him lamely, and without looking back she walked out of the station.

His father arrived with sandwiches and found James drawing trees on a piece of paper.

'What kind are they?' he asked.

James looked up with bloodshot eyes and said, 'Willows.'

Ken processed the boy: his dark wavy hair, the olive skin of his bare arms and legs. He could have been the son of a gypsy. 'Why willows?' he asked sadly, sitting down next to him.

'I am trying to make friends with them. Because sometimes when I go to sleep, I see them and all the leaves make screaming noises.'

'That doesn't sound much fun.'

'It's not fun.'

'Why don't you draw one without leaves?'

'Don't they always have leaves?'

'I don't know, but you can still draw one without them.'

James brightened. It was the most intimate conversation they'd shared. Kenneth had stopped trying to be a father and, for a moment, he was one.

The DI arrived and snapped the moment in two with the click of a ring-binder.

'If we could get started again in about half an hour?'

Ken nodded. He had a tumour of dread growing in his

intestines. He handed James the sandwiches and they sat and ate them slowly, painfully, their mouths so dry that they could barely swallow.

The interview didn't last long. The detective had taken the measure of James now and he knew how to manoeuvre him. The boy was flagging. He was run ragged, worn down. He tried to stay calm but he couldn't keep track of his own admissions and denials. One second he was indifferent, the next he was suddenly frank. He tried being evasive, pleasant, sulky and uncooperative in turns, but his rope was running out and there was already more than enough to hang him with.

'We know that you were seen going towards the woods the day that David F went missing. We also know that you went to the woods the day after, as you've admitted that yourself. You found David Fielding there, but did not touch the body. You then threw up. We know from the medical reports that he did not die until two days later. You say you thought he was dead, but you left biscuits for him in case he was still alive.'

'If he was alive, then why didn't he eat them?'

'Because he wasn't conscious.'

'You mean a coma sleep?'

'If you are in a sleep like that, you can't wake yourself up.'

'How am I to know that?'

'Why didn't you go for help?'

Silence.

'Or tell a grown-up that you'd found him?'

'Because this would happen.'

'What would happen?'

'I would be put in prison and hung.'

'You won't be hung.'

The sandwich – cheese and piccalilli – which resembled sick before it went down, rose up again in Ken's gullet as if he were a bird regurgitating food for its offspring.

'I don't believe you.' James slammed his hands on the grey Formica table.

'Why?'

'Nobody ever believes *me*!' He was marching around the room, shaking his small fists at the injustice of the world.

'James, I think that it was you who trapped and attacked David Fielding.'

'It wasn't me, it was David!' he screamed.

It was like a glass had exploded. The words flew across the room in jagged shards. The rage, the frustration, the fear all quit his body at once. The boy had blacked out.

The following morning James was charged with the murder of David Fielding.

TWENTY

The familiar words that people never imagine being said to them – 'I must tell you that by law you're not obliged to say anything, unless you wish to do so, but that anything you do say . . .' – were said to him.

The clothes had come back from the lab confirming that there were traces of David's blood on the racing car T-shirt and on the sandals. DI Brian Richards had no more doubts. As unthinkable as it was, James Gardner, aged ten, had killed another child. James was expressionless.

It was Sandra who'd accompanied her son to the station when the accusation was delivered. The news immediately made her spill over. All the grief that she'd hidden in the chasms of her body was unleashed: the tears of a wife – the loneliness of two becoming one; then the tears of a mother – the loss of a child, the loss of another.

This overflowing woman was asked if she'd like a tissue. She declined, she had some of her own, but they were exhausted in a moment and a PC replaced them with a stack of phlegm-green paper towels.

'How could this happen to me?' was all she could say.

The DI advised her that she should get a lawyer. There would be further interviews.

'I need to speak to my husband.' The word *husband* was the only trace of family that she still possessed.

She did not look at or touch James. They showed her to a phone. She sobbed into the receiver and her husband translated her tears. His mouth drained of saliva. His wife was all water and he was a desert. Feeling nauseous, he put down the phone and rushed to the bathroom. The receiver slid off the overly polished table-top and hung suspended by its cord, bobbing like a body, the sounds of his wife still pouring out of it, flooding the room like a running tap.

James was allowed home to collect some essentials. Jenny, whom James hadn't seen since the second day of interviews, was given the task, along with another PC, of escorting James and his mother. No one spoke on the journey. Sandra had now lost her concerns about the neighbours seeing a police car on the drive. Soon the whole world would know.

Whitie was waiting behind the glass of the front door. Without a word Sandra scooped her up, ascended the stairs and disappeared into her bedroom. Jenny was expecting her to put the dog in and come back out, but the door shut with both of them behind it.

'Cifer?' James called.

'Who's that?'

'C is for Cat,' he told her with a smile, waiting for her to get the joke.

She laughed, too much, and he raised his eyebrows.

'We'd better get his things together and get back,' the other PC reminded her awkwardly.

'Yes,' she said, remembering herself. 'Where's your room?'

'Up here.' He led the way. 'My playroom is in there.' He gestured efficiently, like an estate agent. 'It is nicer than my bedroom. My bedroom is very yellow,' he explained by way of warning. Walking past his parents' room, they could hear his mother's muffled sobs and James rolled his eyes in apology for her adolescent behaviour.

Taking a vanity case from his wardrobe, which next to his still sleight frame looked full-size, he packed it neatly and adeptly. He'd practised this routine time and time again in readiness for when he ran away from home. He was economical with clothes – nothing warm, due to his dislike of the contact of wool – reserving the space for books, which he selected with care. He was too old for most of them but they'd be an eiderdown world to creep into for comfort.

He slipped two piglets and a prone sow into his pocket – the only survivors of his kingdom's holocaust.

'OK,' he said somewhat breezily. 'I am set!'

He closed the door and retraced his steps along the dim limbo-landing, passing his parents' door again, which he glanced at but did not stop for.

'Don't you want to say goodbye to your mum?'

Without a word he gently took Jenny's hand in his and forced a smile.

'Mrs Gardner, we're leaving now,' she said.

The sobbing subsided for a moment before resuming with greater intensity. The door remained shut.

'Cifer? Cifer the Second?' James called again from the hall. 'Can I go and look for her, so I can say . . .?'

Jenny turned to her colleague, the small request in her eyes. He nodded begrudgingly. James dropped his case and darted from one room to the next, calling the cat's name. No sign. Crestfallen he returned to the hall and picked up his belongings. They let themselves out and walked down the drive to the car. James did not look back. His eyes leapt along the flagstones with their chalked-on numbers: his fading summer hops, skips and jumps. Jenny joined the boy in the back seat and he rested his head on her shoulder.

James was to be held in a secure unit, normally reserved for adults. No concession had been made for his age, despite the fact that it was all that the staff could talk about:

'Ten years old! Can you believe it? Ten! Do you remember what you knew by the age of ten?'

They nodded their heads and sucked their teeth, though they didn't even try to remember. All they knew was that they hadn't killed by then, couldn't have killed by then, by ten.

His pseudo cell was free from anything homely. There were no pictures, no plants, no windows, and the walls could never be described as a soothing green. Jenny sat with him for a while, like a mourner in a pew. She watched him while he unpacked. He did not seem to understand the enormity of what was happening to him, and she didn't have the heart or the stomach to tell him. When he'd arranged his books – in size-descending order – and placed the pigs by his bed on the small shelf, he sat down next to her.

'Is your hair long?'

'To here.' She pointed to halfway down her arm.

He nodded approvingly. 'I bet it looks pretty.'

She felt the beginnings of a blush. Despite what she knew about him and what he'd done, he enthralled her. She eradicated an urge to touch his cheek and tell him it would all be OK. It would have been deeply unprofessional and it would also have been a lie. It wouldn't be OK. It would never be OK for him, ever again. From the tender age of ten, until the age he wasn't anything any more, it would not be OK. There is no way to tell that to a child.

Jenny reminded herself that she was not at liberty to discuss the case, but she felt compelled to tell him something, reach out to him somehow.

'Tomorrow morning you'll be charged in court.' It sounded dry and formal, not much of a concession at all, but it was something.

'I see.'

Did he even understand what she meant? 'How do you feel?'

The detective had asked the boy the same question every day but with a different emphasis and James could smell insincerity. He delighted in the sensation that the word *feel* produced when she said it.

'Feel?' he repeated, echoing her intonation.

She waited.

'I don't feel anything. Do I?'

'You must. Everyone feels something all the time.'

'Not me. Not since David left.'

'David, the boy who . . . died?' she asked, leaning on a euphemism.

'No. My David. The other David, my best friend, the one nobody but me could see. I miss him more. Maybe he will come back. Since he left me, I feel nothing.' It was an untruth: he felt frightened, alone, abandoned, but he clung to his assertion, wanting to believe it.

She was not prepared for this response. 'In the morning a van will take you to court and your lawyer will ask if you can go home until the trial. Do you understand?'

'It doesn't matter. They won't let me go home, will they?'

'I don't know.'

He nodded his head, registering that she'd wanted to shake her own. 'Will you come with me tomorrow?'

'No . . . I can't.'

'OK.' Panic swelled up inside of him like a balloon. Could she see it? He hoped not. Slowly he exhaled and felt it deflate. 'Will the van they take me away in be white?'

'Yes, it probably will.'

'So it will have square wheels then?'

A laugh flew out of her mouth, a tiny wren of mirth. 'No. It won't have square wheels.'

'You have a nice smile,' he said, and she felt another blush press its fingers into her cheeks. He was so direct it was disarming.

'I bet you say that to all the girls,' she said, before she could stop herself. Then, to hide her embarrassment, she released a few more tiny laughing birds out of her mouth. He laughed too, lolling back on the bed so all his curls fanned out into a lazy halo.

The moment was crushed under the approaching sound of sturdy soles on the stone floor. They froze like mice caught feasting in a larder.

'You're supposed to be sitting outside the room,' said a starchy voice.

'Hello, Alice. I know, but he's only – '

'It's WPC Humphries in front of him,' the woman cut in.

'Of course.' Jenny stood, made sure her hair was fastened securely and looked about the barren room.

WPC Humphries sat herself down in the chair in the corridor – an action bereft of any feminine restraint – and opened a tabloid paper.

'Bye, James,' Jenny said and almost abstractedly linked her index finger with one of his curls. 'See you in a couple of days.'

'Two?'

She nodded furtively.

James did not say goodbye, but he did say, 'Please . . . don't . . .' then he stopped.

'What?' Jenny asked.

He shook his head as though he'd forgotten.

'Bye . . .' she said, to her colleague, managing to stop herself from saying 'Alice', but unable to say 'WPC Humphries'. 'Have a good evening.'

'Yeah, right!' her colleague snorted, but she jerked her head as a goodwill gesture – her derision wasn't intended for her fellow officer.

WPC Humphries was determined not to be hoodwinked by the boy. To her mind he was a barbarian, a menace to society. He did not merit her sympathy. If he thought he could butter her up, he had another thing coming. James was not under any such illusion, nor was he inclined to try. Instead he took his copy of *Pinocchio* from the strictly functional chest of drawers and withdrew into its pages.

It was a new set of policemen who accompanied him to the court. A pedestrian pair, who pretended he wasn't there. He could have been a vase they were delivering, or a chest of drawers. The van had bars on the small square windows, which made James feel like a real prisoner, but it still all seemed like a dream that he was too weak to wake himself from. He was dragged along, caught up in the wheels of the story as it raced on before him.

The van slowed down when they neared their destination, and James stood to look out of the windows of his Porta-cell.

A large collection of people had gathered.

'Are they here for me?' he said over his shoulder into the empty belly of the metal van. The men did not reply. James stared hard at the faces on the pavement. The windows were blackened so they couldn't see him, but their eyes stared back, blankly at first. They'd long since waited for this moment, but now that it had arrived, they didn't know what to do with it. Then their mouths opened and their fingers pointed and they sent waves of hate through the dark squares of glass.

The crowd was mainly made up of women – daughters, mothers and grandmothers. On the fringes were men, ubiquitously dressed in tracksuits. They were all baying for blood, for retributive justice.

'Kill the kid who killed a kid. There's no crime worse than killing a kid.'

All irony was lost to them and the inflammatory press presence was fuelling their flames, validating their outrage. The potential lynch mob, frustrated by police, was acting up in front of the cameras, a crowd scene of overzealous film extras.

James wondered how they'd known where he was. He imagined that his mother had told them. He scanned the swarming horde, struck by the idea that David the First might be among them, leading them.

'They can't see in . . . can they?' he asked. 'No, James,' he answered himself, jokily, but he could not extract the terror from his voice. In the distance he could see a few smaller figures huddled together and among them he thought he could make out Christian and Tara.

In court the charge was heard. Bail was denied and he soon found himself back in the van again. The assembly was still outside and its screams cranked up the moment he came in sight. This time James didn't approach the window. He sat slumped inside and slid St Christopher around his throat, each link an invitation to score along the perforated line. James flinched as a missile hit the body of the van with a bang, then a second and a third. When one struck the window, he screamed. He was sure that it was Christian who threw the first stone.

Autumn started packing up her favourite belongings as James had done: systematically. Jenny was still one of his favourites and he'd also grown fond of a policeman called Sam who was dark and thoughtful. James talked quite openly with him, but clammed up whenever he touched upon anything to do with the case. One day, when Alice was on duty, she deliberately left a newspaper lying out so that he'd be sure to see the front page. The headline focused on the funeral of David Fielding and the trauma of his family. James didn't seem to spot it, which infuriated the woman. She wanted him to face the full extent of the havoc he'd wreaked and to rub his *Pinocchio*-reading nose in it.

Often James was in good spirits and made Sam and Jenny laugh doing impressions of their fellow constables.

'Who is this?' he'd say, and mimic Alice limping round on the spot. He'd observed that she had one leg shorter than the other. He'd bark, 'Yeah right!' and 'Pull the other one!'

He also wrote stories for them. He told them that he was going to be a writer when he was taller. It froze Jenny's heart to hear him talk like this. This boy who'd been described by the press as a 'monster', 'a bad seed', 'a little devil' . . . He would never be allowed to grow up. He would remain a child, frozen in time.

The journalists wrote new pieces every day. His name hadn't been released but they didn't need it, not when there were so many other far more emotive words that could be used. They'd worked out where he'd lived and interviewed neighbours and teachers. The local council and social services were approached for comments. Did they have any records? Was there going to be an investigation into negligence? The authorities followed the routine course of self-exoneration, shifting the blame – quite literally – closer to home.

Sandra and Kenneth were terrified. They moved out of their home in different directions. She went, with Whitie, to put strain on her sister's family, and Ken went to his mother's, with the cat, under strict instructions to find a home for it or get it put to sleep.

They didn't visit their son. They convinced themselves that it was for the best, for his sake. They needed to get their own lives in order. Only then could they be strong for him. They were also wrangling with the lawyer about keeping the psychiatrists at bay. James was not allowed any counselling; the consensus was that it could adulterate the evidence. His lawyer mooted claiming manslaughter on the grounds that their son was suffering from diminished responsibility. On the one hand, it would be a weight off his parents' shoulders if James was deemed mad, but in their hearts they did not think, had never thought, that he was and felt ashamed about the idea of packing him off to a mental institution.

In the end he had four visits from four psychiatrists. They were all sent along to establish one thing, and one thing alone: whether he understood the difference between right and wrong. If he did, then he could be tried for murder. They asked no other questions about his mental state: his paranoia; his fears, wishes and dreams. They didn't ask him about his imaginary friend, or his other friends, or his relationship to his parents. It was hard, dry facts they were after. Black and white. Right and wrong. Good and evil. Nothing in-between was relevant, or even existed.

'Good and bad are words. That's all they are,' he told them with the sagacity of a linguistics professor.

They all agreed that he was clever.

His cleverness was the deciding factor against letting him speak at his own trial. How could they allow him to defend himself – for this most indefensible act – when to him what was 'reality' was to many a fantasy and to most a lie? And every lie that was exposed would be a victory to the prosecution. He would be perceived as trying to evade punishment, and in the eyes of the jury this would imply guilt. He was too precocious, too unpredictable, too prone to fabrication. It was considered best that he be silent, as silent as the two phantom witnesses, David and David.

He would be seen, but not heard.

TWENTY-ONE

By the time that James's case went to court, eight months had
passed and another birthday. His parents had visited separately
with gifts that he did not care for. He asked them both how Cifer
the Second was. His mother told him that *it* had gone to stay
with his father, until he was released, and his father said that
she had gone to live on a farm. He smelt two rats. All that he
said was, 'When an animal has been put to sleep, can it wake
up again?'

To which, in both instances, the response was a guilty, 'No.'

Jenny bought him a small, lined notebook for his birthday
for him to write stories in. Sam smuggled him in a copy of *Lord
of the Flies*. Was he telling James that he understood how children
could be savage, just like adults, making wars where there
were none? Poor Piggy! Poor Ralph!

But James knew that his story was Simon's. Simon who
got stuck like a pig.

Jenny put in a request to accompany him to the court,
which was granted. They travelled together and entered with
a social worker. It was a large panelled room and James was as
bewildered as his storybook Alice, but he wouldn't let it show.
He wore his funeral-confirmation suit. The clothes maketh
the man. His hair had been cut short, all his Samson strong curls
hacked clean away. No longer could he be mistaken for a little
angel. It was not seen as fitting for a killer to be crowned with

curls.

People often put on weight in custody, the goose fattened for slaughter, but James had refused to eat properly, sometimes altogether. He'd lost the little puppy fat he had, which prompted descriptions such as 'lean' and 'mean-spirited'. Round his neck was his swinging saint, vainly promising to carry him safely across troubled waters.

This was not a juvenile court. The ten-year-old accused – who'd now turned eleven – would be tried as an adult. The dock-rail was too high for him, the jury would've only seen his wispy hairs sticking up like weedy alfalfa sprouts, so a platform had been built. This way he could see and be seen. He was on show, centre stage; the freak. The Elephant Boy.

The trial began.

The offer to the Crown to plead manslaughter had been rejected. But there was still the small matter of his name. The press were clamouring for its release, as were the prosecution. The defence submitted. Locals had suspected other children and a brick had already flown through the wrong window, so the judge decreed that the boy's identity could be announced. James was being made an example of. He was being used as a deterrent. Odd, when everyone agreed that no other child was capable of such a deed.

He tried to assimilate the scene before him: wigged barristers, ex-teachers, ex-friends, psychiatrists, a gallery of journalists, the jurors and two tribes of relatives, led in procession by the mothers, James's and David's. Jenny had told him that if he got upset he should imagine everyone sitting in underwear. This didn't work for him, but he imagined them all as pigs, pigs in clothes. The last to arrive was the judge, and everyone rose on command. He was enthroned – Chief Pig – in his red robe, white wig and ermine collar. James felt shaky and sick but he wouldn't let it show. He soaked everything up with his peripheral vision. He wouldn't look anyone in the eye, would not meet their accusatory glares. He could see his parents, his mother martyred in starch and his hunched father still missing a spine.

James was directly addressed only twice – once at the beginning of the trial, and once at the end – though he was pointed at and referred to constantly, like a biology lecturer's yellowing skeleton. The proceedings lasted eleven days, one day for each year of his life, and each day was regimented like school; but there was no home time for James.

At the close of each session he was allowed a brief moment with his parents, which was always awkward and tearful. There was little bodily contact. James was stiff and withdrawn and, truth be told, did not want to be hugged wearing wool next to his skin.

No witnesses were called on the first day. It was eaten away at by lengthy, confident speeches from the prosecution, followed by the defence, who nibbled more cautiously at the edges of the litigation. James tried to look interested and not to yawn, but their posturing and their exposition bored him. His eyes soon became fixed while his brain meandered away into daydreams. He'd been told that if he had any questions or if there was anything he didn't grasp, he could ask a barrister, but he didn't want them to think him stupid, so he simply feigned understanding wherever necessary. The tapes of his interviews were played, all of them, without any editing. And for these James was alert and interested.

'Is that me?'

Jenny nodded that it was.

'I sound little, don't I?'

Occasionally he giggled when he heard himself say something witty, and the jury stiffened.

This was no laughing matter.

The witnesses were called the next day like chat-show celebrities. They took the hot seat and recounted their stories. James barely recognised the events described. They were not how he remembered them. The tales had been edited to make them more interesting. The prosecution had coached their protégés and rehearsed them, over and over. Their performances were now polished and smooth and they shone like rubies. Once each impressive gem was strung alongside the next it would make a magnificent choker.

Next the disciples of death were called to the stand, an array of specialists and forensics. And each one was the authority on something: the fingerprints, blood, vomit, bruising, diabetes and digestives. Then the farmer, Mr Howell, the son of the wheelchair-monster mother, was called. He stated his name and profession and swore to tell the whole truth and nothing but. He recalled meeting the accused with a lamb that had been tortured. The farmer neglected to say what had tortured the lamb, so these details were left to the jurors' imaginations.

'The boy behaved suspiciously,' the man told the court without encouragement. 'Told my mother he had a friend with him, but we didn't see one. He looked guilty, like a wrong'un.'

'Guilty of what?' the defence barrister asked. 'Surely you are not saying – with the gift of hindsight – that you thought him capable of murder? Are we to understand from this statement that you are clairvoyant?'

'No. Not murder then, but he had a guilty look. He stole some scissors, like I said. Guilty of stealing, certainly.'

'So you no longer have the scissors? Am I right?'

'No. We've got them.'

'But you said that he stole them.'

'He dropped them.'

'So he didn't actually take them off your premises?'

'No.'

'Theft is what happens when someone steals something from you, so you no longer have it in your possession.'

'I know!' Mr Howell didn't appreciate being condescended to.

'I am glad.'

Theft was wrong, just as murder was wrong. And scissors too. It was not looking good.

Teachers were called as character witnesses. The headmaster, Mr Stewart, spoke of his personal knowledge of the boy. He then launched into a well-rehearsed assembly-style lecture.

'Our school prides itself on teaching Christian values. We say prayers and sing hymns and attend our affiliated local church. The children all know the Lord's Prayer by heart, and the Ten Commandments. In all my experience, I would say with confidence that by as young as five, every child knows that it is wrong to hurt another . . . child. James Gardner was no exception. He was unlike any boy I've had in my school, but he knew right from wrong, even if he chose to ignore it.'

The defence suggested that the headmaster was trying to distance the school from slurs of culpability but he vehemently denied this, embarking for a second time on his prepared speech. The barrister cut him off.

'Would you say that learning the words of the Lord's Prayer parrot-fashion is the same as understanding them?'

'Yes. I would.'

His most recent class teacher, Mrs Grace, was not so absolute. She seemed overcome with stage fright. Occasionally she dried up completely and had to be prompted. Her eyes would not settle, nor would her hands.

'He was a daydreamer . . . always away with the fairies. He had an imaginary friend called David.'

'But would you say that he showed any aggressive tendencies?' The prosecutor was trying to nudge her back to the script.

'He had terrible tantrums. They were quite frightening. And he threw things at me, or the other pupils . . . chairs sometimes.' She almost looked at James – who was busy remembering one chair once – but then her chin led her away at the last moment.

'And did he tell lies?'

'All children – '

'Today we will stick with one child please. No generalisations. Did the accused tell lies?'

'Yes. White ones at first. One time he ranted about his imaginary friend killing people and I couldn't get the class settled all day after that. He was very . . . imaginative.'

The doctors and psychiatrists were split down the middle. He was the Oxymoronic Boy. The prosecution's people had diagnosed that there was no evidence of mental illness or sub-normality; quite the reverse, he had a very high IQ. Though he refused to touch upon the murder with them, they were convinced that he had no qualms about lying. They made it very clear that what he did was lie – not create, not imagine, not dream up. James lied and he lied compulsively. They concluded that David the First was not a condition but a concoction that enabled him to distance himself from blame and his own brutality.

Most of the medical witnesses for the defence claimed that he was suffering from a psychopathic disorder, possibly schizophrenia. The corroborative symptoms displayed by James included a lack of empathy towards others, aggressive behaviour and a lack of remorse. There was only one voice who took a more liberal middle ground, a Dr Giddins, who under cross-examination, when pressed to state whether she believed that James was mentally mature, responded by saying, 'He has mental maturity, but not mental balance. I don't believe that James knew that David Fielding would die, or that he even fully understands the irrevocable nature of death. What this boy needs is treatment. If he has committed this . . . a most extreme offence, he must also be suffering from a most extreme trauma.'

But the prosecution quickly reminded the court that they were there only to establish if James had the maturity to know the difference between right and wrong. James had been leaning forwards, listening to this doctor with special interest.

Not because he agreed with what she said necessarily, but because she was the first person to refer to him in the present tense. Everyone else had said he *was*, as though, like David, he had already died.

The other children were called up to testify: Christian, Rebecca the Second, Paul, Matthew and Graham – his blood brethren. He was not shocked about Tara. She described him as Mr Jekyll and Dr Hyde. James had to bite his tongue so as not to cry out that she'd got the doctor and the mister the wrong way round. But he'd been instructed that he must, at all costs, remain silent. So he had to sit by mutely while his friends denounced him, neatly avoiding saying anything that would stain or stick to their own spotless reputations. One by one the little painted saints were sworn in and took the stand, and they carried their tidy truths like Harvest Festival baskets.

'He told me that he'd killed his sister. And I believed him,' Tara announced to the court in her best public-speaking voice.

James shook his head violently at this, as he did whenever he disagreed with a statement. It was all he could do.

'What makes you say that?'

'Because I could tell he meant it. And I heard him say that he'd hurt Rebecca Clove with the pitchfork.'

'A fork,' repeated one of the barristers. He was fixing the image in everyone's heads, in readiness for the next fork, the fork used to torture David Fielding with.

'Yes. A big one for hay.'

'Who did he say this to?'

'To himself.'

'Didn't that strike you as odd, a boy talking to himself?'

'He was odd.' She looked James directly in the eye when she said this. 'He pretended that he had an imaginary friend . . . but we all knew he was making it up . . . because he's a big baby.' Her voice quivered with spite and she had to be checked and reminded that this was a court of law and not a place for name-calling. James smiled at this reproof and Tara looked suitably shamed.

'Do you know the difference between right and wrong?'

'Of course I do.'

'Do you think that the accused – James – knows the difference between right and wrong?'

'Definitely.' The word was another nail being gleefully hammered into his coffin.

Rebecca the Second tried to help him, tried to make him sound good, but her words were turned against her and she had no evidence that he wasn't capable or guilty of the crime. Yes, he had cut her to make them blood brother and sister. Yes, he could be cruel. Yes, he knew the difference between right and wrong. Yes, he had an imaginary friend. Yes, they were all told to bring weapons. Yes, they'd all been branded. And no, she couldn't say categorically that he hadn't done it.

Rebecca the First was the final child to be called, Rebecca the Resurrected. James's eyes widened with disbelief when he saw her. He wanted to bolt, to scream. He smelt the stench of pig flesh in his nostrils and clasped his hand over his mouth.

Today she sported a tidy bob with a short fringe and was wearing a dress. James had never seen her dressed like a girl before, but it was her, flesh and blood, as far as he could tell. He wanted to stand up and exclaim that it was all OK, that they should call David Fielding to the stand and he would appear too, or his David. But his only defence, he'd been told, was to play dead. He watched her keenly. Would she moan or wail? Would she levitate or become translucent? To James's disappointment and relief, she did none of these things. She spoke, like a young lady. She told them about her accident and how she'd later heard that James had orchestrated it. She said this calmly, as if she bore no resentment. Then she recounted how he'd visited her in the hospital. Finally she reported that he'd informed the gang that she was dead.

The jury donned a uniform mask of shock.

Rebecca explained how they'd decided to play a practical joke on James – 'to get him back,' as she put it – to let him know that they didn't want to play with a liar any more.

'That was the last time I saw him.'

James wanted to cry out, 'You can see me now, right here, you bloody liar!' It was as though he was the ghost. He was the invisible David.

At the end of that day's session, when he met with his parents, he was agitated and chatty.

'Could you see Rebecca . . . Clove?'

'Yes.'

'Have you spoken to David's mummy and daddy?'

'Well . . . we . . .'

'Have they got a new baby yet?'

'No. His mother's pregnant though – how did you know?'

'Oh, good.'

'Have you been reading the paper?'

Before James could answer his mother started crying. 'I never said those things about you James. I never – '

'I haven't read a paper,' James told her matter-of-factly. 'Will they let me off then?'

'What?'

'Now that they're going to get a new baby?'

His parents were at a loss for something to say to this.

'Don't cry, Mum. Have you taken my school clothes back?'

'No,' she said, sobbing even harder.

He reached up and patted her on the shoulder. 'Well, you should, you can get the money back . . . if you have the receipt.'

She tried to touch him but he turned away, as though someone had called his name.

Once the trial was underway, he was distant with Jenny too. He had to behave like a grown-up now. He was, after all, being tried as one. He no longer placed his hand in hers, nor did he lean his head on her shoulder. He stiffened when she touched him.

In the court, he'd been warned not to laugh again and he couldn't speak, so apart from the head-shaking and the furtively sliding of his St Christopher up and down its chain, he was motionless and impenetrable.

The press were quick to pick up on this. They'd done their homework, looking up synonyms for psychopath. They called him callous, resistant, unyielding, unemotional, remote, detached, distant, impassive, unfeeling, aloof. They said he had dead eyes and was ominously mature. If only he'd known that he would lose all sympathy by behaving like one of them, when all he wanted to do was yawn, fidget, bawl, behave like himself – a child. Instead, he forced himself to affect poise, so that they all saw that he knew what a serious business this was.

After the jury had listened to everyone – but James – having their say, it was time for the barristers to sum up.

The barrister for the prosecution spoke at length and with great dramatic effect. He chose his words with extreme care. He understood just how difficult and appalling it must be for the jury. They were trying the murder of a child. And this case was even more difficult and appalling, considering that the accused himself was a child. He then went on, with trowel applications, about the unparalleled wickedness of the crime. He was sure that everyone would agree that this act was a breach of nature. Not only had James destroyed the life of a child and his entire family, but he had destroyed the very notion of innocence itself. It was the murder of faith.

Every piece of evidence placed James – and no one else – at the scene. They'd all heard the taped confessional. The boy had committed the act and of that there was no room for doubt. All the jury had to do was decide whether James knew right from wrong. The intricacies of motive or responsibility were not the issue. This was a motiveless case. The boy was cunning, aggressive and dominating. He had killed the child, and before that he had barbarically held him prisoner and inflicted torture on him.

'You see before you an eleven-year-old, a clever child, an imaginative child, but a child with the heart of a killer.'

James tried his best to follow what this man was saying, but it didn't sound like he was talking about him. He caught hold of the words 'a clever child, an imaginative child', the floating seeds of a dandelion clock, and he held them in his fist. Then the parachute seeds came free and the words dropped him back into a panelled courtroom where a man was talking and talking about evil.

In the afternoon the defence barrister had his say, but James couldn't follow any of it. The minute he opened his mouth the boy was busy thinking about all the names of birds he could remember. The man droned on in a tone that sounded like he wanted pity. All he could claim in James's defence was that he didn't believe that the crime was premeditated and that James felt remorse, hence the sugar lumps and digestives. The man had no conviction, or perhaps he just knew that a conviction was certain.

Sandra and Ken could not face seeing James at close of play. They skulked away to their separate cars and made separate, convoluted journeys to ensure that no one followed them. It was up to Jenny to break the news of this fresh abandonment to James. And he took it – like he'd taken everything over the past ten days – stoically.

TWENTY-TWO

The eleventh day dawned. All that remained was the judge's summing up, and the verdict. Mr Pig Justice, with a voice as droopy as podgy cheeks, advised the members of the jury that in such an emotive case they had to be vigilant and rely on their heads over their hearts. He recapitulated the salient points, reviewing and hinting like an examiner who'd taken a bribe. Then the jury was dismissed to weigh up the evidence on the scales of justice.

While everyone waited, James was taken out for a glass of orange squash. He had his woollen trousers on again and was feeling sticky and irritable.

'Why is it so hot in there?' he asked.

'They had to turn the air conditioning off. It was too loud.'

That seemed as illogical to James as everything else did. Adults were unfathomable.

They were called back in. The jury had not needed long.

'On the count of attempted murder have you reached a verdict on which you are all agreed?'

'Yes.'

'Do you find the defendant James Gardner guilty, or not guilty, of the murder of David Fielding?'

'Guilty.'

'And this is unanimous?'

'Yes.'

The court was taciturn. This was the anticlimax they'd all been waiting for. The specks of dust in the air became visible in the sunlight for a second, before a cloud drew a curtain across the window pane. It was then that James understood what had happened. What it all meant, this charade of pigs in wigs.

Jenny tried to comfort him but he wouldn't be mollified and flicked up his hand, which caught her in the eye. She let out a yelp and another officer was immediately springing to her assistance. Before he could get there, James had passed out. As he fell, he smacked and split open his brow on the golden metal railing of his enclosure.

This was the melodrama the hungry pack had been waiting for. And James had given it to them just when they'd thought all the bones had been picked clean. It was feeding time at the zoo. All the forced formality of the court had been sliced open and words flew about like flies. The chaos was infectious. The people bayed, they barked, they grunted and they howled.

The Pig Judge banged his gavel, but nobody gave a damn.

I would like to dedicate this book to my loving parents and my extraordinary friends. Thank you all for your unwavering support, for all the times you've put up with me and put me up, for all the bars you've propped up with me and the tabs you've picked up. I owe you and adore you…

Mum, Dad, Lady Tinca, Ben, Carole and Dick Leahy, Lynda Ronan, Catherine Kanter and family, Dame (Lucy) Briers, Sarah (Pilks) and Phil Bucknall, Kirsty Morrison, Tom Woodroffe and Gary Sykes, Jon Levene and Karey Fisher, Sophie, Alex – and family – Schneideman, The Duchess (Sarah Thorowgood), Sophie and Gavin Stewart, Lucy – the Dare clan – and Matt Fell, Wendy Wason, Max and goddaughter Bella, David Greer, Hettie Judah, Jo McNeill and Giles Martin, Tim Webster and family, Victoria Grant, Mary Wells, Hetty Haxworth, Victoria Beattie, Rachel Pickup, Michele Moran and Pete Staves, Rhashan Stone, Jan Shepherd, Andrew Fallaize, Luke Healy, Caroline Taylor, David Benedict, Louise Tam, Lija Kresowaty, Caroline Pretty, Frederic Roscop, Preeya Kalidas, Mary Harris and those upstairs, Benn Cunningham, Alex Flache, Paula Spence, Cyril Megret, Kate Ashfield, Philip Kidson, The Soho Scribblers, the staff at Century and the salvation that is the French House.

I am also full of gratitude to all at To Hell – Lucy Owen for your encouragement, tact and intelligence, Emma Young for your work and wit, and Laurence Johns and Dean Ricketts for your inimitable vision.